**Praise for *New York Times* bestselling author
Heather Graham**

"Graham stands at the top of the romantic
suspense category."

—*Publishers Weekly*

"An incredible storyteller."

—*Los Angeles Daily News*

"Graham is the queen of romantic suspense."

—*RT Book Reviews*

**Praise for *New York Times* bestselling author
B.J. Daniels**

"B.J. Daniels is a sharpshooter; her books hit the
target every time."

—#1 *New York Times* bestselling author
Linda Lael Miller

"*Hero's Return* by B.J. Daniels is a creative
masterpiece."

—*Fresh Fiction*

New York Times and *USA TODAY* bestselling author **Heather Graham** has written more than one hundred novels. She's a winner of the Romance Writers of America's Lifetime Achievement Award, an International Thriller Writers Silver Bullet Award and, in 2016, the ThrillerMaster award from International Thriller Writers. She is an active member of International Thriller Writers and Mystery Writers of America, and is the founder of The Slush Pile Players, an author band and theatrical group. An avid scuba diver, ballroom dancer and mother of five, she still enjoys her South Florida home, but also loves to travel.

B.J. Daniels is a *New York Times* and *USA TODAY* bestselling author. She wrote her first book after a career as an award-winning newspaper journalist and author of thirty-seven published short stories. She lives in Montana with her husband, Parker, and three springer spaniels. When not writing, she quilts, boats and plays tennis. Contact her at bjdaniels.com, on Facebook or on Twitter, @bjdanielsauthor.

New York Times **Bestselling Author**

HEATHER GRAHAM

LAW AND DISORDER

⬧ HARLEQUIN® BESTSELLING AUTHOR COLLECTION

ISBN-13: 978-1-335-99621-3

Law and Disorder

Copyright © 2019 by Harlequin Books S.A.

The publisher acknowledges the copyright holders of the individual works as follows:

Law and Disorder
Copyright © 2017 by Heather Graham Pozzessere

Secret Bodyguard
Copyright © 2001 by Barbara Heinlein

Recycling programs for this product may not exist in your area.

HARLEQUIN®
www.Harlequin.com

Printed in U.S.A.

CONTENTS

LAW AND DISORDER

Heather Graham

1

Dakota Cameron was stunned to turn and find a gun in her face. It was held by a tall, broad-shouldered man in a hoodie and a mask. The full-face rubber mask—like the Halloween "Tricky Dickie" masks of Richard Nixon—was familiar. It was a mask to denote a historic criminal, she thought, but which one?

The most ridiculous thing was that she almost giggled. She couldn't help but think back to when they were kids; all of them here, playing, imagining themselves notorious criminals. It had been the coolest thing in the world when her dad had inherited the old Crystal Manor on Crystal Island, off the Rickenbacker Causeway, between Miami and South Beach—despite the violence that was part of the estate's history, or maybe because of it.

She and her friends had been young, in grammar school at the time, and they'd loved the estate and all the rumors that had gone with it. They hadn't played cops and robbers—they had played cops and *gangsters*, calling each other G-Man or Leftie, or some other such silly name. Because her father was strict and there was no way crime would ever be glorified here—even if the place had once belonged to Anthony Green, one of the biggest mobsters to hit the causeway islands in the late 1940s and early 1950s—crime of any kind was seen as very, very bad. When the kids played games here, the coppers and the G-men always won.

Because of those old games, when Kody turned to find the gun in her face, she felt a smile twitching at her lips. But then the large man holding the gun fired over her head and the sign that bore the name Crystal Manor exploded into a million bits.

The gun-wielder was serious. It was not, as she had thought possible, a joke—not an old friend, someone who had heard she was back in Miami for the week, someone playing a prank.

No. No one she knew would play such a sick joke.

"Move!" a husky voice commanded her.

She was so stunned at the truth of the situation, the masked man staring at her, the bits of wood exploding around her, that she didn't give way to the weakness in her knees or the growing fear shooting through her. She simply responded.

"Move? To where? What do you want?"

"Out of the booth, up to the house, now. And fast!"

The "booth" was the old guardhouse that sat just inside the great wrought-iron gates on the road. It dated back to the early years of the 1900s when pioneer Jimmy Crystal had first decided upon the spit of high ground— a good three feet above the water level—to found his fishing camp. Coral rock had been dug out of nearby quarries for the foundations of what had then been the caretaker's cottage. Over the next decade, Jimmy Crystal's "fishing camp" had become a playground for the rich and famous. The grand house on the water had been built—pieces of it coming from decaying castles and palaces in Europe—the gardens had been planted and the dock had slowly extended out into Biscayne Bay.

In the 1930s, Jimmy Crystal had mysteriously disappeared at sea. The house and grounds had been swept up by the gangster Anthony Green. He had ruled there for years—until being brought down by a hail of bullets at his club on Miami Beach by "assailants unknown."

The Crystal family had come back in then. The last of them had died when Kody had been just six; that's when her father had discovered that Amelia Crystal—the last assumed member of the old family—had actually been his great-great-great-aunt.

Daniel Cameron had inherited the grandeur—and the ton of bills—that went with the estate.

"Now!" the gun wielder said.

Kody was amazed that her trembling legs could actually move.

"All right," she said, surprised by the even tone of her voice. "I'll have to open the door to get out. And, of course, you're aware that there are cameras all over this estate?"

"Don't worry about the cameras," he said.

She shrugged and moved from the open ticket window to the door. In the few feet between her and the heavy wooden door she tried to think of something she could do.

How in the hell could she sound the alarm?

Maybe it had already been sounded. Crystal Manor was far from the biggest tourist attraction in the area, but still, it *was* an attraction. The cops were aware of it. And Celestial Island—the bigger island that led to Crystal Island—was small, easily accessible by boat but, from the mainland, only accessible via the causeway and then the bridge. To reach Crystal Island, you needed to take the smaller bridge from Celestial Island—or, as with all the islands, arrive by boat. If help had been alerted, it might take time for it to get here.

Jose Marquez, their security man, often walked the walled area down to the water, around the back of the house and the lawn and the gardens and the maze, to the front. He was on his radio at all times. But, of course, with the gun in her face, she had no chance to call him.

Was Jose all right? she wondered. Had the gunman already gotten to him?

"What! Are you eighty? Move!"

The voice was oddly familiar. Was this an old friend? Had someone in her family even set this up, taunting her with a little bit of reproach for the decision she'd made to move up to New York City? She did love her home; leaving hadn't been easy. But she'd been offered a role in a "living theater" piece in an old hotel in the city, a part-time job at an old Irish pub through the acting friend who was part owner—and a rent-controlled apartment for the duration. She was home for a week—just a week—to set some affairs straight before final rehearsals and preview performances.

"Now! Get moving—now!" The man fired again and a large section of coral rock exploded.

Her mind began to race. She hadn't heard many good things about women who'd given in to knife- or gun-wielding strangers. They usually wound up dead anyway.

She ducked low, hurrying to the push button that would lower the aluminum shutter over the open window above the counter at the booth. Diving for her purse, she rolled away with it toward the stairway to the storage area above, dumping her purse as she did so. Her cell phone fell out and she grabbed for it.

But before she could reach it, there was another explosion. The gunman had shot through the lock on the heavy wooden door; it pushed inward.

He seemed to move with the speed of light. Her fingers had just closed around the phone when he straddled over her, wrenching the phone from her hand and throwing it across the small room. He hunkered down on his knees, looming large over her.

There wasn't a way that she was going to survive this! She thought, too, of the people up at the house, imagining distant days of grandeur, the staff, every one of which adored the house and the history. Thought of them all…with bullets in their heads.

With all she had she fought him, trying to buck him off her.

"For the love of God, stop," he whispered harshly, holding her down. "Do as I tell you. Now!"

"So you can kill me later?" she demanded, and stared up at him, trying not to shake. She was basically a coward and couldn't begin to imagine where any of her courage was coming from.

Instinctual desperation? The primal urge to survive?

Before he could answer there was a shout from behind him.

"Barrow! What the hell is going on in there?"

"We're good, Capone!" the man over her shouted back.

Capone?

"Cameras are all sizzled," the man called Capone

called out. She couldn't see him. "Closed for Renovation signs up on the gates."

"Great. I've got this. You can get back to the house. We're good here. On the way now!"

"You're slower than molasses!" Capone barked. "Hurry the hell up! Dillinger and Floyd are securing the house."

Capone? As in "Al" Capone, who had made Miami his playground, along with Anthony Green? Dillinger—as in John Dillinger? Floyd—as in Pretty Boy Floyd?

Barrow—or the muscle-bound twit on top of her now—stared at her hard through the eye holes in his mask.

Barrow—as in Clyde Barrow. Yes, he was wearing a Clyde Barrow mask!

She couldn't help but grasp at hope. If they had all given themselves ridiculous 1930's gangster names and were wearing hoodies and masks, maybe cold-blooded murder might be avoided. These men may think their identities were well hidden and they wouldn't need to kill to avoid having any eye witnesses.

"Come with me!" Barrow said. She noted his eyes then. They were blue; an intense blue, almost navy.

Again something of recognition flickered within her. They were such unusual eyes...

"Come with me!"

She couldn't begin to imagine why she laughed, but she did.

"Wow, isn't that a movie line?" she asked. "*Terminator*! Good old Arnie Schwarzenegger. But aren't you supposed to say, 'Come with me—if you want to live'?"

He wasn't amused.

"Come with me—if you want to live," he said, emphasis on the last.

What was she supposed to do? He was a wall of a man, six-feet plus, shoulders like a linebacker.

"Then get off me," she snapped.

He moved, standing with easy agility, reaching a hand down to her.

She ignored the hand and rose on her own accord, heading for the shattered doorway. He quickly came to her side, still holding the gun but slipping an arm around her shoulders.

She started to shake him off.

"Dammit, do you want them to shoot you the second you step out?" He swore.

She gritted her teeth and allowed the touch until they were outside the guardhouse. Once they were in the clear, she shook him off.

"Now, I think you just have to point that gun at my back," she said, her voice hard and cold.

"Head to the main house," he told her.

The old tile path, cutting handsomely through the manicured front lawn of the estate, lay before her. It was nearing twilight and she couldn't help but notice that the air was perfect—neither too cold nor too hot—and that the setting sun was painting a palette of colors in the sky. She could smell the salt in the air and hear the waves as they splashed against the concrete breakers at the rear of the house.

All that made the area so beautiful—and, in particular, the house out on the island—had never seemed to be quite so evident and potent as when she walked toward the house. Jimmy Crystal had not actually named the place for himself; he'd written in his old journal that the island had seemed to sit in a sea of crystals, shimmering beneath the sun. And so it was. And now, through the years, the estate had become something glimmering and dazzling, as well. It sat in homage to days gone by, to memories of a time when the international city of Miami had been little more than a mosquito-ridden swamp and only those with vision had seen what might come in the future.

She and her parents had never lived in the house; they'd stayed in their home in the Roads section of the city, just north of Coconut Grove, where they'd always lived. They managed the estate, but even in that, a board had been brought in and a trust set up. The expenses to keep such an estate going were staggering.

While it had begun as a simple fishing shack, time and the additions of several generations had made Crystal Manor into something much more. It resembled both an Italianate palace and a medieval castle with tile and marble everywhere, grand columns, turrets and more. The manor was literally a square built around a center courtyard, with turrets at each corner that afforded four tower rooms above the regular two stories of the structure.

As she walked toward the sweeping, grand steps that led to the entry, she looked around. She had heard one of the other thugs, but, at that moment, she didn't see anyone.

Glancing back, she saw that a chain had been looped around the main gate. The gate arched to fifteen feet; the coral rock wall that surrounded the house to the water was a good twelve feet. Certainly not insurmountable by the right law-enforcement troops, but, still, a barrier against those who might come in to save the day.

She looked back at her masked abductor. She could see nothing of his face—except for those eyes.

Why were they so...eerily familiar? If she really knew him, if she had known him growing up, she'd have remembered who went with those eyes! They were striking, intense. The darkest, deepest blue she had ever seen.

What was she thinking? He was a crook! She didn't make friends with crooks!

The double entryway doors suddenly opened and she saw another man in its maw.

Kody stopped. She stared at the doors. They were really beautiful, hardwood enhanced with stained-glass images of pineapples—symbols of welcome. Quite ironic at the moment.

"Get her in here!" the second masked man told the one called Barrow.

"Go," Barrow said softly from behind her.

She walked up the steps and into the entry.

It was grand now, though the entry itself had once been the whole house built by Jimmy Crystal when he had first fallen in love with the little island that, back then, had been untouched, isolated—a haven only for mangroves and mosquitos. Since then, of course, the island—along with Star and Hibiscus islands—had become prime property.

But the foyer still contained vestiges of the original. The floor was coral rock. The columns were the original columns that Jimmy Crystal had poured. Dade country pine still graced the side walls.

The rear wall had been taken down to allow for glass barriers to the courtyard; more columns had been added. The foyer contained only an 1890's rocking horse to the right side of the double doors and an elegant, old fortune-telling machine to the left. And, of course, the masked man who stood between the majestic staircases that led to the second floor at each side of the space.

She cast her eyes around but saw no one else.

There had still been four or five guests on the property when Kody had started to close down for the day. And five staff members: Stacey Carlson, the estate manager, Nan Masters, his assistant, and Vince Jenkins, Brandi Johnson and Betsy Rodriguez, guides. Manny Diaz, the caretaker, had been off the property all day. And, of course, Jose Marquez was there somewhere.

"So, this is Miss Cameron?" the masked man in the house asked.

"Yes, Dillinger. This is Miss Cameron," Barrow said.

Dillinger. She was right—this guy's mask was that of the long-ago killer John Dillinger.

"Well, well, well. I can't tell you, Miss Cameron, what a delight it is to meet you!" the man said. "Imagine! When I heard that you were here—cuddle time with the family before the final big move to the Big Apple— I knew it was time we had to step in."

The man seemed to know about her—and her family.

"If you think I'm worth some kind of ransom," she said, truly puzzled—and hoping she wasn't sealing her own doom, "I'm not. We may own this estate, but it's in some kind of agreement and trust with the state of Florida. It survives off of grants and tourist dollars." She hesitated. "My family isn't rich. They just love this old place."

"Yeah, yeah, yeah, Daddy is an archeologist and Mom travels with him. Right now they're on their way back from South America so they can head up north with their baby girl to get her all settled into New York City. Yes! I have the prize right here, don't I?"

"I have no idea what you're talking about," Kody told him. "I wish I could say that someone would give you trillions of dollars for me, but I'm not anyone's prize. I'm a bartender-waitress at an Irish pub who's struggling to make ends meet as an actress."

"Oh, honey," Dillinger said, "I don't give a damn if you're a bad actress."

"Hey! I never said I was a *bad* actress!" she protested. And then, of course, she thought that he was making her crazy—heck, the whole situation was making her crazy—because who the hell cared if she was a bad actress or a good actress if she wasn't even alive?

Dillinger waved a hand in the air. "That's neither here nor there. You're going to lead us to the Anthony Green stash."

Startled, Kody went silent.

Everyone, of course, had heard about the Anthony Green *stash*.

Green was known to have knocked over the long-defunct Miami Bank of the Pioneers, making off with the bank's safe-deposit boxes that had supposedly contained millions in diamonds, jewels, gold and more. It was worth millions. But Anthony Green had died in a hail of bullets—with his mouth shut. The stash was never found. It had always been suspected that Anthony Green—before his demise—had seen to it that the haul had been hidden somewhere in one of his shacks deep in the Everglades, miles from his Biscayne Bay home.

Rumor followed rumor. It was said that Guillermo Salazar—a South American drug lord—had actually found the stash about a decade ago and added a small fortune in ill-gotten heroin-sales gains to it—before he, in turn, had been shot down by a rival drug cartel.

Who the hell knew? One way or the other, it was supposedly a very large fortune.

She didn't doubt that Salazar had sold drugs; the Coast Guard in South Florida was always busy stopping the drug trade. But she sure as hell didn't believe that Salazar had found the Green stash at the house, because she really didn't believe the stash was here.

Chills suddenly rose up her spine.

If she was supposed to find a stash that didn't exist here...

They were all dead.

"Where is everyone?" she asked.

"Safe," Dillinger said.

"Safe where?"

No one answered Kody. "Where?" she repeated.

"They're all fine, Miss Cameron."

It was the man behind her—Barrow—who finally spoke up. "Dillinger, she needs to know that they're all fine," he added.

"I assure you," Dillinger continued. "They're all fine. They're in the music room."

The music room took up most of the left side of the downstairs. It would be the right place to hold a group of people.

Except...

Someone, somewhere, had to know that something was going on here. Surely one of the employees or guests had had a chance to get out a cell phone warning.

"I want to see them," she said. "I want to see that everyone is all right."

"Listen, missy, what you do and don't want doesn't

matter here. What you're going to do for us matters," Dillinger told her.

"I don't know where the stash is. If I did, the world would have known about it long ago," she said. "And, if you know everything, you surely know that history says Anthony Green hid his bank treasure in some hut somewhere out in the Everglades."

"She sure as hell isn't rich, Dillinger," Barrow said. "Everything is true—she's taken a part-time job because what she's working is off-off Broadway. If she knew about the stash, I don't think she'd be slow-pouring Guinness at an old pub in the city."

Dillinger seemed annoyed. Kody was, in fact, surprised by what she could read in his eyes—and in his movements.

"No one asked your opinion, Barrow," Dillinger said. "She's the only one who can find it. I went through every newspaper clipping—she's loved the place since she was a kid. She's read everything on Jimmy Crystal and Anthony Green and the mob days on Miami Beach. She knows what rooms in this place were built what years, when any restoration was done. She knows it all. She knows how to find the stash. And she's going to help us find it."

"Don't be foolish," Kody said. "You can get out now. No one knows who you guys are—the masks, I'll grant you, are good. Well, they're not good. They're cheap and lousy masks, but they create the effect you want and no one here knows what your real faces look like. Pretty soon, though, walls or not, cops will swarm the place. Someone will come snooping around. Someone probably got something out on a cell phone."

She couldn't see his face but she knew that Dillinger

smiled. "Cell phones? No, we secured those pretty quickly," he said. "And your security guard? He's resting—he's got a bit of a headache." He shook his head. "Face it, young lady. You have me and Barrow here. Floyd is with your friends, Capone is on his way to help, and the overall estate is being guarded by Baby Face Nelson and Machine Gun Kelly and our concept of modern security and communication and, you know, we've got good old Dutch—as in Schultz—working it all, too. I think we're good for a while. Long enough for you to figure out where the stash is. And, let's see, you are going to help us."

"I won't do anything," she told him. "Nothing. Nothing at all—not until I know that my friends and our guests are safe and that Jose isn't suffering from anything more than a headache."

Not that she'd help them even then—if she even could. The stash had been missing since the 1930s. In fact, Anthony Green had used a similar ruse when he had committed the bank robbery. He'd come in fast with six men—all wearing masks. He'd gotten out just as fast. The cops had never gotten him. They'd suspected him, but they'd never had proof. They'd still been trying to find witnesses and build a case against him when he'd been gunned down on Miami Beach.

But her demands must have hit home because Dillinger turned to Barrow. "Fine. Bring her through."

He turned to head down the hallway that led into the music room—the first large room on the left side of the house.

It was a gorgeous room, graced with exquisite crown molding, rich burgundy carpets and old seascapes of famous ports, all painted by various masters in colors that complemented the carpet. There was a wooden dais at one end of the room that accommodated a grand piano, a harp, music stands and room for another three or four musicians.

There were sofas, chairs and love seats backed to all the walls, and a massive marble fireplace for those times when it did actually get cold on the water.

Kody knew about every piece in the room, but at that moment all she saw was the group huddled together on the floor.

Quickly searching the crowd, she found Stacey Carlson, the estate manager. He was sixty or so with salt-and-pepper hair, old-fashioned sideburns and a small mustache and goatee. A dignified older man, he was quick to smile, slow to follow a joke—but brilliant. Nan Masters was huddled to his side. If it was possible to have platonic affairs, the two of them were hot and heavy. Nothing ever went on beyond their love of Miami, the beaches and all that made up their home. Nan was red-haired, but not in the least fiery. Slim and tiny, she looked like a cornered mouse huddled next to Stacey.

Vince Jenkins sat cross-legged on a Persian rug that lay over the carpet, straight and angry. There was a bruise forming on the side of his face. He'd apparently started out by fighting back.

Beside him, Betsy Rodriguez and Brandi Johnson were close to one another. Betsy, the tinier of the two, but by far the most out-there and sarcastic, had her arm around Brandi, who was nearly six feet, blond, blue-eyed, beautiful and shy.

Jose Marquez had been laid on the largest love seat. His forehead was bleeding, but, Kody quickly saw, he was breathing.

The staff had been somewhat separated from the few guests who had remained on the property, finishing up in the gardens after closing. She couldn't remember all their names but she recalled the couple, Victor and Melissa Arden. They were on their honeymoon, yet they'd just been in Texas, visiting the graves of Bonnie Parker and Clyde Barrow in their separate cemeteries. They loved studying old gangsters, which was beyond ironic, Kody thought now. Another young woman from Indiana, an older man and a fellow of about forty rounded out the group.

They were all huddled low, apparently respecting the twin guns carried by another man in an identity-concealing mask.

"Kody!" Stacey said, breathing out a sigh of relief. She realized that her friends might have been worrying for her life.

She turned to Dillinger. "You'd better not hurt them!"

"Hurt them?" Dillinger said. "I don't want to hurt any of you, really. Okay, okay, so, quite frankly, I don't give a rat's ass. But Barrow there, he's kind of squeamish when it comes to blood and guts. Capone—my friend with the guns—is kind of rabid. Like he really had syphilis or rabies or something. He'd just as soon shoot you as look at you. So, here's my suggestion." He paused, staring Cody up and down. "You find out what I need to know. You come up to that library—and you start using everything you know and going through everything in the books, every news brief, every everything. You find that stash for me. Their lives depend on it."

"What if I can't find it?" she asked. "No one has found this stash in eighty-plus years!"

"You'd better find it," Dillinger said.

"Help will come!" Betsy said defiantly. "This is crazy—you're crazy! SWAT teams aren't but a few miles away. Someone—"

"You'd better hope no one comes," Dillinger said. He walked over to hunker down in front of her. "Because that's the whole point of hostages. They want you to live. They probably don't give a rat's ass one way or the other, either, but that's what they're paid to do. Get the hostages out alive. But, to prove we mean business, we'll have to start by killing someone and tossing out the body. And guess what? We like to start with the big-mouths, the wise-asses!"

He reached out to Betsy and that was all the impetus Kody needed. She sure as hell wasn't particularly courageous but she didn't waste a second to think. She just bolted toward Dillinger, smashing into him with such force that he went flying down.

With her.

He was strong, really strong.

He was up in two seconds, dragging her up with him.

"Why you little bitch!" he exclaimed as he hauled his arm back, ready to slam a jaw-breaking fist into her face.

His hand never reached her.

Barrow—with swift speed and agility—was on the two of them. She felt a moment of pain as he wrenched her out of Dillinger's grasp, thrusting himself between them.

"No, Dillinger, no. Keep the hostages in good shape. This one especially! We need her, Dillinger. We need her!"

"Bitch! You saw her—she tackled me."

"We need her!"

The hostages had started to move, scrambling back,

restless, frightened, and Capone shoved someone with the butt of his gun.

Barrow lifted his gun and shot the ceiling.

Plaster fell around them all like rain.

And the room went silent.

"Let's get her out of here and up to the library, Dillinger. Dammit, now. Come on—let's do what we came here to do!" he insisted. "I'm into money—not a body count."

Kody felt his hand as he gripped her arm, ready to drag her along.

Dillinger stared at him a long moment.

Was there a struggle going on? she wondered. A power play? Dillinger seemed to be the boss, but then Barrow had stepped in. He'd saved her from a good beating, at the least. She couldn't help but feel that there was something better about him.

She was even drawn to him.

Oh, that was sick, she told herself. He was a crook, maybe even a killer.

Still, he didn't seem to be as bloodthirsty as Dillinger.

Dillinger stepped around her and Barrow, heading for the stairs to the library. Barrow followed with her.

"Hey!"

They heard the call when they had nearly cleared the room.

She turned to see Capone standing next to Betsy Rodriguez. He wasn't touching her; he was just close to her.

He moved his gun, running the muzzle through her hair.

"Dakota Cameron!" he said. "The world—well, your world—is dependent on your every thought and word!"

She started to move toward him but Barrow stopped her, whispering in her ear, "Don't get them going!"

She couldn't help herself. She called out to Capone. "You're here because you want something? Well, if you want it from me, step the hell away from my friend!"

To her surprise, Dillinger started to laugh.

"We've got a wild card on our hands, for sure. Come on, Capone. Let's accommodate the lady. Step away from her friend."

From behind her, Barrow added, "Come on, Capone. I'm in this for the money and a quick trip out of the country. Let's get her started working and get this the hell done, huh? Beat her to pieces or put a bullet in her, and she's worthless."

"Miss Cameron?" Dillinger said, sweeping an elegant bow to her. "My men will behave like gentlemen—as long as your friends let them. You hear that, right?"

"I can be a perfect gentleman!" Capone called back to him.

"Tell them all to sit tight and not make trouble—that you will manage to get what we want," Barrow said to her.

She looked at him again.

Those eyes of his! So deep, dark, blue and intense!

Surely, if she really knew him, she'd recognize him now.

She didn't. Still, she couldn't help but feel that she did, and that the man she knew wasn't a criminal, and that she had been drawn to those eyes before.

She shivered suddenly, looking at him.

He didn't like blood and guts—that's what Dillinger had said.

Maybe he was a thief, a hood—but hated the idea of

being a murderer. Maybe, just maybe, he did want to keep them all alive.

"Hey!" she called back to the huddled group of captives. "I know everything about the house and all about Anthony Green and the gangster days. Just hold tight and be cool, please. I can do this. I know I can do this!"

They all looked at her with hope in their faces.

She gazed at Barrow and said, "They need water. We keep cases of water bottles in the lower cabinet of the kitchen. Go through the music room and the dining room and you'll reach the kitchen. I would truly appreciate if you would give them all water. It will help me think."

But it was Dillinger who replied.

"Sure," he said. "You think—and we'll just be the nicest group of guys you've ever met!"

2

Nick Connolly—known as Barrow to the Coconut Grove crew of murderers, thieves and drug runners who were careful not to share their real names, even with one another—was doing his best. His damned best.

Which wasn't easy.

Nick didn't mind undercover work. He could even look away from the drugs and the prostitution, knowing that what he was doing would stop the flow of some really bad stuff onto the city streets—and put away some really bad men.

From the moment he'd infiltrated this gang three weeks ago, the situation had been crazy, but he'd also thought it would work. This would be the time when he could either get them all together in an escape boat that the Coast Guard would be ready to swoop up, or, if that kind of maneuver failed, pick them off one by one. Each of these guys—Dillinger, Capone, Floyd, Nelson, Kelly and Schultz—had killed or committed some kind of an armed robbery. They were all ex-cons. Capone had been the one to believe in Nick's off-color stories in an old dive bar in Coconut Grove, and as far as Capone knew, Nick had been locked up in Leavenworth, convicted of a number of crimes. Of course, Capone had met Nick as Ted—Ted Johnson had been the pseudonym Nick had been using in South Florida. There really had been a Ted Johnson; he'd died in the prison hospital ward of a knife wound. But no one knew that. No one except certain members of the FBI and the hospital staff and warden and other higher ups at the prison.

None of these men—especially "Dillinger"—had any idea that Nick had full dossiers on them. As far as they all knew, they were anonymous, even with each other.

Undercover was always tricky.

It should have been over today; he should have been able to give up the undercover work and head back to New York City. Not that he minded winter in Miami.

He just hated the men with whom he had now aligned himself—even if it was to bring them down, and even if it was important work.

Today should have been it.

But all the plans he'd discussed with his local liaisons and with Craig Frasier—part of the task force from New York that had been chasing the drug-and-murder-trail of the man called Dillinger from New York City down through the South—had gone to hell.

And the stakes had risen like a rocket—because of a situation he'd just found out about that morning.

Without the aid, knowledge or consent of the others, for added protection, Dillinger had kidnapped a boy right before they had all met to begin their takeover of the Crystal Estate.

It wouldn't have mattered who the kid was to Nick— he'd have done everything humanly possible to save him—but the kidnapped boy was the child of Holden Burke, mayor of South Beach. Dillinger had assured them all that he had the kid safely hidden somewhere—where, exactly, he wasn't telling any of them. They all knew that people could talk, so it was safer that only he knew the whereabouts of little Adrian Burke. And not to worry—the kid was alive. He was their pass-go ace in the hole.

That was one thing.

Then, there was Dakota Cameron.

To be fair, Nick didn't exactly know Kody Cameron but he had seen her—and she had seen him—in New York City.

And the one time that he'd seen her, he'd known immediately that he'd wanted to see her again.

And now, here they were. In a thousand years he'd never imagined their second meeting would be like this.

No one had known that Dillinger's game plan ended with speculation—the vague concept that he could kidnap Dakota, take her prisoner—and *hope* she could find the stash!

Dillinger planned the heists and the drug runs; he worked with a field of prostitution that included the pimps and the girls. He had South American contacts. No one had figured he'd plan on taking over the old Crystal Estate, certain that he could find a Cameron family member who knew where to find the old mob treasure.

So, now, here he was—surprised and somewhat anxious to realize that the lovely young brunette with the fascinating eyes he'd brushed by at Finnegan's on Broadway in New York City would show up at the ticket booth at a Florida estate and tourist attraction.

Craig Frasier, one of the main men on the task force Director Egan had formed to trace and track "Dillinger," aka Nathan Appleby, along the Eastern seaboard, spent a lot of time at Finnegan's. The new love of his life was co-owner, along with her brothers, of the hundred-and-fifty-year-old pub in downtown Manhattan.

Nick and Kody Cameron had passed briefly, like proverbial ships in the night, but he hadn't had the least problem recognizing her today. He knew her, because they had both paused to stare at one another at the pub.

Instant attraction? Definitely on his part and he could have sworn on hers, too.

Then she'd muttered some kind of swift apology and Craig's new girlfriend, who'd come over to greet them, explained, "That's Kody Cameron. She's working a living theater piece with my brother. Sounds kind of cool, right? And she's working here part-time now, making the transition to New York."

"What's living theater?" Nick had asked Kieran Finnegan.

"Kevin could tell you better than me," she had explained, "but it's taking a show more as a concept than as a structured piece and working with the lines loosely while interacting with the audience as your character."

Whatever she did, he'd hoped that he'd see her again; he'd even figured that he could. While Kieran Finnegan actually worked as a psychologist and therapist for a pair of psychiatrists who often came in as consultants for the New York office of the Bureau, she was also often at Finnegan's. And since he was working tightly with Craig and his partner, Mike, and a cyber-force on this case, he'd figured he'd be back in Finnegan's, too. But then, of course, Dillinger had come south, met up with old prison mates Capone, Nelson, Kelly, Floyd and Schultz, and Nick—who had gone through high school in South Florida and still had family in the area—had been sent down to infiltrate the gang.

The rest, as the saying went, was history.

Now, if Dakota Cameron saw his face, if she gave any indication that she knew him, and knew that he was an FBI man...

They'd both be dead.

And it didn't help the situation that she was battle ready—ready to lay down her life for her friends.

Then again, there should have been a way for him to stop this. If it hadn't been for the little boy who had been taken...

He had to find out where the kid was. Had Dillinger stashed him with friends or associates? Had he hidden him somewhere? It wasn't as hard to hide somewhere here as one would think, with the land being just about at sea level and flat as a pancake. There were enough crack houses and abandoned tenements. Of course, Nick was pretty sure Dillinger couldn't have snatched the kid at a bus station, hidden him wherever, and made it to the estate at their appointed time, if he had gone far.

But that knowledge didn't help much.

Nick's first case when he'd started with the Bureau in the Miami offices had been finding the truth behind the bodies stuffed in barrels, covered with acid and tossed in the Everglades.

He refused to think of that image along with his fear for the child; the boy was alive. Adrian Burke wouldn't be worth anything in an escape situation if he was dead.

Nick wiped away that thought and leaned against the door frame as he stood guard over Kody. Capone was now just on the other side of the door.

Like the entire estate, the library was kept in pristine

shape, but it also held an air of fading and decaying elegance, making one feel a sense of nostalgia. The floors were marble, covered here and there by Persian throw rugs, and built-in bookshelves were filled with volumes that appeared older than the estate itself, along with sea charts and more.

Kody Cameron had a ledger opened before her, but she was looking at him. Quizzically.

It seemed as if she suspected she knew him but couldn't figure out from where.

"You're not as crazy as the others," she said softly. "I can sense that about you. But you need to do something to stop this. That treasure he's talking about has been missing for years and years. God knows, maybe it's in the Everglades, swallowed up in a sinkhole. You don't want to be a part of this—I know you don't. And those guys are lethal. They'll hurt someone…kill someone. This is still a death penalty state, you know. Please, if you would just—"

He found himself walking over to her at the desk and replying in a heated whisper, "Just do what he says and find the damned treasure. Lie if you have to! Find something that will make Dillinger believe that you know where the treasure is. Give him a damned map to find it. He won't think twice about killing people, but he won't kill just for the hell of it. Don't give him a reason."

"You're not one of them. You have to stop this. Get away from them," she said.

She was beautiful, earnest, passionate. He wanted to reassure her. To rip off his mask and tell her that law enforcement was in on it all.

But that was impossible, lest they all die quickly.

He had to keep his distance and keep her, the kid-napped child and the others in the house alive.

Capone was growing curious. He left his post at the archway and walked in. "Hey. What's going on here? Don't interrupt the woman, Barrow. I want to get the hell out of here! I've done some wild things with Dillinger, but this is taking the cake. Makes me more nervous than twenty cartel members in a gunboat. Leave her be."

"Yeah. I'm going to leave her be. And she's going to come up with something," Barrow said.

He'd barely spoken when Schultz came rushing in. While Capone knew how to rig a central box and stop cameras and security systems, Schultz was an expert sharpshooter. He was tall and thin, not much in the mus-cles department, but Nick had seen him take long shots that were just about impossible.

"News is out that we're here," he said. "Cops are sur-rounding the gates. I fired a few warning shots and Dill-inger answered the phone—told them we have a pack of hostages. You should see them all out there at the gates," he added, his grin evident in his voice. "They look like a pack of chickens. Guess they're calling for a hostage negotiator. Dillinger is deciding whether to give them a live one or a body."

Kody Cameron stood. "They give him a body and I'm done. If he gives them one body, it won't make any difference to him if he kills the rest of us."

"And just how far are you getting, sweet thing?" Schultz asked, coming close to her. He reached out to lift the young woman's chin.

Nick struggled to control himself. Hell, she wasn't just a captive. Not just someone he had to keep alive.

She worked for Finnegan's. She was connected to

Kevin Finnegan and Kieran Finnegan—and therefore, to Craig Frasier.

And he noticed her the first time he'd ever seen her. Known that he'd wanted to see her again.

He'd never imagined it could be in this way.

For a moment he managed to keep his peace. But, damn her, she just had to react. Schultz cradled her face and she stepped back and pushed his hand away.

"Hey, hey, hey, little girl. You don't want to get hurt, do you? Be nice."

Nick stepped up, swinging Schultz around.

"Leave her alone, dammit. We're here for a reason."

"What? Are you sweet on her yourself?" Schultz asked him, his tone edgy. "You think this is merchandise you keep all for yourself?"

"I'm not merchandise!" Kody snapped.

"I want her to find what Dillinger wants, and I want to get the hell out of here!" Nick said. He was as tall as Schultz; he had a lot more muscle and he was well trained. In a fair fight, Schultz wouldn't stand a chance against him.

There were no fair fights here, he reminded himself. He had to keep an even keel.

"Leave her alone and let her get back to work," he said. "Get your mind on the job to be done here."

"Shouldn't you be up in one of the front towers?" Capone asked Schultz. "Isn't that your job in all this?"

Schultz gave them all a sweeping and withering glare. Then he turned and left.

Capone was staring at Nick. "Maybe you should get your mind on the job, too, Barrow," he suggested.

"And you," Nick added softly.

Capone continued to stare at him.

It went no further as Dillinger came striding into the room. He ignored Capone and Nick and walked straight to the desk and Kody.

"How long?" he asked her.

"How long? You're asking me to do something no one has managed in decades," Kody said.

"You're got two hours," Dillinger said. "Two hours. They're bringing in a hostage negotiator. Don't make me prove that I will kill."

"I'm doing my best," Kody said.

"Where's the phone in this room?" Dillinger asked.

"On the table by the door, next to the Tiffany lamp," Kody said.

"What the hell is a Tiffany lamp?" Dillinger demanded, leaning in on Kody.

"There. Right there, boss," Nick said, pointing out the elegant little side table with the lamp and the white trim-line phone. He walked over to it and saw that the volume was off.

"Ready for calls," he told Dillinger.

"Good. We'll manage it from here. Capone, get on down and help Nelson with the hostages. Schultz is in the eagle's seat in the right tower. Floyd's in the left. And we've got our good old boy, our very own private Machine Gun Kelly, in the back. Don't trust those hostages, though. I'm thinking if we have to get rid of a few, we'll be in better shape."

"No, we won't be," Nick said flatly. "You hurt a hostage, it tells the cops that they're not doing any good with negotiation. We have to keep them believing they're getting everyone back okay. That's the reason they'll hold off. If they think we're just going to kill people, they'll storm us, figuring to kill us before we kill the hostages. That's the logic they teach, trust me," Nick told Dillinger.

Dillinger shrugged, looking at the phone. "Well, we'll give them a little time, if nothing else. So, Miss Cameron, just how are you doing?"

Dakota Cameron looked up and stared at Dillinger, then cocked her head at an angle. "Looking for a needle in a haystack?" she asked. "I'm moving some hay out of the way, but there's still a great deal to go. You do realize—"

"Yes, yes," Dillinger said impatiently. "Yes, everyone has looked for years. But not because their lives were at stake. You're holding so many precious souls in your hands, Miss Cameron. I'm just so sure that will help you follow every tiny lead to just where the treasure can be found."

"Well, I'll try to keep a clear head here," she said. "At the moment, my mind is not hampered with grief over losing anyone, and you really should keep it that way. I mean, if you want me to find out anything for you."

Nick wished he could have shut her up somehow; he couldn't believe she was taunting a man who was half-crazy and holding the lives of so many people in his hands.

He had to admire her bravado—even as he wished she didn't have it.

But Dillinger laughed softly beneath his mask.

"My dear Miss Cameron, you do have more balls than half the men I find myself working with!" Dillinger told her. "Excellent—if you have results. If you don't, well, it will just make it all the easier to shut you up!"

She wasn't even looking at Dillinger anymore. She'd

turned her attention back to the journal spread open before her.

"Let me work," she said softly.

Dillinger grunted. He took a seat in one of the chairs by the wall of the library, near the phone.

Nick walked to the windows, looking out at the gardens in the front of the house, the driveway and—at a distance—the wall and the great iron gates that led up to the house.

More and more cars were beginning to arrive—marked police cars, unmarked cars belonging to the FBI and other law-enforcement agencies.

He wondered how Dillinger could believe he might get out of this alive.

And then he wondered just how the hell any of them were going to get out alive.

The phone began to ring. Dakota Cameron jumped in her chair, nearly leaping from it.

Nick nearly jumped himself.

Dillinger rose and picked up the phone. "Hello? Dillinger here. How can I help you? Other than keeping the hostages alive… Let's see, how can you help me? Well, I'll begin to explain. Right now, everyone in the house is breathing. We have some employees, we have some guests… What we want is more time, really good speed boats—cigarettes or Donzis will do. Now, of course, we need a couple because a few of these good people will be going with us for just a bit when we leave. We'll see to it that you get them all back alive and well as long as we get what we want."

Nick wished he was on an extension. He wanted to hear what was being said.

He saw Dillinger nod. "How bright of you to ask so

quickly! Yes, there is a missing child, too, isn't there? An important little boy—son of a mayor! Ah, well, all children are important, aren't they...? Mr. Frasier? Ah! Sorry, Special Agent Frasier. FBI. They've brought in the big guns. Let's go with this—right now, I want time. You give me some time and you arrange for those boats. To be honest, I'm working on a way to give you back that kid I scooped up. Not a bad kid, in the least. I liked him. I'd hate for him to die of neglect, caged and chained and forgotten. So, you work on those boats."

Nick saw Dakota Cameron frown as she'd heard the name Frasier. Not that Frasier was a rare name, but Kody was good friends with Kevin Finnegan and therefore friends with his sister Kieran—and so she knew Craig. She had to be puzzled, wondering first if he was indeed the same man a friend was dating and, if so, what he was doing in South Florida.

She looked up from her ledger. She was staring at Dillinger hard, brows knit in a frown.

A moment later Dillinger set the receiver back in the cradle. He seemed to be pleased with himself.

"You kidnapped a child?" she asked.

"I like to have a backup plan," Dillinger said.

"You have all of us."

"Yes. But, hey, maybe nobody cares about any of you. They will care about a kid."

"Yep, they will," Nick interrupted. "But I think they need to believe in us, too. Hey, man, you want time for Miss Cameron to find the treasure, the stash, or whatever might be hidden? If we're going to buy that time, we need to play to them. I say we give them the security guard. He needs medical attention. Best we get him out of here. An injured hostage is just a liability. Let's give him up as a measure of good faith."

"Maybe," Dillinger said. He looked at Kody. "How are you doing?"

"I'd do a lot better if you didn't ask me every other minute," she said. "And," she added softly, "if I wasn't so worried about Jose."

"Who the hell is Jose?" Dillinger asked.

"Our security guard. The injured man," Kody said.

Dillinger glanced restlessly at his watch and then at the phone. "Give them a few minutes to get back to me."

He walked out of the room, leaving Nick alone with Kody.

"How *are* you doing?" he asked her.

She shrugged and then looked up at him. "So far, I have all the same information everyone has had for years. Anthony Green robbed the bank, but the police couldn't pin it on him, couldn't make an arrest. He wrote in his own journal that it was great watching them all run around like chickens with no heads. Of course, it wouldn't be easy for anyone to find the stash. What it seems to me—from what I've read—is that he did plan on disappearing. Leaving the country. And he was talking about boats, as well—"

She broke off, staring at the old journal she was reading and then flipping pages over.

"What is it?" Nick asked.

She looked up at him, her expression suddenly guarded. He realized that—to her—he was a death-dealing criminal.

"I'm not sure," she said. "I need time."

"You've got time right now. Use it," he said.

"We need to see some of the hostages out of here—returned to safety," she said firmly. "In good faith!"

They were both startled by the sound of a gunshot. Then a barrage of bullets seemed to come hailing down on the house.

A priceless vase on a table exploded.

Nick practically flew across the room, leaping over the desk to land on top of Kody—and bring her down to the floor.

The barrage of bullets continued for a moment—and then went silent.

He felt her move beneath him.

He looked down at her. Her eyes were wide on his as she studied him gravely. He hadn't just been intrigued, he realized. He hadn't just wanted to see her again.

He'd been attracted to her. Really attracted.

And now…

She was trembling slightly.

He leaped to his feet, drawing her up, pulling her along with him as he raced down the hall to the stairs that led to the right tower where Schultz had been keeping guard.

Nick was pretty damned certain Schultz—a man who was crazy and more than a little trigger happy—had fired the first shots.

"What the hell are you doing?" he shouted.

As he did so, Dillinger came rushing along, as well. "What the hell?" he demanded furiously.

"I saw 'em moving, boss. I saw 'em moving!" Schultz shouted down.

The phone started ringing. Nick looked at Dillinger. "Let me take it. Let me see what I can do," he said.

Dillinger was already moving back toward the library. Nick followed, still clasping Kody's hand.

When they reached the library, Dillinger stepped back and let Nick answer the phone.

"Hello?" Nick said. "This is Barrow speaking now. We don't know what happened. We do know that you responded with the kind of violence that's going to get someone killed. Seriously, do you want everyone in here dead? What the hell was that?"

"Shots were fired at us," a voice said. "Who is this?"

"I told you. Barrow."

"Are you the head man?"

Nick glanced over at Dillinger.

"No. I'm spokesman for the head man. He's all into negotiation. What we want doesn't have anything to do with a bunch of dead men and women, but that's what we could wind up with if we don't get this going right," Nick said.

"We don't want dead people," the voice on the other end assured him.

"We don't, either," Nick said.

"Barrow. All right, let's talk. I think everyone got a little panicky. No one wants anyone to die here today. We're all working in the same direction, that being to see that everyone gets out alive. Okay?"

Nick knew who was doing the negotiating for the array of cops and FBI and law enforcement just on the other side of the gates.

He was speaking with Craig Frasier. Nick was glad the FBI and the local authorities had gotten it together to make the situation go smoothly. He knew Craig; Craig knew him. There was so much more he was going to be able to do with Craig at the other end.

"How are they doing on my boats?" Dillinger asked, staring at Nick.

"We're going to need those boats," Nick said. He needed to give Craig all the information he could about the situation, without making Dillinger suspicious, and he wanted, also, to maintain his position as spokesman for Dillinger.

"Yes, two boats, right?" Craig asked.

"Good ones. The best speedboats you can get your hands on. Now, we're not fools. You won't get all the information you need to save everyone until we're long gone and safe. But, right now, we're going to give you a man. Security guard. He's got a bit of a gash on his head. We're going to bring him out to the front and we'll see that the gate is opened long enough for one of you to get him out. Do you understand? The fate of everyone here may depend on this nice gesture on our part going well."

He knew that Craig understood; Nick had really just told him the guard had been the only one injured and that he did need help.

"No one else is hurt? Everyone is fine?"

Craig had to ask to keep their cover. But Nick knew the agent was also concerned for Dakota Cameron. That the Cameron family owned this place—and that Kody was down here—was something Craig must have realized from the moment Dillinger made his move.

"No one is hurt. I'm trying to keep it that way," Nick assured him, glancing over at Dillinger.

Dillinger nodded. He seemed to approve of how Nick handled the negotiations. There was enough of a low-lying threat in Nick's tone to make it all sound very menacing, no matter what the words.

"That's good. Open the gate and we'll get the man.

There will be no attempts to break in on you, no more bullets fired," Craig said.

Nick looked at Dillinger. *Yes?* he mouthed.

Dillinger nodded. "Keep an eye on her!"

As he hurried out, Kody stood and started after him, then paused herself, as if certain Nick would have stopped her if she hadn't. He held the phone and stared at her, wishing he dared tell her who he was and what his part was in all this.

But he couldn't.

He couldn't risk her betraying him.

He covered the mouthpiece on the house phone. "Don't leave the room."

"Jose Marquez…" she murmured.

"He's really letting him go," Nick said.

She walked over to him suddenly. He was afraid she was going to reach for the mask that covered his face.

She didn't touch him. Instead she spoke quickly. "You're not like that. You could stop this. You have a gun. You could—"

"Shoot them all down?" he asked her.

"Wound them, stop this—stop them from killing innocent people. I'd speak for you. I'd see that everyone in court knew that people survived because of you."

She was moving closer as she spoke—not to touch him, he realized, but to take his gun.

He set the phone down and grabbed her roughly by the wrists.

"Don't pull this on anyone else. Haven't you really grasped this yet? They're trigger happy and crazy. Just do as they say. Just find that damned stash!"

Something in her jaw seemed to be working. She looked away from him.

"You found it already?" he said incredulously. "You have, haven't you? But that's impossible so fast!"

She didn't confirm or deny; she gave no answer. He heard a crackle on the phone line and put it back to his ear. As he did so, he looked out the windows.

Dillinger, wielding a semiautomatic, was leading out two hostages carrying Jose Marquez. They brought him close to the gate, Dillinger keeping his weapon trained on them the entire time.

They left Jose and walked back into the house.

Dillinger followed them.

A second later the gate opened. Police rushed in and scooped up the security guard. They hurried out with him.

The gates closed and locked.

"Barrow! Barrow? Hey, you there?"

"Yes," Nick replied into the phone.

"We have the security guard. We'll get him to the hospital. What about the others? Do they need food, water?"

Kody was staring at him. He heard footsteps pounding up the stairs, as well.

Dillinger was back.

"Sit!" he told Kody. "Figure out what we need to do in order to get our hands on that stash."

To his surprise, she sat. She sat—and had the journal up in her hands before Dillinger returned to the room.

"Well?" Dillinger said to Nick.

Nick spoke into the phone. "We've given you the hostage in good faith. We really would like to see that all these good folks live, but, hey, they call bad guys bad guys because…they're bad. So back away from the gates and start making things happen. What about our boats?"

"I swear, we're getting you the best boats," Craig said.

"I want them now," Dillinger said.

"We need you to supply those boats now," Nick said, nodding to Dillinger and repeating his demand over the phone. "We need them out back, by the docks, and then we need you and your people to be far, far away."

"The boats will be there soon," Craig told Nick.

"Soon? Make that six or *seven* minutes at most!" he said.

He hoped Craig picked up on the clue. Stressing the word told him there were seven in this merry band of thieves.

"Don't push it too far!" Nick added. "Maybe we'll give you to ten or *eleven* minutes to get it together, but... well, you don't want hostages to start dying, do you?"

Easy enough. That told him there were eleven hostages, including Dakota Cameron, being held.

Dillinger looked at Nick and nodded, satisfied.

"We've got one of the boats," Craig said. "How do I get my man to bring it around and not get killed or become a hostage himself?" he asked.

"One boat?"

"So far. Getting our hands on what you want isn't easy," Craig said. "If we give you that one boat, what do we get?"

"You just got a man."

"We could find a second boat more quickly if we had a second man—or woman," Craig said.

They had to be careful; the negotiator's voice carried on the land line.

Of course, Craig Frasier knew that. He would be careful, but Nick knew that he had to be more so. Dakota could hear Craig, as well.

"Please," she said softly, "give them Stacey Carlson

and Nan Masters. They're older. They'll just be like bricks around your neck when you need hostages for cover. Please, let them leave."

"Please," Dillinger said, mimicking her plea, "find what I want to know!"

"I might have," Kody said very softly.

"You might have?"

"Give the cops two more hostages. Give them Stacey and Nan," she said. "I'll show you what I think I've figured out once you've done that. Please."

Dillinger looked at Nick. "Hey, the lady said please. Let's accommodate her. Get on the phone and tell them to get the hell away from the gate. We'll give them two more solid, stand-up citizens." His eyes narrowed. "But I want my boats. Two boats. And I want them now. No ten minutes. No eleven minutes. I want them now!"

He looked at Kody. She was staring gravely at him.

"We have a present for you," he told Craig over the phone. "Two more hostages. Only we want two boats. Now. We want them right now."

"And if we don't get those boats soon…" Dillinger murmured.

He looked over at Kody.

And his eyes seemed to smile.

3

"It's done. He's let them go. Three of the hostages. Your security man, Marquez, and the manager and his assistant."

Kody looked up from the journal she'd been reading.

Concentration had not been an easy feat; men were walking around with guns threatening to kill people. That made her task all the more impossible.

But it was Barrow who had walked in to speak with her. And the news was good. Three of her coworkers were safe.

And she was sure it was Craig Frasier out there doing the negotiating with them on the phone. Craig Frasier. From New York. In Miami.

But then, at Finnegan's, Kieran had been saying that Craig was going on the road; they'd been tracking a career criminal who'd recently gotten out of prison and was already starting up in NYC, and undercover agents in the city had warned that he was moving south.

Dillinger?

Was Craig Frasier here in Miami after Dillinger?

The masked man with the intense blue eyes was staring at her. She schooled her expression, not wanting to give away any of her thoughts or let on that she knew the negotiator and might know about their leader.

"So what happens now?" she asked. Capone was once again standing just outside the library, near the arched doorway to the room. He was, however, out of earshot, she thought, as long as they spoke softly.

"We need getaway boats. And, of course, Anthony Green's bank haul stash. How are you doing?" Barrow asked her.

How the hell was she doing?

Maybe—*maybe*—with days or weeks to work and every bit of reference from every conceivable source, she might have an answer. So far she had found some interesting information about the old gangster, Miami in the mob heyday, and even geography. She'd gone through specs and architectural plans on the house. But she was pretty sure she'd been right from the beginning—the stash was not at the house on Crystal Island. It was in the Everglades—somewhere.

To say that to find something in the Everglades was worse than finding a needle in a haystack was just about the understatement of the year. The Everglades was actually a river—"a river of grass," as one called it. On its own, it was ever-changing. Man, dams, the surge of sugar and beef plantations from the middle of the state on down, kept the rise and flow eternally moving, right along with nature. There were hammocks or islands of high land here and there. The Everglades also offered quicksand, dangerous native snakes and now, sixty-thousand-plus pythons and boas that had been let loose in the marsh and swamps, not to mention both alligators and, down in the brackish water, crocodiles, as well.

Great place to hide something!

"Well?" Barrow asked quietly.

"I don't think the stash is here," she said honestly. "Anthony Green talks about having a shack out in the Everglades. My dad and his University of Miami buddies used to have one. They went hunting—they had their licenses and their permits to take two alligators each. But usually they just went to their shack, talked about school and sports and women—and then shot up beer cans. The shacks were outlawed twenty or thirty years ago. But that didn't mean the shacks all went down, or that some of the old-timers who run airboat rides or tours off of the Tamiami Trail don't remember where a lot of them are."

"So, the stash is in one of the old cabins," Barrow murmured. "But you don't know which—or where." He hesitated. "A place like Lost City?"

Kody stared at the man, surprised. Most of the people she knew who had grown up in the area hadn't even heard about Lost City.

Lost City was an area of about three acres, perhaps eight miles or so south of Alligator Alley, now part of I-75, a stretch of highway that crossed the state from northwestern Broward County over to the Naples/Ft. Myers area on the west coast of the state. It was suspected that Confederate soldiers had hidden out there after the Civil War, and many historians speculated that either Miccosukee or Seminole Indians had come upon them and massacred them all. Scholars believed it had been a major Seminole village at some point—and that it had been in use for hundreds of years.

But, most important, perhaps, was the fact that Al Capone—the real prohibition era gangster—had used the area to create his bootleg liquor.

She hesitated, not sure how much information to share—and how much to hold close.

Then again, she didn't have a single thing that was solid.

But...

It was evident he knew the area. Possibly, he'd grown up in South Florida, too. With the millions of people living in Miami-Dade and Broward counties alone, it was easy to believe they'd never met.

And yet, they had.

She knew his eyes.

And she had to believe that, slimy thief that he was, he was not a killer.

Yes, she had to believe it. Because she was depending on him, leaning on him, believing that he was the one who might save them—at the least, save their lives! She had to believe it because...

It wasn't right.

But, when she looked at him. When he spoke, when he made a move to protect one of them...

There was just something about him. And it made her burn inside and wish that...

Wish that he was the good guy.

"Something like that," she said, "except there's another version of the Al Capone distillery farther south. Supposedly, Anthony Green had a spot in the Everglades where he, too, distilled liquor. Near it, he had one of the old shacks. The place is up on an old hammock and, like the Capone site, it was once a Native American village, in this case, Miccosukee."

"You know where this place is?" Barrow asked her.

"Well, theoretically," she said with a shrug. "Almost all the Everglades is part of the national parks system, or belonging to either the Miccosukee or the Seminole tribes. But from what I understand, Anthony Green had his personal distillery on a hammock in the Shark Valley Slough—which empties out when you get to the Ten Thousand Islands, which are actually in Monroe County. But I don't think that it's far from the observation tower at Shark Valley. There's a hammock—"

Kody stopped speaking when she noticed him staring down at one of the glass-framed historic notes she had set next to the Anthony Green journal she'd been cross-referencing.

"Chakaika," he said quietly.

She started, staring at him when he looked up and seemed to be smiling at her.

"A very different leader," he said. "Known as the 'Biggest Indian.' He was most likely of Spanish heritage, with mixed blood from the Creek perhaps, or another tribe that had members flee down to South Florida. Anyway, he was active from the center of the state on down—had his own mix of Spanish and Native American tongues and traded with other Native Americans, but seemed to have a hatred for the whites who wanted to ship the Indians to the west. He attacked the fort and he headed down to Pigeon Key, where he murdered Dr. Henry Perrine—who really was, by all historic record, a cool guy who just wanted to use his plants to find cures for diseases.

"Anyway, in revenge, Colonel Harney disguised himself and his men as Native Americans and brought canoes down after Chakaika, who thought they could not find him in the swamp. But they found a runaway slave of the leader's who led them right to the hammock where the man lived. They didn't let him surrender—they shot him and his braves, and then they hanged him. And the hammock became known as Hanging People Kay. I know certain park rangers believe they know exactly where it is."

Kody lowered her head, keeping silent for a minute. Her parents had been slightly crazy environmentalists. She knew all kinds of trivia about the state and its history. But while most people who had grown up down here might know the capital and the year the territory had become a state or the state bird or motto, few of them knew about Chakaika. Tourists sometimes stopped at the museum heading south on Pidgeon Key where Dr. Henry Perrine had once lived and worked, but nothing beyond that.

"Chakaika," he said again. "It's written clearly on the corner of that letter."

"Yes, well…they found oil barrels sunk in the area once," she murmured. "They were filled with two of Anthony Green's henchmen who apparently fell into ill favor with their boss. I know that the rangers out there are pretty certain they know the old Green stomping grounds—just like they know all about Chakaika. The thing is, of course, it's a river of grass. An entire ecosystem starting up at Lake Kissimmee and heading around Lake Okeechobee and down. Storms have come and gone, new drainage systems have gone in… I just don't know."

"It's enough to give him," Barrow said. "Enough to make him move."

Kody leaned forward suddenly. "You don't want to kill people. You hate the man. So why don't you shoot him in the kneecap or something?"

"And then Capone would shoot us all," Barrow said.

"Do you really think that I could just gun them all down?"

"No, but you could—"

"Injure a man like that, and you might as well shoot yourself," he told her. "And, never mind. I have my reasons for doing what I'm doing. There's no other choice."

"There's always a choice," Kody said.

"No," he told her flatly, "there's not. So, if you want to keep breathing and keep all your friends alive, as well—"

Dillinger came striding in. "So, Miss Cameron. Where is my treasure?"

"Dammit! Listen to me and believe me! It's not here, not in the house, not on the island," she told him. She realized that while she was speaking fairly calmly, she was shivering, shaking from head to toe.

It was Dillinger and Barrow in the room then.

If Dillinger attacked her, what would Barrow do? Risk himself to defend her?

There certainly was no treasure at the house—other than the house itself—to give Dillinger. She'd told him the truth.

"So, where is it?" he demanded.

Thankfully he didn't seem to be surprised that it wasn't in the Crystal Manor.

"I have no guarantees for you," she said. "But I do have a working theory. This letter," she said, pausing to tap the historic, framed note that had been hand-penned by Anthony Green, "refers to the 'lovely hammock beneath the sun.' It was written to Lila Bay, Green's favorite mistress. In summary, Green tells her that when he's about on business and she's missing him, she should rest awhile in the hammock, and find there the diamond-like luster of the sun and the emerald green of the landscape."

"What's that on the corner?" Dillinger demanded suspiciously.

"It's the name of a long-ago chief or leader who was killed there. I think it was a further reference for Green when he was trying to see to it that Lila found the stash from the bank," Kody said.

Dillinger stood back, balancing the rifle he carried as he crossed his arms over his chest and stared at her.

"So, my treasure is in an alligator-laden swamp— along with rattlers, coral snakes, cottonmouths and whatever else! And we're just supposed to go out to the swamp and start digging in the saw grass and the muck?" Dillinger said.

"I'm still reading his personal references," Kody said. "But, yes. I can't put this treasure where it isn't. I'm afraid I'd falter and you'd know me for a liar in an instant."

"And you think you can find this treasure in acres of swamp land?" he asked.

Everything in Kody seemed to recoil. She shook her head. "I'm not going into the swamp. I don't care about the treasure or the stash. You do. I mean, I can keep reading and give you directions, all kinds of suggestions, but I—"

"Come on, Dillinger," Barrow said. "She'd be a pain in the ass out in the swamp!"

Dillinger turned to stare at Barrow. "She's going with us, one way or the other."

"What?" Barrow asked.

"Did you think I'm crazy? No way in hell we're leaving here without a hostage. We'll take Miss Cameron here for sure. I can't wait to see her dig in the muck and the old gator holes until she finds the diamonds and the emeralds! Come on, Barrow, you can't be that naive. They're not going to just give us speedboats. They're going to have the Coast Guard out. They're going to be following us. Now, I'm not without friends, and I'm pretty damned good at losing people who are chasing me, but…hey, you need to have a living hostage." He turned to Kody. "And, of course, Miss Cameron, if you're going to send us on a wild-goose chase, you have to understand just how it will end for you."

The house line began to ring again.

Dillinger looked at Barrow. "Get it! See if they have my boats for me now. You!" He pointed a finger at Kody. "You figure it out—or you will be the one in the snake and gator waters!"

Kody looked down quickly at the journal she was reading. She prayed he couldn't see just how badly she was shaking.

She knew local lore. She'd walked the trails at Shark Valley. She'd driven out from the city a few times just to buy pumpkin bread at the restaurant across from the park.

But she'd never camped in the Everglades. She'd never even gotten out of her car on the trail once it had grown dark.

Tramping out in alligator-and snake-infested swamps? No way.

"Get the line," Dillinger told Barrow again when the phone continued to ring.

Barrow answered.

"Where are the boats? We're doing our best to make sure that this works but you need to start moving on your end. And, be warned—no cops, no Coast Guard, no nothing coming after us!" he said.

He looked over at Dillinger. "He's getting us a pair of Donzi racers."

"That will do," Dillinger said. "As long as he starts getting it done. As long as he backs off some."

"You keep your men in check—I mean stay back," Barrow said to the person on the other end of the line.

Barrow covered the phone with his hand. "He swears they won't fire unless they're fired on. You've made that clear to the others, Dillinger, right? I don't want one of those trigger-happy psychos getting me killed."

"Hey, we fire on them, they fire back," Dillinger said with a shrug. "Like the saying goes, no one lives forever. If they shoot, they take a chance on killing a hostage!"

Barrow politely relayed Dillinger's threat. Then he walked out of the room, leaving Kody alone with Dillinger.

She kept telling herself that Craig was out there. He was playing a careful game, all that any man could do when hostages were involved.

Did Craig know she was in there? Of course, she knew him, she'd had meals with him and Kieran and the Finnegan family, and they'd talked about her home in Miami and the estate on Crystal Island with all its mob ties...

She blinked, determined that she not give anything away.

Dillinger just looked at her and tapped his fingers on the desk. "We need you, Miss Cameron. Isn't that nice? As long as you're needed, you know that you'll live. Remember that."

Then Dillinger, too, walked out of the room.

Kody looked around, wondering what was near her that might possibly be used as a weapon.

Nothing.

Nothing in the room stood up to a gun.

Nick stood with Dillinger in the ballroom—the large stretch on the left side of the house that connected two of the towers. Crown moldings and silk wallpaper made the room a work of real, old-artisan beauty, but, at the moment, it felt empty and their soft-spoken conversation seemed to echo loudly with the acoustics of the room.

"You played us all," he told Dillinger. "You made us all think that coming here was the job—that there was something here we'd be taking. In and out. Quick and easy. Round up people as a safety net and then get the hell out."

"I said the house was the key to great riches!" Dillinger said. "And this is an easy gig. We have some scared people. We have the cops keeping their distance at the gate. The guard is going to be okay. At worst, he'll have some stitches and a concussion. So, Barrow, don't be a pansy. You know what? I'm not so fond of the killing part myself. But, hell, when a job needs to be done…" He let Nick complete the thought himself.

Instead, Nick went on the offensive. "If Miss Cameron is right, we've got to go south from here and then west into the Everglades. Donzi speedboats aren't going to take us in to where we need to be. I don't think you planned this out."

"You don't think?" Dillinger said, tapping Nick on the forehead. "You don't think? Well, my friend, you're wrong. I know where Donzis won't take us—and I know where airboats will take us! I've done lots of thinking."

"This isn't an in and out!" Nick snapped.

"No. But the reward will be worth the effort."

So, Dillinger had known all along that what he'd wanted wouldn't be found on the property. And he had other plans in the works already. Who else was in on it? Any of the men? None of them? Was Dillinger so up-tight and paranoid that he hadn't trusted a single person in their group?

Nick was pretty sure he was doing a decent job of maintaining his cover while giving his real coworkers as much information as possible. Craig and their local FBI counterparts and law enforcement knew how many men were in the house—and how many hostages remained. He hadn't been able to risk a call to Craig—other than those he made as Barrow. While the agent didn't know the who, how or where, he now knew Dillinger had expected he'd have to leave the house to find his treasure. Would he assume that he'd be heading out to the Everglades, given the legends?

Dillinger had to have people lined up and waiting to help him. As he'd said, to get where they wanted to go, a Donzi would be just about worthless. They'd need an airboat.

Dillinger had no doubt been playing this game for the long run from the get-go.

It was still crazy. There was no real treasure they were taking from the house. There was just information—a major league *maybe* on where treasure might be found.

Dillinger was, in Nick's mind, extremely dangerous. He was crazy enough to have taken a house—a historic property—for what might possibly have been found in it.

And while none of them had even so much as suspected Dillinger would go off and do something like kidnap a child, he had done so—and been smug when he'd let them all know that he had the child for extra leverage.

The kid changed everything. Everything.

Nick couldn't wait for that moment when Dillinger was off guard and the others were in different places and he could take him down and then wait for the others. He couldn't risk losing Dillinger—not until he knew where the man was holding the little boy.

First thing now, though, Nick knew, was to get them all out of the house—alive.

Then he'd just have to keep Dakota Cameron—and himself—alive until Dillinger somehow slipped and told them where to find little Adrian Burke. Then he'd have to get himself and Kody away from Dillinger and whoever the hell else he had in on it and—

Baby steps, he warned himself.

"Here's the thing—we haven't done anything yet, not really," he told Dillinger. "Okay, assault—that's what they can get us on. They don't understand what we're doing, why in God's name we've taken this place, why we've taken hostages…and they really don't have anything. What you really want—what we all want—is the Anthony Green bank-job treasure. They just promised that they're getting the boats—that they'll be here right away. The young woman whose family owns this place is still reading records and I do think she's gotten something in two hours that no one else thought of in decades. Not that it doesn't mean we'll be digging in the muck forever but… I really suggest that you let more hostages go," Nick said.

"I don't know," Dillinger said. "Yeah, maybe…maybe we should get rid of that one woman—the one with the mouth on her. She might be stupid enough to attempt something."

"Good idea. Here's the thing—the hostages are weakening us. We have the hostages in the front and the front towers covered, and you've proven you have sharpshooters up there who will pick off men and happily join in a gunfight. But, with everyone moving around and everything going on, we are missing a man for sound protection in back. I'm afraid they'll eventually figure that out. Let go a few more hostages, and we'll be in a better position to control the ones we do keep."

Dillinger seemed to weigh his words.

Then they heard shots—individual rat-a-tats and then a spray of gunfire.

Dillinger swore, staring at Nick. "What the hell? What the bloody hell?"

"I guarantee you, the cops and the Feds were clean on that," Nick snapped. "One of your boys just went crazy with a pistol and an automatic."

He raced down the length of the room to the stairs to the tower. He was certain the first shots had come from that direction.

Another round of gunfire sounded. Nick ran on up the stairs.

Schultz was there, spraying rounds everywhere.

"What the hell is the matter with you?" Nick shouted.

The man was wielding a semiautomatic. He had to take great care.

Schultz gave him a wild-eyed look before he turned back to the window. Nick made a flying leap at him, hitting him in his midsection, bringing him down.

The semiautomatic went flying across the floor.

Nick rose, ready to yell at Schultz. But the man was

staring up at him with swiftly glazing eyes. He was dead. A crack police marksman had evidently returned the spray of bullets with true accuracy.

"Hey, Barrow! Schultz!" Dillinger shouted from below.

Nick inhaled. He stood and went to the stairs.

"You brought in an idiot on this, Dillinger!" he called down. "They've taken down Schultz. The idiot just went crazy and the police returned his fire. A sharpshooter got him. We need to play for a little time while those boats get here. We need to let more of the hostages go—now. If they figure out just how weak we are in numbers, they might storm the house."

"They do, and everybody dies!" Dillinger swore.

"Don't think with your ass, Dillinger. We can pull this off if no one else acts like we're in the wild, wild, West! I want to live. I didn't come in on a frigging suicide mission! We came here for something. We need to keep calm and figure out the best way to get it. Let me offer up more hostages."

"The girl almost has it. We can grab up whatever journals and all she's using and take the boats. I want them now!"

"The boats are coming. Let me free a hostage!" Nick pleaded.

Dillinger was quiet for a minute. "Yeah, fine. Just one."

"Two would be better. There's a young couple down there—"

"No, only one of them. And tell the cops if another one of our number dies, they'll have all dead hostages. One way or the other!" Dillinger snapped. "Schultz is dead," he reminded Nick. "We should retaliate. Kill someone—not let them go."

Nick hurried along the hall back to the library, Dillinger close at his heels.

The phone was already ringing when they reached the room.

Dakota Cameron remained behind the library desk.

Her face was white, but rather than afraid she looked uneasy. Guilty of something.

For the moment Nick ignored her. He picked up the phone. Once again Craig was on the other end and they were going to play their parts.

"What happened?" Craig asked.

"Your people got a little carried away with fire," Nick said. "We now have a dead man. We should kill a hostage."

"No. The boats are coming. And your man started the firing. He was trying to kill people out here. Our people had to fire back."

"Do it again, the hostages die."

"We don't want to fire."

"Yeah, well, we have anxious people up here carrying semiautomatic weapons. But just to prove that we can keep our side of a bargain, we're going to give you another hostage. Then we want the boats."

"Yes, all right. That can be done."

"We'll have someone for you, so watch the gate. No tricks or someone will die."

"No tricks," Craig said.

Nick hung up. Dillinger was looking at him.

"Okay, we give them a hostage," Nick said. "Or two."

"Two? I said—"

"Two. We'll give them the sassy girl—Betsy, I think her name is—and then a guest. All right?"

"Fine. Do it," Dillinger said.

"You want me out there?" Nick asked.

"Yes, you, Mr. Diplomacy. Get out there."

Nick was surprised. "You're leaving her alone upstairs?" he asked.

"No." Dillinger looked over at Kody, smiled and headed over to her. "I'll be close. But just to be careful…" He reached into his pocket and pulled out police-issue plastic cuffs.

"Miss Cameron, one wrist will do. We just need to see that you don't leave the desk. I can attach you right here, to the very pretty little whirligig in the wood," Dillinger said.

Nick was relieved to see that Kody offered him her left wrist and just watched and waited in silence as he secured it to the desk. She didn't protest; she didn't cause trouble. She was probably just glad they were letting another hostage free.

But Nick didn't trust her. She was a fighter.

"Miss Cameron, you have all the clues, clues that are like a road map, right? You know what we need to do?" Dillinger asked her.

"I have an area. I have an idea," Kody said.

"Don't lie to me," Dillinger said.

She shook her head. "I told you—no guarantees. This treasure has been missing for decades. I believe I know where you can dig, but whether it's still there or not, I don't know. Even the earth shifts with time."

"I knew you could find it, my dear Miss Cameron!"

"Me? How did you even know I'd be here? I don't even live here anymore. I live in New York," Kody said.

"Oh, Miss Cameron. Of course, I checked out my information about the stash, the house—and you. It was possible but I doubted that the treasure would be in the house. I knew that you were here. I knew how much you loved this old house…and, yeah, I knew you'd be leaving soon. So it was time to act." He shrugged, as if he was done explaining. "Now let me get rid of your big-mouthed friend. You help me, I help you. That's the way it works."

Dillinger turned and looked at Nick.

Nick gritted down hard on his teeth.

Yeah, they'd all been taken on this one. Dillinger had known damned well that he hadn't gotten them all to take the house for the treasure.

They'd taken the house for Dakota Cameron.

Because Dillinger believed that she was the map to the treasure.

"Get going, Barrow. Do it. I'll be watching from the top of the stairs. I mean, I really wouldn't want to leave Miss Cameron completely alone," Dillinger said.

Nick headed on out and down the sweeping marble stairs to the first floor.

He was loath to leave the upstairs, especially now that Schultz had been killed. He was afraid Dillinger would lose all logic in a frenzied moment of anger and start shooting.

But he had no choice. And Dillinger needed Kody Cameron. He wouldn't hurt her.

Dillinger was at the top of the stairs.

Watching Kody.

Watching Nick.

And there was nothing to do but play out the man's game…

And make it to the finish line.

4

Capone and Nelson were with the hostages when Nick arrived in the living room. The group of them was still huddled together.

The group, at least, was a little smaller now.

"You," he said quietly, pointing at the tiny woman who had given them the hardest time. "What's your name?"

"What's it to you?" she demanded.

He fired his gun—aiming at a mirror on the wall. It exploded. He waited in silence.

"Betsy Rodriguez!" the young woman answered him.

"Thank you," he told her. "Come on."

"What?" she asked.

"Come on. You're going out."

"Me. Just me?"

"No," he said and pointed to another young woman. She appeared to be in her mid- to late-twenties; she was clinging to the arm of the man beside her. They were a couple. It was going to be hard to split them up.

But it was what Dillinger wanted.

"You," he said to the young woman.

"Us?" she asked. As he'd expected, she didn't want to be separated from the man she was with.

"No. Just you," he said softly.

The young woman began to sob. "No," she said stubbornly. "No, no, no!"

"Please, miss," Nick said. "Honestly, none of us wants any of you dead. Help me try to see that no one does wind up dead."

"Go, Melissa, please go," the dark-haired man who was with her said. "Go!" he told her. "Please. I need to know that you're all right."

"Victor, I can't leave you," the woman—whom he now knew to be named Melissa—said.

Melissa hugged the man she had called Victor. He pulled away from her, saying, "You can and you must."

"How touching! How sweet!" Capone said.

"Nauseating!" Nelson agreed. He walked over as if about to strike one of them with the butt of his gun.

Nick moved more quickly, walking through the huddled crowd to reach Melissa and pull her to her feet. He looked down at Victor as he did so. There was something cold and hateful in the man's eyes. Cold, hateful—and oddly calm.

The guy was a cop! Nick thought. Some kind of a cop or law enforcement. He just knew it. He also knew the man wasn't going to cause trouble when he couldn't win.

Nick thought about the situation quickly. It would be good to have another cop around—except this guy didn't know that he was FBI and he could easily kill Nick thinking he was with the bad guys—which he was, by all appearances.

He reached down and grasped the man's arm.

"Victor, you're coming, too."

The man stood and looked at him. "No, don't take me. Take the young woman who is one of the guides here. She's very scared. I'm scared—just not as scared," Victor said.

Nick liked him.

He wished he could keep him around, that they were in a situation where they could trust one another.

They weren't.

"No, I think we're going to let you lovebirds go together. I don't want my friends here becoming nauseated."

"Hey!" Nelson said. "He told you to go. You don't want us shooting up your lovey-dovey young wife, do you?"

Staring at Nick with a gaze that could cut steel, Victor took his wife's arm and started out of the room, followed by Betsy Rodriguez and then Nick.

He had to be careful now. Dillinger was watching from upstairs and Nelson was following him out to the porch.

Nick walked out toward the gate, making his way slightly past Betsy Rodriguez. He came as close to Victor as he dared and spoke swiftly.

"Cop? Please, for the love of God, tell me the truth," Nick said urgently.

Victor stared at him and then nodded.

"Tell Agent Frasier that the main man plans to get out to the Everglades, down south of the Trail, near Shark Valley. Keep his distance. Watch for men abetting along the way."

It was all he dared say. He shoved the man forward, shouting to the assembled police, agents and whoever else at the gate, "Get the hell back! Take these three—

and remember, sharpshooters have a bead on you and inside there are a few guns aimed at the skulls of a few hostages."

Craig Frasier stepped forward, his hands raised, showing that he was unarmed.

"No trouble! And boats will show up at the docks almost as we speak. But what's the guarantee for the rest of the hostages?"

"You'll find them once we're gone. Most of them," he added quietly. "But we need assurances that we won't be followed. Get too close and— Well, just keep your distance."

He stepped back behind the gate and locked it again.

Betsy Rodriguez and Melissa went running toward officers who were waiting to greet them with blankets.

Only Victor held back a moment, nodding imperceptibly to Nick.

"Wait!" Craig called. "I need more…more on the hostages to give you the two boats."

"As soon as I can see them from the back, I'll bring out a few more," he promised.

"I'll be here. Waiting."

Nick nodded gravely. He turned and headed back toward the house.

As he'd suspected, Capone had waited and watched from the porch.

Nelson was with the rest of the hostages. Dillinger was still upstairs and Floyd and Kelly would be manning the towers.

He doubted that anyone other than himself and Dillinger knew Schultz was dead. Dillinger wouldn't have shared that news, fearing the others might have wanted revenge.

Dillinger only wanted one thing: the treasure.

Capone walked with him through the grand foyer and into the music room. "Good call, by the way, on getting rid of that cop," Capone said.

Nick looked at him; Capone was no idiot. "You saw that, too?"

"Yep. That kind of guy is dangerous. We don't want any heroes around here, you know."

"No heroes," Nick agreed. He shook his head. "I've got to admit—it's got me a little worried. Getting out of here, I mean." He hesitated. A man really wouldn't want to be bad-talking an accomplice in an evil deed. "I kind of thought that Dillinger was sure what he wanted was here. I guess he had the idea we might be heading someplace else to find it all along—and that's why he took the kid. More leverage."

"Yeah, I'm figuring that's the leverage he's using to get us all out of here. Do the cops even know he's the one who took the boy?" Capone asked. "You know, I've done some bad things, but I've never hurt a kid. That's why he didn't tell us. Hell, even in prison, the men who hurt, kill or molest kids are the ones in trouble. I'd never hurt a kid!"

"Nor would I—and probably not our other guys, either, but who knows. And I don't know if the cops know that Dillinger took the boy yet, but I'm figuring they do. And if they find the kid…"

"If they find the kid, we may all be screwed," Capone said.

"Do you know where he stashed him?"

Capone shrugged. "He didn't tell me. Dillinger isn't the trusting kind. Let's just hope he knows what the hell he's doing."

Nick nodded.

He really hoped to hell he knew what he was doing himself.

Kody had a letter opener.

Not just any letter opener, she told herself. This was a letter opener that was now considered a historic or collectible piece. It was fashioned to look like a shiv—the same kind of weapon often carried by Anthony Green and his thugs. They'd been sold at almost every tourist shop in Miami right after Green had been gunned down on the beach.

Now, they were rare. And collectible.

And she had slid the one the property had proudly displayed on the library desk into the pocket of her jeans.

Yep, she thought, a letter opener. Against automatic weapons. Still, it was something.

Maybe it would help once they got to the Everglades. She didn't imagine it would do much against a full-size alligator if one came upon her while she was trying to find the place in the glades where Anthony Green might have hidden his stash—or even one of the thousands of pythons. But at least it was something.

She looked up as Dillinger came striding back into the room.

"How are you doing?" he asked her.

She stared back at him. "Um, just great?" she suggested.

He laughed softly. "You are something, Miss Cameron. You see, I do know what I'm doing. I know that you know what you're doing. See, if you were to go online and Google yourself, you'd find some of your acting pages or your SAG page or whatever it is, and you'd find some promo pictures and play reviews and things like that. But when you keep going, you find out that you were quite the little writer when you were in college and that you did a feature for the school paper on the mob in Miami. You'd already done a lot of studying up on Anthony Green—and why not? Your dad inherited this place! Now, of course, I know you're not rich, that he runs it all in a trust. But I knew that if anyone knew how to get rich, it would be you. As in—if anyone could find the stash, it would be you."

Kody tried not to blink too much as she looked back at him. The man wasn't just scary. He was creepy. He was some kind of an intellectual stalker—and knew things about her that she'd half forgotten herself. It was terrifying to realize he'd really gone on a cyber-hunt for her—and that he'd found far more than most people would ever want to find.

Her skin seemed to crawl.

"I keep telling you this—there's no guarantee. Most people who have studied Anthony Green and Crystal Island and even the mob in general have believed that Green stashed his treasure out in the Everglades. I think I've found verification of that—and that's all," she said.

"But you know just about where. Everyone has looked around Shark Valley—but you know more precisely where. Because you also studied the Seminole Wars, and you loved the Tamiami Trail growing up—and made your parents drive you back and forth from the east to the west of the Florida peninsula all the time."

"I didn't make them," Kody protested, noting how ridiculous her words were under the circumstances. "And you really are counting on what may not exist at all."

"The stash exists!"

"Unless it was found years ago. Unless it's sunk so deep no one will ever find it. Oh, my God, come on! Criminals have written volumes on people killed and tossed into the Everglades, criminals through time who never did a day of time because the Everglades can hide just about anything—and anyone! I can try. I can try with everything I've learned now that I've been put to the fire, and everything that I know from what I've heard and what I've read through the years. But—"

She broke off. He was, she was certain, smiling—even if she couldn't exactly see his face.

"That's right," he said softly. "Bodies have disappeared out there. You might want to remember that."

"Maybe you should remember not to threaten people and scare them and make them totally unnerved when you want them to do calculated thinking!" she countered quickly.

He held still, quiet for a minute. "It will be fun when we reach the peak, Miss Cameron. It will be fun," he promised.

Ice seemed to stir and settle in her veins.

It would be fun...

He meant to kill her.

And still, she'd play it out. Right now, of course, because many lives were resting on her managing to keep this man believing...

And then, of course, because her life depended on it.

Barrow came striding into the room, his blue eyes blazing from his mask. As they lit on her, she felt the intensity of their stare and once again she had a strange feeling that she'd been touched by those eyes before.

"We're closing in on time to go. What are you going to need here, Miss Cameron?" he asked. Then he turned to Dillinger. "I'd wrap up whatever books and journals she wants to take. We'll be getting wet, getting out of here in speedboats."

"Well, what do you need, Miss Cameron?" Dillinger asked.

Barrow had walked over to the windows that looked out over the water.

"They're coming now," he said.

Dillinger walked over to join him. "They've stopped about a mile out."

"I'll give them a few more people and they'll bring the boats in to the docks. Their people will clear the area and we'll leave the last of the hostages on the dock for them," Barrow said.

"Not good enough," Dillinger said. "We need at least a couple of them with us."

"All right, how's this? We let three go. We take two with us—and leave them off once we're a safe distance away."

"I say when it's a safe distance. And if they follow us, the hostages are dead," Dillinger said flatly.

"I'm telling you, hostages will be like bricks around our necks once we start moving," Barrow said.

"Let the guests go. There are a couple of people who work here left—keep them," Dillinger said.

Kody jumped up. "If you're taking them, let me talk to my friends. The guides who work here. Let me talk to them. It will make it easier for you."

Dillinger pulled out a knife. For a moment she thought that Barrow was going to fly across the room and stop him from stabbing her.

But he didn't intend to stab her.

He cut through the plastic cuffs that held her to the desk.

"Go down. I'll warn our guys in the turrets about what's going on," he said.

Barrow caught Kody by the arm. She wanted to wrench free but she didn't. She felt the strength of his hold—and the pressure of her shiv letter opener in her pocket.

She glanced at him as they headed down the stairs.

"This isn't the time," he said.

"The time for what?"

"Any kind of trick."

"I wasn't planning one, but if I had, wouldn't this be the right time—I mean, before we're in a bog or marsh and saw grass and Dillinger shoots me down?"

Those blue eyes of his lit on her with the strangest assessment.

"Now is not the time," he repeated.

She looked away quickly. The man put out such mixed signals. He didn't like blood and guts, yet he didn't want any escape attempts.

He headed with her into the music room where they joined Capone and Nelson.

"You, you, and you!" he said, pointing out the two male and the one female guests.

They stood, looking at one another anxiously. Kody was amazed at how clearly she remembered their names now. The men were Gary Goodwin and Kevin Dean. The woman was Carey Herring.

"No, no, no! They're getting out—and we're not!"

Kody turned quickly to see that Brandi Johnson, her face damp with tears, was looking at the trio who was then standing.

She left Barrow's side, hurrying over to the young woman. "It's okay. It's okay, Brandi," she said. She squeezed the girl's hand and then pulled her close, talking to her and to the young man with the thick glasses at her side. "Brandi, Vince, we're all going to be together. We're going to be fine. Don't you worry. They need us."

"I'm good, Kody. I'm good," Vince told her. She smiled at him grimly. She really loved Vince; he was as smart as a whip and loved everything about his job at the estate. He had contacts that he seldom wore and he was a runner—a marathon runner. He'd told her once that he liked to look like a nerd—which, of course, he was, in a way—because nerds were in.

He would be good to have at her side. Except...

She was very afraid that Brandi was right; they were the ones who would end up dead.

But not now. Right now, she was still needed. All she had to do was to make sure that Dillinger believed they could all be important in finding his precious Anthony Green treasure.

"Come on, you three, it's your lucky day," Barrow said quietly to the guests. "Let's go."

Kody stayed behind with the two guides, taking their arms in hers. "Just hang tight with me," she whispered to a trembling Brandi.

"Stop it. Move away from each other," Nelson told them.

"She's scared!" Kody informed him. "We're not doing anything. She's just scared."

Barrow—who almost had the three being released out the door—paused and looked back. "They're okay, Nelson. Trust me." He turned to Kody. "No tricks at this moment in time, right?"

She met those eyes and, for whatever reason, she had a feeling he was giving her advice she needed to heed. "No tricks."

All the way to the gate, the young woman who was being set free looked back at Nick, tripped and had to grasp someone to keep standing.

"We're almost at the gate," Nick told her. "Look, it's all right. You're going!"

"Someone is going to shoot me in the back!" she whispered tearfully.

"No, you're safe. You're out of here."

When he got the gate open, Craig Frasier raised his arms to show that he was unarmed then stepped forward to accept the hostages.

As he did so, they heard a short blast of gunfire.

"What the hell!" Nick muttered, spinning around furiously. The angle meant the shot had come from one of the towers—and it hadn't been aimed at one of the hostages, him or Craig.

The shot had been aimed at the sky.

Dillinger. He'd headed up to one of the towers himself.

He leaned out over the coral rock balustrade to shout out to the FBI.

"We've got three young people left. They will die if you don't back off completely. You follow us, they die. It's that simple. Do you understand?"

Craig pushed the three hostages through the gate, then stepped back from the fence, lifting his hands. "We aren't following. How do we get the last three?" he shouted.

"We'll call you. Give Barrow there a number. If we get out safe and sound, they'll be safe. Even deal. Got it?"

Craig reached into his pocket and handed Nick his card. Nick shoved the card into the pocket of his shirt. Barely perceptible, Craig nodded. Then he shouted again, calling out to Dillinger, "You have someone else. The boy that was kidnapped this morning. When are you going to give us the boy?"

For a moment Dillinger was silent. Then he spoke.

"When I'm ready. When you keep your word. When you get these hostages back, you'll know how to find the boy."

"Give us the boy now—in good faith. He's just a kid," Craig said, looking at Nick for some sign. But Nick shook his head. So far, he hadn't gotten Dillinger to say anything.

"Kids are resilient!" Dillinger called. "You keep your word, you get the kid."

Craig looked at Nick again. Nick did his best to silently convey the fact that he knew it was imperative they keep everyone alive—and that he figured out where Dillinger had stashed Adrian Burke before it was too late.

The cop—Victor Arden—had apparently repeated word for word what Nick had said earlier. Craig knew what Nick knew so far; they wouldn't have to follow the Donzis at a discreet distance. Dillinger would take his band the sixty-plus miles from their location there on the island down and around the peninsula, curving around Homestead and Florida City, to Everglades National Park.

Every available law-enforcement officer from every agency—Coast Guard, U.S. Marshals, State Police,

Rangers, FBI, Miccosukee Police and so forth—would be on the lookout. At a distance.

While that was promising, the sheer size of the Everglades kept Nick from having a good feeling. Too many people got lost in the great "river of grass" and were never seen again.

He needed to actually speak with Craig—without being watched or heard.

"The boats are docking now in back," Craig told him. "How will my men get back?" He looked up at the tower and raised his voice. "If they're assaulted in any way—"

A shot was fired—into the sky once again.

And Dillinger spoke, shouting out his words. "They just walk off onto the dock. You stay where you are. My friend, Mr. Barrow there, is going to walk around and bring them to you. You know that I have sharpshooters up here in the towers. No tricks. Hey, if I'm going to die here today, everybody can die here today!"

"We don't want anyone to die," Craig said.

"So, my boats best not run out of gas," Dillinger said. "Fix it now…or a hostage dies, I guarantee you."

"You're not going to run out of gas. You have good boats, in sound working order," Craig promised him. "My men will leave the boats' keys in the ignitions, and give Barrow here backups. As soon as my men are safely off the property, we'll all back away."

"Go get 'em, Barrow!" Dillinger shouted.

Nick backed away from the fence and then turned to follow the tile path around the house and out to the back. He traversed the gardens to the docks.

There were two Donzis there, both a good size, both compact and tight. They were exactly what Dillinger had wanted.

Two men, Metro-Dade police, Nick thought, leaped up onto the dock as they saw Nick. They eyed him carefully as he came to meet them. He figured they knew his undercover part in this, but they would still carry out the charade for his safety.

He reached for the keys then he pretended to jerk the two men around and push them forward. He lowered his head and spoke softly. "Tell Frasier and the powers that be to concentrate south of Shark Valley. Around Anthony Green's old distillery grounds."

"Gotcha," one of the men murmured, turning back to look at Nick and raise his hands higher, as if trying to make sure Nick wouldn't shoot him.

"They're after Green's treasure?" the second man asked, incredulous. "Asses!" he murmured. "Everyone is still...okay?"

"Yeah. I'm trying to keep it that way," Nick said. He fell silent. They had come closer to the house on the path. In a few steps they'd be turning the corner to the front. He couldn't risk Dillinger so much as looking at his lip movement suspiciously.

He got the two men to the gate, opened it and shoved them out.

He carefully locked the gate again, looking at Craig.

There was no shout and there were no instructions from the tower. Dillinger, he knew, had already moved on. He'd have gotten what books and materials Dakota Cameron was using and he'd have headed on down and out.

Nick walked backward for a few minutes and then headed back into the house.

As he'd expected, it was empty.

He went through the music room, checked the courtyard and made his way through the vast back porch to look out to the docks.

The cons were already on their way to the boats with the hostages. Dillinger himself was escorting Kody Cameron.

Nick reached the docks just as Dillinger was handing out boat assignments.

Nelson, Capone, Kelly and the young woman, Brandi Johnson, were to take one boat.

Dillinger would take the second with Floyd, Vince and Kody Cameron.

And Barrow, of course.

"Barrow, move it!"

"No!" Brandi cried, trying to break free from Capone to reach Kody and Vince. "No, please, no. Please don't make me be alone, please…"

"You don't need to be alone. I can shoot you right here," Dillinger said.

"Then you can shoot me, too!" Kody snapped. "You let her come with us or you let me go with her, one or the other!"

"I should shoot you!" Dillinger flared, gripping Kody by the front of her tailored shirt.

"Hey!" Barrow stepped in, extracting Kody from Dillinger's grip—a little less than gently—and staring down Dillinger. "Eyes on the prize, remember? Can we get out of here, dammit! Let's go while the going is good. Vince, just go with the nice Mr. Nelson, nice Mr. Capone, and nice Mr. Kelly, please. Brandi—Miss Johnson, step aboard that boat, please!"

Everyone seemed to freeze in response to his words to Dillinger for a minute.

Then Dillinger ripped off his cheap costume shop mask and glared around at everyone.

Nick had his hand on Kody's arm. He could feel the trembling that began.

Now they all knew what Dillinger looked like. They could identify him. Until now, the hostages weren't at much of a risk.

Now they were.

"What are you doing?" Capone began.

"What's the difference?" Dillinger spat. "Who cares? We'll be long gone, and we'll leave these guys in the Everglades. By the time they're found—if they're found—we'll be gone."

The others hesitated and then took off their masks.

And Barrow had no choice. He took off his mask and stared at Kody—praying.

The instant he pulled it off, he detected the flare in her eyes.

She recognized him, of course. Knew that she knew him…immediately. He'd always had the feeling she'd suspected he was familiar, but now that she could see his face, she was certain.

But from the look of confusion that overtook her face, he knew she couldn't place him exactly. And if she did figure it out, he'd have to pray she was bright enough to not say anything. She had to be. Both their lives depended on it.

"Let's get going!"

Nick moved them along, hopping into the front Donzi himself without giving Dillinger a chance to protest.

Dillinger followed, allowing his changes.

Nick turned the key in the ignition, shouting back

to Capone after his boat roared to life, "You good back there?"

"She's purring like a kitten!" Capone called to him.

Nick led the way. He looked anxiously to the horizon and the shoreline. He skirted the other islands, shot under the causeway, joining the numerous other boats.

There was no way to tell which might be pleasure boats and which might be police. He had to trust in Craig to see that law enforcement got in front of them, that officers would be in the Everglades to greet them.

He drove hard for forty-five minutes. The day was cool and clear; under different circumstances, it would have been a beautiful day for boating.

Dillinger suddenly stood by him at the helm. "Cut the motor!" he commanded.

"I thought you wanted—"

"Cut the motor!"

Nick did so. "What are you doing?"

"See that fine-looking vessel up there? Not quite a yacht, but I'd say she's a good thirty feet of sleek speed."

"Yeah, so?"

"We're taking her."

"Ah, come on, Dillinger! She's not the prize," Nick protested.

The second Donzi came up next to them. "That one?" Kelly shouted to Dillinger.

"Looks good to me," Dillinger shouted back.

Nick realized they'd come up with this game plan while he'd been working with the hostages.

"No," Nick said. "No, no, this isn't good."

"What are you, an ass?" Dillinger asked him. "You don't think the cops won't be looking for these Donzis

soon enough? Even if they know we have hostages—
even they know I took the kid. We're taking that boat!"

Kelly was already moving his boat around the larger
vessel. He started shouting. A grizzly-looking fellow
with bright red skin and a captain's hat appeared at the
rail. "What the hell are you carrying on about, boy?"
he demanded.

Kelly lifted his semiautomatic and pointed it at the
old man. "Move over, sir! We're coming aboard!"

"Son of a bitch!" Nick roared. He kicked his vessel
back into gear, flooring it on a course toward the second Donzi.

Kelly turned to him, gun in hand.

"What the hell is the matter with you?" Nick demanded of Kelly.

"What the hell is the matter with *you*?" Dillinger
asked him.

"We're not killing the old bastard," Nick said, snapping his head around to stare at Dillinger. "We're not
doing it. I am not risking a death penalty for you stupid asses!"

Huddled together in the seat that skirted the wheel,
Kody and Brandi Johnson were staring at him.

For the moment, he ignored them.

They were safe for now.

The old man wasn't.

Not giving a damn about damage or bumpers, Nick
shoved the Donzi close to the larger vessel; she was
called *Lady Tranquility*.

Nick found a hold on the hull and lifted himself up
and over onto the deck. The old man just stared at him,
shaking his head. "You think I'm grateful? You think

I'm grateful you didn't kill me? You're still a thug. And you should still be strung up by the heels."

"You got a dinghy of any kind?" Nick asked, ignoring him.

"Yeah, I got a blow-up emergency boat."

"This is an emergency. Blow it up and get the hell out of here!" Nick said.

By then, he heard Dillinger yelling at him again. Floyd was coming up on board, using a cleat the same way Nick had, and Dillinger was pushing Kody upward.

He helped Floyd on, and Kody, and then Brandi.

"Get him in his inflatable dinghy and get him out of here!" Nick urged Floyd.

Floyd stared at him. Then he shrugged and grabbed the old man. "Let's do it, you old salt. Let's do it."

"Make sure he stays the hell away from the radio!" Dillinger ordered, crawling up onto the deck at last. "Come on, get on up here!" Dillinger called to the men in the second Donzi.

Nick left them at the bow, heading toward the aft. He got a quick look down the few stairs that led to the cabin. Seemed there was a galley, dining area, couches—and a sleeping cabin beyond.

The storage was aft; the old man had gotten his inflatable out.

Floyd was keeping an eye on him. "Hurry it up, geezer!" Floyd commanded.

Nick took a quick look down into the cabin and toyed with the idea of using the radio quickly. He made it down the steps, but heard movement above.

"Who the hell does he think he is?" Nick heard. It was Kelly—and he was furious that Nick had stopped him. "Like he thinks he's the boss? Well, the pansy sure as hell isn't my boss!"

Nick looked up the stairs and saw Kelly's gun aimed at the old man again.

Nick couldn't shoot but he couldn't let the man die. His hand reached out for the nearest weapon—a frying pan that hung on a hook above the galley sink. He grabbed it in an instant and aimed it at Kelly's head.

His aim was good—and the old frying pan was solid. Kelly stumbled right to the portside and over the deck and into the water.

Floyd stared at him.

"We're not killing anyone!" Nick snapped.

Floyd shrugged and turned to the old man. "Better get in that boat, then, mister. If he's alive, Kelly will be coming back meaner than hell."

Nick looked at Floyd.

Floyd wasn't a killer, he realized.

Good to know.

Of course, Floyd wasn't a model of citizenry, either.

It was still good to know that in this number, there was at least one more man who didn't want the bay to run red with blood.

"Hey, Barrow!"

It was Dillinger shouting for him. He hurried around to the front.

"Get her moving!" Dillinger said.

"Aye, aye, sir," Nick said. He hurried back to the helm, set the motor and turned the great wheel.

A minute later Dillinger came and stood by him. "Hey, where the hell is Kelly?"

Nick tensed. "I think he went for a swim." Dillinger was silent.

"Hmm. At this point, good riddance." Dillinger shrugged and then turned toward the cabin. "Well, I'll bet the old guy didn't know much about fine wine, but there's bound to be some beer aboard. You know the course, right? Hold to it. We'll be around the bend to some mangrove swamps I know and love soon enough."

Dillinger left him, heading down to the cabin.

Nick spared a moment to take stock. This mission was definitely not going the way they'd planned when he'd signed on to go undercover. But he was playing the hand he'd been dealt. He had no other choice.

At least they were down to three hostages. Dakota Cameron, Brandi Johnson and Vince Jenkins.

And down to four cons. Nelson, Capone, Floyd and Dillinger.

And, of course, there was still a kidnapped boy out there...

And they were heading for the Everglades. Where, soon enough, the winter sun would set.

5

"God, it's dark!" Brandi whispered to Kody.

"Yes, it's dark," Kody whispered back. She wasn't sure why they were whispering. She, Vince and Brandi were the only ones down in the cabin. They were hardly sharing any type of useful secrets.

Above them, on deck, were their captors. Men she could see clearly now.

Dillinger, the oldest and the craziest in the group, had a lean face with hollow cheeks, and eyes that darted in a way that made her think of a gecko. Floyd was almost as much of a "pretty boy" as his borrowed gangster name implied. Nelson, also whipcord-lean, tense, reminded her of a very nervous poodle. Capone was muscular and somewhat stout, with brown eyes and chubby cheeks.

And Barrow.

Yes, she knew him. She knew his face. She recognized him.

From where? She still couldn't pinpoint just when she'd seen him before. So how could she possibly be so certain they had met? But she was.

Why did she feel a strange sense of attraction to him,

as if he were some kind of an old friend, or an acquaintance, or even someone she had seen and thought…

I need to know him.

"Where are we? Do you think we're still in Florida?" Brandi asked. "I mean…we're on the water, I know that, but we're not really moving anymore. I don't think. Or we're going really slow."

"We're right off the tip of the peninsula," Vince said. "Kind of out in the swamps that would make us really hard to find. But, in truth, a pretty cool place, really. You know crocodiles usually hang out in salt water, and alligators like fresh water, but here, we have both—yeah, both. Alligators and crocodiles. 'Cause of the way the Everglades is like a river of grass, you got the brackish thing going…"

Brandi was staring at him in horror.

Kody set a hand on his arm. "Come on, all three of us grew up here. I know I've been to Shark Valley a couple of dozen times. The wildlife is just there—snakes and alligators in the canals and on the trails—and people don't bother them and they don't bother people. We're going to be fine," she told Brandi.

"They're going to leave us out here, aren't they?" she asked, tilting her head to indicate the men on the deck.

"Don't be silly," Kody said.

"Yeah, don't be silly," Vince said. "They're not going to leave us—not alive anyway."

Brandi let out a whimper; Kody pulled her in close and glared at Vince.

"Sorry!" he whispered. "But, really, what do you think is going on?"

"I don't know," Kody admitted.

Vince looked over at her, obviously sorry he'd been so pessimistic when Brandi was barely hanging in.

"I've come down this way a lot," he said. "Hop on the turnpike and take it all the way down to Florida City, hop off, take a right and you get to the Ernest F. Coe Visitor Center, or head a little farther west and go to the Royal Palm Visitor Center and you can take the Anhinga Trail walk and see some of the most amazing and spectacular birds ever!"

Brandi turned and looked at him sourly. "Birds. Yep, great. Birds."

Vince looked at Kody a little desperately.

"Let me see what's going on," she whispered.

She left her position at the main cabin's table and inched her way to the stairs.

As she did so, she heard a long, terrified scream. She ran up the few stairs to reach the deck and paused right when she could see the men. Vince and Brandi came up behind her, shoving her forward so that she nearly lost her balance as the three of them landed on the highest step.

"What the hell?" Dillinger demanded angrily.

Yeah, what the hell? Kody wondered.

The boat's lights cast off a little glow but beyond that the world seemed ridiculously dark out on the water. Except, of course, Kody realized, the moon was out—and it was high up in the sky, bathing in soft light the growth of mangroves, lilies, pines and whatever else had taken root around them.

Kody wasn't a boater, or a nature freak. But she did know enough to be pretty sure they were hugging a mangrove shoreline and that the boat they were on had basically run aground—if that was what you called it when you tangled up in the mangrove roots.

And now it appeared that Nelson was heading back to the boat across the water, walking—or rather running—on water. He wasn't, of course. He was moving across submerged roots and branches and the build-up of sediment that occurred when the trees, sometimes in conjunction with oyster beds, formed coastlines and islands.

"What the hell are you doing, running like a slimy coward?" Dillinger thundered. "Where the hell is Capone?"

"Back there... We were shining the lights and trying to see around us but it's pitch-dark out here. We were a few feet apart. We kept flashing the lights, trying to attract your friend who is supposed to come help us, just like you told us... There was a huge splash, a huge splash, can't tell you how it sounded," Nelson said. He held a gun. He was shaking so badly, Kody was afraid he'd shoot somebody by accident. He worked his jaw and kept speaking. "I saw... I saw eyes. Like the devil's eyes. I heard Capone scream...it was...it was...not much of a scream...a choking scream... It's out there. A monster. And it got him. It got Capone."

"You mean you two were attacked by the wildlife and you just left Capone out there to fight it alone? You have a gun! No, wait! You don't just have a gun—you have an automatic!"

"I couldn't see a damned thing. I couldn't shoot—I couldn't shoot. I could have hit Capone."

"You left Capone!" Dillinger said.

Nelson stared back at him. "Yeah, I left Capone. He was—he was being eaten. He was dead. Dead already. There wasn't anything I could have done."

Kody heard a shot ring out. She saw Nelson continue to stare at Dillinger as if he was in shock. Then, he keeled over backward, right over the hull of the boat, gripping his chest as blood spewed from it.

He crashed into the water.

And Brandi began to scream.

Dillinger spun around. "Shut her up!" he ordered. He was still holding his smoking gun.

Kody was ice cold herself, shaking and terrified. She turned to Brandi and pulled her against her, begging, "Stop, Brandi. Stop, please!"

Vince caught hold of Brandi, pulling her back down the stairs to the cabin, out of harm's way.

There was silence on deck then.

Barrow, Floyd and Dillinger—and Kody—stood there in silence, staring at one another.

"He was one of us!" Floyd said.

"He wasn't one of us!" Dillinger argued. "He let a prehistoric monster eat Capone, eat my friend." He swore savagely and then continued. "Capone was my friend. My real friend. And that idiot led him right into the jaws of a croc or gator or whatever the hell it was!"

"I don't think it was his fault," Floyd said. "I mean—"

Dillinger raised his gun again. Barrow stepped between the two men, reaching out to set his hand on the barrel of Dillinger's gun and press it downward.

"Stop," Barrow said. "Stop this here and now. What's happened has happened. No more killing!"

Dillinger stared at Barrow. Maybe even he saw Barrow as the one voice of sanity in the chaos of their situation.

But, Kody realized, she was still shaking herself.

Cold—and shaking so badly she could hardly remain on her feet.

She shouldn't be so horrified; the two dead men were criminals. Criminals who had been threatening her life.

But it was still horrible. Horrible to think that a man had been eaten alive. Horrible to have watched a man's face as a bullet hit his chest, as he splashed over into the water…

"I never heard such a thing," Floyd murmured as if speaking to himself. "An alligator taking a full-grown man like that."

"Maybe that idiot Nelson panicked too soon and Capone is still out there?" Dillinger asked.

Kody jerked around, startled when she heard Vince speaking from behind her.

"In the Everglades, alligator attacks on humans are very rare. I think the worst year was supposed to be back in 2001. Sixteen attacks, three fatal. You know all those things you see on TV about killer crocodilians are usually filmed in Africa along the Nile somewhere. Crocs are known to be more aggressive, and of course, we do have them here, but… Capone is a big man…not at all usual." He spoke in a monotone; probably as stunned as she was by the events in the last few minutes.

"Someone has to look," Dillinger said. "The airboat is still due. Someone has to look, has to find Capone. Has to make sure…"

No one volunteered.

"Go," Dillinger told Barrow.

"What about the hostages? Three of them and three of us," Barrow noted.

Kody had to wonder if he was worried about Dillinger managing the hostages—or if he was afraid for the hostages.

"I've got the hostages," Dillinger said. "Floyd is here with me. We're good. Go on, Barrow. You're the one with the steel balls—get out there. Find Capone. See if—"

"Alligators drown their victims. They twist them around and around until they drown them," Vince offered.

Kody gave him a good shove in the ribs with her elbow.

He fell silent.

Luckily, Dillinger hadn't seemed to have heard him.

Barrow had.

He suddenly turned and pointed at Vince. "Right, you know a fair amount, so it seems. You come with me."

Kody could feel Vince's tension. Huddled behind him, Brandi whimpered.

Kody had to wonder if Barrow hadn't told Vince to come with him because he was afraid for Vince—afraid that Vince would say something that would send Dillinger into a fit of rage again.

"Um…all right," Vince said.

He looked at Kody, his eyes wide with fear. But then, as he stared at her, something in him seemed to change. As if, maybe, he'd realized himself that Barrow was actually trying to keep them all alive. He smiled. He crawled on past her up the rest of the cabin steps and out onto the deck.

Barrow was already crawling over the hull.

"There's a good tangle of roots right here," Barrow said. "Watch your step, and cling to the trees this way. Dillinger!"

"Yeah?" Dillinger asked.

"The boat's spotlight—throw it in that direction," Barrow said.

"Yeah, yeah, should have done that before."

Kody heard some splashes. For a few minutes she could see Barrow leading, Vince following, and the two men walking off into the mangrove swamp. Then they disappeared into the darkness of the night.

Everything seemed still, except for the constant low hum of insects...

And the occasional sound of something, somewhere, splashing the water.

Victim or prey.

"They really don't," Vince said, his voice still a monotone as he followed Nick across the mangroves, slipping and sliding into several feet of water here and there. "Alligators, I mean. They don't usually attack people. We're not a good food supply. And since the python invasion down here, gators don't get big enough anymore."

"Tell that to the alligators," Nick murmured. He didn't know what the hell had happened himself. It was unlikely that a man Capone's size had been taken down by an alligator, but it wasn't impossible.

And he didn't know who the hell Dillinger was supposed to be meeting, but it was someone coming with an airboat.

Dillinger had taken over at the helm once they'd headed around the tip of the peninsula; Nick had known that he'd force them to come aground. But Dillinger had a one-track thing going with his mind. There'd been no stopping him.

Now, of course, he'd taken Vince with him to keep him alive. Dillinger was trigger happy at the moment.

Nick had been stunned himself when Dillinger had gunned down Nelson without blinking. They were all at risk. What he really needed to do was to take Dillinger down. Take him out of the equation altogether—no matter what it took.

But what about the boy? Adrian Burke. Where was the child? Only Dillinger knew.

Then again, what about the hostages?

Dillinger seemed to get even crazier the deeper they got into the Glades. Did Nick risk Vince, Brandi and Kody in the hope of saving a child who might be dead already by now?

"Help!"

He was startled to hear someone calling out weakly.

"Hey...for the love of God, help me. Please..."

The voice was barely a whisper. It was, however, Capone's voice.

"I hear him!" Vince said.

"Yeah, this way," Nick murmured.

He was startled when Vince suddenly grabbed him by the arm, so startled, he swung around with the Smith & Wesson he was carrying trained on the man.

"Whoa!" Vince said. "I guess you are one of them!"

"What?"

"You, uh, you've kept us alive a few times. I thought that maybe you were a good guy, but, hey...never mind."

Nick said nothing in response. He couldn't risk letting Vince in on the truth. The man talked too much. Instead, he turned, heading for the sound of Capone's weak voice.

Nick came upon him in a tangle of mangrove roots.

Capone seemed to be caught beneath branches and roots that had actually tangled together.

"We thought a gator got you," Vince said.

"Gator? That Nelson is an idiot!" Capone said. "The branch broke, splashed down and pinned me here like a sitting duck. If there is some kind of major predator around… " He paused, looking up at Nick. "My leg is broken. I won't be able to make it to…wherever it is exactly that Dillinger wants to go. You gotta help me somehow, Barrow. You gotta help me. He'll kill me if I'm useless. Dillinger will kill me!"

Nick hesitated but Vince didn't.

"No, no, he likes you!" Vince said. "He just shot that other guy—Nelson—for leaving you!"

"He shot Nelson?" Capone demanded, staring at Nick.

"Yeah," Nick said quietly.

He reached down. First things first. He had to get Capone out of the mire he was tangled in.

There was a sudden fluttering sound as Nick lifted a heavy branch off the man. He had disturbed a flock of egrets, he saw. A loud buzzing sounded; he'd also attracted a nice swarm of mosquitos.

Vince swore, slapping at himself.

"Help me!" Nick snapped.

Vince went to work, slapping at his neck as he did so. "Amazing. Amazing that people actually came and stayed to live in these swamps."

He rambled on but Nick tuned him out. He was too busy detangling Capone.

When they lifted off the last branch and pile of brush, Capone let out a pained cry.

"My leg," he wailed. He looked at Nick desperately. "What the hell do I do? He'll kill me. No, no, we have to kill him, Nick. We have to kill him before he kills all of us."

"We can't just kill him, Capone," Nick said.

"Why the hell not? The hostages are free or with us. Once we kill him—"

"We don't know who he has coming. He made plans for this. Someone is bringing an airboat here. We're stuck, if you haven't noticed. And this may be a national park, but if you've ever spent any time in the Everglades, you know that we could be somewhere where no one will ever find us."

"We have guns."

"And he's got a kid stashed somewhere, too, Capone. A little kid."

"I know. He made sure we all knew. I'm sorry about the kid but—"

"I won't tell him that you wanted to kill him," Nick said firmly.

Capone stared at him and nodded.

"Yeah. Okay. But you watch. He's going to want to kill me."

"I can see that you're left behind. On the boat. The one we stole from that poor old man. Someone will come upon it eventually," Nick said.

"You can make that happen?"

Nick shrugged. "I can try. If you stay behind, it'll probably be the cops who find you. But, hey, these guys might speak nicely for you when it comes to sentencing."

Capone suddenly pulled back and shot him a look. "You're a cop!"

Nick didn't miss a beat. "I swear I am not a cop." Without a moment's hesitation he called to Vince for help lifting Capone.

With Capone shrieking in pain, they got the man up on his one good leg.

Just as they did, they heard the whirr of an airboat and saw a blinding light flood the area.

Sleeping birds shrieked and fluttered and rose high in flight.

Nick noticed the glassy eyes of a number of nearby gators; they'd been hidden in the darkness.

The sound of one engine sputtered and stopped; a second did so just a moment after.

Two airboats had arrived.

"Hey, are you having trouble?" someone shouted.

Nick couldn't see a thing; he was blinded.

But he didn't have to. He knew this had to be Dillinger's associate, whoever he had been waiting for to bring him the airboat.

"Broken leg!" Nick shouted.

The light seemed to lower. He saw the first airboat and a second airboat in back.

A man jumped off the first one and came sloshing through the water. He was quickly followed by another. Both men were tall and muscular and quick to help support Capone.

"Where's Dillinger?" the older of the two, a man with dark graying hair and a mustache and beard to match, asked Nick.

"Back at the boat we took this afternoon," Nick said.

"Cops have been looking for that ever since the old man who owned her got picked up by a Coast Guard vessel about an hour ago."

"You gotta ditch it," the younger man said. He looked just like the older man.

Father and son, Nick figured.

"Everyone is all right?" the older one asked, sounding nervous.

"Do I look all right?" Capone moaned.

"I meant…"

"The hostages are all alive. We've had a few difficulties," Nick said. "There—ahead, there's the boat!"

"Dillinger!"

Dillinger looked over the bow as Nick, Vince, Capone and the two unnamed newcomers came along, nearing the boat.

"Capone!" Dillinger cried. "I knew it. I just knew you weren't dead. You're too damned mean for any alligator to eat!" He frowned then, realizing how heavily Capone leaned upon the men at his sides. "What happened?" he asked darkly.

"We've brought you an airboat—just as you asked," the older of the men shouted.

"Good. How will you get back?" Dillinger asked.

"We've got a second boat. We'll get out of here and back to our business," the older man said.

"All right, go."

"We're even then, right?" the older man demanded. "We did what you wanted."

"Yep. You did what I wanted. Head to the old cemetery in the Grove. Find the grave of Daniel Paul Allegro. Dig at the foot. You'll find what you want. You've evened the score enough, so go," Dillinger said.

"How do I know that the papers are there?" the older man asked.

"You're going to have to trust me. But I've always been good to my word," Dillinger said.

The man with the graying dark hair and beard looked at Nick. "If you would help us…?"

"Yes, of course," Nick said. He took Capone's arm and wrapped it around his shoulder. The night was cool but Capone was still sweating profusely.

The men who had brought the airboat nodded and walked away.

Nick watched as they left, water splashing around them as they returned to the second airboat.

They'd owed Dillinger; he'd been holding something over them. Now all they wanted was to get away as quickly as possible, get to a graveyard and dig something up.

What hold could Dillinger have had on the men?

It didn't matter at the moment. What mattered was the fact that one man was dead and Capone couldn't move an inch on his own.

"My leg is broken!" Capone shouted up to Dillinger. "I'm in bad shape. I tripped, fell, Nelson went running off…"

Dillinger started swearing. "We've got to get you up here." He paced the deck, grabbing his head, swearing. "Floyd! Floyd, get up here, help!"

Floyd appeared on deck, looking around anxiously. He saw Capone. "Hey, you're alive!"

"Well, somewhat," Capone said.

It wasn't easy, but with help from Floyd and Vince, they got Capone onto the boat.

Nick crawled over the hull.

By then, Kody and Brandi had pillows and sheets taken from the boat's cabin stretched out and ready on the deck. In a few minutes, they had Capone comfortably situated. Vince had noted a broken plank caught up in a nearby mangrove. He hurried to get it and, between them all, they splinted Capone's leg.

"He needs medical care," Kody said.

"He can't go slogging through the Everglades, up on the hammocks, through the saw grass and the wetlands," Nick agreed quietly.

"I'll make it! I'll make whatever!" Capone said. "Don't…don't…"

"He thinks you're going to kill him," Vince told Dillinger.

"What?" Dillinger asked. He truly looked surprised.

"I'm like a lame horse," Capone said quietly.

Kody had been kneeling on the deck by him. She stood, retreated down the steps for a minute, and came back with a bottle of vodka.

"This will help," she said.

"I killed Nelson for leaving you, because we don't turn on each other," Dillinger said. He looked at his friend and reassured him.

"Then you have to leave me," Capone said, looking at Dillinger and taking a long swig of the vodka. He sighed softly, easing back as the alcohol eased some of his pain. "I swear there's nothing I will tell them. There's nothing I can tell them. I don't even know where you're going. Just leave me."

"You'll do time. You know you'll do time," Dillinger told him.

"Yes, yes, I will. But I may live long enough to get out," he said. "If I try to go with you…"

Dillinger thought about his words. He lowered his head. After a long moment he nodded.

He walked over to the big man on the ground, leaned down and embraced him.

Then he jerked up, his gun trained on the others.

"He stays. We go," he said.

Nick was startled when Kody spoke up. "You can't leave him, not like this."

"Miss Cameron," Nick said, trying to step in, trying to stop whatever bad things her words might do to Dillinger's mind.

"He needs help. Look," Kody said, determined. "Brandi is screaming and scared and freaking us all out. She needs to be picked up as soon as possible. And Capone here needs help. Leave the two of them. Capone still has his gun, and Brandi isn't a cruel person. They have enough supplies on the boat to get them through the night okay. I say we leave them both." She turned to Dillinger. "That leaves five of us. Five of us in good health and good shape and not prone to hysterics in any way. We can make it."

Dillinger stared back at her. Nick barely dared to breathe.

Dillinger smiled. "You are quite something, Miss Cameron. I think you might have something. All right! Get supplies together. We leave Capone and little Miss Cry Baby here. Actually, Blondie, you really were starting to get on my nerves. Let's do it."

"You want to move deep into the Everglades by night?" Vince asked Dillinger.

"Well, hell, yes, of course!" Dillinger said. "The cops or someone will be around here very soon. We've got to get deep into the swamp and the muck and the hell of it all before the law comes around. Darkness, my boy! Yes, great. Into the abyss! Indeed, into the abyss!"

6

The airboat was a flat-bottomed, aluminum-and-fiberglass craft with the engine and propeller held in a giant metal cage at the rear. Dillinger prodded everyone in.

Kody recalled the two men who had come to deliver the boat. They hadn't looked like bad men.

Once again she asked herself, *So what did bad men look like?*

Why didn't Barrow look like a bad man? Was he a good man—somehow under the influence of real criminals because he was between a rock and a hard place? He had a child somewhere being held, perhaps. Somehow, he was being coerced…either that, or she was simply being really drawn to someone really, really bad—and she couldn't accept that!

She had a hard time understanding what was going on with any of the men. She wished she could close her eyes and open them to find out that everything that had happened had occurred in her imagination.

But it was real. Too real.

At least she was grateful that Dillinger had listened to her and left both Capone and Brandi behind.

Alive.

As she was. For now…

Amid the deafening sounds of the motors she looked out into the night.

It was dark. Darker than any darkness Kody had ever known before. There was a haze before her to the north, and she knew the haze she saw was the light that illuminated the city of Miami and beyond up the coast.

But it was far away.

Out here Kody had no concept of time. She realized suddenly that she was tired, exhausted. It had to be getting close to the middle of the night. It seemed they'd been moving forever, but, of course, out here, that didn't mean much. Unless you were a ranger or a native of the area, each canal, new hammock and twist and zig or zag of the waterways seemed the same. The glow of gator eyes—caught by the headlights of the airboat—was truly chilling.

And despite it all, she'd nearly drifted to sleep twice. Vince had caught her both times.

Suddenly the whirr of the airboat stopped. She jerked awake—as did Vince at her side.

"Where are we?" Vince murmured.

Kody didn't know. But as she blinked in the darkness, Barrow and Floyd jumped out of the airboat and caught hold of the hull, pulling it—with the others still aboard—up on a hammock of higher, dry land. The lights still shone for a moment, long enough for Kody to see there was a chickee hut before them. It was the kind of abode the Seminole and Miccosukee tribes of Florida had learned to use years before—built up off the ground, open to allow for any breeze, and covered with the palms and fronds that were so abundant.

She was still staring blankly at the chickee hut when she realized Barrow had come back to the airboat—and that he had a hand out to assist her from her chair.

She was so tired that she didn't think; she accepted his hand. And she was so tired that she slipped coming off the airboat.

He swept her up quickly. Instinctively she wound her arms around his neck.

It felt right; it felt good to hold on to him...

She wanted to cry out and pull away. And she didn't know why she felt with such certainty that he would protect her and that he'd keep her from harm.

He set her down on dry ground. "Hop on up. I'm going to light a fire," he said, indicating the chickee hut.

It was just a few feet off the ground. Vince was already there. He offered her an assist up and she took it.

There was nothing in the little hut—nothing at all. But it was dry and safe, Kody thought. Floyd was up on the platform with them and he indicated that the two of them should sit. "Make yourselves as comfortable as you can. Grab what sleep you can. This isn't exactly the Waldorf but..."

Kody took a seat in the rear of the chickee hut and Vince followed her. She could hear Dillinger and Barrow talking, but they kept their argument low and nothing of it could be heard.

Vince shook his head. "What the hell?" he murmured.

Kody reached for his hand and squeezed it. "Hey. We're going to be okay."

"Yeah."

"Just follow directions and you'll be okay," Floyd said.

They were both silent. Then Vince spoke, as if he just had to have something to fill the silence of the night.

"Did you know that Alexander Graham Bell led the team that created the first airboat?" Vince asked idly as they sat there. "And it was up in Nova Scotia? The thing was called the *Ugly Duckling.* Cool, huh? The things are useful down here—and on ice for rescues. Go figure."

"Sure, cool," Kody agreed. "I had not known that," she said lightly.

"Alexander Graham Bell, huh, go figure!" Floyd said.

Kody thought Floyd was just as interested in what the others were saying as she and Vince were. He kept trying to listen. He had his gun on his lap—ready to grab up—but Kody was getting a different feeling from the man than she had earlier. Somehow, right now, he didn't seem as dangerous.

Floyd inched closer. "Do you really think you can find this treasure stash Dillinger thinks you can find?" he asked, looking first at Kody and then on to Vince. "I guess I never knew the guy. I mean, I hope you can find that treasure. Seems like the only one who can kind of keep Dillinger in check right now is Barrow, but even then…" His voice trailed. He squinted—as if squinting might make him hear more clearly.

Kody glanced at Vince and then at Floyd. "I don't know. I mean…we're following a written trail. Things change. The land out here changes, too." She hesitated and then asked, "Do you think he's going to kill us all?"

Floyd shrugged. "Hell, I don't know. I actually wish I was Capone! Yeah, they'll get him. Yeah, he'll go to jail. But he won't die out here in this godforsaken swamp!"

"Why don't you just shoot him?" Vince asked. "You just shoot Dillinger dead when he least expects it. Kody and I disappear until we can get help. You disappear into the world somewhere, too. You don't want to hurt us, and we won't turn you in. The three of us—we live."

Floyd hesitated, looking away. "Dillinger won't do it—he, um, he won't kill us."

"He might! Why take a chance?" Vince said.

Floyd smiled. "Don't kid yourself. I could never out-draw Barrow. I could never even take him by surprise." He lifted his shoulders in a hunch and then let them fall. "If I could…no. You've got to be careful, toe the line! Barrow is freaked out that Dillinger kidnapped that kid. Barrow can't take the kid thing and I think he's pretty sure the boy is stashed somewhere and he'll wind up dying if we don't get the truth from Dillinger. He won't do anything until Dillinger gives up the kid, and now that we're out here… I don't know how in hell that's going to happen."

Kody swatted hard at an insect, her mind racing. "If the police just got their hands on Dillinger, they could make him talk."

Floyd shook his head. "Dillinger's real name is Nathan Appleby. I'm not supposed to know any of this. None of us is supposed to know about the others. But I was at this place Dillinger was staying at in the Grove one day and I found some of his papers and then I looked up anything I could about him. He served fifteen years of a life sentence up north. He and some other guys had kidnapped a white-collar executive. He wouldn't give up the guys he was working with to the cops—or the old crack house where they were holding their hostage. The hostage wound up dying of an overdose shot up into his veins by the people holding him. Nathan's gang on that one did get away with the money. But one of them betrayed Nathan. That guy wound up in the Hudson River.

"See, that's just it—he holds things over on people. Like the guys who brought the airboat. He had papers on them, I'm willing to bet, which would have proven the older man's—the dad's, I'm pretty sure—illegal status here in the USA. And, I'm willing to bet, when Nathan gets what he wants here, he's got some other poor idiot he's blackmailing somehow to have a mode of transportation available for him that will get him out of the country. Not so hard from here, you know. He can get to the Bahamas or Cuba damned easily, and move on from there."

Kody had been so intent on Floyd's words that she didn't hear or see Dillinger approaching until Vince nudged her. She turned to see that Dillinger and Barrow had come up on the platform. She wasn't sure if Dillinger had heard what Floyd had been saying.

"What's going on here?" Dillinger asked.

"I'm telling them that they'd be crazy to try to escape," Floyd said. "Nowhere to go."

"I don't believe you," Dillinger said. There was ice in his voice. He raised his gun.

Kody wasn't sure what might have happened if she hadn't moved, and she wasn't the least sure of what she was doing.

She was just very afraid that Dillinger was about to shoot Floyd.

She rolled off the ledge of the chickee hut and landed down on the ground of the little hardwood hammock they had come upon.

And she began to run.

He wouldn't fire at her, would he? Dillinger wouldn't fire at her!

She heard a shot. It was a warning shot, she knew. It went far over her head.

And she stopped running. She couldn't see anything at all, except for large shadowlike things in the night, created by the weak moonlight that filtered through here and there. She tried to turn and her foot went into some kind of a mud hole. She stood for a moment, breathing deeply, wondering what the hell she had done—and what the hell she could do now.

She could hide and maybe they wouldn't find her.

"Kody."

She heard her name spoken softly. It was Barrow. She turned but she couldn't see him.

"Stay where you are," he whispered. "Don't move."

She stood still, puzzled, afraid—and lost.

And then she understood. At first it sounded as if she was hearing pigs rooting around in a sty. Then she realized the sound was a little different.

She felt Barrow's hand on her upper arm, at the same time gentle and firm. He jerked her back, playing a light over the muck she'd just stepped into.

And right there in the mud hole she saw a good-size group of alligators. They weren't particularly big, but there were plenty of them gathered together on the surface of the mud.

She froze and her breath stalled in her throat.

"Come on!" he said, pulling her away.

With his urging, she managed to move back. She realized she had come fairly far—the chickee hut and the fire Barrow had built were a distance ahead through a maze of brush and trees. She knew then that this was the opportunity she'd been waiting for. She turned to Barrow.

"He's going to kill everyone and you know it," Kody said.

"I don't intend to let him kill everyone," he said. "You have to believe me."

He looked directly into her eyes then and, in the light of the flashlight, she saw his face clearly. She wasn't sure why, but at that moment she remembered where and when she had seen Barrow before.

In New York City. She and Kevin had been walking out of Finnegan's. He'd been telling her that he had a secret new love in his life, and he was very excited. And she had been laughing and telling him she was glad she was all into her career and the move to New York, because she didn't have anyone who resembled a love—new or old—in her life at all.

And that's when she'd plowed into him. Run right into him. He'd been there with another man—Craig Frasier. Of course, she knew Craig Frasier because she knew his girlfriend Kieran Finnegan.

They paused to look at one another, both apologizing and then...

She'd thought instantly that he felt great, smelled great, had a wonderful smile, and that she wanted to find out more about him. She'd hoped he wasn't married, engaged or dating, that she'd be able to see him and...

Then Kevin had grasped her arm and they'd hurried on out and...

Her mind whirled as the memories assailed her.

"You're FBI!" she said.

His hand on her arm tensed and he pulled her closer. "Shh!"

"All along, you're FBI. You could have shot him dead several times now. We're here, out in the true wilds, the Everglades where even the naturalists and the Na-

tive Americans and park rangers don't come! You could
have shot him, you—"

"Shh! Please!"

"You didn't say anything to me! Not a word," Kody
told him. She was shaking, furiously—and still scared
as could be.

"I couldn't risk it," he said.

"But I recognize you—"

"It took you a while," he said. "Look, if you'd recognized me and it had shown, and Dillinger had known, or
Schultz, or even one of the others, we could all be dead
now. I just infiltrated this gang not long ago. It should
have been easy enough. We should have gotten into the
house. I should have been able to design a way in for
the cops and the FBI, but…there's a little boy out there.
Dillinger kidnapped a kid. I have to get him to tell me
where he's holding that boy."

She stared at him, sensing his dilemma, because she
herself felt torn.

On the one hand, her desire to survive was strong.

And on the other hand, she couldn't let an innocent
child die.

"You've had opportunities to tell me," she said. "I
could maybe help."

"How?"

"You're forgetting—he believes he needs me. He
thinks I know all about Anthony Green and the stash
of riches from the bank heist Green pulled off years and
years ago. Maybe he'll talk to me. Maybe he will—you
don't know!"

"And maybe he won't. And maybe he'll figure out that
Vince is really more up on history than you are and that

he needs him—and doesn't need you. Dammit, I'm trying to keep everyone alive," Barrow said to her.

Barrow. His real name was Nick. Nicholas Connolly. Now she remembered clear as day.

She remembered everything. She'd asked Kieran and Craig about him later, and they'd told her his name—and what he did!

"You're on some kind of a team with Craig Frasier. He's the one you've been talking to all along on the negotiations," Kody said.

"A task force. And, yes. Our task force has followed Dillinger—actually, Nathan Appleby—from New York on down. And now…we've got to stop him here. But we've seen what he's capable of. We have to find that boy before Nathan knows that he's trapped." He was staring at her and he let out a long breath.

"What do we do?" she whispered. "He's—he's crazy. Even Floyd thinks he's crazy. He shot and killed one of his own men!"

"We go back. We make it through the night," he told her. "There's nowhere to go out here. We're north of the tip of the peninsula and south of Tamiami Trail and the Shark Valley entrance up that way. A mile here is like a hundred miles somewhere else. The chickee is the safest place to be for the night." When she shivered, he added, "One of us will be on guard through the darkness."

She looked at him.

He was right about one thing.

She didn't want to just walk into the darkness of the Everglades.

Vipers, constrictors and crocodilians, oh, my.

"Okay," Kody said quietly. "Okay. So we go back. Morning comes. We head to what I believe to be the area where Anthony Green had his distillery, his Everglades hideout. And what happens if I can't find the treasure he wants? What happens if you can't find the boy?"

"I have to believe that we'll get what we need—that somewhere in all this, Dillinger will trust me and that I can get him talking. And if not, I pray that the cops and the FBI and everyone else working the kid's disappearance will find a clue. One way or the other, I will see to it that you and your friend, Vince, are safe by tomorrow morning. I got information to Craig. They know where to go. They'll have a very carefully laid ambush for tomorrow. We just have to get to that time."

Kody nodded dully. Okay. She'd go back.

He suddenly pulled her into his arms; she swallowed hard, looking up at him, seeing the emotion conflicting in his eyes.

"I'll keep you safe!" he vowed. "I'll keep you safe!"

"I know!" she whispered, hoping there was more courage in her voice than she felt.

"I have to make this look real," he told her.

She felt the muzzle of his gun against her back. "Of course."

Dillinger was standing by the edge of the chickee hut ledge when they returned—watching for them.

"My dear Miss Cameron! Foolish girl. Where were you going to go?" he asked.

"She's not going anywhere. She's going to be by my side from here on out," Barrow—or, rather, Nick Connolly—told him.

"Let's hope not. It's getting late. We could all use a little sleep. Oh, but, please, don't go thinking that my fellows are sweet on you, Miss Cameron, or that if I sleep, you can run again," Dillinger said. "I wake at a whisper in the wind. You will not pull things over on me.

"Not to mention…the coral snake doesn't have much of a mouth span, but the bite can be lethal. There are pygmy rattlers out there and Eastern diamondbacks. And the cottonmouth. Nasty, all of them. Not to mention the pythons and boas. But, since I'm being honest here, I haven't heard of anyone being snuffed out by one of them yet. There are the alligators and the crocs—mostly alligators where we are right now, but, hey, if you're going to get mauled or eaten by an alligator or a croc, do you really care which one?"

"I'm not going anywhere," Kody said. "You scared me. You scared me worse than the thought of a snake or an alligator or whatever else might be out here." She inhaled air as if she could breathe in courage. So far, it seemed to work with him. "You have to stop. You got mad at your own man for nothing. You—you shot one of your own men."

"He betrayed the brotherhood," Dillinger said.

"I want us all to live. You want Vince and me to find your treasure. So quit scaring everyone so much and we'll find your treasure."

Dillinger smiled and glanced at Barrow where he stood right behind her.

"This one is a little firecracker, isn't she?" Dillinger asked.

"And you need her," Barrow said softly. "And you do have your code of honor, Dillinger. None of these people has betrayed anyone, so let's just let them be. Meanwhile it's you, me and Floyd taking turns on guard. We'll get some sleep."

"Sure," he said. "Floyd, there's some water and some kind of food bars on the airboat. Go get 'em."

"On it, boss," Floyd said.

Kody realized that she was desperately parched for water—and that she was starving, too.

Barrow—Nick—walked around her, leaped up onto the platform and then reached a hand down to help her up.

She accepted it.

And when Floyd came with the water and power bars, she gratefully accepted those, as well.

After she ate, she found herself curling into a little ball on the wooden platform. Vince was to her one side. Nick was to her other side, leaning against one of the support poles.

"I'll take the first hours," Dillinger said. "Floyd, you're up next."

Hours later, Kody realized she had fallen asleep. She opened her eyes and Nick was still by her side, sitting close beside her, awake, keeping guard. She could feel his warmth, he was so close, and it was good.

The night had been cold, and she was scared, but she'd slept, knowing Nick Connolly remained at her side.

She looked up at him. His eyes were open and he was watching her. She was startled to feel a flood of warmth streak through her.

Of course, she remembered now when she had initially met him. Her reaction had been quite a normal one for a woman meeting such a striking man. He was really attractive with his fit build and dark blue, intense eyes. She'd had to hurry out that night at Finnegan's, but she'd thought that maybe she'd see him again.

Then life, work and other things had intervened.

And now…

He was good, she thought. Good at what he did. He had kept all the hostages alive so far. He had gotten many of them to safety.

He was still a very attractive man. Even covered in Everglades' mud and muck. With his broad shoulders and muscled arms he looked like security. Strength. And she was so tempted to draw closer to him, to step into the safe haven of those arms…

What was she thinking? This had to be some kind of syndrome, she told herself. Kieran Finnegan would be able to explain it to her. It was a syndrome wherein women fell in love with their captors.

No, she wasn't in love. And he wasn't really a captor. He was as G-man and he worked with Craig Frasier!

"You okay?" he whispered.

She nodded.

"I will get you out of this."

"Yes… I believe you."

He nodded grimly.

"Vince? Is Vince all right."

"Right now? He's quite all right. Take a look."

Kody rolled carefully to take a look at Vince. He was actually snoring softly.

She turned back to Nick. She nodded and offered him a small, grim smile.

"Hey! You're up, Barrow!" Dillinger suddenly called out.

"Yep, I'm on it," Nick called back to him.

He stood. Kody saw that he'd never let go of his gun, that it was held tightly in his hands.

It would be so easy! So easy for Nick just to walk over

and shoot the man who was holding them all hostage, threatening their lives.

But she saw the way that Dillinger was sleeping. His gun in his lap.

The man even slept with his damned eyes open!

Kody didn't sleep again. She watched as the sun came up. It was oddly beautiful. The colors that streaked the sky were magnificent. Herons and cranes, white and colorful, flew to the water's edge. Then nature called.

She stood and saw that Floyd and Dillinger and Nick were all up. Nick had gone over to kick the fire out. There was little preparation to be made for them to move on, but they were obviously ready to go.

She cleared her throat.

"I… I need a few moments alone," Kody said. "I need privacy."

"Don't we all," Dillinger said.

"I'm serious. I need to take a little walk. As you've pointed out, there's really nowhere for me to go. I insist. I mean it, or you can shoot me now!"

Dillinger started to laugh. "Okay, Barrow, take Miss Cameron down a path. Give her some space—but not too much. You seem to be good at hunting her down, but we're ready to move on and I don't want to waste any time."

"Yeah, fine," Nick said.

"Don't worry. Hey, I'm fine right here!" Vince said. "It's a guy thing, right? No one cares about my privacy, huh?"

They all ignored Vince.

"Go. Move! There's a trail there," Nick told her.

She walked ahead of him, aware that Dillinger was watching. Nick kept his gun trained on her.

A great blue heron stood in her way. The bird looked at her a moment and then lifted into flight. It was beautiful...and it was all so wrong.

Fifty feet out and into the trees, she turned and told Nick, "I really need privacy. I won't go anywhere, I swear."

"Scream bloody murder if you need me," he said and stopped.

She'd really only need a few seconds—what they used to call *necessary* seconds for the nonexistent facilities out here—but she was one of those people who absolutely needed to be alone.

The hammock was riddled with what they called gator holes—little areas of mud and muck dug out by gators when they tried to cool themselves off in summer. It was winter now, but the holes remained. One was full of water and she dared dip her hands in, anxious to pretend she was dealing with something that resembled normalcy and hygiene.

She looked up, ready to rise—and a scream caught in her throat.

She was staring at a man. He had coal-dark eyes and long dark braids, and he was dressed in greenish-brown khaki jeans and a cotton shirt. He was, she knew, either Miccosukee or Seminole, and he was capable of being as silent as a whisper in the air.

He quickly showed her a badge and brought his finger to his lips. "Tell Nick that Jason Tiger is here," he said softly. Then he disappeared back into the brush by the gator hole.

He might never have been there.

7

"Jason Tiger," Kody said, whispering as she returned to Nick. "He showed me his badge!"

Instead of taking her by the arm to lead her back, Nick reached down and pretended to tie his shoes. "Tiger?" he said. He didn't know why he needed the affirmation. If Kody had said the name, she had certainly seen the man.

His heart skipped a beat.

He silently sent up a little prayer of thanks.

He'd known Jason Tiger from years before, when they'd both attended the same Florida state university. Neither of them had been FBI then. Since then he'd seen Jason only once, just briefly, right before he'd gone undercover.

The name Tiger signified one of the dominant clans of the Miccosukee. Jason had been proud to tell him that his family clan was that of William Buffalo Tiger, who was just recently deceased, and had been the first elected tribal chairman when the Miccosukee had been recognized as a tribe in the 1960s. Jason knew the Everglades as few others. He'd been recognized by the FBI for the contributions he'd made in bringing down murderers and drug lords—those who had used what Jason considered to be the precious beauty and diversity of the Everglades to promote their criminal activities.

If Kody had seen Jason Tiger, they were going to be all right.

Jason would be reporting to Craig and the county police and the tribal police and every other law enforcement officer out there.

It was good.

It was more than good; it was a tremendous relief. Jason was out there and Nick wasn't working this alone anymore.

He stood and grabbed her arm. "All right." He nodded, knowing that was all the reassurance he could give her right now. Just fifty feet away, he felt Dillinger looking their way.

He held her arm tighter as they returned to the chickee. He couldn't show the relief he was feeling. He didn't dare defy Dillinger as yet—not until they knew the whereabouts of the boy. And still, the lives of Kody and Vince were at stake.

Kody wrenched free from his hold as they neared the airboat. He wasn't prepared. She managed the feat easily.

She walked over to Dillinger. He followed closely, ready to intervene.

"I don't care about the money or your treasure or whatever," she told him. "I'm more than willing to help you find it and you are just welcome to it. But if you want my help—or Vince's help—you better tell us where that little boy is. You kidnapped a kid. We've been out overnight now. That little boy is somewhere terrified, I imagine. Let him go, and I will dig from here until eternity to find the treasure for you."

Nick realized he was holding his breath, standing as

tense as steel—and ready to draw on Dillinger or throw himself in front of Kody Cameron.

But Dillinger laughed softly.

He stared at Kody, obviously amused. "Wow. Hey, Vince, is that true? You don't care about yourself, right? You'll work yourself to the bone for me—if I tell you where the kid is, right? Yeah, Vince, you ready to throw your own life away for a kid you've never seen?"

Vince didn't answer. He pushed his glasses up the bridge of his nose, looking nervous.

"Okay, Miss Cameron, you want to know where the kid is? He's up in the northwest area, an abandoned crack house that's ridiculously close to the fancy new theater they've got up there north of the stadium. So, there's your kid. Yeah, it's probably getting bad for him. He was a pain in the ass, you know. I had to tie him up and stuff a gag in his mouth. So, I'm going to suggest you find this treasure for me as quickly as possible. Then I'll leave you where—if you're lucky—some kind of cop will find you before the wildlife does. And you can tell the cops where to look. You happy now?"

For a moment the air seemed to ring with his words. And then everyone and everything was silent, down to the insects.

"Yes, thank you!" Kody snapped at last, and she hurried past Dillinger, ready to hop aboard the airboat.

Dillinger studied Nick for a long moment. Nick was afraid he was on to something.

Then Dillinger smiled. "I will get what I want!" he said softly.

"I'm sure you will. I have to tell you, I'm confused. What the hell is the idea with the boy? I mean, we're in the Everglades. The boy is in an abandoned crack house."

"If they find us—not an impossible feat, even out here—I may need to use that boy to get free," Dillinger said.

"You have hostages."

"And by the time we find the treasure, we may not," Dillinger said. He shook his head, swearing. "Here we are, end of the road, the prize in sight. And I'm down at the finish line with you and Floyd, the two most squeamish crooks I've come across in a long career."

"I told you, I'm not in this to kill people. I never was. I like the finer things in life. I've been around, too. You can survive without killing people," Nick said. "I'm also against the jail terms or the needle that can come with killing people."

"Ah, well, they can only stick a needle in once," Dillinger said. "And we've already killed people, haven't we?"

"You killed Nelson. I sure as hell had no part in that. The hostages... Thanks to me, we're not going to die because of them."

"Ah, but you did kill Schultz, didn't you?" Dillinger accused him. "It's so obvious, my friend. You've got a thing for the woman. Schultz was getting too close. You took care of him, huh?" Barrow asked, his grin broad—eerie and frightening—as he stared at Nick.

And Nick was good at this, the mind game—delving into the psyche of criminals, following the trails of sick minds.

But he wasn't sure about Dillinger. Nick had studied this man. But, right now, he wasn't sure.

"You'll never really know, will you?" he asked Dillinger quietly, and he was pleased to see a worried frown crease the man's brow. Dillinger didn't know; the man really didn't know if Barrow would go ballistic on him or not.

Pull a trigger—or not.

It was good. It was very good to keep Dillinger off guard.

"Thing is, no one has any idea who killed old Schultz. You shot Nelson in front of the hostages. Oh, yeah, so you don't intend that Dakota and the young man should live, right? Well, start thinking anew. I'll help make sure you get the hell out of here. But you aren't killing that girl. You've got it right. I've got a thing for her. And she's coming with me."

"And then what, you idiot?" Dillinger demanded angrily. "You're going to just keep her? Keep her alive? You will rot in jail, you idiot."

"You'll be long gone—what will you care?"

"She'd better find what I want, that's all I've got to say. You want her alive? She'd better find it."

Nick looked at the ground and then shook his head as he looked back up at Dillinger. "You want to know if I can be a killer? Touch a hair on her head. You'll find out."

"Really?" Dillinger said, intrigued.

"Yeah. Really."

With that he shoved his way past Dillinger and headed toward the airboat.

In minutes, it seemed that they indeed flew, the craft moving swiftly across the shallow water and marshes of the Everglades.

"Such an interesting place," Dillinger said, "this 'River of Grass!' If one wants to be poetic, I mean. Imagine Anthony Green. Out here, in pretty good shape. But he's out of ammunition and there are a dozen deadly creatures you can encounter in every direction—with no real defense. Imagine being here. Deserted. Alone. With nothing."

Kody didn't answer him or even respond, even though Vince looked at her nervously, apparently praying she had some clue as to what they were doing.

They'd traveled for hours until she'd told them to stop. Now she held a map unfolded from the back page of one of the journals. She pointed in what she truly hoped was the right direction. "Anthony Green's illegal liquor operation was out here, right on this hammock. When he had the place, he had workstations set up—chickees. But there was a main chickee where he set up a desk and papers and did his bookkeeping."

"Obviously, not here anymore, right?" Dillinger asked, eyes narrowed as he stared at her.

"You're sure this is the right place?" Floyd asked her.

"I'm not *sure* of anything," Kody said. "I know that there were four chickees and all the parts for having a distillery. I'm thinking that they were set about the hammock in a square formation, with the 'cooking' going on right in the middle by the water. Remember, land floods and land washes away. But I do think that we have the right hammock area…" She paused and looked over at Vince. "Right?"

"The Everglades is full of hammocks," Vince murmured. "Hardwood hammocks, with gumbo limbo trees, mahogany and more, and there are pine islands. Unless you really know the Everglades, it can all be the same."

"My sense of direction isn't great," Kody said. "But I believe that we did follow the known byways from the southern entrance to the park and that, if we were to continue to the north, we would come upon Shark Valley and Tamiami Trail. Naturally, we've really got to hope that this was the hammock. But—"

"Great," Floyd murmured. "We have to hope!"

Kody ignored him. "Okay, so, the heating source they used was fire, but anything they might have used to create fire would have been swallowed up long ago into nature. But Green had a massive stainless-steel still and a smaller copper still—a present to Green from the real Al Capone—and other tools that were made of copper or stainless steel. If we can find even the remnants of any of the containers, we'll know we're in the right place."

"This is ridiculous," Floyd told Dillinger. "Even if we find a piece of stainless steel, how are we going to find out where the chickees were? This has been an idiot's quest from the get-go, Dillinger!"

The way Dillinger looked at Floyd was frightening.

Floyd quickly realized his mistake and lifted a hand. "Sorry, man. I just don't see how we're going to find this."

"There is hope," Kody said quickly. "There are notes in Anthony Green's journal about his chickees. He didn't intend that his operations be washed away in a storm. Each one of the chickees was built with pilings that went deep into the earth. If we see any sign of pilings or of the remnants of a still, we'll know we're in the right place."

"Well, we know what we need to do." Nick stepped forward, defusing the tension and getting the group to focus on the task at hand. "We need to all start looking. Span out over the hammock, but be careful. There are snakes that like to hide in the tall grasses. Vince and Kody, you stay to the center and see if you can find remnants of a still. Floyd, you and Dillinger, try the upper left quadrant over there. I'll head to the right. We're looking for any one of the sections where the workmen's chickees might have stood."

It was like looking for a needle in a haystack. Time passed. Decades. There were so few of them; there was so much ground to cover.

"Let's cover each other, crossing positions around here," Vince suggested to Kody.

She looked at him, smiled and nodded. He was a good guy, she thought. Afraid, certainly, but doing his best to be courageous when it didn't look good at all for them.

Vince didn't know that "Barrow" was FBI. She longed to tell him but she wasn't sure if that would be wise. Vince could still panic, say something.

"We're going to be okay," she told him.

"Yeah. We're going to have to make a break for it somehow," he told her. "Do you realize that if we really find this stash—oh, so impossible!—Dillinger will kill us?"

"Maybe he'll let us go," Kody said.

"He killed one of his own men!"

"Yes, but that man deserted one of his friends. Maybe he does have some kind of criminal code of honor," Kody said.

Vince shook his head. "We have to get out of here," he said.

"But what is your suggestion on how?" Kody asked. "We're in the center. The three guys with guns can focus on us in a matter of seconds."

"Two of them won't kill us—neither Floyd nor Barrow," Vince said, his voice filled with certainty. "We just have to watch out for Dillinger."

"Who has an automatic weapon," Kody murmured. "We might be all right, Vince. Help will be on the way."

Vince let out a snort. "Yeah. Help. In the middle of the Everglades."

"Okay, so, to us it's a big swamp. But there are people who know it well, down to each mangrove tree, just about. It's going to be okay."

"Hey!" Dillinger suddenly called. "Are you two working out there?"

"Yes!" Kody shouted.

"Anything?" Nick asked.

Kody turned, hearing Nick's voice behind her. He was walking in quickly toward where they stood.

But before he could speak, Vince stood and stared at her, shaking his head, a look of desperation in his eyes. "We're going to die. If we just stay here, we're going to die. I'd rather feed a gator than take one of that asshole's bullets. I'm sorry, Kody."

He turned, ducking low into the high grasses, and began to run.

"What the hell?" Dillinger shouted.

He began to fire.

Nick threw himself on top of Kody, bringing her down to the damp, marshy earth. The gunfire continued and then stopped.

"Now, take my hand. Run!" Nick told her. He had her hand; he was pulling her. He came halfway to his feet and let go with a spray of bullets.

Then, hunched low, and all but dragging her behind him, he started to run.

Kody was stunned; she had no idea where they were going or why they had chosen that moment to leave. Vince had wanted to run...

Where was he?

Had he been shot?

What about Floyd? Was he shooting at them along with Dillinger?

Kody just knew that, for the moment, they were racing through a sea of grass and marsh. Her feet sank into mush with their every movement. Grass rose high around her, the saw grass tearing into her flesh here and there.

"Low! Keep low!" Nick told her.

Keep low and run? So difficult!

She could still hear Dillinger firing, but the sound was nowhere near as loud as it had been.

While Kody had no idea where they were running to, apparently Nick did. She felt the ground beneath her feet harden. They had come to a definite rise of high hammock ground, possibly a limestone shelf. She was gasping for breath and tugged back hard on Nick's hand.

"Breathe. Just breathe!" she gasped out.

And he stood still, pulling her against him as she dragged in breath after breath.

Suddenly the sound of gunfire stopped.

Now they could hear Dillinger shouting. "You're a dead man, Barrow! You're dead. I'll find you. And I'll let you watch me rip your pretty little pet to shreds before I kill you both. You're an ass. If the cops get you, you'll face a needle just like me!"

Nick remained still, just holding Kody.

"You can come back! You, too, Floyd! You can come back and we'll find the treasure, and we'll go on, free as the birds. I know where to go from here. I've got friends, you know that! They'll see that we get out of here safely. We can be sipping on silly drinks with umbrellas in them. Hey, come on now. Barrow, just bring her on back. I won't kill her, I promise. I just want that damned treasure!"

Nick held still and then brought his finger to his lips. He started to walk again—away from the sound of Dillinger ranting.

As they moved, though, they could still hear the man. "Vince! You idiot. Why did you run? I wouldn't have killed you. I just need the knowledge that you have. You're going to die out here. You have no way back in. I'm your way back in. Floyd! Oh, Floyd. You'd better be running. You are such a dead man. Such a namby-pamby dead man. I will find you. I will see that you die in agony, do you hear me? You are dead! You're all dead! I will find you!"

Only when Dillinger's voice had grown fainter did Kody dare to speak. "What the hell was that? What just happened? You said that a child would die. That—"

"Jason Tiger is out here," Nick said. "I'm going to get you to him as quickly as possible, and then I'll try to find your friend Vince."

"But the child. The little boy…"

"Adrian Burke," Nick said, smiling at her. He was studying her with a strange mixture of awe and disbelief. "Jason was still out there when we took off this morning. I met up with him earlier, looking for the pilings. Jason overheard Dillinger give up the boy's location. He got a message through to Craig Frasier and the local cops. They searched all the buildings in the area that Dillinger mentioned and they found the little boy. He's safe."

"Oh, my God! Really?" Kody asked. She wasn't sure if she believed it herself. She was so relieved that she felt ridiculously weak—almost as if she would fall.

"They found him—because of me confronting Dillinger?" she asked incredulously.

"Yep." He looked uncomfortable for a minute. "I should have trusted you," he said softly. "I should have trusted in you earlier."

"I'm just—I'm just so grateful!"

"Me, too. The kids…finding kids. It's always the hardest!"

She was still standing God-alone-knew-where in the middle of deadly wilderness, and it would be wise not to fall. She blindly reached out. Nick caught her hands, steadying her.

"I have to get back around to where I can leave you with Jason Tiger," he told her. "Then I can look for your friend."

"There was so much gunfire," Kody said. "But Vince… Vince is smart. There's a chance he made it." She paused, as if to reassure herself, then said, "He was determined to escape. He was certain that Dillinger would have killed us."

Nick was quiet.

"He would have killed us," Kody said.

"Most likely. Come on. We're on solid ground here, and I think I know where I'm going, but I haven't worked down here in Florida for years."

"You worked here—in Florida?"

"I did. I'm from Florida."

"Ah. But…you know Craig?"

"I work in New York City now," he told her. "I often work with him there. I've been on a task force with Craig and his partner. We've been following Dillinger—Nathan Appleby—all the way down the coast. I was the one who had never been seen, and I know the area, so I fit the bill to infiltrate. Especially once we knew that Dillinger was down here. That he was forming a gang and pulling off narcotic sales, prostitution, kidnapping…murder."

She was really shivering, she realized.

But it wasn't just fear. The sun was going down.

A South Florida winter was nothing like a northeastern winter, but here, on the water, with the sun going down, it was suddenly chilly. She was cold, teeth chattering, limbs quaking. And he was watching her with those eyes of his, holding her, and he seemed to be a bastion of heat and strength. She didn't want to lean on him so heavily. They were still in danger—very real, serious danger. And yet she felt ridiculously attracted to him. They'd both been hot, covered in swamp water, tinged with long grasses…

She was certain that, at the moment, her hair could best be described as stringy.

Her flesh was burned and scratched and raw…

And she was still breathing!

Was that it? She had survived. Nick had been a captor at first, and now he was a savior. Did all of that mess with the mind? Was she desperate to lean on the man because there was really something chemical and physical and real between them, or was she suffering some kind of mental break brought on by all that had happened?

She never got the chance to figure out which.

"Come on," he urged her.

And they began to move again, deep into the swamp. She felt his hand on hers. She felt a strange warmth sweeping through her.

Even as she shivered.

* * *

They weren't in a good position, but once Vince had suddenly decided to run, there had been no help for it.

Nick couldn't have gone after Vince and brought him down and go on pretending he was still part of Dillinger's plan. If he'd brought Vince back to Dillinger, the man would have killed Vince.

There had been nothing else to do but run then. Now all he could do was hope that Vince was smart enough to stay far, far away from Dillinger. And while Nick hadn't seen Floyd disappear, it was pretty clear from Dillinger's shouting that he'd used the opportunity to get away, as well.

It was one thing to be a criminal. It was another to be a crazed murderer.

Hurrying along at his side, Kody tugged at his hand, gasping.

"Wait, just one minute. I just have to breathe!" she said.

And Kody breathed, bending over, bracing her hands on her knees, sweeping in great gulps of air.

Nick looked around anxiously as she did so. Naturally, Dillinger had seen the direction in which they had run.

Nick believed he knew the Everglades better than Dillinger, at any rate. But, even then, he was praying that Jason Tiger had been watching them, that Tiger had followed him after they had spoken.

"You…you think that Vince will be okay?" Kody asked him.

"He's smart. He needs a good hiding place and he needs to hole up. Dillinger has studied the Everglades on paper, I'm sure. Though he was hoping that the treasure might have been at the mansion, he thought that it might be out here. He had communication going with men who owed him or needed him. I'm sure he has someone coming out here for him soon. But he's not a native. Vince is, right? He seems knowledgeable."

Kody stared at him. "He's knowledgeable. I'm knowledgeable. But this? We're on foot in the swamps! Oh, please! Who is at home out here and knows what they're doing—except for the park rangers and maybe some members of the local tribes and maybe a few members of the Audubon Society. Dillinger was right—we don't know what we're doing out here."

"But Jason Tiger does," Nick reminded her gently.

"Oh! But where is he?"

"He's been watching, I'm sure. He'll find us. Don't worry. Ready?"

She nodded. He grabbed her hand again and hurried in a northwesterly direction, hoping he had followed the directions he'd received from Jason Tiger.

He'd been out in the Everglades often enough. His dad had brought him out here to learn to shoot, and his grandfather had kept a little cabin not far from where they were now. But most of what he knew about the Everglades he'd learned from a friend, Jimmy Eagle. Jimmy's dad had been a pilot from Virginia but his mom had been Miccosukee.

One of the most important things he'd ever learned from Jimmy was that it was easy to lose track of where you were, easy to think one hammock was another. Waterways changed, and there could be danger in every step for the unsuspecting.

He heard a bird call and stopped walking, returning the call.

A moment later Jason Tiger stepped out onto the path, almost as if he had materialized from the shrubs and trees.

"Right on the mark," he told Nick. "Miss Cameron, excellent."

Kody flushed at the compliment.

"I was excellent at running," she murmured. "But…" She paused, looking at Nick and telling him, "Your expression when you came toward me…it was so…determined."

"I was trying to let you know that we'd be able to do something," Nick told her. "I was going to let you know that Jason had found me while I was looking for the pilings of Anthony Green's distillery operations."

"And Vince chose that moment to run," Kody murmured.

"You think he's alive?" Jason Tiger asked Nick.

"I think it's possible."

"I'll get you to the cabin, then I'll look," Jason said.

"I wanted Kody safe with you," Nick said. "As long as Kody is safe, I can go back out and search until I find Vince—and Floyd. Floyd deserves jail time, but he doesn't deserve a bullet in the back from Dillinger."

"This way," Jason Tiger said.

He led them through a barely discernible trail until they came to the water.

He had a canoe there.

"Hop in," he told them.

Nick steadied the craft and gave Kody a hand. He stepped in carefully himself. Jason hopped in after, shoving his oar into the earth to send them out into the water.

They were in an area of cypress swamps; the trees grew here and there in the water. Egrets, cranes and herons seemed to abound and fish jumped all around them. Nick saw a number of small gators, lazy and seeking the heat of the waning sun.

The sun was going down, he realized. Night was coming again.

Jason drew the canoe toward the shore and then leaped out. Nick did the same, helping to drag the canoe up on the shore.

He wasn't sure what he was expecting, but not the pleasant cabin in the woods he and Kody saw as they burst through the last thick foliage on the trail.

It wasn't any kind of chickee. It was a log cabin, on high ground.

Nick looked at Jason Tiger, who seemed amused.

"There are a lot of houses out here. A lot on tribal lands. We're not completely living in the past, you know. Hey, guys, if it were summer, there's even an air conditioner. Everything here is run on a generator," Jason told them.

"Wow, so, there are a lot of these out here? For the Miccosukee and Seminole?" Kody asked.

Jason laughed. "No. Actually, this one belongs to the United States government. A lot of drug traffic goes through here."

Jason had a key; he used it, letting them into the cabin. It was rustic, offering a sofa in worn leather, a group of chairs, a center stove and a few throw rugs.

"There are bedrooms to the right and left. Hot showers are available—naturally, we ask you to conserve water. I have lots of coffee and power bars and other food."

"You live out here?" Kody asked him.

"When I need to. When we're watching the flow

of illegal drugs through the area. I work with a new-bie, Sophia Gray, and when she's in residence, she uses the second bedroom. You'll find clean clothing there, Miss Cameron. Anyway, I've been in touch with Special Agent Frasier and the police. We are actually on the edge of National Park land. You're at a safe house. You'll be fine, and we'll have you out of here by morning," Jason told Kody. "And now…"

"I need to get back out there," Nick said. "Find Vince first…and hope that I can find Floyd, as well."

"And Dillinger," Kody said. "He's still out there. He has to be stopped. I think that he really is crazy—dangerously crazy."

"Yes, and Dillinger," Nick said. "And, yes, he is crazy. Functionally crazy, if you will, and that makes him very dangerous." His tone softened as he added directions. "You stay here and obey anything Jason says, and stay safe."

"Of course," Kody said.

"Wait, this is backward. You need to watch over Miss Cameron," Jason said. "I'll see if I can find your friend, Vince, and the others."

"I can't ask you to take on my case," Nick said.

"You have to ask me. I know these hammocks and waterways like the back of my hand. You don't. I'll find them." When Nick was about to protest, he added, "I'm right, and you know that I'm right. I'm better out here than you are, no disrespect intended."

Nick was quiet for a moment and then lowered his head. "All right," he said.

"You're still armed?" Jason asked Nick.

Nick reached for the little holster at his back and the Glock there. "I am armed."

"All right, then. I'm going to head right back out. My superiors at the FBI know this place. We're remote, but they'll get here."

"I should go out with you—"

"But you won't," Jason told him.

Nick nodded. "You're right. You're far better for this job than me."

He felt Kody's fingers slip around his arm. "I'm sorry. You could both go if it weren't for me. Honestly, I know how to lock a door. I can watch out for myself here."

"No way. You're a witness who can put Dillinger away forever," Jason said.

"He's right. We can't risk you."

"Great. Because I'm a witness," Kody murmured.

Jason smiled at them both. "You're okay here for the moment. Take showers, relax. You were both amazing. Miss Cameron, you behaved selflessly, with great courage, and Special Agent Connolly, you're the stuff that makes the Bureau the place to belong. So, take this time. Sit, breathe… Hey, there's real coffee here."

"Thanks, Jason," Nick murmured.

Kody stepped over to Jason and took his hand, shaking it. "Thank you! And the child…the child is really all right?"

"Yes. Thanks to you, they knew where to search. He's safe and sound."

"I'm so glad," Kody murmured.

Jason nodded then and headed to the door. "Lock up," he told Nick. "Not that I'm expecting you'll have any company, but—"

"You just never know," Nick finished for Jason. He offered him a hand, as well. "Thank you, my friend."

"We're all in this together," Jason assured him.

When he left, Nick locked the door.

Kody was heading toward the kitchen. "Coffee!" she said. "Food."

"Yes."

"He's an agent. You're an agent." She spoke while searching the cabinets.

"Yes."

"But you didn't know him before?"

"Yes."

"He's from here and you're from here."

Nick laughed softly. "A lot of people are from here. But, yes—Jason and I went to college together," he said.

"It's ironic, isn't it, that I saw you in New York City? Never here," she said.

He grinned at that. "Millions of people live in this area. I don't suppose it's odd in any way that people from South Florida never met. It's just odd that we wound up here together in this way after we did see each other in New York. I was probably a few years ahead of you in school. I went to Killian—and then on to the University of Florida. I was in Miami-Dade Homicide…and then the FBI," Nick told her. "And, for the last ten months or so, I've been on the task force with Craig. For the last few weeks, I've been undercover as Barrow."

"Incredible," she murmured.

"Not really."

She stared at him a moment longer and then smiled. And he thought that she really was beautiful—a perfect ingénue for whatever play it was she was doing.

She walked over to him.

"Well, I'm alive, thanks to you," she murmured.

"It's my job," he said. "It never should have gone this

far. I should have been able to stop Dillinger at the mansion. I should have—"

He suddenly remembered the day she'd brushed by him at Finnegan's. He knew then he would have liked to have met her. Now…

They were safe—relatively safe, at any rate. They'd come far from Dillinger and his insanity. Jason Tiger was a great agent who knew this area and loved it, knew the good, the bad and the ugly of it, and would find and save Vince and Flynn if anyone could.

He would have given so much to smile, think they were back, way back before any of this, imagine that they'd really met, gone out…that he could pull her into his arms, hold her, feel her, kiss her lips…

But Nick was still an agent.

He was still on duty.

"Should have what?" she asked softly.

"Should have been able to finish it all earlier," he said softly.

She still held the bag of coffee. He took it gently from her fingers and headed into the kitchen to measure it out. In no time, he heard the sound as it began to perc.

She still stood in the living room of the cabin, looking out. He saw that she walked to the door to assure herself it was locked. She turned, probably aware that he was studying her.

"Windows?" she asked with a grimace. "I'm usually not the paranoid type."

"They've got locks, I'm sure," Nick said. He crossed the room to join her at the left window to check.

It was impossible.

They'd been crawling around in fetid swamp water,

muck and more. Yet there was still something sweet and alluring in her scent.

She looked at him. Her face was close, so close. Her lips…so tempting.

Get a grip! he told himself.

"We should check them all," she said.

"That's a plan. Then all we need fear is a raccoon coming down the chimney," he said, grinning at her.

They checked and double-checked one another, close and closer. He headed to each of the two bedrooms. Simple, rustic, charming, clean…

Equipped with beds.

"This is good, right?" Kody asked him, tugging at the left bedroom window. It was evidently Jason Tiger's room. It was neat as a pin, but there were toiletries on the dresser and some folded clothes on the footrest.

"Yeah." Nick double-checked the window. "One more room," he said.

In the second room, the guest room, he could almost smell the scent of crisp, cool, cotton sheets.

Kody checked a window; he walked over to her.

How the hell could her hair still smell like some kind of subtle, sweet shampoo?

"Good, right?" she asked.

He inhaled the scent. "Yep, excellent."

"And you're still armed?" she asked.

"I am. Glock in the holster at the back of my belt."

"Then it's good. It's really all good. We aren't in any danger."

Nick arched a brow.

They weren't in any danger?

He was pretty sure he was in the worst danger he'd been in since he'd started on his undercover odyssey.

Because she was danger.

Because he was falling into love/lust/respect/admiration...

And he was an agent.

And she was the bartending actress he was duty-bound to protect.

And yet the mind could be a cruel beast at times. No matter what the circumstances, no matter what their danger, his position, her position, he couldn't help but believe there was a future. And in that future they were together.

Or was that just his mind teasing him?

For the moment he needed to shape up and damn the taunting beast of a voice within him that made him picture her as she headed for the shower.

8

Clean!

There was nothing like the feeling of being clean.

Kody could have stayed in the shower forever, except, of course, she knew the water was being heated by a generator. Special Agent Nick Connolly certainly deserved his share of the water.

And Vince was still out there, somewhere. Was he safe? He surely knew more about the Everglades than Dillinger, but just living in the area and knowing history and geography did not ensure survival. There were just too many pitfalls. Crocodilians, snakes, insects—and, of course, a madman running around with a gun.

And what about Floyd?

Floyd was a criminal but not a killer; he had never wanted to hurt them.

She couldn't help but be worried about them both.

She had to believe that Jason Tiger would find Vince. Meanwhile, Vince was smart enough to watch out for sinkholes, gator holes and quicksand. He knew which snakes were harmful and which were not. He probably even had a sense of direction. He would head straight for the observation tower at Shark Valley—and the Tamiami Trail. He was going to be okay.

Hair washed, flesh scrubbed, Kody emerged from the shower. A towel had been easy to find in the bathroom. She hesitated when she was dry, feeling as if she was somewhat of an invader as she headed to the dresser and found clothing that belonged to Jason Tiger's "newbie" associate. "Forgive me," she murmured aloud, finding panties and a bra and then a pair of jeans and a tailored cotton shirt.

When she returned to the living room, Nick was sipping coffee at the little dining table that sat between the kitchen and the living room. He'd obviously showered; his hair was wet and slicked back. She couldn't help but notice the definition of his muscles in a borrowed polo shirt and jeans. She met his eyes, so beyond blue, and she felt such a tug of attraction that she needed to remind herself they were still in a perilous position.

And that Nick had been her captor—who had turned into her savior.

There was surely a name for the confusion plaguing her!

"Hey," he said softly.

"Hey."

"Feel better?"

"I feel terrific," she told him. "Clean. Strong. Okay—still worried."

"Jason will find Vince," he assured her.

She nodded and pulled out a chair to join him at the table. "What are you doing?" she asked him.

He swept an arm out, indicating the maps on the table. "I'm following your lead. This map was created by a park ranger about ten years ago. Now, of course, mangrove islands pop up here and there, water washes away what was almost solid. You have your hardwood hammocks and you have areas where the hardwood hammocks almost collide with the limestone shelves. From what I'm seeing here and where we've been, I'm convinced that we were in the right place. Anthony Green's still sat on a limestone shelf."

"Where we were today, I'm pretty sure," Kody agreed.

"Exactly. Well, on this map, the ranger—Howard Reece—also made note of the manmade structures he found, or the remnants thereof. Kody, you were right, I believe." He paused and pointed out notations on the map. "There are the pilings for different chickee huts he had going there. Back quarter—that's the one where Anthony Green did his bookkeeping. So, if you're right, that's where we'll find the buried treasure."

"If it does exist," she said.

"I believe that it does."

"And you want to go find it—now?"

He laughed softly. "Nope. I want to stay right here now. Stay right here until you're picked up by my people and taken to safety. Then I want to help Jason Tiger and the forces we'll get out here to find Vince and Floyd. And then, at some point, get the right people with the right equipment out here to see if we're right or wrong."

She nodded and bit into her lower lip.

He reached out, laying his hand over hers where it rested on the table. "I know that you're worried. It will be okay. Jason will find Vince, and, I hope, Floyd."

"What if he can't find them? What if he can't find either of them?" Kody asked.

"He will." The conviction with which he spoke the words sank into her, giving her hope. "For now," he said, "let's find something to eat. There's not a lot of food here, nothing fresh, but there are a lot of cans and, as Jason said, power bars."

"There's soup," Kody said, pointing to a shelf in the kitchen area.

"Anything sounds good. Want me to cook for you?"

"You mean open a can?"

"Exactly."

Kody laughed. "Yes, I'd love you to open a can for me."

They both rose. Nick dug around for a can-opener. Kody found bowls, spoons and even napkins. She set the table.

"Nice," Nick told her.

"Well, we want to be civilized, right?"

"I don't know. I could suck the stone-cold food out of a can right now, but, hey, you're right. Heated is going to be better."

She smiled. It was an oddly domestic scene as they put their meal of soup and crackers together. Jason kept a hefty supply of bottled water at the cabin, and the water tasted delicious.

"So, when you're not playing the part of a thug and holding up historic properties, what are you doing?" Kody asked as she ate.

"I'm with the same unit as Craig Frasier—criminal investigation," Nick told her. "New York City is my home office. The man you know as Dillinger was carrying out a number of criminal activities in New York that included extortion and murder. He served time. He should have served more time, after. The cops had arrested him again a few years ago on an armed robbery, but the one witness was found floating in the East River.

Then he started to move south, so we followed his activities. And as I said, I was a natural to slide into the gang he was forming down here."

"And you like your work?" Kody asked. "I know that Craig likes his work and his office."

"I love what I do. It feels right," he said. "What about you—what do you do when you're not guarding the booth? Ah, yes! Acting. And you're friends with Kevin Finnegan." He was quiet for a minute. "Well, this is just rude, but what kind of friends?"

She laughed. "Real friends. We've struggled together on a number of occasions. We met on the set of a long-running cop show that we both had a few short roles on." She grinned. "He was the victim and I was the killer once in the same episode. And we've gone to some of the same workshops together. But, trust me, we were never anything but friends."

"Kevin is a good-looking, great guy," Nick said.

"That he is," she agreed. "And it's cool to have a friend like him for auditioning and heading out and trying to see what's going on. We were both accepted to a really prestigious class once because we could call on one another right away and work together. We decided long ago that we'd never ruin what we had by dating or becoming friends with benefits, or anything like that." She hesitated, flushing. That was way too much information, she told herself. "And, by the way, Kevin is in love. It's even a secret from me, it's such a hush-hush thing. I hope it works out for him. I do love him—as a friend."

"Nice," he murmured.

He was watching her, his eyes so intense she looked away uncomfortably.

She rose uneasily, afraid it sounded as if she was determined he know she wasn't involved with Kevin. She wandered closer to the stove and nervously poured more coffee into her cup. "So. What happens now? I mean, Jason Tiger has been in contact with Craig and the FBI and the local police, right? They'll be out soon, right?"

"They'll be out soon," he agreed. "We're just in an area where there is no easy access. But they'll get here. Why don't you try to get some sleep? You have to be exhausted."

"I'm fine, really. Well, I'm not fine. I'm worried about Vince. I just wish—"

"Jason Tiger is good. For all we know, he might have found Vince by now."

"Right," she murmured. She smiled at him. "I can't believe that I didn't know you right away. I mean, it's not as if we got to know one another that night at Finnegan's. But you do have a really unusual eye color and…"

"I was afraid that you'd recognize me," he said quietly. "That, naturally, you would call me out, and we would all be dead."

"Yes, well…"

"I just wasn't that memorable," he said, a slight smile teasing his lips.

"Oh, no! I had been thinking…"

"Yes?"

Kody flushed, shaking her head.

"You know what I was thinking?" he asked.

"What's that?"

"I was thinking that it was a damned shame that I was on this assignment, that I never had asked you out, that I was meeting you as an armed and masked criminal."

"Oh," she said softly.

He stood and joined her by the stove. Stopping close to her, he touched her chin, lifting it slightly.

"What if it had been different? What if we'd met again in New York and I'd asked you to a show…to dinner? Would you have said yes?"

Kody was afraid her knees would give way. She was usually so confident. Okay, so maybe being under siege, kidnapped at gunpoint and still trapped in a swamp was making her a little too emotional. She was still shaky. Still caught by those eyes. And she was attracted to him as she couldn't remember being attracted to anyone before.

"Yes," she said softly.

He smiled, his fingers still gentle on her chin. He moved toward her and she could almost taste his kiss, imagine the hunger, the sweetness.

Then there was a pounding on the door.

Dropping his hands from her chin, he moved quickly away from her, heading to the door.

"It's Tiger!" came a call.

Nick opened the bolt on the door. Jason Tiger was there with Vince. Vince was shaking.

And bleeding.

"Oh, get in, get in! Sit him down. I'll boil water. Is an ambulance coming? Can an ambulance come?" Kody demanded.

Nick took Vince's weight, leading him to a chair. Apparently both men were adept at dealing with wounds. Nick had Vince's shirt ripped, while Jason went for his first-aid box.

Kody did set water to boil.

"It's just a flesh wound," Nick said.

"We'll get it cleaned, get some antiseptic on it," Jason murmured.

Nick took the clean, hot towel Kody provided and in moments they discovered he had been right; it was just a flesh wound.

"Dillinger didn't shoot you?" Kody asked.

Vince looked up at her with a shrug. "I tripped on a root. Scratched myself on a branch."

"Oh," she said, relieved, sliding down to sit in one of the chairs.

"Floyd?" Nick asked Jason Tiger.

"No sign of him—nor have I been able to find Dillinger. The airboat is where it was. He hasn't taken off from where you were, by the old distillery."

Vince suddenly turned and grabbed Nick's arm. "You weren't one of them. You're not a crook."

"No," Nick said, hunkering down and easing himself from Vince's hold. There wasn't time to give him the background of his undercover investigation right now. They had to find Dillinger. "You were smart—and lucky. When Dillinger started shooting, you went down low. But he is still out there. As long as he's out there, other people are in danger. Did you see him again? Did you hear him stalking you?"

Vince looked from Nick to Jason and then at Nick again. "I think he chased me through half of the hammock. Then he was gone."

"I didn't see him," Jason said.

Nick stood. "All right." He looked over at Jason Tiger. "This time, I think it's me. I think that I need to go," he said.

Tiger nodded.

"You're going out there again?" Kody asked him.

"Yes, we need to stop Dillinger and, hopefully, find Floyd alive."

He turned, heading out of the little cabin in the swamp. Even as he did so, they heard shouts. Kody hurried to the door behind Jason.

An airboat had arrived; it bore a number of men in khaki uniforms.

Men with guns.

They were going after the killer in the swamps.

"Kody!"

One of the men, she saw, was hurrying toward her. It was Craig Frasier. He caught her up in a hug.

"Thank God. Kieran and Kevin have been going insane, they've been so worried about you. Not to mention your family. We'll get you home. We'll get you back to safety."

She gave him a hug back. Craig was truly an amazing man. Kody was happy that he and Kieran Finnegan were together—and happy that he was a good friend to Kevin and all of the Finnegan family.

She was grateful to know him, and everyone involved with Finnegan's on Broadway.

He was there for her.

She and Vince were safe.

And yet, at that moment—right when she was surrounded by law enforcement—she felt bereft.

Nick was gone. He was off with the teams of officers that had come out to find Dillinger and Floyd.

EMTs had arrived with the officers; they were looking at Vince's wounds. They were asking her if she was all right.

Soon, she was escorted onto an airboat. And before she knew it, she was back on the Tamiami Trail, headed toward downtown Miami and to the home in the Roads section of the city, just north of Coconut Grove, where she had grown up. A policewoman came with her, took her statement and promised to watch her house through the night—just in case Dillinger found his way to her before they were able to find Dillinger.

And there was nothing left to do except watch the television to see how the rest of it all began to unfold. Dillinger was out there. He was determined to get the treasure, and so, Nick was certain, he had to have stayed in the general area where they had been.

Law enforcement had fanned out, but by the time they reached the hammock again, the airboat that Dillinger had extorted from the men he had been blackmailing was gone. He was off, somewhere.

The forces that had come out for the search were from Miami-Dade and Monroe counties, Florida Highway Patrol, the U.S. Marshal's Office and the FBI.

But, as the hours went by, they found nothing.

Nick was about to give it up himself when he determined one more time to search the original hammock. The grasses grew high there, and a twisted pattern of pines might hide just about anything along the northern edge of the hammock.

He came out alone and stood in the center, as still as he could manage. And that was when he was certain he heard movement. He cautiously took a step, and then another, and drew his weapon and gave out a warning. "FBI. Show yourself, hands above your head."

Floyd emerged out of the grass. He was shaking visibly.

"I don't want to die. I don't want to die. They can lock me up, but I don't want to die."

"You're not going to die. But you are under arrest."

"Barrow. You," Floyd said. "I should have known you were a cop. I mean, I don't like blood and guts. But you...? Wow. I should have guessed it. It's cool. It doesn't matter. Get me in. Protect me. He was running around here crazy. Dillinger, I mean. He wants me dead. He wants you dead more but..." He shook his head as he stepped forward. "Get me out of here. Quickly. He'll shoot me dead right here in front of all of you, he just wants me dead so badly."

"All right, all right," Nick said, and cuffed the man. He caught him by the elbow and hurried back toward the airboat where other officers were waiting. "Come on, we'll get you in. You'll be safe."

"Did you get him? Did you get Dillinger?" Floyd asked.

"Not yet."

"You have to get him."

"Yes, we know."

But while Floyd was brought in, and they worked through the night, there was no sign of Dillinger to be found.

When morning dawned, he was still on the loose.

Kody sipped coffee and watched the news.

She should have slept, but she hadn't.

Her parents had arrived as soon as humanly possible, of course. They'd been worried sick about her, and she understood.

They'd nearly crushed her. Her mother had cried. Her father had cursed the day he'd discovered he'd been related to the Crystal family. Emotions had soared and then, thankfully, fallen back to earth and she had finally managed to make her parents behave normally once again.

She'd gotten a call from Mayor Holden Burke. He'd nearly been in tears as they had spoken. He'd been told by the police that it had been her courage against the kidnappers that had led to his son being found. She'd told him how grateful she was that the boy, Adrian, was alive, and she'd begged him not to do anything publicly for her—she wanted it all to remain low key.

"Yes, but I hear you're an actress—don't you want the publicity?" he'd asked.

She'd laughed. "No, I want to create characters and read well for auditions and, of course, get great reviews," she told him. "The only publicity I want is for great performances. As far as my home goes… I just worry."

"Oh, trust me," he assured her, "more people than ever will want to tour the house now. And I will thank you with my whole heart and remain low key."

When she hung up, she'd smiled, glad of a new friend.

She needed to sleep.

But hours later she was back up, staring at the television. She wanted to hear about Nick.

Every local channel and even the national channels had covered the news.

Nathan Appleby, aka Dillinger, was still on the loose. The FBI had been on his trail for nearly a year, from the northeast down to the far south. Thanks, however, to the combined efforts of various law-enforcement groups, the hostages taken at the Crystal Manor were safe, as were those who had been forced to accompany the criminals. Three of the gang had been killed; their bodies had been recovered by the Coast Guard and the Miccosukee police.

Dillinger, however, was still at large. The local populace was advised that he was armed and extremely dangerous.

There was nothing said about Nick Connolly.

"Hey!"

She had been sitting in the living room, quietly watching the television. She turned to see that her father was already up, as well.

She smiled and patted the sofa next to her. He came and sat with her.

"The manhunt continues?" he asked.

"Here's the thing. Dillinger manipulates people. The men who brought him the airboat—they weren't bad. I mean, I don't think they would ever want to hurt anyone. Dillinger put them into a desperate situation, like he does with everyone."

With an arm around her shoulders, her father said, "I didn't want you moving to New York. And I didn't want to stop you. You have to follow your dreams, and you're responsible and…well, now I'm glad you're going to be in New York—far, far away from wherever the Anthony Green stash might be. I thank God that you were rescued. I can't imagine what your mom and I would have gone through if we had made it home and…and you hadn't been found."

"I'm very thankful."

"You don't ever have to work at that awful mansion again—under any circumstances!"

"Dad, the house wasn't at fault. I love the old house and the history—and we don't throw it all away because of a very bad man. They will find him."

He nodded. "I know. For your mom and me, you're everything, though. We thought it was tough when you decided to move to New York, when you landed the role and you got the part-time gig at Finnegan's. But...you were safer there."

"None of us can ever expect something like what happened, Dad. Anywhere. Bad people exist everywhere."

"I know," he told her quietly. "Because of New York, though, you already knew that FBI man who brought you home."

"Craig Frasier. Yes, I know him through Kieran Finnegan, who is Kevin's sister. You met Kevin—I introduced you to him when we were in an infomercial together."

"Right."

"His family owns the pub where I'll be working part-time. And you will love it when you come up," Kody assured her father.

"And he's the one who saved you?"

Kody shook her head. "No. That was Nick."

"They haven't even mentioned a Nick on the news, you know."

"I know. He was working undercover. But... " Her voice trailed.

"Well, if he weren't all right and still working this thing, you'd be hearing about a dead agent," her father said.

"Dad!"

"Am I right?"

"Yes, you're right."

She leaned against his shoulder. "Don't blame the house on Crystal Island, Dad. Don't stop loving it. Don't stop caring about it. If we do that, we let the bad guys win, you know."

"Very nobly said," her father told her, a slight smile

twisting his lips. "But… I say screw all noble thoughts when it comes to your safety!"

"Dad!"

"Not really. I just want them to catch that guy!"

Kody agreed.

And she longed to hear that Nick Connolly was fine, as well.

Two days later there were still a number of officers searching through the miles and miles that encompassed the enormous geographical body known as the Everglades.

Nick was no longer among them.

The chase now would fall to the men who knew the area.

He spent a day being debriefed and a day on paperwork. That was part of it, too.

He was going to be given a commendation. Thanks to his work, according to Director Egan via a video conference, a kidnapped child had been found and not a hostage had been harmed.

In his debriefing, Nick was determined that the agency understand it had been Dakota Cameron who had gotten the information out of Nathan Appleby and that Jason Tiger had been the one to convey it to the police and the FBI back in Miami. He was told that Kody had completely downplayed her role in the entire event, hoping that life could get back to normal.

He, too, would stay out of the public eye. It didn't pay, in his position, to have his face plastered on newspapers across the country.

Floyd—aka Gary Forman—had told the police everything he knew about Dillinger, the gang and the various enterprises that Dillinger had been into. What seemed surprising to Nick at the end of it all was that Dillinger was an amazing crook. The man had worked with a scope that Nick, even as part of the gang, had merely been able to guess about.

Sitting with Craig Frasier in the Miami Bureau offices, he shook his head and said, "Why did the man become so obsessed with a treasure that may not exist? If he stayed away from Crystal Island, he could still be fronting all his illicit operations."

"Who says he isn't? The man is still out there," Craig reminded him.

"So he is. But he's known. His face is known. The thing is, of course, that he does use people."

"Exactly. He may well be deep in Mexico now, on an island somewhere—or headed for the Rockies. No one knows with a man like that."

"True," Nick said. "There was just something about him and that treasure. He was obsessed, like an addict. He still means to get that treasure somehow."

"Well, Jason Tiger and the local Miccosukee police as well as the FBI and city and county police are still on it."

"Yes," Nick murmured. "Good people. And still… I don't feel right. I don't feel that we should be turning it over now. You and me—we followed Nathan Appleby all the way down the east coast. I was the one chosen to go undercover."

"Something that is completely blown now, of course—albeit in the best way."

"Yes. It doesn't feel right, though."

"And we're due on a plane back to New York tomorrow. It's over for us. I thought you'd be glad. I know that you didn't mind and accepted the undercover—but, it's also damned good to get out of it."

"I am ready, I don't mind doing what's needed, but you're right—there's a time you're ready for out. There's always the point where you may have to give yourself away or commit a criminal act. And then you have guys like Nathan Appleby—guys who kidnap kids and don't give a damn if they live or die, as long as the act gives them their leverage. I am glad it's over. I just wanted it to be over with Nathan Appleby behind bars."

"We don't win every time. We try our best. That's what we do."

Nick stood and grinned at Craig. "Tomorrow, hmm. What time?"

"Plane leaves at 11:00 a.m."

"I'll be there."

"And tonight?"

"Tonight… I want to stop by and see a girl. I want to pretend that months and months haven't gone by and that I just saw her say hi to you and smile at me as she left a restaurant."

"And?"

Nick laughed softly. "And, hopefully, I'm going on a date."

9

An iconic pop singer died. An earthquake rattled Central America. A boatload of refugees made landfall just south of Homestead, and a rising politician threw his hat into the ring for a vacated senate seat.

Given all that, the news about the assault on the historic mansion on Crystal Island at last died down.

Kody had spent hours with her folks, assuring them she was fine. She had made arrangements for them to fly to New York when the show opened, and she'd told them about her apartment, her part-time job and her friends, especially the Finnegans. She told them about the four siblings who owned the pub. How Declan was the boss and Kieran was a clinical psychologist and therapist who often worked with the police and the FBI. How Danny was a super tour guide and would take them around and, as they knew, Kevin was an actor.

It was all good.

She went back out to the mansion. She and her co-workers and friends who had been taken hostage hugged and cried and did all the things that survivors did. She was somewhat surprised to discover that none of them was leaving.

"I just don't see it happening again," Vince said.

"You don't give in to violence," Stacey Carlson told her.

Nan Masters, his supportive assistant, as always, smiled. "Stacey does not give in. He hires more security. That's the way we roll."

Jose was still in the hospital, but doing well.

Brandi was fine, as well—traumatized, but fine.

Kody felt relieved and almost happy when she left them. Everything was perfect.

She'd called Craig; he'd assured her that Nick Connolly was fine. They were all disappointed, of course, that they hadn't been able to find Nathan Appleby.

Her parents were still at a board meeting, seeing to the trust, when Kody came back from the mansion and turned on the news.

Yes. The story had already fallen to the back burner.

The doorbell rang as she was staring at the television.

When she looked through the peephole, her heart skipped a beat. It was Nick.

She instantly thrust the door open.

"Hey! You're supposed to be cautious!" he began.

He was barely able to speak. She threw her arms around him, holding him fiercely.

"Um, cautious…or not!" he said, looking down into her eyes, half detangling himself and half sweeping her closer. And he just looked at her and then his mouth touched down on hers and he kissed her.

Her mouth parted and she tasted the sweet heat of his lips and tongue. The warmth swept into her limbs, magical and wonderful, and causing her to tremble. He lifted his mouth from hers, searching out her eyes.

"You're okay," she said as if she needed him to confirm it.

"Yes. And you?"

"Absolutely fine, thank you. I... You're here. Thank you. I mean, thank you for knowing that I would be worried about you. And thank you for letting me know that you're okay."

"That's not why I'm here," he said. "Although I'm grateful to know that you were worried."

"Of course," she murmured. "So, why are you here?"

"Ah, yes. Well, you're not being held by a demonic kidnapper anymore. I'm not working undercover. In fact, I'm free until tomorrow, when I fly back to New York. I'm here to ask you to dinner. This is your family home, though, I understand. Should I ask your folks, too?"

"No! Oh, don't get me wrong. I love them dearly. But I don't need their approval to tell you this. I would love to go to dinner with you. That would be great. Where should we go?"

"I'm staying at the Legend, the new place on the bay. They have a chef who just won the grand prize on a reality show," he said with a rueful smile. "Want to try it?"

"Yes. Give me one minute." She started into the house, leaving him on the steps, then went back to invite him in. Gathering her wits, she ran to the kitchen counter to leave a note for her parents so they wouldn't worry, grabbed her purse and headed back. He smiled, watching her.

"What?" she asked.

"I was nervous coming here to ask you out, and I can see you're nervous, too. But we shouldn't be so nervous. We know each other, right? We slept together—kind of—in a hut."

"Yes…but it's different now, huh?"

He offered her his arm. She took it and then headed down the walk to his rental car, a black Subaru. He opened the door for her; she slid in.

"They still haven't found Dillinger—Nathan Appleby?" she asked.

"No. It's amazing that he's managed to disappear the way he has—and yet, not. He has such a network going. He had a way to reach someone who got him out—or got him into hiding in the Everglades, one or the other."

"But you're going home, right?"

"Yes. I wouldn't be useful anymore undercover. He knows me. Craig Frasier is heading back, too. The operation will be handled from here now. Every agency down here is on the lookout."

"You don't sound happy about it," Kody said.

"I'm not. I hate it when we haven't finished what we started out to do. Dillinger has been a step ahead of us down the eastern seaboard. I'm not happy, but…" He shrugged, glancing over at her. "But you're heading to New York City, too, right?"

"The play opens in a few weeks."

"Living theater?" he asked. "I mean, isn't most theater living? Not to sound too ignorant or anything, but…"

Kody laughed. "Interactive would be a better description. It's been done before in a similar manner. We're doing a Shakespeare play, except that it all takes place on different floors within an old hotel. I love what we're doing. It's never the same thing, different every night. Basically, we are the characters. We work with the script and draw people in from the audience. And the audience moves from place to place while we have our scenes in which we work."

"I can't wait to see it."

"You'd really come?"

"Sure. We can have FBI night at the theater."

"Very amusing."

"I'm serious. I'm sure that Craig and Kieran will come, and Craig's partner. And once I'm home, I'm hoping to be paired again with my old partner, Sherri Haskell."

"Ah, Sherri."

"Married to Mo."

"I didn't ask."

"Yes, you did."

Nick drew up to valet parking and they left the car behind.

He caught Kody's hand, hurrying up the planked ramp that led out to the bay and along the water. The moon was a crescent, dozens of stars were shining and the glow of lights from the hotel and restaurant on the water was magical.

"Florida will always be home," Nick said.

"Always," Kody agreed. He pulled her into his arms and he kissed her again, and she thought that, indeed, it was all magic. She couldn't remember when she had met someone who made her feel this way, when she had longed for just such a touch and just such a kiss.

He drew away from her and leaned against the rail, just holding her, smoothing her hair, looking out on the water.

"You have a room?" she asked softly.

"That's a leading question, you know."

"Yes, I know."

He studied her eyes. "Room service?"

"That would be lovely."

He caught her hand again and led her to the elevator. When he opened the door to his room, she went straight to the large window that looked out on the night.

"Sorry, there's no balcony. Not on taxpayers' money," he said. "However, it is much better than the place I had before, when I was hanging with Dillinger's gang."

She turned to look at him.

"It wouldn't matter to me where you stayed," she said.

He strode to her, taking her into his arms. She drew the backs of her fingers down his face. He kissed her again, his fingers sliding to the zipper at the back of her dress. She allowed it to slip from her body.

"I wasn't… I'm not really prepared," he told her. Then he laughed. "I'm sure I can be—there're a dozen stores nearby."

"I'm on the pill," she told him.

"I'm not— There's no one else at the moment?" he asked.

She shook her head. "I've been working on the play, on the move…on life. But I've always been an optimist."

He laughed at that, pulled her closer. And he slid from his jacket, doffed his holster and gun, and kissed her neck and throat while she struggled with the buttons on his shirt. Still half dressed, they fell back on the bed. He kissed her again and then again, and stared down at her, and she reached up to him, drawing him back and tugging at his belt and his waistband.

Rolling, mingling passionate kisses with laughter, they finally stripped one another completely and lay breathlessly naked together, frozen for a moment of sweet anticipation and wonder. Then they tangled together again, seeking to press their lips upon one another's flesh here and there. He rose above her, staring down at her, straddled over her, and she reached for him, amazed that however it had come about, they were here together, and she was simply grateful.

He kissed her lips, her throat, and his mouth moved along her body, teasing her flesh. She lay still for a moment, not even breathing, swept up by the sensation. He caressed and teased, lower and lower, until she could stay still no longer, and she arched and writhed and rolled with him, and allowed her lips and tongue to tease in turn, bathing the length of him in kisses until breathless, they came together at last. He moved within her slowly at first. Their eyes were locked as the pace of their lovemaking began to increase, bit by bit, to a fever pitch.

Outside, the stars shone on the water. A breeze drifted by. The night was beautiful and, for Kody, these were intricate and unbelievable moments in which the world was nothing but stars, the scent of shimmering seawater and the man who held her.

Their climax was volatile and incredible, and holding one another in sweet aftershocks seemed just as wonderful. And then whispering and laughing and talking—and wondering if they should indeed order room service or just let the concept of dinner go—seemed as natural as if they had known one another forever.

"So there's been no one in your life for a long time?" he asked her.

"Not in a long time. I do love what I do. Rehearsals are long and hard—then there is the part-time work, as you know. And you?"

"Long hours, too. But I was engaged. To a designer."

"A designer?"

"Marissa works for a major clothing line. She wants her own one day."

"What happened?"

"Off hours, not enough time…we drifted apart. I have nothing bad to say about her. We just—we just weren't meant to be. Being with an agent isn't easy. Takes someone who understands that time is precious and elusive."

"It's a give and take," Kody said softly. She hoisted up on an elbow and smiled down at him. "I had a similar problem with my last ex. Gerard."

"Ah. And what happened to him?"

Kody hesitated. "He met a teacher. She didn't work a second job to pay for the privilege of doing her main job. She just had much better hours."

"I'm sorry."

"I introduced him to the teacher," Kody said. "He was a good guy. I wasn't right for him."

"You think we might be right for each other?" Nick asked softly.

"I just… I hope," Kody said.

"Hmm. What made you…care about me?"

"Your ethics."

"As a crook?"

She laughed. "You wouldn't hurt people. That mattered. And you?"

"Well, there's nothing wrong with the way you look, you know," he teased.

"Ah. So it's all physical attraction, then?"

"And your courage, determination and attitude," he said.

She laughed softly. "For me it was your eyes. I knew your eyes. And I knew you, because of your eyes."

He smiled and pulled her down to him again. And what started as a kiss developed into another session of lovemaking.

By the time they finished, Kody jumped up after looking at her watch. "Oh! I have to go back. My parents… I mean, I was just home here to tie up loose ends. My mother and father are already a bit crazy."

"Say no more. I'll get you home right away," Nick promised.

They dressed quickly. "I really did intend to wine and dine you with a sumptuous meal," Nick said, his hand at the small of her back as they left the room and headed down.

"We'll both be in New York. There are tons of fabulous restaurants there, too, you know. I mean, I am assuming that we'll see one another in New York? Or is that maybe too much of an assumption? I was really worried about myself, you know. I was attracted to you— when you were with Dillinger. You weren't a killer—I knew that much…well, my feelings did make me question myself."

He smiled, holding her hand tight.

"Time is precious and elusive," he said. "I will gratefully accept any you can give me in the city—especially with your show starting."

"I'll find time," she promised. "I'm partial to old, historic restaurants."

"I know a great pub. I think we both get a discount there, too," Nick teased.

"A great pub!" she agreed.

The valet brought Nick's car. Kody glanced at her watch again. It was nearly 1:00 a.m. She was surprised that her mother or her father hadn't called her yet. Maybe they were happy she was out with an FBI agent.

The distance between the hotel and her parents' home wasn't great; she was there within minutes.

Nick walked her to the door.

"I'll really see you in New York?" she murmured.

He pulled her into his arms. "You will see me. You'll see so much of me…"

She moved into his kiss. The wonder of the night seemed to settle over her like a cloak. She was tempted to walk into her house and check on her family—and then just tell them she was off to sleep with her FBI agent before he had to get on his plane.

Kody managed to gather a sense of decorum.

"I should meet your parents," Nick said. "But I guess you shouldn't wake them up."

"Probably not the best idea," she agreed. "You'll meet them. They're coming up for opening night."

They kissed again. It seemed all but impossible to stop—to let him drive away.

But, finally, he broke away. "Kody, I…"

"Me, too," she said softly.

Then she slipped into the house, closed the door behind her and leaned against it. A sense of euphoria seemed to have settled over her.

She was walking on air.

But as she moved away from the front door, the lamp above her father's living room chair went on.

"Dad," she murmured.

Then she fell silent.

And she dead-stopped.

It wasn't her father, sitting in his chair.

It was Nathan Appleby—aka Dillinger.

Nick headed down to the rental Subaru but paused as he reached the car. He looked up at the sky. It really was one of the most fantastic winter nights in Miami.

Stars brilliant against the black velvet of the sky, a moon that seemed almost to smile in a half curve and a balmy temperature of maybe seventy degrees.

He would always love South Florida as home. There was nothing like it—even when it came to the Everglades with all its glory, from birds of uncanny beauty, endangered panthers—and deadly reptiles.

It would always be home to both of them, even as it seemed they both loved New York City and embraced all that could be found there. Actually, Nick had never cared much which office he was assigned to; he was just glad to be with the Bureau. Even if they didn't win every time.

Nathan Appleby was still out there.

But the hostages were safe. The hostages were alive. It was out of his hands and, after tonight, he could say that it had ended exceptionally well. The future loomed before them.

He turned the key in the ignition and drove out onto the street. His phone rang and he glanced at the Caller ID. It was Kody. He answered it quickly. "Hello?"

At first there was nothing. He almost hung up, thinking maybe she had pocket dialed him.

Then he heard Kody's voice. "You know me, Mr. Appleby. You know that I won't help you unless I'm sure others are safe. And this time, you have my parents. Do you really think that I'll do anything for you, anything at all, when I'm worried about their safety?"

"Right now, Miss Cameron, they are alive. You know me. I don't care a lot whether people live or die. You get that treasure for me and your parents live. It's that simple."

Nick quickly pulled the car to the side. He hadn't gone

more than a block from the Cameron house. He cursed himself a thousand times over.

They had underestimated Nathan Appleby. They hadn't comprehended the depth of his obsession, realized that he would risk everything to find the Anthony Green treasure.

Appleby had known everything about the Crystal Island mansion, about Anthony Green. It was only natural that he should have known where the Cameron family lived, only natural that he had made his way out of the Everglades and into the city of Miami—and on to the Cameron house.

"You left Adrian Burke bound and gagged in an abandoned crack house," Nick heard Kody say. "I need to know where my parents are—that they will be safe. That's the only way I help you."

"Okay, here it is. They are not in a crack house. They're out on a boat belonging to some very good friends of mine. Now, you help me and I get the treasure, I make a call and they go free. If you don't come with me—nicely!—I call and they take an eternal swim in Biscayne Bay. Oh, and added insurance—if they don't hear from me every hour, your parents take a dive."

"I'll go with you. But what guarantee do I have?"

"You don't have any guarantees. No guarantees at all. But… I can dial right now. Mommy and Daddy do love the water, right?"

"Do you mind if I put sneakers on?" Kody asked. "They beat the hell out of sandals for scrounging around in the Everglades!"

Torture was illegal.

But Nick still considered slipping into the Cameron

house and slicing Nathan Appleby to ribbons in order to
force him to tell the truth about Kody's parents.

But there were inherent dangers—such as Appleby
getting a message through to the people holding Kody's
parents, Kody herself protesting, and a million other
things that could go wrong—along with torture being
illegal. Appleby had said he had to make a call once an
hour. The man was mean enough, manic enough, to die
before making a call.

Nick didn't want to give up the phone; he couldn't
reach Craig or anyone else unless he did hang up the
phone.

He knew where Appleby would take Kody.

"Let's go!" he heard Appleby snap. "Ditch the purse—
you have a phone in there, right? Ditch the purse now!"

The line was still open but nothing else was coming
from it. Nick hung up quickly and called Craig.

"We'll get the Coast Guard out in the bay along with
local police," Craig said as soon as Nick apprised him
of the situation. "We'll find them. Swing by for me at
the hotel. We'll head out together. They'll alert Jason
Tiger and he'll see that everyone out there is watching
and ready."

"We know where they're going," Nick said.

"How damned crazy can that man be? He intends to
dig in the swamp all night by himself?"

"He's not alone. He has Kody."

Nathan Appleby made Kody drive.

Her own car.

She wasn't sure why that seemed to add insult to in-
jury.

She didn't know how he'd gotten to her house; she

hadn't seen a car, but then, he might have parked anywhere on the street.

Wherever he had come from, he had come to her house and kidnapped her parents. They were out somewhere in the bay. He'd come prepared; he had two backpacks—one she was certain she was supposed to be carrying through the Everglades. He'd managed all this with the news displaying his picture constantly and every law-enforcement agent in the city on the lookout for him.

He kept his gun trained on her as they drove, held low in the seat lest someone note that she was driving under stress.

Not that there were that many people out. Miami was truly a city that never slept, but here, in the residential areas that led from her home close to downtown and west toward the Everglades, there were few cars on the road.

"I'm not sure how you think I'm doing this. I mean, honestly? I don't know how I'm doing this. I've only ever dropped by the Everglades by daylight. I'm pretty sure there are gates or fences or something when you get to the park entrances," Kody said.

"We won't be taking a park entrance," he told her.

"What? You just happen to have friends with access driveways?" she asked, unable to avoid the sarcasm.

"I happen to know where to go," he said.

Kody checked the rearview mirror now and then, but she couldn't tell if any of the cars she saw behind them were following her or not.

She was fairly certain she had gotten a call out—that she'd managed to dial Nick's number without Appleby noting what she was doing as they'd spoken. Then, of course, he'd made her leave her purse.

But he'd never looked at the phone. He didn't know what she had done...

If, of course, she had actually done it.

She had, she assured herself.

They passed the Miccosukee casino where lights were still bright and the parking lot abounded with cars.

Then, as they continued west, there were almost no cars.

Businesses advertising airboat rides seemed to creep up on them. The lights were low and the darkness out there at night seemed almost surreal.

Kody had been driving nearly an hour when Appleby picked up his phone.

"My parents?" she asked.

"Yes, Miss Cameron. I'm making sure they'll be just fine."

Someone answered on the other end.

"Everything is good," he said. And he smiled at Kody and hung up. "Just keep on helping me and we'll be fine."

"You need more than just me," she said. "This is the kind of project you need a host of workers to accomplish. We have to find the pilings. We think we know that he buried the stash at the corner of the main chickee, but we're not sure. And how deep? Exactly where? We need more people to look."

"Maybe," he told her.

"Just how many friends do you have? And do you really trust these people? Okay, so I've seen you in action. You extorted an airboat from people who were forced to help you. But remember, people you bribe and threaten just might want to bite back, you know," Kody told him.

"Would you bite back?" he asked her.

"If you keep threatening my parents, I promise you, I'll bite back!"

"Not if you want them alive. And slow down!"

Kody slowed down. She had no idea what he was looking for. If she were to turn to the right at the moment, she'd wind up in a canal. Not a pleasant thought. If she turned to the left, as far as she could see, there was nothing but soupy marsh. They were, she knew, near Shark Valley, but it was still ahead of them on the trail by a mile or two.

"Here," he said.

"Where's 'here'?" Kody demanded.

"Slow down!"

She slowed even more and glanced in the rearview mirror.

There were no lights behind them.

She wasn't being followed. Her heart seemed to sink.

"Right there!" Appleby told her. "See there? See the road? And don't get any ideas. You sink us in a canal or a bog out here, your parents die. Oh, and you die, too. So, drive, and drive carefully."

"Do you know how pitch-dark it is out here?" Kody demanded.

"Do you know that's why they give cars bright lights?" Appleby retorted.

Kody grated her teeth. She turned to the left and slowly, carefully, followed the dirt road Appleby had indicated. It seemed to head into nothing but dense green grass and it slowly disappeared.

"That's good," Appleby said. "Here. This is fine. It's as far as we go by car, my dear."

She's already been dragged through the swamp. She'd spent a night in a chickee. She'd walked, not knowing if she'd disturb a rattler or a coral snake, or if she'd step on a log that turned out to be an alligator. She shouldn't have been so terrified.

And yet she was.

Appleby shoved his gun into his waistband and tossed her a backpack. "Get your flashlight," he commanded her.

She found a large flashlight in the pack along with water, a folded shovel, a pick and a power bar.

They might have been on a planned hike or tour into the wilderness!

"Turn your light on," he said.

She did so, as did he. The flashlights illuminated great circles of brush and grass and trees. "There," he said.

Where?

And then she saw an airboat before them.

"Let's go!" he said.

She took a step; the ground was no longer solid.

She stepped into swamp and prayed she wasn't disturbing a cottonmouth.

It was only a few steps to the airboat. She was grateful to climb aboard it.

And then Appleby was with her, the motor was revving and they were moving deeper into the abyss of the night.

"I will be there when they arrive," Jason Tiger assured Nick. "I'll have Miccosukee police with me. They know how to hide in the night. We'll be on it, I promise."

"But don't approach until we're out there," Nick said. "We're trying to find her parents. We'll be behind them. We have a ranger meeting us to take us out to the hammock. We'll take the first miles by airboat and then switch to canoes so that we're not heard."

"We won't approach. Unless, of course, we see that Miss Cameron is in imminent danger."

"Of course," Nick agreed.

Nick spoke with Tiger as he waited for Craig to join him. He hung up just as his teammate joined him in the car.

"You know, I keep thinking about this," Nick said.

"We haven't thought of anything but for days now," Craig said grimly.

"No. I mean the timing. I went to Kody's house at 8:00 p.m. Her mom and dad were still out—at a board meeting. We came to the hotel. We were at the hotel about three hours or so. That would mean that Appleby got to her house, either charmed or laid a trap for her parents when they returned, and then found someone to threaten who had a boat, and got Kody's mom and dad out on the boat. At least, that's what he told Kody."

"And?" Craig asked him. "Ah. Yeah, timing. You don't think that he really got them out on a boat. We have the Coast Guard out, but, of course, there are so many boats out there. And they can search for the Cameron couple. Thing is…"

"There are hundreds of boats out on the water. It's dark, and the bay stretches forever, and boats move," Nick said. He shook his head. "But I don't think they're on a boat."

"Where do you think they are?"

"Somewhere near the house," Nick said. "I can't look, though. I have to get out there. I have to get out there as quickly as possible. I know what Kody was doing, where she was looking, what she believed. I need—"

"To be there. I get it. Drop me at the Cameron house. I'll find her parents, if they are anywhere near the house," Craig said firmly.

Nick nodded. "Thank you."

"It's a plan, my friend. It's a good plan. I'll get some help out to the house with me. If Mr. and Mrs. Cameron are anywhere near, we'll find them. And, if they're on the water, the Coast Guard will find them. Appleby knows Kody. He knows that she'll do anything he says as long as she's worried about her parents."

"We're ahead of him by one step this time," Nick said. "He didn't know that she got a call through on her phone, that I heard what went on between them. As far as he knows, we don't have a clue that Kody has been taken, that he has her out in the Everglades."

"She's really the right stuff," Craig said lightly.

She's perfect! Nick thought, and it felt as if the blood burned in his veins.

He knew he probably shouldn't be on the case now. Because he would kill, he would die, to see that she was safe. And that was just the way it was.

10

The airboat drifted onto the marshy land just before the rise of the hammock.

Kody's heart sank when she thought about the impossibility of the task before them. People had known about the Anthony Green stash forever. Scholars had mused and pondered on it.

They'd agreed that the treasure was in the Everglades.

Where bodies and more had disappeared since the coming of man.

"Get your pack. We'll head straight back," Appleby told her. "That bastard G-man had it down right, just before everything went to hell, before your silly friend freaked out and ran. You know, this could have all been over. We could have found the treasure. I'd have left you out here, where one of those rangers or Miccosukee police would have found you.

"Yep. It could have all been over. You know, letting that man in was the only mistake I made," Appleby said, and shrugged. "He talked a good story—he pulled it off. He acted as if he could be tough when needed." He grinned at Kody. "Maybe that's why you two hit it off so well. Two actors, cast in different roles in life."

Appleby laughed, amused by his observation. "Okay, let's go. Get back there. We're going to find the site of the pilings, and we're going to start digging."

"Don't you think that this is a little crazy?" Kody asked him. "The local police know that you were here, the FBI know that you were here…they'll have someone out here."

"Why would they have someone out here?"

"It was a crime scene!"

Appleby laughed. "They looked for me here. They didn't find me here. They've moved on. They're checking the airlines and private planes. They're going to be certain that I've fled the area. They won't be looking for me here. So let's get started."

"This is ridiculous. It's dark. I can step on a snake. You can step on a snake. I saw gator holes back there. You could piss off a gator—"

"Yep. So let's hurry. Over here. That's where your lover boy seemed to be when all hell broke loose. And he was going by your determination."

It was insane. Maybe by daylight. Maybe with a dozen people digging and working…

"It could be worse," Appleby said.

"Really?"

"It could be summer." Appleby laughed and swatted his neck. "If it was summer, the mosquitos would be unbearable."

Every step in the night was torture. At least, once they had moved in from the edges of the hammock, the ground was sturdy, a true limestone shelf.

It was difficult to get a bearing in the darkness. While the stars remained in the sky, the glow of the flashlights only illuminated circles of light; large, yes, but not large enough. She heard the chirping of crickets and, now and then, something else. Something that slunk into the water from the land. Something that moved through the trees. There were wild boars out here, she knew. Dangerous creatures if threatened. There were Florida panthers, too. Horribly endangered, and yet, if one was there, and threatened…

She kept walking, searching the ground, a sense of panic beginning to rise within her as she thought about the hopelessness of what she was doing. And then she came upon an indentation in the earth. She paused and shone her light down.

The dry area of the heavy pine piling would have eroded with time. But beneath the limestone and far into the water, the wood had been preserved.

She'd found it.

A piling that indicated the corner of the main chickee where, decades ago, Anthony Green had maintained the Everglades "office" for his illicit distillery.

She looked up; Appleby was staring at her.

"Time to dig!"

"We've been watching her. She has been safe," Jason Tiger told Nick. "You don't see them, but there are three men with me, watching from different angles. Oliver Osceola is in a tree over there—he's closest. Appleby has kept his gun out, so we've been exceptionally careful not to be seen or to startle him in any way." He was quiet for a minute. "We have a sniper. A good one. David Cypress served three tours of duty in the Middle East. If we need—"

"We need to keep watching now. My partner is searching for Kody Cameron's parents. She'll throw herself in front of him, if she's worried about what will happen to her folks." The burning sensation remained with Nick, something that he fought—reminding himself over and over again that he was a federal agent, responsible to his calling. He would make every move the way a federal agent would—and that included killing Appleby point-blank if necessary to save a civilian.

The time taken to reach the hammock deep in the Everglades behind Shark Valley had seemed to be a lifetime.

He was here now.

He could see Appleby and Kody.

"All right, we're ready," Jason Tiger said. "You call the shots."

Nick nodded and ducked low into the grass. He kept as close to the ground as he could, making his way around to the area where Kody and Appleby were standing. He came close enough to hear them speaking.

"That's it! Now dig. It's there somewhere! You see! Ah, you were such a doubter, Miss Cameron! Dig! We have found it."

Kody was trying to assemble a foldable spade.

"You need to make a phone call," she said.

"I need you to dig."

"Make the call. It's been an hour again. I mean it—make the call."

"What if I just cut you up a little bit, Miss Cameron?"

"Then you'd have to dig yourself," Kody told him. "Make the call."

"You want me to make a call? Fine, I'll make a call."

Appleby pulled out his phone. He placed a call. He appeared to be speaking to someone.

But Nick wondered if there was actually anyone on the other end.

Had the man really taken Kody's parents out on a boat somewhere? Did he have new accomplices watching over them, actually ready to kill?

Or had Nick been right? Were they somewhere near their own home?

Still a safe distance, hunkered low in the rich grasses, Nick put a call through to Craig. "Anything yet?"

"No. But we have search-and-rescue dogs on the way. We're going to find them. What's going on at your end? Have you found Kody and Appleby?"

"We have them. Jason Tiger has had them in sight. We're good here. Just…just find Kody's parents."

As he spoke he heard the dogs start to bay. They were on to something. He suddenly found himself praying that Craig and the men and the dogs weren't going to find corpses. The corpses of two people he had never met.

"Bones," Craig said over the phone.

"Bones?"

"And a little gravestone. For JoJo, a little dog who died about a decade ago."

"Oh, lord. Craig—"

"Hold up. We've got something. The dogs are heading across the street. There's a park over there. I think he has them in the park, Nick. Right back with you!"

Kody didn't trust Appleby. She knew the man really didn't care if people lived or died.

She wondered with a terrible, sinking feeling if her parents weren't already dead. If Appleby hadn't come into the house, waited for them and shot them down in cold blood…

"I want to talk to my mother," she said.

"What?"

"I want to talk to my mother. I want to know that she's alive. I don't believe you and I don't trust you. And this is sick and ridiculous, and if I'm going to continue to search and help you, I want to know that my mother is alive!" Kody said determinedly.

"Do you know what I could do, little girl?" Appleby asked her. "Do you have any idea of what I could do to you? Let me describe a few possibilities. Your kneecaps. You can't imagine the pain of having your kneecap shot out. I could shoot them both—and then leave you here. Eventually birds of prey and other creatures would come along and then the fun would really start. They would eat you alive. Slowly. They're very fond of soft tissue, especially birds of prey. They love to pluck out eyes…you can't begin to imagine. With any luck, you'd be dead by then."

Kody wasn't about to be swayed. "I want to talk to my mother."

"You can't talk to your mother."

"Why not? Is she dead? If she's dead, I don't give a damn what you do to me."

"She can't talk because there isn't anyone with her to hand her a phone!"

"I thought she was being held on a boat by people who would kill her."

"She's alive and well, Kody. Okay, maybe not so *well*, but she is alive. She's just tied up at the moment."

"Tied up where?"

"Does it matter? She can't talk right now." Appleby let out a growl of aggravation. "She can't talk. I knocked them out, left them tied up. They're alive, Kody."

"How do I trust you?"

"How do you not? You don't have a choice. Start moving. The longer you take, the more danger there is for your mom and dad."

"Maybe you've never even had them!" Kody said.

Appleby grinned. "Mom. Her name is Elizabeth, nickname Beth. She's about five feet, six inches. A pretty brunette with short, bobbed hair. Dad—Daniel. Six-two, blue eyes, graying dark hair. Yep, not to worry, Kody, dear, I do know the folks."

Kody managed to snap her shovel into working condition. For a moment she stared at Appleby, then she studied the ground and jumped back.

"What?" Appleby demanded.

"Snake."

"It will move."

"Yes, I'm trying to let it. It's a very big snake."

"It's just a ball python," Appleby said. "Someone's pet they let loose out here. Damn, but I hate that! People being so irresponsible. They've ruined the ecosystem."

Kody stared at him. He hadn't minded shooting an accomplice at close range. But he was worried about the ecosystem.

Thankfully, the snake at her feet was a non-native constrictor instead of a viper.

She swallowed hard.

The snake was gone.

She started to dig.

"Tell me you've got something!" Nick whispered to Craig.

"Yes! We've got them. They were left under the bridge at the edge of the park. They couldn't twist or turn a lot or they'd have been in a canal. But we have them. We have them both. Elizabeth and Daniel Cameron are safe."

"Roger that. Thank you," Nick said. He clicked the phone closed, then inched through the grass and rose slightly, giving a signal to Jason Tiger to hold for his cue.

Kody suddenly let out a little cry, stepping backward.

"What?" Appleby demanded.

"Another snake…it's a coral snake. A little coral snake, but they can be really dangerous."

"No, that's not a coral snake. It's just a rat snake. Rat snakes are not poisonous."

"'Red touch yellow, kill a fellow. Black touch yellow, friend of Jack,'" Kody said, quoting the age-old way children were taught to recognize coral snakes from their non-venomous cousins.

"Yeah! Look, black on yellow!" Appleby said.

"No, red is touching yellow!"

"You want to get your nose down there and check?" he demanded.

"I am not touching that snake!" Kody said.

Appleby made a move. Nick could judge the man's body motion, the way that he crouched. He was getting ready to strike out.

And that was it.

Nick went flying across the remaining distance between them.

Appleby spun around, but he never knew Nick was coming, never saw what hit him. Nick head-butted the man, bringing him down to the ground.

The man's gun went flying.

They could all hear the popping sound as it was sucked into the swamp.

Appleby made no effort to struggle. Nick had raised a fist; Appleby just stared at him. He started to laugh. "You won't do it, will you? Pansy lawman. You won't do it. In fact…"

Nick didn't listen to the rest; he was already rising. Jason Tiger and his men were coming in to take the prisoner.

He looked over at Kody, who was standing there, shaking. She hadn't moved from her position; she was just staring at him.

Then she flew at him, her fists banging against his chest. "Nick! You idiot, he has my mom and dad. He's going to kill my mom and dad. He'll never tell us—"

"That's right! They'll die!" Appleby chortled.

Nick caught Kody's hands. He turned and glanced at Appleby. "No, actually, Dan and Beth are just fine. They're being checked out at Mercy Hospital as we speak, but I imagine they'll be home by the time Kody and I manage to get back in."

Kody went limp, falling against him. "Really?"

"Really," he said.

He started to lead her back toward the police boat that had brought him to the hammock.

"Thank you!" she whispered.

"You did it, you know. Getting the call through. If you hadn't managed that, no one would have known. You did it, Kody."

She looked up at him. "I called the right guy, huh?" she said softly.

He kissed her lightly, holding her close, and heedless of who might see.

Appleby let out a horrendous scream. "It got me! It got me! Son of a bitch, it got me! Help, you've got to get

me help, fast. You have to slice it, suck the poison out…
It got me. You bastards, do something!"

"Oh, I don't know," Jason Tiger said. "David, did you
see the snake?"

"Had to be a rat snake."

With Appleby supported between them, Jason Tiger
and David Cypress walked by them. Jason Tiger winked.
Rat snake, he mouthed to Nick.

And Nick grinned.

Yep…

Let Appleby do a little wondering, after what he had
done to others.

The winter's night was nearly over. Morning's light
was on the way. And with it, Nick felt, all good things.

It was done. Case over, the way he liked it.

Appleby would rot beyond bars.

And Kody was safe, in his arms.

"'He hath, my lord, of late made many tenders of his
affection to me!'"

Beyond a doubt, Dakota Cameron made the most
stunning Ophelia that Nick had ever seen.

The play was definitely different; not that, until now,
he'd really been an expert on plays.

He was learning.

But even with what he knew, *Hamlet Thus They Say*
was a different kind of show. Of course, Kody was beyond stupendous and Nick could hear the buzz among
the people around him.

It was going to be a hit.

There was no real curtain call; the play just continued
for four hours each night. There was no intermission. It
was "living theater."

And it was FBI night.

Craig was there with Kieran. Mike, Craig's partner, was there. Nick had been glad to learn that he would be repartnered with Sherri Haskell, and she was there with her New York City cop husband, Mo.

Director Egan had even come out for the night.

They waited in front of the theater for the last of the attendees to leave.

"I can't believe that they didn't break character—not once!" Kieran said, smiling at Nick. "Okay, so, actually, I can't believe you disappear, Kody goes home to settle some things, and you come back a duo, having caught a man who held a spot on the Ten Most Wanted list— and found a treasure that's been missing for decades."

"Ah, but we didn't find the treasure!" Nick told her.

"I think you did."

Nick laughed softly, looking at Craig. "Poor Ophelia, going mad for love! I think Craig and I did a bit of the same. The county, the federal government and the Miccosukee Tribe all got together—and that's when they found the treasure. None of us stayed because, as we know, the FBI is a commitment—and because the show must go on. That's a commitment for Kody.

"We stayed in Miami just long enough for her to spend a day with her parents. Then we all had to be back up here. But, yes, Kody's research and logic led those forces to the stash. They had to dig pretty deep. I don't think that Nathan Appleby would have managed to get it all out. He might have found some pieces, though. It had been buried in leather cases, and they were coming apart. But, yes, the stash was filled with gold pieces— South African—and emeralds, diamonds, you name it."

"What will happen with it all?" Kieran asked.

"I understand some of the pieces will wind up in a museum. Some will go to the state and some will wind up helping to keep the Crystal Manor going. It will be part of the trust that runs the place—along with Kody's family. And speaking of Kody's family…" He paused, waving as Daniel and Beth Cameron exited the theater. Nick drew them over and introduced them to those in their group they hadn't met already.

Of course, on arrival in the city, they'd been brought to Finnegan's and feted with stout from excellent taps and the world's best shepherd's pie.

"Wow. And you're FBI, too?" Daniel asked Sherri.

"Yes, sir. I am."

"Well, our girl will be hanging around with a good crowd," Daniel told his wife.

"Yes, certainly," Beth Cameron said, but she looked a little puzzled.

"Is anything wrong?" Nick asked her.

"No, no, of course not. I'm not so sure that I get it. I mean, living theater, or whatever it is. I'm used to the actors just…acting on stage. I've never talked with the actors before during a performance," she said. "But, of course, Kody and Kevin were wonderful!"

Kieran laughed. "Yes, they were. They were both wonderful."

"She talked to me—but as if she didn't know me!" Daniel said.

"Well, she doesn't know you. Not as Ophelia," Nick explained.

"Yes, yes, of course. She's playing a role. I guess. I mean, of course. It's just strange," Beth said. She sighed. "She has a beautiful voice. Maybe it will be a musical next. Oh, look!" she murmured, catching Nick by the hand. "There—do you know who that is?"

Nick looked. No, he didn't.

"That's Mayor Holden Burke. With his little boy, Adrian. And his wife, Monica."

The man, next to the boy who appeared to be about nine, noted Beth just as she was whispering about him.

He waved and came over, catching the hands of his wife and son so they would join him. Adrian Burke was carrying a large bouquet of flowers.

Beth introduced people all around.

"We're so grateful," he said, and his wife nodded, looking around. "You're the agents who were involved?"

"Craig and I were down there," Nick said. "But, like I said in my debriefing, in all honesty, Kody was the one who got Nathan Appleby to say where Adrian was being held. And an agent down in South Florida, Jason Tiger, got the information back to the city."

The cast door opened and the actors were all coming out. There was a round of applause that sounded up and down the street.

Nick saw Kody, and saw that she was searching through the crowd.

Looking for him, he thought. He waved and then watched her chat and smile with grace and courtesy as she spoke to fans and signed programs.

"Excuse us," Mayor Burke said.

Nick realized, as the mayor and his family approached Kody, that she'd never actually met them.

She took the flowers from Adrian, hugged him and planted a kiss on his cheek. She was hugged by the mayor and his wife.

The three left then, waving to the others.

And, finally, the crowd around the performers had just about thinned out.

He, Kody's parents, the Finnegans and the extended FBI family made their way over to the group, congratulating the actors. Nick bypassed everyone, going directly to Kody and taking her in his arms.

Her kiss was magnificent. Her eyes touched his with promise. She was filled with the excitement and adrenaline of opening night; she was also anxious, he knew, for their time together.

But first, of course, they all made their way to Finnegan's for a late-night supper and a phenomenal Irish band.

And, at last, it was time for him and Kody to leave.

In his company car they saw her parents to their hotel in midtown. Then they headed for his apartment.

When they'd first returned to the city a few weeks ago, they'd kept both apartments. That had proved to be a total waste. They both worked, and worked hard, but their free time was spent together.

When a night bartender at Finnegan's was about to lose his lease—his apartments were being turned into condos—Kody offered her apartment to him, and so, just last week, she had made the official move into Nick's place.

It was simply the best accommodation: a full bedroom, an office, a parlor, two baths. Plus it was situated right on the subway line that connected Finnegan's and the FBI offices and midtown.

Kody, of course, had already made some changes, and Nick loved them.

There were posters on the wall—show posters and band posters—and there was artwork, as well. Seascapes, mostly, from Florida, and paintings from New York City, too.

One of his favorite pieces they had bought together down in the Village. It was a signed painting of the Brooklyn Bridge.

"A new artist—who will be a famous artist one day," Kody had said. "And if not, it's still a brilliant painting and I love it."

She was, he thought, everything he needed.

Life, as he saw it, was too often grim. But Kody looked for the best, always. And she saw the best that way. She showed it to him, as well.

"So, what did you think of the play? What did you really think?" she asked when they stepped into the apartment, alone at last.

"I loved it," he said.

"Really?"

"I really did. But I do believe you have to have the right cast for that kind of theater. Your cast is truly amazing. Powerful performers—they all engaged the audience."

"I don't think my mom saw it that way."

Nick laughed. "She admitted to a bit of confusion."

"But you really thought that it was good?" she asked.

"I, like the critics, raved!"

She flew into his arms, kissing him. "Are you a liar?" she asked.

"No!"

She laughed. "Doesn't matter," she said. "You were there for me, on FBI night."

"I'll come to the show whenever I can."

"You don't have to. It's okay. We'll settle in and we'll figure it all out—the time, the FBI, the theater…"

"I know we will," he told her. And he kissed her

again, shrugging out of his jacket as he did so. It had been a chilly night. Kody was in a heavy wool coat and it, too, hit the floor.

She kicked off her shoes, their lips never parting.

Nick suddenly dipped low and swept her off her feet. She laughed as she looked up at him.

"It's been a dramatic night. Thought I should be dramatic, too."

"You really are quite the actor. You know, down in Florida when I first saw you, I really thought you were a bad guy."

"But not really. You said you knew I wasn't a killer."

"You played the part very well."

"Thank you. If the law-enforcement thing fails…"

She touched his face gently, studying his eyes. "It won't. You love what you do, and you're very good, and I would never want anything different for you."

"Nor would I change a thing about you," he told her huskily.

She smiled.

They headed into the bedroom and Nick laid Kody carefully upon the sheets, kneeling beside her. He kissed her lips again, but she was impatient and rose against him, crawling over him, straddling him, while she tore away her clothes.

"Ah, my lady! Wait, I have a surprise for you," he said.

She laughed softly. "And I have a surprise for you! I can wait for nothing." And she shoved him down. She lay against him, teased his shoulders, chest and abdomen with her kisses as she tugged at his clothing, entangled them both in it, and laughed as they finally managed to strip down completely. She whispered to him, touching him, making love to him with a combination of tenderness and fierceness that drove him wild.

It was later, much later, when he lay sated and incredulous, cradling her to him, his chin atop her head, that she said, "You told me you had a surprise for me."

"Ah, yes!"

He got out of bed and Kody sat up to watch him, curious as he left the room.

He'd never been with an actress before.

This one, he knew he would love all his life. Therefore, he had figured, he would get it right.

He plucked the champagne from the refrigerator and prepared the ice bucket.

The plate of chocolate-covered strawberries was ready, as well.

Along with the long-stemmed roses. And a tiny box.

He swept up the bucket, the plate balanced atop it, the roses in his mouth. And he walked back into the bedroom.

Kody cried out with delight, clapping her hands.

"Oh, but you are perfect! Perfect! Roses, chocolate-covered strawberries, champagne—and a naked FBI guy! What more could one want?"

They both burst into laughter.

And he joined her in the bed.

They popped the cork on the champagne, laughed as it spilled over. They shared the strawberries and Kody smelled the roses and looked at him seriously.

"I love you so much," she whispered. "Is it…is it all right to say that? I tend to speak quickly, rashly, sometimes. I mean…well, you know. I probably could have gotten myself or someone else killed back in Florida if you weren't you. If you hadn't been undercover. If—"

He pulled her into his arms. "I wouldn't have you any other way at all. I love that you said what you did. I love you. And…"

He realized he was terribly nervous. He might be a well-trained agent, but his fingers were trembling as he reached for the little box.

Kody took the box, her eyes on his. She opened it and stared in silence.

His heart sank. "It's too soon, too much," he murmured. "I—"

She threw her arms around him, and kissed him, and kissed him, and kissed him.

"Is that a yes?"

"Yes!" She laughed. "Not even I am that good an actress!"

He took the ring and slipped it on her finger. "Since we're living in sin…?"

"This kind of love could never be a sin," she assured him.

"You're really so beautiful…in every way," he told her.

She smiled—a mischievous smile. "With the pick-up line you gave me in Florida, who would have thought that we would wind up here!"

"Go figure," he agreed.

He kissed her and lay her back on the bed.

"Go figure," he repeated.

And he started kissing her again and again…

It was, after all, opening night. For the show.

And for the rest of their lives.

* * * * *

Also available from B.J. Daniels

HQN Books

Sterling's Montana

Stroke of Luck
Luck of the Draw

The Montana Cahills

Wrangler's Rescue
Rancher's Dream
Hero's Return
Cowboy's Redemption
Cowboy's Reckoning
Cowboy's Legacy
Outlaw's Honor
Renegade's Pride

Harlequin Intrigue

Cardwell Ranch: Montana Legacy

Steel Resolve

Whitehorse, Montana: The Clementine Sisters

Hard Rustler
Rogue Gunslinger
Rugged Defender

The Montana Cahills

Cowboy's Redemption

Don't miss *Just His Luck*,
the next book in the Sterling's Montana series!

Visit the Author Profile page
at Harlequin.com for more titles.

SECRET BODYGUARD

B.J. Daniels

To my aunt Eleanor,
who took me to my first scary movie
and taught me what suspense was all about,
and to my uncle Jack, the best of the Johnsons
and my first real hero.

1

She'd sneak out tonight. He could feel it, the way he always could. A kind of static in the air. Something electric. Something both reckless and dangerous.

Jesse rubbed the cloth over the thin coat of wax on the hood of the black Lincoln town car. Reflections danced in the shine at his touch. He avoided his own reflection though, his gaze on the massive main house across the Texas tiled courtyard.

The curtains were closed in her window, but the air-conditioned breeze on the other side teased them coyly open allowing him to catch glimpses of her.

It was just like Amanda to have the window open in her wing of the air-conditioned hacienda. No wonder her scent moved restlessly through the hot, humid night. Tantalizing. Tempting. He breathed it in, holding it deep inside him as long as he could before reluctantly releasing it. Her music also drifted from her open window and hung in the thick air between the house and the chauffeur's quarters above the garage. She had the radio on the local Latin station she listened to, the music as hot and spicy as the food she liked to eat.

He rubbed his large hand over the dark, slick hood,

wondering if her skin felt like this. Smooth and cool to the touch.

When she came out, it was through the side door. He stepped back into the shadows, not wanting her to see him. At first he thought she'd take the new Mercedes her father had given her for her twenty-fifth birthday, but she headed for the separate garage on the far side of the house. He watched her stick to the shadows and climb into the older model BMW parked in the first stall.

Slumming it tonight?

He waited until she'd pulled away, her taillights disappearing down the long, circuitous, tree-arched drive of the Crowe estate before he climbed on his motorcycle and followed her at a discreet distance.

Hidden cameras recorded all movement in the house and on the grounds, which meant she couldn't leave without being noticed. And yet the guard in the small stone building at the edge of the property that acted as the hub of the Crowes' all-encompassing, high-tech security system wasn't at his post as she and then Jesse breezed past.

Before she even got to the massive wrought-iron gate that kept the rest of the world out of the sequestered compound, the gate swung open wide as if she were the princess of the palace. Which, of course, she was.

He barely slipped through behind her before the gate slammed closed, staying just close enough on his bike as she headed for Dallas, that he didn't lose her.

Night air rushed by thick and hot as he wove in and out of the traffic along the outskirts of the "Big D," keeping her in sight ahead of him, just as he had all the other nights.

Only tonight felt different. Tonight, after all his

waiting, something was going to happen. He sensed it, more aware of the woman he tailed than ever before. He couldn't still the small thrill of secret pleasure that coursed through him. His heart beat a little faster.

Ahead, Amanda pulled over along a dark, nearly isolated street. He swung in behind a pickup parked at the curb and watched her get out. She glanced around as if worried she might have been followed. As if she had something to hide. He smiled to himself. Oh, she had something to hide all right.

Down the block bright red and yellow neon flashed in front of one of those late-night, out-of-the-way Tex-Mex cafés found in this part of Dallas. She walked toward it.

He waited until she was almost there before he pulled his bike back onto the street. As he cruised by, he saw her go to an outside table and sit down with a woman he'd never seen before.

At the end of the block, he turned down the alley and ditched the bike to work his way back toward the café on foot, running on adrenaline, anticipation and enough fear to know he hadn't lost his mind.

He found a spot to watch her from the shadows, close enough he could see but not hear what was being said. She was crying. He could see that, crying and talking hurriedly, nervously. He'd give anything to hear what she was saying and wondered when his heart had grown so cold, so calculating. Mostly, why he believed that Amanda Crowe was lying.

Just over twenty-four hours ago, she'd called her father to tell him that her six-month-old baby, Susannah, had been kidnapped. Her story was that she and Susannah were alone in the ladies' room of a large department store when a man burst in, knocked her out and grabbed the baby. No witnesses were in the room. Also no cops were called.

J. B. Crowe had insisted on handling the kidnapping himself and Amanda had gone along with him. In the Crowe compound, it was commonly believed that the kidnapping was part of some vendetta between Amanda's father, J. B. Crowe, and Governor Thomas Kincaid. If you believed Kincaid capable of kidnapping. Crowe, on the other hand, was an altogether different animal, capable of anything. And, Jesse feared, so was his daughter.

Jesse watched her wipe her eyes as the waiter slid a steaming plate of food in front of her and thought about the man who'd fathered Amanda's baby. Amanda hadn't even kept him around long enough to give the baby his name. Not that Amanda needed a husband. She was a Crowe. She'd never want for anything. Nor would Susannah, for that matter, if she was ever found.

The other woman was talking now, squeezing Amanda's arm, intent, leaning in so no one could hear even though there were few diners and no one at a nearby table.

Jesse wasn't sure why or what exactly he didn't believe. That Susannah Crowe had been kidnapped? Or that Amanda really was the grieving mother she appeared to be? Something just didn't sit right. His gaze narrowed as he watched her. Amanda Crowe was lying. He'd stake his life on it. He smiled at that; he'd already risked more than his life just being here tonight.

She picked nervously at her food but the tears had stopped, her iron-clad control back, a steeliness in her that she shared with her father. Part determination. Part ruthlessness.

A baby began to cry. Amanda turned abruptly, almost spilling her water. A Mexican woman carrying an infant sat down two tables over from Amanda, pulled the baby from its carrier and rocked it, trying to still the shrill cry. Amanda turned back to her food, apparently mesmerized by what was on her plate.

A new thought struck him like a fist. Was it possible?

The waiter brought out an order to go for the woman with the baby. Amanda motioned for her check.

His pulse began to pound. The woman with the baby busily strapped the infant back into its carrier. He was too far away to see the baby's face.

Amanda didn't wait for her check. She got to her feet, tossed a bill on the table, hugged her dinner companion and rushed off toward her car.

But Jesse didn't follow her. The woman with the baby started to leave as well. His mind roiled. What he was thinking didn't make any sense, but with the Crowes, anything was possible.

He moved toward the café, not letting the woman with the baby out of his sight.

It was just some woman and her baby. No kidnapper in her right mind would bring the Crowe baby to a public restaurant. And wouldn't Amanda have raced over to the table if she thought there was even a chance that the baby might be hers?

Unless the woman wasn't the kidnapper. Unless Amanda Crowe had had her own baby abducted. But what kind of sense did that make?

The woman with the baby was leaving. He wove his way through the tables, his heart racing, as he hurried to cut her off.

She looked up, startled and a little frightened to see

him. He glanced into the baby carrier, ready to grab both the woman and the child.

The baby was brown skinned, with a thick head of black hair and a pair of eyes to match. While close to the same age, the little boy looked nothing like Susannah Crowe.

He stumbled back, mumbling, "Sorry," to the startled mother as she hugged the baby protectively to her. Whatever had made him think the infant would be Susannah? Because he was convinced Amanda had done something with her baby. Made it look like a kidnapping. But why?

Feeling foolish, he moved on through the café and out the back door to the alley. Amanda was gone. So was her companion. So much for his hunch. He was letting Amanda Crowe get to him. Letting her mess with his mind. A sliver of doubt worked its way under his skin, just as she had. What if he was wrong?

Amanda had almost raced from the café at the sight and sound of the baby. But wouldn't that have been the reaction of any grieving mother whose baby had been kidnapped?

The voice in the darkness startled him. He spotted two figures at the end of the alley in the shadows, one large, one small. He flattened himself against the rough rock wall, hoping they hadn't seen him.

"You *have* to do this," the man said quietly, urgently. "*We* have to do this. There is no going back now."

Jesse had heard the voice somewhere before but couldn't place it.

"Don't pressure me," the woman snapped back. "I'll do it. I just need more time."

This voice Jesse recognized immediately. Amanda

Crowe. But who had she met in the alley? And what did she need more time to do?

"We don't have time," the man said, sounding frustrated and angry with her. "Stop stalling. You know what's at stake. Just do it. Get it over with. Tonight."

Jesse heard the sound of hurried footfalls headed in his direction. He held his breath as the man stomped past him. In the light bleeding out into the alley from one of the open doorways, Jesse got a look at him. Even from the back, he recognized Gage Ferraro, the man who'd fathered Amanda's baby.

He swore under his breath and waited, pressed to the rock wall, expecting Amanda to follow her former lover. After a few minutes when she didn't appear, he glanced down the alley only to find she was gone.

He stood for a moment longer, thinking about what he'd overheard. What was Gage Ferraro doing back in town? The answer was obvious. The kidnapping. Gage and Amanda must have cooked up a plot to fleece her father. Jesse couldn't imagine anything more dangerous. Or lucrative.

He headed down the alley to where he'd left his bike, amazed at this woman. Amazed even more that he still found her intriguing. And, against his better judgment, incredibly desirable. It defied logic.

A figure suddenly stepped out of a doorway a few feet in front of him, snapping him out of his troubling thoughts. Startled, he almost pulled the piece he kept at his back before he recognized the silhouette.

Five feet four inches of spitfire, Amanda Crowe stood with her hands cocked on her hips, her feet apart, her body language nothing short of enraged.

Physically, he could have taken her with one hand tied

behind him. And lord knows he wanted to take her, all right. However, Jesse was a lot of things, but he wasn't stupid. If he touched her, he'd be dead before daylight.

Nor was he about to underestimate her. Quite frankly, he thought her as ruthless as her father. More so, after what he'd heard tonight. As she stepped closer, he could see her hair, thick and wheat-colored, cropped to her arrogant chin and her eyes, light brown with an edge to them that could cut like the shattered glass of a beer bottle.

Even if she hadn't been J.B.'s daughter he'd have taken her seriously. But she was the pride and joy of the biggest mobster this side of the Rio Grande and messing with her was messing with more than trouble.

"What the hell do you think you're doing spying on me?" she demanded.

Oh, she was something. Righteous and raging. He gave her his best grin, one that had gotten him out of a lot of tight spots. He might as well have spit in her eye for all the good it did.

"Does my father *know* you're spying on me?" she demanded, raising one fine brow.

He wiped the grin off his face and glared at her. "What do *you* think?"

She regarded him, taking his measure and making it clear she found him wanting. Some people thought his dark looks intimidating, even dangerous. But it was obvious, she wasn't one of those people.

"I think," she said dragging out each word, "that Daddy made a mistake. Surely he can do better than sending a *chauffeur*." She brushed past him, one soft, full breast grazing his bare arm, her scent lingering on his skin long after she was gone.

He stood, his back to her as she retreated down the alley. Slowly he released the breath he'd been holding, his body vibrating with a combination of lust and disgust. How the hell could he want a woman he so despised?

Had she known what she was doing just now when she'd brushed against him? Had she known the effect it would have on him? He shook his head and smiled wryly. If he was right about her, they were both playing dangerous games, risking everything. The difference was, she was a Crowe and the odds were always stacked in their favor.

He rubbed the back of his neck and stopped smiling, suddenly aware of that distinctive prickle along his spine, the one that warned him someone was behind him, watching him.

Had she stopped up the alley to look back? Not likely. The woman hadn't given him the time of day since he went to work for her father several weeks before. No, he thought, as he quickly turned, his hand going to the small of his back and his piece.

But the alley was empty. And yet he'd have sworn someone had been there just a few moments before. Gage?

Paranoia. It went with the job. He walked to his bike, swung his leg over and started the motor. It purred in the hot darkness. He considered for a moment what J.B. would do if his precious daughter told him the chauffeur had been spying on her, lusting after her. But worse, if Jesse's instincts had been right a few moments ago, then someone had been spying on him as well. Might even suspect what he was up to. That thought was enough to give him nightmares.

He cruised back to the Crowe estate, jumpy and irritable. The guard buzzed him in. He took the service road through the trees and went straight up to his apartment over the garage. On the way home, he'd invented a plausible story just in case he needed one, although in that case, he doubted he'd live long enough to tell it. But J.B. wasn't waiting for him. Nor any of the mobster's henchmen.

As he slipped his key into the lock, he noticed the corner of a piece of paper sticking out from under his door. Cautiously, he turned the key.

The piece of paper appeared to be a photocopy of a newspaper article. Frowning, he picked it up, pushed open his door and reached for the light switch. The headline leapt off the page: Infant Abandoned Beside Road.

He stepped into the apartment, locking the door behind him and read the story.

A baby had been discovered in the wee hours of the morning north of Dallas along a dirt road. The abandoned infant's parents hadn't been found yet. Police were making enquiries.

Could the baby be Susannah Crowe? Had Amanda and Gage abandoned the baby beside a road and pretended the infant had been kidnapped?

He tried to imagine a woman that cold-blooded. Amanda Crowe, he reminded himself, was a mobster's daughter. This mystery baby could be Susannah.

He glanced at the name of the town in the article. Red River, Texas? He'd never heard of it. There was no date on the article. Nor any way of knowing in what paper the story had run.

Why had someone put it under his door unless they wanted him to know what had happened to Susannah?

A thought rattled past like a freight train. If someone really did have information about Susannah Crowe, why tell the chauffeur? Unless—

His heart jackhammered and he felt oddly light-headed. Unless someone knew why he'd followed Amanda tonight. The same someone he'd sensed in the alley earlier? Someone who knew exactly what Jesse was doing here.

He moved to the window and parted the curtains, startled. Amanda's light was on in her room and she was standing at the window, staring in his direction as if waiting for him to look out. Had she put the article under his door? A cry for help. Or a dare? Catch me if you can. Was she that sure he couldn't?

Her light snapped off.

He stared at the dark window, wondering what the hell was going on, suddenly terrified of the answer.

2

Amanda stood in the dark, telling herself Jesse couldn't possibly know. But he'd been in the alley. He might have overheard her and Gage. She tried to remember exactly what had been said. Nothing about Susannah. At least not by name.

And even if Jesse did suspect something, what could he do about it? Go to her father with his vague suspicions? She realized with a start, that was exactly what he would do. Her father's men would do anything for him, including spy on her. Jesse was no different.

In his simmering dark-eyed look she'd seen more than raw hunger. She'd seen contempt. His look said he knew her. Knew her every secret. Her every thought. Could see into her heart and see things that repulsed him.

Damn the man! She tried to calm herself, but couldn't still the shaking inside her. How dare he judge her, let alone track her down like a dog? Did he hope to get something on her he could use to get closer to her father? Or something to use as leverage to get her into his bed?

She understood men like him only too well. He'd take advantage of any opportunity. Had she given him the one he needed? She'd been so careful. Everything so deliberate, so calculated. She had tried to think like her father. The thought made her shudder. But she *was* her father's daughter, wasn't she?

Her father, she thought grimly. It would be like him to tell the chauffeur to follow her and report where she'd gone, whom she'd met. But why the chauffeur when J.B. had an assortment of trained thugs?

It definitely raised the question: had her father asked Jesse to follow her tonight? Or had Jesse done it on his own?

She hugged herself, fear making her weak at the thought that her father might know what she'd done. Had she messed up somehow, left a trail that would lead back to her and eventually destroy her?

Worse, she knew she'd passed the point of no return. She couldn't turn back now. It was too late. She had to go through with it. To the end.

She shuddered at the thought of how it could end. Especially now that she had Jesse after her. Across the courtyard she could see the window of the chauffeur's quarters clearly from her room. He'd turned out his lights as she had. Was he looking out just as she was? Staring at her as she'd often caught him doing before?

She trembled, aware that more than fear and anger coursed through her veins tonight. As she pressed her fingers to the cool glass, her body ached for something she knew she'd never had, something she couldn't even put words to. This ache had nothing to do with her baby daughter or the trouble she was in and everything to do with the sultry Texas night and the man across the courtyard. How stupid she'd been to brush against him. Taunting him had been a very big mistake.

She hadn't expected to feel anything when she

touched him but revulsion. But he'd made her long for release, a powerful, purely physical need that ignored what also simmered between them, mutual contempt and mistrust. Worse, he made her feel vulnerable.

Crowes never let themselves be vulnerable. Ever.

She'd have to do something about him. Something drastic. After all, she was her father's daughter. And he'd taught her that the world revolved around her. She could have anything she wanted. Do anything she wanted. It was the unlimited credit card that came with being his only child—and a daughter, at that. And she'd never needed that credit line more than she did right now.

She forced all thoughts of Jesse Brock from her mind and concentrated on a much more pressing problem. Her father. If he had ordered the chauffeur to follow her, then did he know something or was he just being protective?

Either way, she didn't like it.

A light knock at her bedroom door made her jump. She stood perfectly still, not making a sound. Go away.

"Miss?" Eunice Fox called through the closed door.

Hurriedly Amanda climbed into her huge poster bed, having long outgrown the frilly decor her father had insisted on, and pulled the covers over her to hide the fact that she was still fully clothed.

"Miss?" the housekeeper persisted.

Amanda didn't answer. Whatever it was, it could wait until morning.

"Miss, it's your father," Eunice said more forcefully. "He insists on speaking to you. Even if I have to wake you."

Amanda heard Eunice start to open the door and swore under her breath. "Tell him I'll be right down."

She waited until she heard Eunice's retreating steps on the tile hallway, before she flung back the covers.

Her father didn't allow locks in the house, except for his wing, which was off-limits to everyone, including staff and Amanda.

Her father's security system allowed little privacy, something she only recently had come to hate. The irony of her father's idea of security didn't elude her. For all the house's hidden cameras and state-of-the-art surveillance equipment, the place made her feel anything but secure and yet allowed secrets. More secrets than even her father knew. She hoped.

Hurriedly she stripped, then dressed in a nightgown, robe and slippers. As she stepped to the door, she wondered what could be so important that he would have her awakened at this time of the night. Her footsteps slowed. News of Susannah? Her heart drummed heavy in her chest. Dear God.

She braced herself for bad news. Very bad news.

The moment Jesse walked into the late-night coffee shop and spotted Dylan Garrett, he saw the former cop's concerned expression.

"What's wrong?" Dylan asked before Jesse could sit down.

Jesse slid the now bagged copy of the newspaper article across the scarred Formica table and motioned for the waitress to bring him a cup of coffee. As Dylan read the short news article, Jesse studied the man across from him. They were about the same age but as different as night and day in both looks and temperament.

Dylan Garrett was a cowboy, rugged, muscular and tanned from hours spent on his ranch. His light-brown hair was sun streaked and he had laugh lines around his blue eyes and a dimple when he smiled, which was often.

But as Dylan looked up from the article, he wasn't smiling, let alone laughing. "Who gave you this?"

Jesse shook his head. The coffee shop was empty except for a male cook in the back and the waitress. Both looked tired and distracted. Neither was within earshot. "I found it under my door."

Dylan frowned. He'd been one hell of a cop before he quit the force to return home to the ranch and Jesse trusted him with his life. "Then someone on the Crowe compound gave it to you?"

Jesse's nodded. "It has to have something to do with the Crowe baby."

The waitress put a cup of coffee as black and thick as mud in front of him. The pot must have been on the burner for hours, turning the brew to sludge. He picked it up and took a swallow. It was god-awful stuff but he noticed that Dylan had already downed his and was working on a second cup. The man was as tough as he looked.

"Why *would* someone give it to you?" Dylan asked. "Unless your cover is blown."

"Amanda caught me following her tonight." He hated to admit it.

Dylan looked worried. "She'll go straight to her father," he said with certainty. No one knew more about J. B. Crowe than Dylan. He'd spent a year of his life working undercover for the mob.

"Yeah, I figure she will." At the very least, she'd try to get him fired. At the most... "What if the newspaper article is her way of telling me she did something with the baby?"

"Good Lord," Dylan said and shook his head. "Pull

out now. I know J. B. Crowe. You're as good as dead if he finds out who you are and what you're up to."

That wasn't exactly news to Jesse but he was too close to back out now. "There is a chance that she'll slip up and make a mistake now that she suspects I'm on to her."

"Don't forget who you're dealing with here," Dylan said with obvious distaste. "On the surface, J.B. might seem like any other successful businessman. But believe me, he's into a lot more than just running numbers and racketeering. I saw and heard things—" He looked away. "Pretending to be one of them, I got to the point where I didn't know who I was. Or where the real me began or that other Dylan ended. These people are more dangerous than you think. Before they kill you, they expose you to a way of life that leaves you empty inside, without hope. If people like this can thrive around us and we can't stop them—"

"We can stop them." But he knew what Dylan was saying. For men like J. B. Crowe there were no rules. And no consequences. He called the shots; there was no higher power. And sometimes Jesse did wonder if there was any way to bring down a man like J. B. Crowe. Or his daughter. "We *will* stop them."

Dylan smiled. "I once believed that."

Jesse changed the subject to something more pleasant. "Tell me about your ranch. The Double G, right? I heard about the business you started there with your sister. How is Lily, anyway?"

"Bossy as ever."

"And Finders Keepers?" Jesse asked, more than a little interested in the detective agency Dylan and Lily had opened last fall.

"Keeps us busy," Dylan said modestly. Jesse had heard it was very successful.

"I was hoping you'd do a little investigating into this," he said, picking up the bagged article again. "I'd do it myself but I can't leave right now. Even if this baby isn't Susannah, there has to be some connection."

Dylan looked skeptical as he picked up the bagged newspaper clipping. "I should be able to track down the article and find out whether or not the baby is the missing Crowe infant. Anything else?"

"See if there are any other fingerprints on the copy other than mine. I'd like to know who gave it to me." He hesitated. "One more thing, I overheard Amanda talking to Gage Ferraro in the alley tonight. I think the two of them are working together. Maybe trying to ransom the baby."

"Just when you think things can't get any worse." He shook his head. He looked tired and worried.

"Any news on that friend of yours from college?" Jesse asked, remembering hearing about Julie Cooper's disappearance.

Dylan shook his head.

Jesse felt the clock was ticking. Since he'd gone undercover only a few weeks before, the Crowe grandchild had been kidnapped. He felt as if he were sitting on a powder keg that was about to blow.

Dylan finished his coffee and got to his feet. "I'll get back to you on the newspaper article by tomorrow afternoon."

Jesse rose and shook his hand. "Thanks."

The cowboy just nodded. "In the meantime, mind what I say about watching your back. J. B. Crowe loves money and power but family means everything to him. When Amanda tells him you've been tailing her, you're a dead man. And she will tell him."

3

The moment Amanda saw her father, she knew it wasn't going to be good. He stood in the main room amid the heavy masculine western decor, his back to her and the door, his stance rigid, anxious. She knew he wouldn't have called her down this late unless something was terribly wrong.

She braced herself, glad at least that her stepmother Olivia, distraught over Susannah's kidnapping, had taken off on a shopping spree in New York. Olivia only seemed to make matters worse when J.B. was in one of his moods.

"Daddy?" Amanda asked, the childhood endearment now sounding all wrong, as if she'd aged overnight and everything had changed. The realization surprised her: she was no longer J.B.'s little girl. Had he realized that yet?

J. B. Crowe wasn't a tall man, just barely five foot ten inches, but he was extremely fit, trim and athletic, making him appear much larger, much more powerful. She'd never feared her father. Until recently.

He turned, his dark eyes warming only slightly at the sight of her. He wore one of his favorite tailored suits as he always did when he went into Dallas for dinner. She suspected he'd gone because he knew the governor was in town, probably had known where the governor would dine just so he could run into him.

She felt a shiver, aware that he believed Governor Thomas Kincaid had kidnapped Susannah. She was glad she'd begged off dinner. She hated scenes.

But she also couldn't keep kidding herself. Time was running out. It might have already run out.

"Is anything wrong?" he asked frowning.

She surfaced from her thoughts, pasting a smile on her face as she stepped to him, hurriedly giving him the perfunctory kiss on the cheek before moving behind the bar to make herself a drink, putting as much distance as she could between them. The realization surprised her. Saddened her. They had once been so close.

"I'm fine," she said quickly, filling a glass with ice. "I was worried about you since Eunice said you wanted to see me. It's so late."

"I'm sorry, my dear," he said, not sounding sorry in the least. "I hope I didn't wake you."

"No." He knew he hadn't awakened her. She suspected he knew a lot more than that.

She looked down at the array of liquor bottles. Her hand suddenly shook, the ice in her glass rattling faintly.

"Here, let me do that." He took the glass from her and stepped behind the bar, forcing a closeness that made her feel trapped, his intent gaze unnerving. Did he know what she'd done? Worse, what she planned to do next?

Her heart drummed. "Maybe just a club soda," she said, moving out of his way. "My stomach is a little upset." At least that wasn't a lie but then lying came as naturally as breathing for Crowes, didn't it? Unfortunately, she wasn't half as good as her father and she knew it.

"You're feeling well, I mean, as well as can be expected under the circumstances?" he enquired still studying her.

She'd always been his pride and joy. His precious princess. The thought turned her stomach because it had been a role she'd been happy to play. Until recently.

She met his gaze and felt tears rush into her eyes. Now wasn't the time to think about all that she'd lost. Or how much more she stood to lose. She nodded, unable to speak.

He reached for her hand and squeezed it, then handing her the glass of club soda, he led her over to the dark leather couch and motioned for her to sit down.

She cupped the cold sweating glass in her hands, her heart a drum in her chest, and waited for him to tell her that he knew everything.

"Gage is back in town," he said at last.

Her head jerked up. She'd anticipated the worst. But this completely threw her. He knew that Gage Ferraro, the son of her father's sworn enemy and Susannah's natural father, was back in town? Part of Gage's attraction had been his good looks. And the fact that her father despised him even more than he did Gage's father, Mickie Ferraro. But Gage, it appeared, had had his own agenda. She knew now that he had never cared anything for her and suspected the seduction had been to get at J.B. in some way. She'd been played for a fool and put her father in a very precarious situation. But she believed Gage did care about his daughter, Susannah. She had to believe that.

She'd only seen Gage a few times. A few times too

many, she thought, unable still to remember the night she'd conceived Susannah. Gage told her later that she'd drunk too much. But she'd suspected he had put something in her drink. Otherwise she was sure she never would have slept with the man.

But she had Susannah, and Gage was gone from her life as if he'd never existed, so she had no regrets. She would just be much more careful in the future. Had she told her father, Amanda had no doubt he would have killed Gage. She suspected all that stopped him when he found out about the pregnancy was rumor of an investigation into some of his so-called business deals. Also, the Organization wouldn't have liked it. At first J.B. had threatened a shotgun wedding, but Amanda had known her father wasn't about to let Gage become his son-in-law. Gage's loyalties were to his father, a competing mobster boss who had been trying to take over some of J.B.'s territories. He'd never let a man he didn't trust marry into the family.

So with the promise of peace, her father had seen that Gage was given a job in Chicago and literally escorted out of town within hours. No one had asked Amanda what she wanted. J.B. always knew what was best for her and the baby.

She said nothing now, waiting for the other shoe to drop.

"Gage believes he can find Susannah and bring down Kincaid," her father said, a note of grudging respect in his voice.

She stared at him, dumbstruck. Why hadn't Gage told her this? And yet it was so like Gage. Pretending to get into her father's good graces by bringing Susannah home safely—and seeing that Kincaid took the rap for the kidnapping. Why hadn't she thought that Gage might pull something like this?

"While Gage is in town," J.B. said, "I want you to stay away from him."

There was a severity to her father's voice that surprised her. He thought she'd go to Gage. Probably already knew she had, thanks to Jesse.

"You're not to see him under any circumstances." Her father smiled, lightening his tone. "As a favor to me. And only because it's for your own good."

As if he knew what was good for her. She would have reminded him that she was twenty-five, of legal age, and that she would decide who she saw and what she did. But she'd only dated Gage Ferraro to show her father that he couldn't tell her what to do, a childish, stupid thing to have done. She'd underestimated Gage and paid the price.

The truth was, she had never known independence, having lived her entire life under her father's roof, under his rules, and she never would, if he had his way.

She gave him what she hoped was a reassuring smile, not feeling in the least bit guilty for lying to him. "It's not a problem."

He returned her smile but she noticed it never reached his eyes. He hadn't forgiven her for Gage. He saw it as a betrayal and her father did not forgive easily. Even his own daughter. Especially his own daughter.

"Good," he said. "Then there is nothing to worry about. Soon Susannah will be home, Kincaid will be neutralized and we can put all of this behind us." His eyes narrowed. He knew her too well. "Are you ill, my dear? Maybe it was something you ate? I understand you went out tonight and only recently returned. I do hope you're getting enough rest."

She felt shaken. She'd taken care of the guard at the gate—and the cameras. She'd even waited until Eunice and the other hired help had gone to bed. The only way her father could have known that she'd left and gone to a café was if Jesse had already reported to her father.

The bastard. "I met a friend," she said and waited for J.B. to ask the friend's name and if he knew her. When he didn't, she knew he'd had the chauffeur, of all people, follow her. That was a new low, even for her father.

"I hope you had Jesse take you in the car," he said, killing any question in her mind. Why did anything her father do still shock her?

"No, actually, I drove the BMW."

He raised a brow. "Not the Mercedes convertible I got you for your birthday?"

She felt her heart rate quicken. Why did he care which car she took unless—She felt sick. Had he put some sort of tracking device on the Mercedes? Or had he wanted her to use it because it was parked in the garage near the chauffeur's quarters?

"I just felt like driving the BMW," she managed to reply. "For old times' sake."

He nodded, still watching her, reminding her of when she was a child and he suspected she was lying. "I don't like the idea of you going out alone. Not after what happened with Susannah—" He stopped, his gaze boring into her. "I couldn't bear it if anything were to happen to you."

She felt a chill, his words a warning she couldn't ignore. She had betrayed him once. She was not to do it again.

"Don't worry," she said quietly. "I am always very careful." Now she would be even more careful. "But if it makes you feel better, I will have Jesse drive me."

That seemed to satisfy him. At least temporarily. He patted her shoulder. He didn't ask her anything else about tonight. Obviously he already knew. Damn Jesse Brock.

"You didn't ask if I'd received a ransom note yet," he said, catching her off guard.

"Have you?" she asked, sounding breathless, sounding scared.

"No," he said studying her. "Odd isn't it? Unless Susannah has been kidnapped for some other reason."

"What other reasons are there besides money and power?" she asked.

He smiled at that. "None, that I can think of. But don't you worry, my dear, I will get my granddaughter back. One way or the other."

Trembling at the certainty she heard in his voice, she kissed her father's cheek and left him to finish his drink alone, acutely aware that he was suspicious of her comings and goings. Hopefully he just thought she was meeting Gage Ferraro behind his back. That was much safer than the truth.

She hurried up to her room, not turning on the light as she went to the window. The darkness smelled of hyacinths, the air sweet and sweltering. She closed the curtains and went into the bathroom where she'd long ago disabled the surveillance camera.

Still shaking, she pulled out the equipment she would need, then pushed it back into its hiding place. Not tonight. No matter what Gage said. It was too dangerous. Tomorrow night. Her last chance. She'd do it then.

Her heart beat faster. If she failed tomorrow night—

She refused to consider that possibility. Too much was at stake. Tomorrow night. Come hell or high water. Or even Jesse Brock.

Across the courtyard, the light glowed in his apartment and she could see him moving behind the curtains, a shadow as dark as the man himself.

With a lot of luck and every ounce of deceitful Crowe blood that ran through her veins, she would see that no one ever found out what had really happened to her baby, especially her father. Jesse Brock didn't know it yet, but he was going to help her. It would be his last good deed.

The phone rang, making Jesse jump. He stopped pacing and reached for it, expecting the worst.

"Bring my car around," J.B. ordered and hung up.

Jesse looked at the clock, instantly uneasy. J.B. seldom went out this late. And yet, Jesse had been expecting trouble. Amanda had obviously told her father that he'd followed her tonight and now the old man wanted to go for a ride. Great.

Jesse figured he had two options: Run. Or stay and tough it out. In which case, he wanted to take a weapon. But he knew that would be the wrong thing to do. If one of J.B.'s goons frisked him... No, it would be better to play it straight. Even when the old man got around to asking Jesse about earlier tonight.

He took a breath and let it out slowly, then he went to get the car.

As he pulled up in front of the house, J.B. came out with his two bodyguards, two big bruisers with pug faces and bad attitudes whom Jesse had nicknamed Death and Destruction. It was no secret that neither man liked him. Probably because Jesse had been able to gain J.B.'s trust so quickly.

It had been a simple setup. Wait until Amanda and her father got out of their car at J.B.'s favorite restaurant. Add one speeding, out-of-control car and a chauffeur waiting by his boss's car who just happened to be able to jump in at the right moment and save the damsel in distress.

Shocked and grateful, Crowe had played right into his hands. He'd hired Jesse away from his "former" boss with a substantial raise and the rest was history. The almost hit-and-run had happened so fast Death and Destruction hadn't even had a chance to move, something Crowe had never let them forget. They'd hated Jesse ever since.

Jesse got out of the large, freshly waxed and polished Lincoln to open the back door for his boss. Death, the slimmer of the two, slid in, followed by J.B., then Destruction. Not one of them even gave Jesse a second glance.

As he closed the door and went around to the driver's seat, he wondered if that was a bad sign. With men who would kill him without a moment's hesitation behind him, he began to sweat as he waited for instructions.

"Johnson Park," J.B. ordered.

Jesse shifted into gear and got the car moving, not liking the sound of this. Johnson Park was an old industrial area outside of Dallas that had been closed for a good twenty years, maybe more. Not a good place to go this time of the night. It was the kind of place you could dispose of a body too easily.

Prolonging the trip was out of the question. Traffic was light and Johnson Park wasn't far. He drove, acutely aware of the men in the back seat and the position he'd put himself in.

When he slowed for the park, he glanced in his rearview mirror and wished he hadn't. The old man met his gaze and what Jesse saw there turned his blood to block ice.

He pulled into the park. The night was black, no stars, no moon, only an occasional unbroken streetlight along the long rows of abandoned warehouses. He drove to the end of the row J.B. indicated and stopped, turned off the lights and killed the engine, unconsciously holding his breath, waiting for the distinct sound of the slide on a weapon being readied.

"Stay here," the mobster ordered him as the two goons opened their doors and J.B. slid out of the car.

Inside the dark stillness of the car, Jesse released the breath he'd been holding, his relief so intense he felt sick to his stomach. He took a few long breaths and tried to quiet his banging heart. That had felt too close. And he still wasn't out of the woods.

It took a moment for his eyes to adjust. A single bulb burned in a building off to his right, in the same direction J.B. and the two bodyguards had gone. A dark-colored Cadillac was parked at the edge of the building.

What the hell were they doing out here at this time of the night? And, although he didn't recognize the Cadillac, he had a bad feeling it had something to do with him.

After a few moments, he cautiously popped open his door and slipped out, closing it quietly behind him. As he moved through the darkness toward the light, he heard J.B.'s voice raised in anger. He crept along the side of the building, following the sound. Above him he could see a broken, dirty window. Cautiously, he climbed up onto a pile of old crates and peered in through the opening in the glass. He could see nothing but shadows and dark shapes off to the left but he could hear J.B. still talking.

"You're telling me that you didn't know this guy you saw her with?" J.B. demanded, his tone hard enough to crack concrete.

"I told you, I didn't get a good look at him. It was dark. It was an alley for hell's sake and I had to get out of there or Amanda would have seen me watching her." The voice had a distinct whine to it. A very familiar whine.

"What I don't understand is what you were doing there in the first place," J.B. said evenly.

"Look, I leveled with you. I'm going to find your granddaughter for you. Nothing's changed. The only reason I called you was to let you know what I'd seen. As a favor. So what is this all about, getting me down here tonight, interrogating me like this?" Gage Ferraro demanded.

Gage had seen Jesse and Amanda in the alley earlier. That much was clear. But if Amanda had told her father about her encounter with Jesse, this should have been old news. Unless she hadn't told him. Yet.

"I just want to make sure your plans don't change," the mobster warned. "I don't want you having anything to do with my daughter. Or my granddaughter."

"Hey, we're talking about my daughter, here," Gage said. The soft scuff of soles on the concrete drowned out whatever J.B. said back to him.

Suddenly all four men came into view beneath the stark light of the single bulb hanging from the rafters.

Destruction had Gage in a headlock and J.B. was close enough to Gage to steal his breath.

"You have no rights to that child," J.B. said in a tone that curdled Jesse's blood. "I thought we agreed to that?"

Gage was trying to nod.

"As far as I'm concerned," J.B. was saying, his voice low and as dangerous as Jesse had ever heard it, "you have no daughter and you don't know mine, either. Is that understood?"

"Yeah, yeah, J.B.," Gage croaked.

Destruction released him.

Gage rubbed his throat. "I told you," he said, sounding hoarse. "I'm going to do this for you. As a favor. That's all."

J.B. nodded. "Let's hope for your sake you're telling me the truth."

Gage looked worried.

J.B. patted Gage on the face. "Find my granddaughter." The mobster turned and walked toward the door, but stopped at the sound of his cell phone ringing. He motioned for Death and Destruction to go on ahead of him with Gage, then reached in his pocket and pulled out the phone.

"Yes?" he barked, then listened. "You got Diana? Does Kincaid know yet? Good." He smiled as he snapped the phone shut and put it back in his pocket. "So now Governor, I have *your* daughter and soon to be born grandchild. How does it feel?"

Jesse winced as if he'd been kicked in the stomach. Crowe had kidnapped the governor's daughter, Diana. The governor's pregnant daughter.

He swore under his breath and he jumped down from the crate and ran along the edge of the building. He knew how dangerous it would be for Diana and her unborn baby to be taken in retaliation for Susannah's kidnapping.

There was no love lost between J. B. Crowe and Governor Thomas Kincaid, not since the governor had declared war on the mob in Texas. But Jesse suspected there was something else between J.B. and Thomas, something more personal.

Hurriedly, Jesse ran along the edge of the building. He could see the Lincoln and knew he couldn't reach it in time. Nor could he let Gage see him again.

Jesse stopped at the corner of the building, caught. He watched as Gage went straight to the dark-colored Caddy. The driver hopped out as if surprised to see Gage back so soon. It was obvious he'd been asleep, Jesse realized with silent thanks. There was a good chance the driver hadn't seen Jesse get out of the Lincoln then.

Gage climbed into the back of his Cadillac and the driver closed the door.

J.B. stood with Death and Destruction as if waiting for Gage to leave. Gage looked as if he couldn't wait to get away as his driver climbed back into the front of the car and started it.

Forgetting about Gage, Jesse considered the spot he found himself in. There wasn't any way he could get to the Lincoln without J.B. seeing him. For a moment, he actually considered just taking off and not looking back.

But blowing his own cover now, when he was so close, wasn't his style. He'd bluffed his way into the chauffeur job, he could bluff his way through this. He hoped.

Gage's driver gave the Caddy a little too much gas as he left. Jesse saw J.B. smile in the glare of the Cadillac's headlights. About then, however, J.B. seemed to notice that his own driver wasn't at his post, and the smile faded.

Jesse ambled out from the dark edge of the building and walked leisurely toward the Lincoln.

"I thought I told you to stay in the car?" J.B.'s voice sounded at once suspicious and furious.

"I had to take a leak," Jesse snapped and moved ahead of the mobster to open his door. He could feel J.B.'s gaze on him and looked up to meet the man's dark eyes without flinching. It took all his nerve.

J.B. held his gaze for a long heart-stopping moment, then he shook his head as if in disgust or disbelief, and slid into the back seat. *It's so hard to get good help these days,* Jesse thought sarcastically.

Death slid in beside the mobster and Destruction strutted around to the other side, giving Jesse a smug grin that hinted that he was looking forward to the day that he got to kill Jesse.

Jesse had made it a point to never be cowed by J.B., but it was getting harder and harder not to let the mobster see him sweat.

"Home," J.B. ordered the moment Jesse slipped into the driver's seat.

Still shaking inside, he gripped the wheel and drove. He didn't dare look in the rearview mirror again. No one said a word from the back seat.

Jesse tried to relax but he couldn't forget how close he'd come to having his cover blown. Gage Ferraro had seen him talking to Amanda in the alley earlier. Fortunately, Gage hadn't gotten a good look at him.

But now Jesse wasn't sure how long his luck would hold. It seemed he and Gage were looking for the same thing. Amanda's baby, Susannah. And even if, as Jesse suspected, Gage was lying through his teeth to Crowe, their paths were bound to cross again. And it was just a matter of time before Gage recognized Jesse as the cop who'd arrested him for drug possession three years ago.

4

The phone rang early the next morning, jerking Jesse from a not so sound sleep.

J.B.'s deep voice filled the line. "I won't be needing your services today but should Amanda want to go anywhere, I want you to take her. I don't want her driving herself. Do you understand me?"

"Yes, sir," he said, heart pounding.

"By the way, I appreciate you keeping an eye on my daughter last night when she went out again."

He swore softly under his breath and sat up, suddenly wide awake. "Yes?"

But J.B. hung up without another word, leaving Jesse off balance. Had Amanda told him just as Jesse and Dylan had known she would? Or had J.B. just figured it out from what Gage had reported to him? The guard at the gate hadn't been at his post but the surveillance cameras would have picked up both Amanda—and Jesse right behind her. Still, Crowe couldn't know that Jesse had followed Amanda to the café.

Either way, it did not bode well. But why would J.B. order him to drive Amanda? Why didn't J.B. fire him? Or have him killed? And why hadn't he asked him to report back on where Amanda went? Maybe J.B. had Gage for that. Or at least J.B. thought he did.

One false move, Jesse knew, and he was toast. Who was he kidding? His cover could already be blown wide-open. He could be living on borrowed time and just not know it. J.B. was probably setting him up. Giving him enough rope to hang himself.

He shook his head, amazed at the spot he found himself in this morning. Right between Amanda and her old man, a very dangerous place to be.

But in the meantime… He tried to still his racing heart. Amanda couldn't leave the Crowe estate without him. He couldn't help but grin, thinking how furious that must make her. Would she be angry enough to finally show her hand? He could only hope.

While he knew he could be walking into a trap J.B. had laid for him, Jesse still felt pretty cocky as he headed for the shower. This might prove to be just the break he'd been waiting for. If he was right, and Amanda and Gage had done something with the baby, then she must be running scared now that her father had people spying on her. She'd try to cover her tracks. She'd slip up. And when she did, Jesse would be there to nail her. So to speak.

He drowned that thought in a cold shower, disgusted with himself because of his body's reaction to the woman. Afterward, he called the main house to let Amanda know he'd be available to drive her and maybe to rub it in a little. He could only assume that she'd tried to get him fired. Or killed. And had failed. At least temporarily. He was feeling pretty pleased about that.

But he couldn't get his call past the housekeeper. Ms. Crowe, Eunice said, wasn't up yet.

He polished several of J. B. Crowe's fleet of expensive cars, watching for any sign of life behind Amanda's closed curtains. None.

As he worked, he found his thoughts divided between worrying that Amanda might have found a way to sneak out without him noticing, and trying to make sense of the newspaper clipping that had been slipped under his door last night. It had to have been someone inside the estate who'd given it to him. He ticked off the few hired help who lived on the premises.

Not the tiny, gray-haired Eunice Fox who'd been with the Crowe family for years. Nor Consuela Ruiz, the family cook. Nor the gardener, a withered, little old man named Malcolm Hines, who had been one of J.B.'s first bodyguards.

Jesse couldn't imagine any of them being disloyal to J.B. or any member of his family. And not just for fear of their lives. That left only Death and Destruction, but Jesse doubted either of them even knew how to read.

So who did that leave? J.B. Not likely. And Amanda.

Jesse called the house again after lunch.

"Ms. Crowe isn't up," Eunice informed him in a tone that dared him to insinuate that it wasn't Amanda's right to sleep all day if she so desired. He knew the housekeeper had been up for hours working and wondered how she could be so protective of such a spoiled, young woman who had never worked a day in her life and no doubt ever would.

"Should she get up—"

"I'll let her know you're available," the elderly woman cut him off icily. "I'm sure she will appreciate knowing that." She hung up, convincing Jesse that Eunice definitely hadn't been the one who'd put the copy of the newspaper clipping under his door.

While he polished J.B.'s fancy fleet and waited for Dylan to call with news on the baby, Jesse found himself thinking about Gage Ferraro and wondering what Amanda saw in the man. Obviously, there was no accounting for taste, but it did make Jesse wonder. Why had J.B. taken his daughter's dishonor so lightly? The J. B. Crowe Jesse had come to know would have had Gage swimming with the fish in cement shoes at the bottom of White Rock Lake.

Jesse wondered what J.B. would do if he found out that Amanda was consorting with the enemy again? If Gage and Amanda had kidnapped Susannah as some sort of scam, Jesse didn't want to be around when J.B. found out.

Meanwhile, he wondered how Gage's father, Mickie Ferraro, had taken losing his first grandchild. Especially considering that he and J.B. were rumored to be fighting for control inside the Organization. Mickie and J.B. had reportedly started with the mob as little more than kids.

Gage was a two-bit hoodlum who was trying to work his way up in the mob. If he really could find Susannah and bring down Kincaid, J.B. would owe him. But somehow Jesse didn't believe that was Gage's game.

Gage Ferraro was a wild card and one Jesse didn't like seeing in the deck. And Amanda… It was just a matter of getting her in a compromising position. The thought had too much appeal—and was damn dangerous.

He just wished he could figure out how all the pieces fit together, especially how the newspaper clipping fit into the mix.

Dylan, true to his word, contacted him a little after two. "We should meet," the cowboy said.

Jesse picked a meeting place nearby and called the

main house a third time, only to be told that Ms. Crowe had finally gotten out of bed and planned to spend the day beside the pool. Mr. Crowe would be home soon. The two would be spending the rest of the afternoon and evening together. Jesse wouldn't be needed.

Anxious to hear what Dylan had discovered, he left, confident Amanda couldn't leave with her father expected home any minute.

The small Texas barbecue joint served cold beer and chipped pork sandwiches with hot sauce. Because of the time of day, the place wasn't busy. He took a table at the back so he could watch the door.

Dylan joined him ten minutes later.

"So is the baby Susannah?" Jesse asked without preamble.

To Jesse's disappointment, Dylan shook his head.

"The baby found beside the road was a boy, a newborn," Dylan said.

Jesse frowned. "Then how could the clipping be connected to Susannah Crowe's disappearance?"

"I don't think it is," Dylan said. "The baby boy left beside Woodland Lake Road just outside of Red River, Texas, had dark hair and dark eyes. He was only a few hours old, leading police to believe he was born on June 5." He paused.

Jesse felt a jolt. The baby had been born on his birthday?

"June 5," Dylan continued, "thirty years ago, 1971."

Jesse's heart took off at a sprint. He stared at the cowboy for a long moment. "June 5 is my birthday."

Dylan nodded. "I had a feeling it was. That's why I did some more checking. I couldn't find out who adopted the baby. Texas adoption laws won't allow that. So I went from the other direction." Dylan seemed to hesitate. "I checked your birth certificate."

Jesse was already shaking his head.

"I don't know how to say this, Jesse. I checked with the hospital listed as your place of birth. You weren't born in Dallas, at least not to Pete and Marie McCall."

Jesse could barely find breath to ask, "What are you saying? That you think I'm that abandoned baby?" He shook his head and rubbed the back of his neck. "I was the middle son, with two brothers and three younger sisters, the perfect family. I had this great childhood. If anything, I was my parents' favorite—" He stopped and shook his head again, all the little things now making him doubt who he was and everything he'd once believed. "There is no way I was adopted. There has to be some sort of mistake. Of course I was born in Dallas, just like my brothers and sisters. Why would my parents lie about where I was born?"

The answer was obvious. If he was that abandoned baby, his parents would have lied to protect him from the truth. They wouldn't want him to know that his birth mother had cared so little that she'd left him beside a dirt road in a cardboard box.

"I'm sorry, Jesse," Dylan said.

He looked past Dylan to the bartender punching up numbers on the jukebox. A Bob Wills and His Texas Playboys song filled the air, Texas swing. He felt sick. And scared. "Who the hell am I, then?"

"You're still Jesse McCall, the man you've always been," Dylan said.

Jesse shook his head. He'd been Jesse Brock since he'd become Crowe's chauffeur two weeks ago. And now he had a bad feeling he wasn't even Jesse McCall, the person he thought he'd been for thirty years. "I have to know."

Dylan nodded almost sadly but didn't seem surprised. "You realize you're probably not going to like what you uncover, if you're even able to dig up anything after all these years."

He nodded, trying to think of a good reason a mother would abandon her baby.

"Do you want me to keep digging?" Dylan asked. "I have another case that's going to tie me up for a while but after that—"

Jesse nodded. He couldn't leave the Crowe case, not now. And after thirty years, what was a few more days?

"Then you're going to stay on the Crowe estate?" Dylan asked.

He nodded, his thoughts torn between this shocking news and Amanda Crowe. "The old man called me this morning and told me he wants me to drive her wherever Amanda wants to go. He thanked me for keeping an eye on her. And obviously someone on the Crowe estate thinks they know who I am or they wouldn't have put the newspaper clipping under my door."

Dylan looked uneasy and Jesse nodded in agreement.

"I know I'm walking a tightrope here," Jesse acknowledged and told him about Gage Ferraro. "Now everyone is looking for Susannah, including Gage, if he isn't just stringing J.B. along. But I overheard him prodding her to make her move. I intend to be there when she does."

Dylan studied him for a long moment and Jesse wondered if the cowboy realized just how involved Jesse had gotten in this case.

"She's a beautiful woman," Dylan said quietly.

Jesse laughed. "She's also a Crowe and she'd cut your throat in a heartbeat."

"Just don't forget that. Jesse, I know this news about the newspaper clipping comes as a shock to you," Dylan said.

"Yeah." He loved his parents, his family and he'd always felt a part of them. This was more than a shock. He felt as if the earth under him was no longer solid. As if nothing was as it seemed.

"Take it slow, okay?" Dylan advised. "Give it a little time."

Time. Right. Too bad that wasn't his nature.

Jesse called the Crowe compound at a little after three. Mr. Crowe was with his daughter. Both had asked not to be disturbed. Nor had they changed their minds about needing Jesse's services, Eunice assured him. They would be dining in tonight together.

After he left the compound, he called his boss at the Dallas P.D. and told him what he'd overheard J.B. Crowe say the night before about the governor's daughter Diana. His boss said he'd handle it and hung up.

He had time. Enough time he could drive up to his parents' house in Pilot Point and back. It wasn't but a couple of hours. Amanda wouldn't dare try to sneak out with her father home and dinner planned for the two of them. Would she?

Marie McCall met him at the door, excitedly kissed him on the cheek then noticed something was wrong. "What is it, honey?"

His mother. She knew him as no one else did. Her hand went to his forehead, just as it had when he was a child.

"Are you feeling ill?" she enquired, regarding him with concern as she ushered him in.

"Stop fussing over him," Pete McCall called jovially from the kitchen. "You're just in time," he said to Jesse. "How about a beer before dinner? We were getting ready to throw some steaks on the grill."

"I made your favorite," his mother said still eyeing him. "Strawberry-rhubarb pie for dessert. I must have known you'd stop by."

"Thanks but I can't stay for dinner." Both his parents looked disappointed. "But I will take that cold beer."

He followed them to the wide redwood deck that overlooked the lake. The air was scented with fresh-mown grass, lake water and glowing briquettes beneath the grill. His father opened a bottle of cold beer and handed it to him.

Now that he was here, he felt foolish. Everything was so normal, just as it had been growing up. These were his parents. How could he doubt that? He was the middle son, wedged in neatly between Alex and Charley, with three great sisters, and this was the perfect family with the split-level house, deck, basketball hoop, horseshoe pit, lake out the back door and parents who doted on him. This was home.

He felt guilty. They were so glad to see him and he realized he hadn't been home for several months because of his undercover work. He hadn't even thought about them.

"I need to talk to you," he said, just wanting to get it out. Obviously there was some mistake. They would clear it up and he would feel foolish but they would forgive him.

They looked worried. "What is it, honey?" his mother

asked, taking a seat on the arm of his father's deck chair. Her hand went to the tiny gold heart she wore on a chain around her neck. She stroked the unusual-shaped heart with her thumb, just as she always did when she was worried or upset. He knew her so well. Just as she knew him.

Still standing he took a sip of the beer, almost talking himself out of even bringing up the subject. But he had to get this settled so he could get back to his undercover assignment, get his head back where it belonged.

"I know you're going to think this is crazy..." Was it his imagination or did his father tense? "Is there any chance I might have been adopted?"

His mother froze, her eyes suddenly swimming with tears. His father said nothing as he put an arm around her.

Oh, God. Jesse sat down heavily in one of the deck chairs, the earth beneath him no longer stable and in that moment, he knew that nothing would ever be the same. "Was I the baby found outside of Red River?" he asked when he found his voice.

Neither answered but his mother began to cry. His father looked pale, his face drawn, older than Jesse had ever seen him.

Jesse closed his eyes for a moment. "How—" He heard the strangled emotion in the word, felt the panicked knocking of his heart and struggled for his next breath. "How did you get me?" He looked from his father to his mother.

She said nothing as she reached behind her to unclasp the gold chain. He'd never known her to take it off before and for a moment, he didn't move.

She held it out to him. "I suppose it was wrong, but we never wanted you to know."

As if in a trance, he lifted his hand to take it from her. The gold chain with the heart pooled in his palm, oddly cold and heavy. He wondered if taking it off had lifted a weight from off his mother's shoulders. Or just the opposite after all these years of keeping this secret.

He looked down at the funny little heart, then at her.

"I found it in your baby blanket." Her voice broke.

He didn't know what to say. He stared down at what looked to him like a broken heart, so like his own. The memory came out of nowhere. He'd been no more than three or four when he'd asked his mother about the strange heart she wore. Her words came back to him, their meaning suddenly clear.

"I prize this heart because a special woman gave it to me," his mother had said.

He gazed at his parents now. He had never thought he looked that much different from them, from his siblings or his other relatives. He'd always been a little darker, looked a *little* dissimilar, but because he'd had no reason to think otherwise, he'd always felt like one of them. Why hadn't he noticed that he was different?

"Why did you adopt me?" he had to ask. "It wasn't like you didn't already have children."

"Because you needed us and we loved you the moment we saw you," his mother said a little too quickly as if she'd been rehearsing that line for thirty years.

He nodded, having never felt so alone, so absolutely desolate. He wondered what else they'd lied to him about. What else they were keeping from him. And who at the Crowe compound had known that he wasn't the son of Marie and Pete McCall? More important, why

did they want him to know? Anyway he looked at it, he
knew he was in trouble. Someone at the compound knew
he wasn't who he was pretending to be. Someone knew
more about him than even he knew about himself—and
that scared him more than he wanted to admit.

5

The hot Texas afternoon sun shimmered off the turquoise of the pool, but Amanda hardly noticed the sun or the water. She felt deathly cold inside and scared, more scared than she had ever been.

"Your father suggested you get some sun by the pool," Eunice had told her when she'd gone downstairs. "He thought it would do you some good. Also he asked Consuela to make your favorite dinner tonight. He'll be joining you."

Amanda recoiled as if struck by a blow. She fought not to stagger.

"If you need anything, I will be here," Eunice continued. "So will Consuela and Malcolm. The chauffeur has been dismissed for the day."

She'd stared at the gray-haired woman, too shocked to speak. J.B. had never ordered her to stay on the estate before, let alone told the hired help to spy on her.

She felt sick. This was her father's way of trying to scare her. And she *was* scared. Because she understood the threat perfectly. Her father either knew the truth. Or suspected it.

It took everything in her not to run. But she knew

the guard at the gate would be expecting that. She was trapped. All the more so because she hadn't finished what she had to do here.

So she'd spent the day beside the pool, just as her father had ordered her to do. She would play the dutiful daughter. One last time.

Eunice had come out to check on her periodically. Even Malcolm Hines, the gardener, had spent the day weeding a flower bed not far from the pool, his presence leaving little doubt that he, too, was keeping an eye on her. The only person she hadn't seen was Jesse. She'd been surprised when she heard him leave just after lunch. And as far as she knew, he hadn't returned.

Consuela, the family's longtime cook, had brought her food and drinks. But while Amanda felt closer to the cook than to her own mother, who had been about the same age as Consuela, she knew she would find no allies on the estate. And certainly none in Olivia, her stepmother, who still had not returned from her New York shopping spree.

Like Olivia, the servants were loyal only to J.B. Amanda had never understood their devotion to him and wondered now what debts these servants owed that required them to indenture themselves to him for life. Whatever the debt, she suspected they would kill for him if he asked them.

She felt like a prisoner. But when her initial shock wore off, she realized she had always been a prisoner here—she just hadn't realized it until now. Her father had manipulated her to get what he wanted: Her and then Susannah under his roof, under his thumb. She shivered, afraid what he would do if he knew about her plans.

Her only hope was to be as cold and heartless as he

was should she get caught. The thought chilled her to the bone.

As the sun sank behind the oak trees, she heard the tinkle of ice. Consuela placed a tall glass on the table next to her.

"I thought you might like some lemonade, it is so hot out." The large, good-natured Mexican woman smiled warmly.

"Thank you, Consuela."

"Have you heard anything about the baby?" the woman asked in a whisper as if the kidnapper might be listening.

"Still no word," Amanda lied.

Consuela crossed herself and muttered something in Spanish that Amanda didn't understand. Something about history repeating itself. Impulsively, the cook bent to hug her fiercely, and Amanda realized Consuela was referring to when someone had tried to kidnap Amanda when she was just a baby. That's when her father had installed the security system.

"Your father will find her," Consuela said, voicing exactly what Amanda feared most. "Mr. Crowe, he always take care of his own. Look how good he take care of you."

After Consuela returned to the kitchen, Amanda heard her father's car and wasn't surprised that he'd returned early. She braced herself, determined to hide her fear of him—and the power he had over her.

It was dark and late when Jesse returned to the Crowe estate. He'd been driving aimlessly for hours, letting the wind and the dark rush past as wildly as his thoughts. He felt dazed and lost, haunted by his talk with his parents.

He'd grilled them, desperate for information about his birth parents. But both had insisted they knew little. He'd been found beside the road. They'd taken him in and later adopted him. They'd never known who his mother was. Or his birth father. They'd left Red River and never looked back. Their story never varied.

Why then did he sense they were keeping something from him? Something they couldn't bear to tell him?

His head swam. He had so many unanswered questions. Why had his birth mother left him beside a dirt road in a cardboard box? And how was it he'd been miraculously found by Marie and Pete McCall?

He breezed up to the guard at the entrance, waited for the gate to swing open and followed the hot, melting rope of blacktop that wound through a thick-leafed arch of oaks, maples and crepe myrtles. A cool breeze seeped from the darkness under the trees.

He breathed it in, trying hard to concentrate on his job. He'd always prided himself on being able to put his personal life on hold while on assignment. That ability had only been tested a few times, however. Most recently by Amanda Crowe. And *now*—finding out that his whole life had been a lie.

Through the trees, he caught the flicker of lights from the hacienda. He slowed, not in the least bit anxious to see Amanda and let her stir him up. Not tonight. He felt torn, desperately needing the truth and yet sick that he would hurt the only parents he'd ever known. They had begged him not to try to find out who he was.

"You're our son," his father had said, his voice breaking. "Nothing is to be gained by digging in the past."

"Jesse, please don't do this," his mother had pleaded. "I don't want you to be hurt."

But he was already hurt. If only he could just let it go. Why did it have to matter?

But it did matter. It mattered a whole hell of a lot and he knew he couldn't let it alone. As soon as he found out what happened to Susannah Crowe he was going to find out about that little baby boy someone had abandoned beside the road thirty years ago.

Ahead, the trees opened a little to make room for the sprawling structures of the Crowe compound. He took the delivery road that went past the garage. The road was dark, cloaked in trees, and far enough from the house that there was little chance he'd run into any of the Crowes tonight.

The garage and his apartment loomed, large and unlit. Ahead, the trees made a dark canopy over the narrow road. Suddenly, he felt the skin on the back of his neck prickle. Something moved off to his right.

He brought the cycle to a stop in the deep shadows next to the garage and his apartment. The stifling Texas spring night quickly settled around him, heavy as hot tar. In the distance, he thought he heard music. Latin music. Coming from the main house. Coming from Amanda's room.

He'd convinced himself that he was imagining things when he spotted the dark figure skulking along the edge of the main house, headed toward the far wing of the main house. J.B.'s wing. An area considered extremely off-limits. One even Jesse hadn't dared explore.

He swung off the bike, intrigued, and slipped through the pools of shadows, following the same path the intruder had taken, wondering why the security system hadn't picked them up yet.

J.B.'s wing ran east of the main house, stretching back

into the trees. A fortress of wrought-iron barred windows and massive wooden doors, it would take a tank to get into without a key.

Jesse gaped in amazement to see one of the iron grates hanging to the side and the window open. He reached automatically for his weapon and realized belatedly that he'd left it in his apartment when he went to see his parents.

As he neared the window, he could hear someone quietly opening and closing drawers in an adjoining room. He tried to imagine the fool who would break into J.B.'s office. As he slipped through the window, he tensed, waiting for the security alarm to go off.

When it didn't, he felt a cold chill run up his spine. Whoever was in the next room had somehow disarmed the system. *Damn,* he thought as he edged toward the faint sound of shuffling papers. He wished he had a gun.

On the wall of the adjoining office, the narrow beam of a flashlight flickered. It bobbed and dipped like a firefly to the sound of drawers being opened and closed in a filing cabinet.

Jesse looked around for something to use as a weapon. A small statue of a woman near the door caught his eye. He wrapped his fist around her slim waist and carrying her like a club, edged toward the open doorway.

He shouldn't have been surprised by what he saw when he peered around the doorjamb. Nothing the woman did should still surprise him. But it did.

Amanda was bent over an old oak desk, going through the drawers.

"What the hell are you doing?" he demanded, stepping into the room.

She jumped and spun around. She had a small book in one hand, like a ledger, and a flashlight in the other.

Her eyes looked golden in the light, like a cat's. He half expected her to pounce.

She eyed him, then the statue in his hand. "It isn't what you think," she said, her voice a low purr.

The sound skittered across his skin, sending a shiver through him. "What do I think?" he managed to rasp.

She smiled then and stepped toward him, the flashlight beam a golden disk on the floor at her side.

He didn't move. Couldn't. She closed the space between them, stopping within a hairbreadth of him. Not touching, but so close he could feel her body heat, smell her exotic, haunting scent, feel the electricity arcing between them. But it was the look in her eyes that was his downfall. The promise of all that he had longed for. And more.

"Jesse?" she breathed and she leaned up as if to kiss him.

The cold barrel of the gun in his ribs snapped him right out of the fantasy.

"Do as I say or I'll kill you," she ordered.

It had been one hell of a day. Not his best. Everything about it seemed surreal. Even comical on some level. Except for the business end of the weapon pressed into his ribs and the desperation he heard in his attacker's voice.

"I know how to use this and I will," Amanda said as she jabbed him with the gun. "You just saved me a trip to your apartment. Now let's get out of here and don't forget who you're dealing with."

Not likely. He put down the statue carefully and let her lead him at gunpoint out of the office. He might have called her bluff, but being taken her hostage was the perfect way to end the perfect day. He didn't think she'd kill him in cold blood. But then he couldn't be sure of that.

Mostly, he wondered what had caused her to do something this desperate—breaking into her father's office. Was this what she and Gage had been discussing in the alley? He noted that she'd put the ledger—if that indeed was what it was, into the canvas bag she carried, along with the flashlight.

They went back out the open window, with her right at his heels. "Where is your bike?" she whispered as she closed the window and locked the iron bars again, keeping the gun on him.

"My bike?" he asked stupidly. "You don't think you can handle a bike that size—"

"I just need to handle you," she interrupted. "You're getting us both out of here on that bike," she said, pressing the barrel of the weapon into his back as they moved through the shadows to the garage.

He wondered where she planned to take him as he climbed on the bike and she slid in behind him. Several possibilities crossed his mind. One involved a bullet to the back of the head and a ditch.

"Whatever you say, sweetheart."

"Don't call me sweetheart," she snapped.

"Whatever you say. But you'd better put this on if you hope to get out of here." He took the helmet from where he'd hooked it over the handlebar earlier. She snatched it out of his hand.

He could have taken her down right then fairly easily. After all, he was trained for this sort of thing. But he reminded himself that she believed he was nothing more than a chauffeur. Also, she needed him. There was no way she could handle the bike alone even if she did know how to ride and she apparently was desperate enough to take him with her. That meant he had her right where he wanted her. Kinda.

He punched the gas. She hurriedly wrapped one slim arm around him and held on, her body pressed tight to his. He felt her hand go up under his shirt until she found bare skin, her touch tantalizing torment. She pressed the cold barrel of the weapon against his ribs.

"Don't do anything stupid at the gate," she whispered next to his ear.

The guard at the gate didn't seem that surprised to see him come back through. The man was, however, surprised to see that Jesse had picked up a woman. Fortunately, the surprise gave Jesse just enough time to speed out of the gate before the guard could react.

"He's going to call your father," Jesse yelled back at Amanda.

She jabbed the gun into his side in answer. "Head south."

It would take only a few minutes for J.B. to verify that Amanda was gone before he sent his goons looking for her—and the chauffeur, who it appeared had helped her escape. Great.

Night lay over the city like a warm, wet blanket. In the distance, he saw the flicker of lightning but while he couldn't hear the rumble of the thunder over the roar of the bike, he could see that the storm was moving their way.

The air crackled with electricity but not all of it from the storm. He'd never felt her touch before. Except for that quick brush in the alley. Now her body clung to his, hotter than the Texas night. Her breasts crushed against his back, soft and rounded through her thin clothing;

her spicy scent deadly. Amanda, armed and as always, dangerous.

His need made him ache; the wanting made him disgusted with himself. He knew who she was, what she was capable of, but the disgust seemed minor compared to the need. God, how he wanted her. And if he had the chance, he feared he'd take her. That scared him more than the gun in his ribs. Or the woman with her finger on the trigger.

She took him down a series of back roads outside of Dallas. He'd seen her checking her watch before they left the estate. She seemed anxious as if she had someplace she had to be.

He could feel her anxiety growing as if time were running out.

"Turn here," she ordered.

He recognized the neighborhood. It was just south of where she'd met the woman at the out-of-the-way Mexican café. Except this area was part of a city renewal program. The houses stood empty, windows broken out, graffiti scrawled on the weathered siding, waiting to be torn down. Almost all of the street lamps were out, and even what had once been a park stood empty, knee-deep in grass.

He felt his skin crawl, recalling his original fear: a ditch and a gunshot to the back of the head. *A fitting end for someone who'd started out in a ditch beside the road,* he thought bitterly.

"Stop the bike," Amanda ordered with another jab of the gun barrel.

He stopped, his patience wearing thin. And her desperation was starting to scare him a little.

"Get off," she ordered as she started to ease the gun from under his shirt. "Slowly."

He considered his options. He could let her kill him. He could let her leave him out here. Or…

He brought his arm down hard. She let out a cry. The weapon clattered to the concrete. In one swift movement, he jerked her off her feet and around onto his lap.

He'd had enough of her orders, enough of her. His body hurt from need, making him tense and irritable. Just being this close to her made him want to take her and get it over with. He knew it would be only the one time. He'd never want her again. He just needed to get her out of his system. Damn the consequences.

He stripped his bike helmet from her blond head and, trapping her arms, pulled her into him hard. His mouth dropped to hers. He would have one kiss. One taste of her.

In the distance, he thought he heard thunder but in his fevered state of mind, it could just have easily been his own thunderous heart.

She fought for only a moment, then surrendered to his arms around her, his mouth on hers, his kiss. Her lips parted with a low moan and she softened against him.

Lightning lit the sky like fireworks. The answering thunder reverberated through him, making the night seem as alive as the rarified air around them.

And for a few moments, she was just a woman, not a mobster's daughter, but flesh and blood and more female than any woman he'd ever known. He freed her arms, deepening the kiss as she placed her palms on his chest.

Suddenly, she shoved him back. Before he could react, she snatched the cycle helmet from his hand and swung. He dodged. The helmet missed his head but glanced off his shoulder as he grabbed for her. But she'd already dropped the helmet, slid off the bike and was running toward the park.

His pride as well as his shoulder hurting, he went after her. Lightning splintered the sky. Thunder rumbled, closer this time.

He tackled her, throwing her down, landing with her under him in the cool, damp grass. She let out a grunt and a curse and fought beneath him. He held her down until she stopped resisting. He could hear her labored breathing but she didn't fight him as he rolled her over and looked down into her face.

In the faint light from one of the few remaining streetlights, he could see her hair fanned out over the dark-green grass, her face pale, her brown eyes wide. He leaned over her, his hands pressing her arms above her head, his body pinning hers to the ground.

She licked her lips and met his gaze, her eyes glittering with rage.

"What the hell is the deal with you?" he demanded, his head spinning from the kiss, from her behavior. For just a moment during the kiss, he'd thought she'd wanted him as much as he wanted her. Wrong. Obviously the kiss had only been a ruse for her. His aching shoulder could testify to that. He was just lucky it hadn't been his head.

"You have to let me go," she commanded through gritted teeth.

"So you can try to brain me again? Not likely."

"If my father finds out what you've done—"

"What *I've* done?" he interrupted. "Something tells me kissing you would be way down on the list long after breaking into his office. Try again."

She took a ragged breath. Tears glittered in her eyes. He could feel the fight go out of her.

"You don't understand," she whispered.

"Boy, you can say that again. Why don't you try to explain it to me." He had no idea what he didn't understand. Highest on his list would have been the kiss.

Over them, lightning lit the sky, thunder boomed as he held her down, determined to finally get some answers. One way or the other.

She looked up at him, her eyes swimming in tears. "Let me up and I'll tell you everything."

He really doubted that but she no longer seemed armed, although everything about Amanda he realized would always be dangerous. At least to him.

He let go of her arms. She lay still for a long moment. A voice inside his head warned him he was being played for the fool. Again. But he started to ease off her.

Suddenly she shot a furtive glance to her right. The canvas shoulder bag she'd been carrying was lying within her reach. She made a grab for it.

He'd seen her put the ledger and the flashlight in the bag, but he had no idea what else was in there. His mind screamed, *She's going for a weapon.*

He grabbed the strap of the bag before she could and tossed the bag just out of her reach.

The bag hit the edge of the sidewalk. Something inside shattered. The sound made him start as if it had been a gunshot.

She let out an oath and attacked him like a hellcat. He fought to hold her down. What had been in the bag that would break and make her this upset?

"What was that?" he demanded as he braved releasing her with one hand to lean out and snag the bag. He dragged it back over to them; it left a wet trail in the grass.

She squirmed under him, cursing.

He frowned as he opened the bag to see what appeared to be a bottle of teething medicine. A pale liquid puddled in the bottom of the bag. No weapon.

His gaze flicked to hers in surprise.

She groaned, closed her eyes and lay still, no longer fighting. A tear squeezed from beneath her dark lashes. For a moment, he thought it might be a real tear with some emotion behind it. But then her eyes flew open and all he saw was anger.

"Get off me, you big oaf," she said through gritted teeth.

His head swam as he eased off her, but he still kept close enough that he could grab her again if it proved necessary.

But she made no move to take off or to attack. She knelt beside the bag in the grass, dumped out the pieces of the bottle, and carefully removed the ledger, checking to make sure the pages hadn't been ruined.

He watched her get to her feet and carefully turn the bag inside out and put the flashlight and the ledger inside again. "The medicine was for Susannah," he said, unable to hide his disgust. The woman was a liar. Her baby hadn't been kidnapped.

"What do you care about my baby?" she demanded angrily.

He opened his mouth, then closed it again. Why would a mobster's chauffeur care about the missing baby? "Maybe I could help you."

"Oh, sure, like you helped last night? Spying on me for my father?"

"J.B. had nothing to do with me following you last night," Jesse said, remembering too clearly the brush of Amanda's breast against his arm. Unconsciously, he rubbed the spot with his hand.

"Then how did he know about me going to the café?"

"Didn't you tell him about me following you?"

"I never told my father anything," she said flatly.

Jesse stared at her. She hadn't gone to her father. That shouldn't surprise him in light of everything else he'd learned about her tonight but it still did. It suddenly hit him. When J.B. had thanked him for keeping an eye on Amanda, he'd just been fishing. And Jesse had taken the bait.

"Gage told him about seeing the two of us together."

She blinked in surprise. "Gage?"

He nodded. "I overheard them."

Her jaw tightened. "What did Gage say?"

"That he was looking for Susannah."

She nodded as if she already knew that.

"You know it crossed my mind that you and Gage might have cooked this whole thing up to extort money from your father," he said, aware he was wading into dangerous waters. "Extortion does run in your family. But now I'm thinking J.B. didn't go for it. So you stole the ledger to give yourselves more leverage."

She shot him a look so deadly it should have killed him on the spot. "I can't stand Gage Ferraro and I don't want anything from my father."

Between her look and her tone, he tended to believe her. Her anger toward both men did make him curious, though.

"What is it you want from me?" she asked out of the

blue. Her gaze searched his face, probing, intimate, disarming.

He swore silently at just the thought of what he really wanted from her as a man. As a cop, it was a whole different story. "I like you. I just—"

"You hate the sight of me," she corrected.

He took a breath. "I think you're rich and spoiled," he admitted, knowing he'd have to be as truthful as he dared. Amanda might be a lot of things, but she wasn't stupid.

"But...?" she asked, cocking her head to one side to study him.

The truth? "But I still want you."

Her lush mouth curved into a humorless smile, her eyes sultry and hotter than the Texas night. "You have a lot of nerve even saying something like that to me let alone kissing me without my permission. Do you have any idea what my father would do to you if he knew?"

"I have a pretty good notion."

"Doesn't that bother you?"

"Not as much as you bother me," he said, surprised at how honest he could be once he got started.

She shook her head and let out a low, sexy laugh. "You are one sure fool."

"Are you going to try to tell me you feel nothing?" he asked.

They stared at each other for a long moment, gazes locked. Lightning electrified the sky. Thunder boomed overhead. The first few drops of rain began to fall, hard and wet from the blackness.

"No," she said slowly, dragging her gaze away. "I feel contempt."

She glanced at her watch and let out a curse. Her

gaze shot up to him. He watched her trying to decide what to do.

"Look," he said carefully. "It's obvious you need to be somewhere. Isn't that why you hijacked me and my bike? I'll take you there." He was afraid she'd changed her mind since hijacking him. Since he'd kissed her and acted like a fool.

Rain slashed downward in large, soaking drops.

For a moment she looked like she might cry again. This time though, he definitely wasn't going to buy it.

"What if I told you my life was in danger?" she asked.

Right. "Did you mention this to your father? I'm sure he has the manpower to do something about it." If it were even remotely true.

"He might have ordered the hit," she said, seemingly oblivious to the rain that now soaked them to their skin.

He frowned, getting real tired of her lies. "Your father adores you and wouldn't touch a hair on your head. At least he did before you broke into his office and took—" he waved a hand at the bag she now clutched to her chest "—whatever is in that book." What *was* in that ledger?

"You think this is a game," she said shoving her wet hair back from her face as she glared up at him.

"I think you're playing with me, yes."

She raised one fine brow in answer. He saw her shiver and look again at her watch, the dial lighting up for an instant in the dark and rain. "There isn't time to talk about this now."

She turned and strode in the direction of the bike. She was back on her high horse.

He watched her strut her stuff, head high, princess of the palace, swinging that cute little behind as she just walked away from him toward the bike as if she'd never held him at gunpoint, or broken into her father's office, or kissed him with a passion like she meant it or tried to coldcock him with a bike helmet. This was probably just another run-of-the-mill day for a woman like her.

He swore and followed her, frustrated in more ways than he wanted to count. Where was she taking him? He could only hope it was to Susannah. Spending time around this woman was pure torture. And he sensed she was enjoying putting him through it.

He also knew going with her would be dangerous. Being within a mile of her was dangerous. Gage and his goons could be waiting for them. J.B. could already know about the missing ledger. Just about anything could be waiting for them.

But wherever she had to be was important. Important enough that she was now willing, although reluctantly, to let him take her. He tried to look at it as a victory of sorts.

The rain fell, hard and wet and unrelenting. The sky over the city crackled with light. Thunder rumbled as it moved off.

Closer he heard a car engine. At first just a low throbbing pulse. He glanced up the empty street. No lights. But the car was close, the engine had a distinct knock to it.

His heart took off at a sprint. They'd been followed. "Amanda!"

She didn't turn, just kept walking through the rain as if she hadn't heard him. She scooped up the helmet from the grass and started across the street toward his motorcycle.

"Amanda!"

The car came out from behind one of the deserted buildings just on the other side of Amanda. It headed right for her, tires screeching on the wet pavement.

6

Amanda heard the car too late. She turned, instantly blinded by the sudden flash of headlights and the realization that the car intended to run her down.

Before she could react, Jesse slammed into her, driving her from the street. They landed in the weeds at the edge of the pavement. The car sped past, so close she heard the crunch of tires next to her and felt the breeze it made as it passed.

"Are you all right?"

She lay in the dirt, too shocked to move.

"Amanda?"

"Yes?"

"We have to get out of here," he said, his voice seeming far away. "They might come back."

She let him help her to her feet. As she glanced after the speeding car, a quiet despair filled her. If she had any doubts about how much trouble she was in, she didn't anymore.

"Come on." Jesse half dragged her to his bike. "We have to get out of here," he repeated urgently.

She glanced down the street. No car lights. No sound of an engine. "They won't be back," she said. "It was just a warning. My father only wanted to scare me. This time."

Jesse stopped walking abruptly and spun around to face her. "You're not going to tell me *that* was your father's doing?"

She wasn't going to tell him anything. She stepped around him, feeling coming back into her limbs, back into her numb mind. She walked toward the bike. He worked for her father. Surely he knew the kind of man J. B. Crowe was.

"You could have been killed!" Jesse called after her.

She hadn't expected things to escalate this quickly, this radically, but she should have. How far would her father go? That's what frightened her most now.

She heard Jesse behind her.

"Even if your father found out about the break-in and that the ledger was missing—"

"Believe me, if my father already knew, that car would not have missed."

He stared at her, disbelieving, and she wondered again if he had no idea what kind of man he worked for. Surely...

"If this isn't about the ledger, then...this is about Susannah, isn't it?" he said, drawing in a breath.

She felt her heart jump inside her chest as she looked at him. "I thought you said we had to get out of here?"

"Listen to me," he said grabbing her shoulders and turning her to face him. "Whatever is going on, it isn't just your life and Susannah's you're jeopardizing but also Diana Kincaid's."

She frowned in confusion. "The governor's daughter? What does she have to do with me or my father?"

"Don't tell me you're that naive." He released her as

if touching her repulsed him. "Your father thinks Governor Kincaid is behind Susannah's kidnapping. Did you really think he wouldn't retaliate? Especially since Diana Kincaid is pregnant."

Her legs suddenly felt boneless. She leaned against the bike for support. There was a time when she would have argued vehemently in her father's defense. Now it would have been a waste of breath. She knew better than anyone what her father was capable of. This news just confirmed her worst fears.

But what about Jesse, she thought, studying him in the dim light of the solitary street lamp. How did he know Diana Kincaid had been taken? As far as she knew, it hadn't been on the news. "What does J. B. Crowe's chauffeur care about the governor's daughter?" she asked, her heart in her throat.

"Maybe I just don't like to see innocent people hurt," he said. "Anyway, I would think the two of you have a lot in common. Daughters of powerful fathers. Both young women with a baby or one on the way, and no husband."

Both being used as pawns.

"Both afraid." He reached out to touch her cheek, his look filled with compassion.

She stepped back, afraid that if she let him get too close, if she let him comfort her, she would break down. The thought of finding comfort in his arms was much too appealing. All the pain and anger and fear would come out in a rush of tears and she would bury her face in his shoulder and, in his arms, tell him everything in her need to confide in someone the awful truth.

But forgetting he worked for her father, forgetting that this man had followed her last night, wasn't something she was apt to do.

"The difference is," she said drawing on her anger to give her strength, "Diana still has *her* baby."

"If you tell the truth before it's too late—"

"It's already too late," she snapped. "I can't help Diana Kincaid. Isn't it obvious I can't even protect *myself* from my father? Now are you going to take me where I have to go or not?"

"Let's go."

He followed her to the motorcycle, chilled by the coldness he'd heard in her voice. Coldness and anger and hurt. Was it possible she was as much a victim as Diana Kincaid?

"Just a minute."

She turned to frown over her shoulder at him.

He held out his hand. "Give it to me."

Surprise and innocence flickered in her eyes.

"The gun," he said, still holding out his hand. The one that had clattered to the concrete beneath his motorcycle when he'd disarmed her. He wasn't sure when she'd picked it up without him seeing her do it. But he was damned sure she had.

With obvious reluctance, she reached up under her jacket and fished the pistol out of the waistband of her jeans and handed it to him.

He stuck it in his own jeans. "Now the ledger."

Her eyes glittered in the dim light with anger and she stepped back as if he'd slapped her.

"Just until I find out what's going on," he said.

For a moment, he thought she would fight him on this. To his surprise, she handed him the ledger without a word. He couldn't shake off the worry that she'd given in way too easily. He desperately wanted to open the book and see what was so important that she would risk everything to get it. But it was too dark and she seemed in a hurry, so he stuffed it in his jacket pocket.

He swung onto the bike, wondering why she hadn't used the gun against him when she'd had the chance.

She climbed on behind him, still silent, and circled his waist with her arms, pressing her face and body against his back as if needing his warmth, his strength. He sensed a vulnerability in her that gave him a twinge of guilt.

If Amanda had kidnapped Susannah with Gage's help as Jesse believed she had, then Jesse would have to arrest her when the time came. What bothered him as he started the bike was that when he did, he'd be throwing her to the wolves. A cold dread filled him at the thought of what J. B. Crowe would do when he found out everything his precious daughter had done.

"Where to?" he asked over his shoulder.

She took him straight to a house not far down the road. In the motorcycle's headlight, he could see that the place was old, isolated and in need of a lot more than paint, though paint would have helped. He could only assume after seeing the teething medicine in her bag that she was taking him to Susannah. It seemed an odd place for Amanda to have left her baby based on her father's net worth.

"This is it?" Jesse asked shining the cycle's headlight at the groves of trees off three sides of the house. It appeared to be a pecan orchard.

No lights burned inside the house. Nor was there a vehicle around. For not the first time, he wondered if she'd led him into a trap. Or another wild-goose chase.

She swung off the bike and started for the house.

"Hold on a minute."

She turned, her look impatient, wary. She no longer seemed vulnerable and now he wondered if she ever had been or he'd just imagined it.

He killed the motor, stood the bike on its kickstand and swung off, keeping his eye on her.

She'd stopped at the foot of the dilapidated steps. She watched him walk toward her, her expression worried as she glanced out into the night, as if looking for the dark car.

He slowed at the sound of a baby crying softly and something beyond that sound. The soft murmur of a woman's voice trying to still the infant.

He glanced at Amanda. She seemed anxious to get into the house. And nervous.

He looked over his shoulder, also half expecting to see that same dark car parked up the road, motor idling. He recalled the knock of the engine.

But there was no car idling nearby, no distinct knock of the engine, no sound at all. The road was empty this far out of town, this late at night and he was pretty sure they hadn't been followed. Then again, he'd been pretty sure before and look what had happened. But unlike Amanda, he didn't think J. B. Crowe was behind it.

They climbed the steps to the wide, worn wooden porch. Amanda rushed ahead to knock on the front door. He heard footfalls inside. The porch light came on. The faded curtains at the window parted. The lock thunked and the door opened.

The woman standing framed in the door was younger than Amanda with black hair and obviously of Mexican heritage.

"Buenas noches," she said to Amanda, then looked at Jesse with concern.

Amanda kissed the woman's cheek and rattled off something in Spanish, most of which Jesse didn't catch. His Spanish was passable at best. Obviously Amanda was fluent.

"English, please," he said catching hold of Amanda's arm.

"This is my friend, Carina." She wiggled out of his hold. "This is my father's chauffeur, Jesse."

He didn't miss the way she'd put him in his place, reminding them all who he worked for.

"The baby has been fussy all night," Carina said and looked hopefully at Amanda.

Amanda shook her head. "It was broken." She shot Jesse an accusing look.

"It will be fine," Carina said. "I was just heating a bottle." She headed toward the kitchen.

The house was small inside. Just the one floor and he could see all of the rooms with the doors standing open. From inside one of the rooms, a baby began to cry again.

He moved toward the bedroom, following the sound, eager to see Susannah.

He heard Amanda right behind him as he entered the small bedroom. A single baby carrier sat beside a narrow unmade twin bed. He moved to it and the sound of the crying baby, expectation making his legs strangely weak.

The baby was beautiful, her skin a rich, warm bronze, eyes dark and wide and filled with tears.

"This isn't Susannah," he said in disbelief as Amanda pushed him out of the way and picked up the baby. The infant quit crying instantly. There was no other carrier in the room, no other baby.

"Of course it isn't Susannah," Amanda said tersely. "Susannah's been kidnapped."

He looked around the room, wondering why she'd brought him here. This couldn't be why she'd been in such a rush. Not to deliver teething medicine to this baby.

He looked at her. Her hair was wet and dark against her lightly suntanned skin. Her eyes were wide and golden. She looked young and scared and surprisingly innocent. And holding another woman's baby with such obvious love and compassion.

"I know you're in trouble," he said quietly. "I can help you."

"Yeah, so far, you've been an incredible help," she said sarcastically, as the baby in her arms began to fuss, its little mouth opening and closing like a bird's.

Short of admitting he was a cop working undercover, he didn't know how to convince her to trust him.

He stared at her as she rocked the baby in her arms and cooed softly to it. He wanted to shake her until her teeth rattled. But the anger dissipated in an instant at the heart-wrenching look on her face as she gazed down at the other woman's child. The suffering he witnessed in her expression made him doubt everything he had believed about this woman and left him stunned. She wasn't the heartless, unfeeling woman he'd wanted to believe she was. She wouldn't have harmed her own baby. Not this woman.

He thought of her desperation, of the gum medicine she'd brought the baby, of the car that had tried to run her down. Dear God. What was Amanda Crowe running from? The answer seemed all too obvious. Her father.

Jesse could believe she had someone to fear. He just didn't believe it was J. B. Crowe.

Her gaze raised to his and the pain he saw almost leveled him. He stood looking at her, shaken. The cop in him reminded him that Susannah was still missing. And until she was found, another mother and her child were in jeopardy. All of this had to be stopped before J. B. Crowe retaliated further. But the man in him could only wonder what had happened to bring Amanda to this point in her life.

Carina came into the room with the bottle of milk.

"You have a beautiful baby," he managed to say.

Carina gave him a worried smile. Whatever was going on, she knew, he realized.

Amanda seemed reluctant to give up the infant, but slowly handed the baby to Carina who offered the bottle of formula. The baby sucked greedily and Jesse felt a pull inside him, an ache that he couldn't put a name to.

"We have to go," Amanda said checking her watch again. She added something in Spanish.

Carina frowned and looked worried, then kissed Amanda's cheek, hugged her and thanked her. *"Vaya con Dios."*

"What did you say to her?" Jesse asked as they headed for the front door.

"I told her I wouldn't be able to visit for a while," she said.

"Oh?"

She stopped at the door, turning unexpectedly. He saw the gun in her hand and swore. Carina must have slipped it to her when they'd hugged.

"Give me the ledger," she said quietly.

He shook his head. "I can't let you do this."

"You can't stop me, Jesse. I need the ledger. Now."

Outside, he heard a sound like the creak of a porch floorboard.

"You don't want to go out there alone," he said, every instinct telling him it was true.

"I need the ledger to trade for my baby," she said, her voice almost a whisper. "Don't make me shoot you for it."

"You're making a mistake," he said, but he pulled the ledger from his pocket. For some reason he believed she was desperate enough to pull the trigger. He'd already witnessed the extremes she'd gone to to get the ledger.

He held it out. When she reached for it, he jerked it back with one hand and grabbed the gun with the other, twisting the weapon from her fingers.

"Now," he said, his voice as low as hers had been, "we're going out there together and face the kidnappers."

"You're the one who's making the mistake now," she said angrily. "You don't have any idea what you're getting involved in."

"I appreciate your concern," he said sarcastically. He could feel her gaze boring into him.

"Who are you?" she asked. "You aren't a chauffeur."

"Not anymore." Holding the gun out of sight, he opened the door and listened. Silence answered him and for a moment, he thought he might have been wrong about a lot of things.

Then he caught movement out of the corner of his eye at the edge of the porch railing.

Instinctively, he grabbed Amanda as he raised the gun, already pulling her back.

A set of headlights flashed on. "Police!"

7

Jesse swore as he pulled Amanda back into the house, slammed the door and locked it behind them.

"You bastard," Amanda spat and tried to squirm out of his grip. "I knew I couldn't trust you."

So had this been some sort of test? "This sure as hell isn't my doing, sweetheart," he said as he snapped off the porch light and pulled her over against the wall beside the door. "Tell Carina to turn out the other lights, get the baby and stay down."

But the moment he said it, he realized the lights were already out and Carina and the baby were gone. In the distance he heard the sound of an engine dying away in the darkness. Out front one of the cops was calling for them to come out with their hands up. He tried to tell himself that the cops had made a mistake.

But he knew better. Amanda had been set up. Or he had.

"What are you trying to pull?" he demanded, tightening his hold on her. Her body felt hot to the touch. Soft, supple and full, yet strong. A body that held more secrets than he cared to contemplate.

"What am I trying to pull? You don't think *I* called the cops?" she snapped.

"Well, you *know* I didn't call them. What about your friend, how did she know to hightail so fast?" he demanded.

"She's an illegal. She's always ready to take off at a moment's notice. She must have heard the police and thought they were after *her*."

He considered that, wondering if Amanda might be telling the truth this time. He doubted it. At least not in its entirety. "That story about trading the ledger for Susannah—"

"That wasn't a story," she snapped.

"Look, *someone* called the cops."

"Or maybe you have some sort of tracking device on your bike."

"Yeah, right, just in case I'm ever hijacked at gunpoint." He didn't tell her that he rode a bike for that very reason. Easy to sweep and something he did regularly. He liked to know if he was being tracked.

She swore. "Or the kidnapper set me up," she said angrily.

Now would probably be a good time to tell her he was an undercover cop. And tell the guys outside as well. A thought struck him. He groaned. "Any chance your father has someone on the force in his pocket?"

In the light filtering in from the cop car's headlights outside, she gave him a look that said even he couldn't be *that* stupid. "My father's never had so much as a parking ticket in the city of Dallas since he took over as the head of the Organization. Does that answer your question?"

"Great." He wasn't sure what bothered him most— her nonchalant view of her father's life of crime or the fact that some of Jesse's brothers in blue were on J.B.'s payroll. "Do you know which cops are on your father's payroll?"

"Don't you?" she asked.

So now she thought he was a dirty cop. Things just kept getting better.

He parted the curtains and looked out. He could see one of the officers outside on the porch. The same one he'd caught sight of moments before. Sergeant Brice Olsen. A cop from another division he knew and who knew him.

There appeared to be just one other officer out front. Possibly another one or two out back. Not exactly a large raid and he couldn't hear any backup on its way. At least not yet. Was it possible Brice was on J.B.'s payroll? Or did this raid have something to do with Diana Kincaid's disappearance?

Jesse figured he and Amanda could have been followed. After all, she'd almost been run down not far from here. But it seemed doubtful. More than likely someone had known exactly where Amanda was going to be.

Not that it mattered now. If Brice was legit, then Jesse knew he could clear this up in a matter of minutes— if he wanted to blow his cover. But if Brice worked for J. B. Crowe, or worse, a competing mobster like Mickie Ferraro—

Outside the cop hollered for them to come out on the count of ten or they were coming in.

"They can't get their hands on this ledger," Amanda said, desperation in her voice.

"The ledger. Yeah, forget the fact that they might kill us," he said, unable to hold back the sarcasm.

"If they get this ledger, my baby will die," she snapped and jerked free of him. "There is only one thing to do. You're going to have to take me hostage."

He stared down at her. "You have to be kidding. Do you realize how dangerous—"

"At this point, getting shot by dirty cops is the least of my worries," she snarled. "Put the gun to my head and you'd damned well better be convincing or we are both dead."

Outside the cop was nearing the number ten.

Jesse swore. "No way."

"Or I could take you hostage," she suggested.

At least the woman had a sense of humor.

Jesse swore again and called out, "We're coming out! Don't shoot!" He looked at Amanda. "And if this doesn't work?"

"Then you'll just have to shoot me," she said.

"Don't tempt me," he growled into her ear as he pulled her to him.

He pressed the end of the barrel snugly against her chin until she raised her head and was forced to look up at him as she leaned against him.

"Ready?" he enquired. His traitorous body didn't have the good sense not to react to the feel of her compact behind pressed against his thighs.

"Not as ready as you, it seems," she said lightly.

Outside the cop yelled again for them to come out.

"Look," she said sounding dead serious again. "There's a car hidden out in the pecan trees off to the left of the house."

His first instinct was not to believe her. "How do you know that?"

"I hid it there."

He tried to imagine what she had to gain by lying, but he suspected lying came as naturally to her as breathing. "Where are the keys?"

"On the top of the front right tire."

He hesitated, but only for a moment. Outside one of the cops yelled for them to come out now. At this point, he had little choice.

"We're coming out!" He opened the door a crack, using Amanda as a shield. It had to be the riskiest, craziest thing he'd ever done. But she was right. There didn't seem to be any other way. No cop, clean or dirty, was going to shoot a woman down in cold blood. Especially the daughter of mobster J. B. Crowe. At least he hoped not.

He shoved Amanda through the door in front of him, hoping he was right about her being the key to getting them out of there alive.

"Cut the lights!" he yelled once he was sure they'd seen his hostage.

The headlights blinked off. It took a moment for his eyes to adjust. "Don't shoot!" He moved them slowly out onto the porch as he looked for a sniper.

The storm had passed, leaving the sky scrubbed clean. Stars glittered brightly. The moon lit the pecan trees ringing the house and the stretch of dried yard in front.

He could see there were three cops; Brice was the only one he recognized. He could also see that this wasn't a standard raid. "Drop your weapons and move back or I'll kill her," he ordered.

Brice saw him and a look passed between them in the moonlight. The cop dropped his weapon first. "Do as he says," he ordered the others. Reluctantly, they dropped their guns and moved back.

Jesse worked his way with Amanda in front of him toward the pecan trees off to his left where she said the car would be waiting for them. He hoped she was telling the truth. His motorcycle lay on its side, obviously disabled. The only other option was taking the cop car he saw parked up the road—a little too conspicuous a ride.

"Don't follow us and no harm will come to the woman," he said, realizing he sounded like a late-night B-movie villain.

"Let him go!" Brice said, sounding dubious. It was obvious Brice wasn't sure what Jesse was up to or which side he was on, but the cop was going to go along with it.

The other two cops didn't seem happy about the turn of events, but they didn't move as Jesse dragged Amanda farther back into the trees.

Just to make sure Brice and his buddies didn't change their minds, Jesse fired a couple of shots into the two front tires of their police car.

"Now!" he cried to Amanda and grabbing her hand, ran.

Amazingly, the getaway car was just where she said it would be. A minivan, a nondescript tan, the keys on the right front tire. He took the keys, opened the passenger side door and pushed her over behind the wheel as he followed her inside.

"Drive!" he ordered, handing her the keys.

The van engine turned over on the first try. She swung the van around and headed in the opposite direction of the house as if she knew where she was going.

He quickly glanced over his shoulder into the back, afraid he'd walked into another trap. The rear of the van was filled with a half dozen suitcases and an assortment of cardboard boxes.

Out the rear window, he could see nothing but darkness. He didn't think Brice would come after them. At least not until the cop checked with his superior. If that was J. B. Crowe, then it would be just a matter of time before Jesse saw the cop again.

Amanda took off through the pecan trees along a dirt track, sans headlights, following the pale silver path of moonlight between the limbs.

As soon as he was sure they weren't being followed, he reached back and pulled a carry-on flight bag to him. What he found inside wasn't much of a surprise. Baby clothes. And tucked in the side of the bag, plane tickets and a passport. He opened the passport in the light from the dash and saw that it was for Elizabeth Greenough.

He glanced over at her, but she didn't look at him as he put everything back where he'd found it and sat holding the weapon in his hand, trying to decide what to do now.

"You can put the gun away," she said as they bounced along beneath the dark branches of the pecan trees. "I don't want to be caught by those men any more than you do. And you aren't going to shoot me."

There were moments he might have argued that. This wasn't one of them. He now had both of Amanda's weapons. He checked the clip on each, then slipped one gun into the waist of his jeans and the other into the glove box.

He glanced over at Amanda as she swung the van onto a narrow tree-lined dirt road. The limbs of the trees scraped the top of the van as she drove. Through the leaves he caught glimpses of the full moon.

He studied her, trying to put all the pieces together, all the different Amandas he'd witnessed over the last two weeks. She was a mystery to him. One he desperately needed to solve if he hoped to keep them both alive.

The problem was, he didn't know what to believe. Back at the house she'd convinced him that her baby had been kidnapped. Now he couldn't even be sure the hit-and-run hadn't been staged for his benefit and maybe even the raid on the house back there. He couldn't be sure of anything. Not with this woman. And yet he sensed he'd only run into the tip of the iceberg. Either way, his ship was sinking.

He'd blown his assignment. He was no longer working undercover to try to bring down J. B. Crowe and his empire. Now he was on the run with Crowe's daughter. If that didn't get him killed he didn't know what would.

On top of that he didn't know where Susannah was, who had her, if she'd really been kidnapped or not. And now his cover was blown with J.B. even if the mobster didn't find out he was a cop. To make matters worse, both his life and Amanda's were on the line and he didn't even know for sure who they had to fear.

He glanced back. No sign in the moonlight of another vehicle following. Nothing but the moonlit darkness.

Amanda had driven down a series of narrow, dirt roads until even the distant sky no longer glowed with the lights of Dallas. She drove with more skill than he would have guessed, but no less self-assurance. The woman was gutsy, he'd give her that.

He glanced over at her again as she wheeled the van down the dirt road, the moon flickering through the trees, the sweet hot Texas air blowing in through the vents.

His heart picked up a beat as he realized how alone they were in this isolated place, how impossibly alluring she was even now, still wet from the rain, still as deceptive and devious as ever.

Her T-shirt hugged her full curves, molding her breasts, the hard buds of her nipples pushing against the cloth. He could almost taste them. He breathed in her scent—a combination of wet and warm—and let out a tortured breath.

"Pull over."

8

Amanda glanced at the empty stretch of dirt road ahead. No cars. No houses. Just the limbs of the trees etched black against the night sky, leaves dark and restless in the breeze. She felt a sliver of fear as she reminded herself that she didn't really know this man or what he was capable of. She'd already misjudged him on several occasions. Misjudging him now could prove fatal.

"Pull over," he repeated, his voice deadly quiet.

She slowed the van to a stop. He reached over, and for a moment, she thought he was going to touch her. He turned off the lights, the engine. Darkness and silence settled around them, wrapping them in its humid cloak.

She had thought Jesse was nothing more than her father's chauffeur. She had thought she could handle him. Neither, it seemed, was the case.

She inched her left hand to the door handle. The metal felt cool to the touch.

"We have a problem," Jesse said in that same quiet voice.

He didn't know how much of a problem they had, she thought. She said nothing, waiting, heart hammering as she measured her chances of getting the door open and throwing herself out before he could grab her. Not good. Especially since she needed the ledger—and he had it.

"I'm not a crooked cop," he said softly. "I'm not on your father's payroll. Not even as a chauffeur as of tonight."

"Why should I care?" she asked, trying to adopt a nonchalance she didn't feel.

"But I *am* a cop."

She dropped her gaze. She didn't dare look at him. He thought being a cop would relieve her mind? That that would make her trust him? Confide her deepest secrets to him?

She wanted to laugh. And cry. A cop. She swallowed, feeling sick to her stomach. One of her earliest memories was of the police coming to the door late at night and dragging her father out while she and her mother cried and tried to fight them off. One cop called her names, meaningless words to her at that age and yet she had understood perfectly what the man had thought of her and her family. Cops had always been the enemy. Even the ones her father now could afford to buy.

"I've been working—"

"I don't care who you are," she interrupted quickly. She didn't want to hear it.

"I don't want you thinking I'm one of your father's dirty cops."

Something in his voice made her look over at him. The moonlight captured his features, giving her a jolt. Sometimes she forgot how dangerous he looked. Or how handsome, which made him all the more dangerous.

"I told you, I don't care," she said.

"Doesn't it make any difference that I'm a cop?"

She let out a groan. "Oh, yeah. I trust you even less than when you were just my father's chauffeur."

He shook his head. "I can't win for losing with you, can I?" His look was full of hunger. It made her skin warm from its heat. Made her body ache just seeing the desire in his eyes. He wanted her. Maybe more than he wanted the truth.

But it would be a cold day in Texas before he'd have her. She knew that was her only weapon against him. His desire.

And her greatest weakness. Her own.

He was a cop. The enemy. And cop or not, as long as he had the ledger she would have to handle him very carefully. The problem was, now she also knew that he wasn't going to just give her the ledger and let her go. And that was going to be a problem.

Jesse blamed the heat, his growing frustrations and the intimacy of the moonlight and pockets of darkness inside the van. "I need the truth." He needed a lot more than that. He needed her and that shook him to his very foundation.

She was the daughter of a mobster, involved in who only knew what and as far as he could tell up to her pretty little neck in deep doo. And now she'd pulled him in with her. And all he could think about was taking her in his arms and ending whatever this was between them, this desire that demanded satisfaction, this terrible ache that clouded his thinking.

What was it about this woman? Any fool could see behind that wide-eyed, injured innocence of hers. Why her?

"You already know the truth," she said, an edge to

her voice. "What are you so afraid of? That you might be wrong about me? Or that you might be right? Worse, that it doesn't matter either way?"

He shook his head, angry with her, angry with himself. What she said was true. Worse, she'd seen his futile struggle to resist her. They both knew she was a deadly temptation. The problem was, he'd always believed himself above such captivation.

"The only truth I know is that you're a thief and a liar," he returned, wanting to hurt her, wanting to push her as far away as he could.

She brought up her hand to slap him but he caught it before her palm reached its mark.

He jerked her to him and groaned as he dropped his mouth to hers, his kiss punishing. She seemed small in his arms. Small and vulnerable. She put up no resistance. Made no sound. Her resignation proving to them both how right she was about him.

He shoved her back, despising himself for wanting her and despising her for having this power over him. His palm felt burned where her hand had been, he could taste her on his lips and her scent infused his senses as permanently as a brand. Somehow he'd let this woman get under his skin. And she would get him killed if he didn't get her out.

"Those suitcases back there, Susannah's clothes, the passport, the airline tickets for the two of you, they're all proof that you're a liar."

She brushed her fingers slowly over her bruised lips, tears welling in her eyes. "I know I'm a lot of things you abhor, Mr. Brock, but even I wouldn't lie about my daughter being kidnapped," she said, her voice dangerously soft. "Or is Brock even your real name? Who is the liar here?" Her eyes fired with anger. "Would you even recognize the truth if you heard it?"

"Try me," he challenged. "Let's hear some truth from those lips of yours."

She glared at him for a long moment, then took a breath. "The day my daughter Susannah was kidnapped, I got a call from Gage Ferraro. He told me he'd been contacted by the kidnappers and that they had demanded a ransom for our daughter."

"The kidnappers went to Ferraro instead of your father?" he asked, already having trouble believing her story. Gage was small potatoes. If they wanted any large amount of money they'd go to J.B. But they didn't want money, did they? "They demanded evidence against your father."

She nodded. "I was to make the trade tonight. But when the police showed up…"

He heard the pain in her voice. Was it possible she hadn't kidnapped her own daughter, hadn't been working with Gage, that she was telling the truth for once?

He pulled out the ledger he'd taken from her and opened it. He shot her a look, his heart pounding. He recognized the handwriting. J. B. Crowe had left him several messages during the time he'd worked as the mobster's chauffeur, all in a small, neat, very vertical, very distinctive script.

And even in the dim light from the dash and the moonlight filtering in through the windows, he could see that the pages were filled with numbers and dates. "Is this what I think it is?"

She nodded. "An account of my father's illegal activities. Enough to send him to prison."

Jesse let out a low whistle. "You planned to trade this for Susannah."

The look in her eyes told him how painful that decision had been. She'd betrayed her father to save her daughter. He no longer doubted that Susannah really had been kidnapped.

He looked again at the book, realizing just what he held in his hands. Something that could bring down J. B. Crowe and his empire.

Amanda touched his arm as if she could see what he desperately wanted to do with the evidence against her father. "If you turn that over to the police, it will be a death sentence for Diana Kincaid and her baby as well as mine."

"It would stop your father," he said.

"Do you really believe that putting him behind bars will stop him?" She shook her head. "The kidnapper will kill my daughter if he doesn't get that ledger. And believe me, my father will see that the same thing happens to Diana and her child."

Jesse swore. She was right. This was a helluva lot more complicated that he'd first imagined. He looked down the road and realized they'd been sitting still too long.

But he didn't know where to go. Or what to do. Crowe would be looking for them. And the cops and the kidnapper. And God only knew who else.

"Tell me about the trade," he said.

"The kidnapper was to bring Susannah to the house and we would make the trade there," she said.

"Whose idea was that?"

"Mine," she said. "I wanted some control. My father owns the place. I knew Carina would be there and could get some things ready, like the car and the items I needed for after the trade."

"You trust this woman?" he asked, recalling how the police had suddenly appeared—and Carina had disappeared.

"Carina is one of the few people I do trust," she said flatly.

"What about your father?" Jesse had to ask. "If you had gone to him about this—"

She shook her head adamantly, reinforcing the sense that something had happened between Amanda and her father. "My father is a mobster."

He looked at her to see if she was serious. "You make it sound as if you just found out what your father does for a living."

Her look was lethal parts anger and hurt. "I've known he was a mobster since I was a kid. But I didn't know about some of his…activities until I started looking for evidence to trade for my daughter."

Jesse held his breath. "What did you find?"

"My father is running a black market baby ring," she said quietly. "He buys some babies, steals others from their mothers, and sells them to the highest bidder." Her voice reeked with contempt.

"How do you know this?" he asked. "Is this in the ledger?"

She shook her head. "Carina worked at the estate until about four months ago, when she had her baby," she said. "My father's men tried to buy her baby. They put pressure on her since she has no husband and she's an illegal immigrant. When she refused to give up her daughter, they tried to steal her." Amanda's gaze settled on his. "They tried to kill Carina. I just found out about it."

Jesse didn't know what to say.

"Now do you understand why, once I get my daughter, I'm leaving the country?" she asked. "I have to. To my father, family is everything because our blood binds us together, family is ownership," she said. "Susannah's curse is that Crowe blood runs through her veins. For that we are all going to suffer because my father will not rest until he has what he considers his."

Jesse wondered what blood ran through his own veins. And what curse it would bring with it. "What happens now?"

"I contact Gage and have him set up another trade."

"You trust him?"

She shot Jesse a look. "Only as far as I can throw him. But he's more upset over Susannah's kidnapping than I would have ever expected. I'd never seen him like that. Scared. He was practically in tears when he came to me about the trade, afraid I couldn't do what had to be done."

He heard the sorrow and pain in her voice, understood for the first time how hard this had been on her and just what extremes she would go to to save her daughter. The brave front she'd put on after the kidnapping had made him think she was lying. Now he realized acting tough was all that had kept her going—being strong, doing what needed to be done, keeping it together—until she could get her daughter back.

"You seem confident the kidnapper will agree to another trade," he said. She nodded. "He wants that ledger. I need to call Gage and set it up."

Jesse nodded. "But how do you know the kidnapper— or Gage—didn't set you up back there?"

"I don't. But I still have the ledger and I know how badly the kidnapper wants it. He'll set up another trade."

That's what Jesse was worried about. Another trade. Another trap.

She pulled a cell phone from the compartment between the seats.

He watched her tap out a number and hoped to hell he wasn't making another mistake with this woman. She could be calling anyone.

"I want to hear what's being said," he told her.

She looked over at him, seemingly amused by his continued lack of trust. "You really are a cop, aren't you?" She leaned toward Jesse, tilting the phone so he could hear the conversation. "Gage?"

"Where the hell are you?" Gage demanded. Amanda was right, he sounded panicked.

"The trade didn't go down," she said. "But I would imagine you already know that."

"You're telling me? I got a call from the pickup person. He's furious. He saw the cops and took off. He thinks you pulled a fast one. What the hell went wrong?"

"You tell me," she said.

Gage let out a nervous laugh. "Yeah, right. *I* called the cops. Not even you believe that. You must have been followed. Probably your old man. I thought you said you'd be careful."

She glanced over at Jesse. "I'm doing my best." She sounded close to tears. He almost felt sorry for her.

Gage swore. "But you still have the ledger?"

"Yes, I want you to set up another trade."

Gage let out another oath. "Let me handle it this time."

"No, I make the trade, that's the deal."

It was obvious that Gage didn't like that. Jesse could hear him slamming things around on the other end of the line.

"It's going to take time," he said finally, sounding angry, frustrated. "A day or two at least. The kidnapper is demanding his own site this time. He's suspicious now. Where are you so I can let you know?"

"I'll contact you tomorrow," she said and clicked off.

Jesse stared out the windshield, unable to shake off the ominous feeling that had settled over him.

The moonlight paved a silver path between the trees and down the long narrow dirt road. The night air drifted in through their open windows, muggy and hot. He could smell something rotting in the trees.

"You act like you know who the kidnapper is," he said.

She didn't answer.

He looked over at her. She had her head down and he realized she was crying softly. It surprised him because for the first time he didn't think the tears were for his benefit.

Her short blond hair was spun silver in the moonlight. She raised her face slowly. The light turned the tears on her cheeks to sparkling diamonds. She brushed them away with her hand, seemingly embarrassed to be crying real tears.

Her gaze locked with his, challenging in its intensity. "Governor Kincaid had my daughter kidnapped."

9

She expected him to call her a liar again. She expected him to at least argue with her. The last thing she expected was him to say, "I'll drive."

"Wait a minute, where are we going?" She didn't like the look in his eyes.

"Red River, Texas," he said and motioned for her to switch seats with him. "I have some business there and we have at least a day before the next trade."

"What about the ledger?" she demanded as she reluctantly relinquished the driver's seat. She didn't give a damn about his other business. "You aren't going to keep me from making the trade."

"I'm not about to stop the trade," Jesse said without looking at her as he started the van. "Gage said it would be at least one day, maybe two. Red River is only a few hours' drive from here. We can be back in plenty of time. And obviously we can't stay in Dallas. No one will be looking for us in Red River."

His argument made sense. "Then you promise to give me the ledger when I need it and stay out of my way?" she persisted, wondering why she thought she could trust him even if he did agree to her terms. As if she were in any position to be laying down terms.

"I told you," he said as he drove. "I'm a cop. I want the kidnapper as much as you do."

"I could care less about the kidnapper," she snapped. "I just want my daughter."

He looked over at her as if surprised by her attitude. "You don't care if a guilty man goes free?"

"Lots of guilty men go free," she said, thinking of all the men she'd grown up around who she now realized had been guilty as sin.

"We'll make the trade," he said after he'd turned onto the highway. "We'll get your daughter back, but if staying out of your way means letting the kidnapper go, we might have a problem."

She eyed him in the flickering light of the street lamps flashing past. "You should know, if I get the opportunity, I intend to take the ledger back and make the trade without your interference. I'll do whatever I have to do to get my daughter back. Including stopping you from risking her life just so you can play hero and bring in the bad guy in the name of justice."

He shook his head at her. "You are something, you know that? I have *both* weapons, I have you and the ledger and you're telling me how it's going to be?"

"I won't let you jeopardize my daughter's life," she repeated.

"Being J. B. Crowe's only grandchild has already done that," he retorted.

She couldn't argue that, but soon she and her daughter would have new names, new identities, new lives. It wouldn't be easy to escape her father and his legacy. Amanda might still have his blood running through her veins, but she wouldn't be J. B. Crowe's daughter ever again. And Susannah would never know about her grandfather, the mobster.

The thought make her sad. But it was J.B.'s own fault that he was about to lose his daughter—and granddaughter.

But first she had to get Susannah back and that was becoming more difficult all the time, she thought looking over at Jesse. Especially since he didn't believe that Kincaid had kidnapped her baby.

As he drove through the thick Texas night toward Red River, he felt as if he'd been heading in this direction all his life. His life must have begun there. And it was there he would find out the truth.

But what was the truth? And was it something he could live with?

He couldn't help but feel disloyal to his family, the people who had loved him and raised him. And torn. He was a cop. Going to Red River, digging into the past, finding out the truth. It all made sense to the cop in him.

But still he felt guilty. He should be thankful for everything Pete and Marie McCall had done for him.

Unfortunately, he couldn't forget the copy of the newspaper clipping. Nor could he not worry about the person who'd put it under his door at the Crowe compound. He had to go to Red River. He had to uncover the truth. It was the kind of man he was. Come hell or high water.

He used Amanda's cell phone to call his boss at home, waking him up, to tell him that he was headed for Red River. His boss hadn't been happy to hear it since Jesse didn't offer any explanation. But he felt someone should know where he was.

To make matters worse, he had to worry about keeping himself and Amanda alive.

He had the ledger and Amanda Crowe. Having either could get him killed. Having both was suicide.

If that wasn't bad enough, Amanda would be looking for an opening to take the ledger back the first chance she got. He'd have to sleep with one eye open. Or not sleep at all until they made the trade.

He glanced over at her. She had settled into her seat as if nothing could budge her from his side. He was sure that was true as long as he had the ledger.

Nor did he plan on letting her out of his sight. That meant they'd be inseparable. And he knew how dangerous that would be.

"You don't believe me, do you?" she said.

He didn't really want to get into this with her but he could hear the determination in her voice and by now he knew when she wasn't going to let something go.

"I understand why you believe that Kincaid is behind this," he said. The kidnapper wanted a ledger that would damage Crowe—maybe even destroy him. Of course, Amanda would suspect Governor Thomas Kincaid. After all, Kincaid's campaign platform had been to eradicate the mob—more accurately, his nemesis, J. B. Crowe.

But kidnapping? It seemed awfully risky for a man in Kincaid's position. And the bottom line was, if Kincaid got caught, it would do more than just destroy his career. He wouldn't last long in prison, not after all the men he'd sent up as a former district attorney. Kincaid was a man known for being tough on criminals.

"You know Kincaid is the kidnapper for a fact?" he asked, all cop again.

"You mean can I prove it?" she asked bristling at his tone. "Not yet. But based on everything I know about the kidnapper, yes. It's Kincaid. Who else would ask for the ledger as ransom?"

"Any enemy your father ever made who now wants to bring him down," Jesse suggested. "And I would imagine J.B.'s made quite a few."

"You don't understand. My father and Governor Kincaid are at war. Diana and I and our babies are just casualties of that war."

He could hear the anger in her voice, the tears just behind them. "It isn't unusual for a governor to want to get rid of the mob," he said quietly.

She gave him a pitying look. "You really think that's what this is about? My father and Kincaid have a history that goes back to when they were boys growing up in Dallas—on the wrong side of the tracks, so to speak."

Hadn't he suspected as much? "What kind of history?"

She sighed. "Kincaid had a little brother, Billy. Billy and my father were best friends, inseparable as kids and later teenagers. Unfortunately, Thomas Kincaid wasn't happy about their relationship. He knew my father did errands for members of the Organization. He didn't want his little brother getting involved with the mob."

She took a breath and met his gaze. "My father swears that Billy wasn't involved in anything illegal, in fact, Billy was trying to get J.B. to go to college. Billy thought my father would have made a great lawyer." She smiled at this.

"What happened?" Jesse said, knowing it could only have ended badly.

"Billy was killed. Shot down by cops during a convenience store robbery that went bad." She shook her head, anticipating his next question. "My father had nothing to do with the robbery. Nor anyone in the Organization. He was devastated. He loved Billy. And he blamed the cops and Kincaid. You see, Kincaid saw the neighborhood market being robbed that night and called the police not knowing J.B. and Billy were inside. Afterward, Kincaid blamed J.B. because of his friendship with Billy. Kincaid was convinced J.B. had something to do with the robbery. Kincaid became governor. My father became a mobster. The rest is history."

Jesse let out a low whistle. That definitely could explain some of the animosity between J.B. and Kincaid.

"Now do you understand why my father and Kincaid are obsessed with destroying each other at any cost?" she asked.

He still found it hard to believe that Kincaid would do anything to jeopardize his career—let alone his life— to get J. B. Crowe after all these years, but at least Jesse better understood now why Amanda believed it.

They drove in silence for a few miles.

"By the way, my name's not Brock," he told her. "It's McCall. Jesse McCall. At least it was when I went undercover two weeks ago."

10

They drove through what little remained of the night, stopping only for gas for the van or coffee to stay awake. Amanda wasn't the least bit sleepy. She watched the dark landscape blur past and thought of Susannah. Had it only been a little over three days since Susannah had been kidnapped? It seemed like weeks. She should have been holding her daughter in her arms right now, not traveling across the state of Texas with an undercover cop. She ached with the need.

She had cried so many tears, she felt as if the well had gone dry. Soon, she told herself. Soon, she would have her daughter. Only the next time, she wouldn't let anything go wrong because she would be alone and in control of the trade. She had no intention of putting Susannah's welfare in Jesse's hands. Even if he was a cop.

That meant getting the ledger and that would mean getting rid of Jesse Brock—McCall, she corrected.

In the meantime, she had little choice but to go along with him. He had the ledger and her daughter's life in his hands. Temporarily.

She felt a moment of guilt. She'd seen how desperately he'd wanted to take the ledger to the cops. But he hadn't. And for that she was grateful. They still had a long way to go until she was contacted for another trade. Jesse might weaken. Or she might get the ledger away from him. A lot could happen.

She thought about what would happen after the trade. The new life she would make with Susannah. For Susannah. She clung to that.

"I think you should call your father." It was the first thing Jesse had said in miles.

"You have to be kidding," she said incredulous. "And tell him what?"

"He might think you've been kidnapped."

"You mean I haven't?" she asked sarcastically.

"I'm serious. Tell him you're all right. That you're being held in protective custody for twenty-four hours."

"You are serious," she said studying him.

"He's your father," Jesse said. "He'll be worried."

She nodded, wondering just how worried her father would be as she pulled out her cell phone. Her father answered in the first ring. "It's me."

"Amanda, my God, I have been out of my mind with worry," he said, sounding like he meant it.

"I'm sorry. It's a long story. All I can tell you is that I'm all right."

He was silent for a long moment.

She thought he might be crying. J. B. Crowe? She must be hallucinating from lack of sleep. "Don't look for me, all right? I'll call you in twenty-four hours. I'm… okay." She hung up, shaken.

"Well?" Jesse asked.

"He took it well," she said, wondering how many men he'd sent out trying to find her. Or if he'd do as she'd asked and call them off.

Jesse slowed the van at the Red River city limits sign and she wondered for the first time what they were doing here. It was the intensity of his expression as he drove into the dusty, little town that suddenly had her worried. What was this about?

He made a pass through town. It didn't take but a few minutes. Main Street was only a few blocks long. Bank, grocery, gas station, café, newspaper, dry goods store.

She was looking at the small sleeping town, wondering what it would be like to raise a daughter in a place like this when Jesse pulled up in front of the *Red River Weekly* and cut the engine.

He glanced over at her. "You can stay in the car if you want."

Yeah, right. "I go where the ledger goes," she said.

"That's going to make bathing interesting," he said as he climbed out of the van, locking it behind him.

The thought had its appeal. In fact, it was the first pleasing thought she'd had in hours. She smiled and followed after him.

He tried the door to the newspaper office, but it was too early according to the sign in the window. "How about some breakfast?"

As far as she was concerned, it was also way too early for breakfast, but she could use more coffee. She watched the reflection of the street in the windows of the businesses as they walked the half block down to the Lariat Café and realized she and Susannah would stand out too much in a town like this. She'd thought about nothing else but how to disappear once she had her daughter.

A bell chimed as Jesse pushed open the door. It was cool inside, the interior sparse. Only a few well-worn tables and chairs sat on the black-and-white-tiled linoleum between a short row of booths and the lunch counter.

Several older men hunched over coffee cups on the blue vinyl stools along the counter. They turned as she and Jesse entered and kept watching as he led her to a booth. She slid into the vinyl and felt a chill. Was there any chance her father had contacts this far north? It didn't seem likely. But of course the governor's contacts extended across the entire state.

The men at the stools finally turned back to their conversation and their cups.

"Howdy," said a pert older waitress as she slid two glasses of ice water and two plastic-covered menus across the marred tabletop. "Get ya'll some coffee?"

"Please," Amanda said. She would have killed for a latte but she could see that strong and black, straight from the pot, was all she was going to get in this town.

The waitress plopped a cup and saucer down in front of her and poured. Amanda took a sip and grimaced.

"Not the expensive Colombian blend you're used to?" Jesse asked wryly after the waitress left.

"You really think I'm just a spoiled kid, don't you?"

He raised a brow in answer.

She would have loved to argue differently but it was true. "All that's going to change," she said taking another drink of the coffee and this time not making a face.

"How will you live once you leave?" he enquired.

She could detect only a faint touch of sarcasm in his tone as she met his gaze over the top of her cup. "I plan to *work*. I might not be able to use my degree but I can find something in my field."

"And what field would that be? Art history? Philosophy? Or maybe interpretive dance?"

"Electrical engineering."

His jaw dropped.

She smiled and took another sip of her coffee. It wasn't so bad, after all. "How do you think I was able to get the ledger with all the hidden cameras and the security system at the house?" He was staring at her as if he'd never seen her before. His look was different. Not sexual. More like just plain interested in her.

She felt a little buzz at the thought and smiled to herself. Maybe Jesse was starting to see her as a person, more than just female body parts. The thought brightened her day because it had obviously upset him—and the closer she got to him, the harder it would be for him to be a cop, and not a man.

And the easier it would be for her to get the ledger back and make the trade—without him.

Jesse discreetly took the ledger from his pocket and opened it, thumbing slowly through the pages. She watched him. His strong jaw was dark with stubble, his eyes black as obsidian.

She'd never noticed the small curved scar over his left eyebrow before and wondered how he'd gotten it. She knew so little about him—and yet so much, she thought. She knew how desperately he wanted to catch the kidnapper, to send her father to prison, to see that justice was done. It made her sad for him. In this world, there was little justice. She feared his battle was futile and would only bring him pain and disappointment.

He grew very quiet as he closed the ledger.

She waited for him to say something. He seemed lost in thought and not good thoughts from the look of him.

"You aren't still thinking of taking it to the police?"

she asked hesitantly. It wasn't an option and she'd fight heaven and hell to stop him from it.

She was relieved when he shook his head.

"No," he said. "I told you I would let you use it to get your daughter back. You'll find I stick to my promises."

She looked down at her menu, almost feeling guilty about her plans to keep him from the trade. Almost.

She studied her menu, antsy. Hers was a waiting game now. Waiting for Gage to set up the next trade. Waiting for Jesse to slip up and give her the opportunity to get the ledger back and get away.

She glanced up at him. If he wanted to play detective in the meantime, what did she care? He was looking at the ledger again, his brows furrowed in a frown. Everything about him looked dangerous. But as she studied him she sensed the only thing she had to fear was the desire he invoked within her.

When the waitress returned, Jesse ordered chicken fried steak, grits and biscuits with milk gravy. Amanda ordered a Spanish omelette. She'd never liked breakfast—especially at this hour.

"So what made you become a cop?" she asked as they ate. She hadn't realized how hungry she was and the omelette was good, the sauce hot and spicy and just what she needed.

"I don't know," he said after a moment. "I guess I believe in justice."

She should have known.

"You don't like authority figures, do you?" he asked between bites.

Did anyone? "I'll admit I had some bad experiences with cops as a child. It might have prejudiced my feelings."

"Maybe I can change that," he said.

Don't hold your breath, she thought, but when she looked up and met his gaze, she said, "Maybe. So tell me about yourself," she said as she studied him, wondering about him more than she wanted to.

He shrugged. "I was raised north of Dallas on a lake. I have," he seemed to hesitate, "two brothers and three sisters."

She lifted a brow. "That's a big family. I'm envious."

He nodded. "Yeah, they're really something. You'd like them." He flushed as if realizing too late that she would never have a reason to meet them.

"And your parents?" she asked, betting they were still together.

"My father is an accountant and my mother is a substitute grade school teacher," he said slowly.

She blinked. "Wow, can't get much more normal than that. Your mother probably volunteers at the hospital and bakes bread for the food bank."

He shook his head. "She volunteers at the senior center and makes quilts for the poor."

She laughed.

"My family is very dull by your standards," he said and turned his attention to his breakfast.

"I would love dull, believe me." She didn't want to get on the subject of her so-called family. "So, let me guess, you were very popular in high school, star quarterback of the football team and…" She squinted at him. "King of the senior prom and your date, the queen of the prom, was named… Brittany."

He looked up from his breakfast, humor in his eyes as he smiled at her. He had a great smile. "You're wrong. Her name was Tiffany."

Amanda laughed. "I knew it."

"What about you?" he asked, his gaze turning serious.

"I was one of the nerds, the .com, chess club, honor roll crowd."

"No prom?"

"Not my thing," she said, surprised how defensive she sounded. "I was your classic Stephen King Carrie."

"I really doubt that. I'm sure there were lots of guys who wanted to ask you but were intimidated. And I don't blame them," Jesse said.

"Because of my father," she said, dismissing his comment.

"No, because you were the smartest, prettiest girl in the school."

She eyed him suspiciously, but couldn't help but smile. "Okay, what do you want?" she asked, only half joking.

"You already know what I want," he said, his heated gaze warming her to her toes. "I told you during one of my weaker, more honest moments."

"More than you want to put my father in jail?"

"More than even that," he said.

She laughed, but her gaze never left his face. Like him, she was only too aware of the chemistry between them. Worse, the more she was around him, the more she was starting to like him.

After breakfast while Jesse paid the check, she stepped outside for some fresh air. The street was still practically empty, the town slumbering in the warming sun.

She waited, feeling anxious. She just wanted her daughter. The ache in her heart felt heavy as stone. She tried not to think of Susannah's smile. Or her bright eyes.

Or the way she curled her tiny fingers around Amanda's finger. Her baby.

Jesse came out of the café and looked around for her as if he thought she might have taken off. Not likely.

As they walked down the street to the *Red River Weekly,* he seemed as nervous and anxious as she felt. And wary. He appeared to be studying the faces of the people they passed as if looking for something. She realized how exposed they were in a town like this. Easy pickings.

A young woman looked up from her desk as they walked into the newspaper office.

"Can I help you?" she asked, peering at them through a pair of pink-framed glasses. Her eyes were lined in black, her cheeks two startling red slashes of blush. A necklace of blue plastic beads noosed her neck above a T-shirt and jeans. Around her floated an aura of grape-flavored bubble gum and open curiosity. The name plate on her desk read: Aimee Carruthers.

"I'd like to take a look at your morgue," Jesse said.

"What year are ya'll interested in?" she asked, studying them intently through her glasses.

"June, 1971."

Aimee Carruthers looked surprised.

Not as surprised as Amanda.

The woman recovered quickly and got to her feet. "June, 1971?" She seemed to wait for Jesse to say more, but he didn't and finally she led them back to a small room.

The morgue had only one window, which was thankfully hanging open. A faint breeze hardly rustled the papers on the top of a filing cabinet under it, but made the tiny warm room bearable.

"That'd be on microfiche." Aimee motioned to a set of small metal drawers each labeled with dates. "You know how to work it?" she asked.

Jesse nodded. "Thanks."

It was obvious she didn't want to leave the room, but it was equally obvious Jesse wasn't going to start his search until she did.

"If ya'll need any help—"

"We'll holler," he said, cutting her off.

She left but not before propping the door open to give them a little more air. Right.

The moment the nosy Aimee Carruthers was gone, he pulled out the drawer labeled 1971 and extracted the spool of film that contained June.

Amanda walked over to the window and looked out onto the alley. The air smelled of red Texas dust and sunshine. When she turned, Jesse was staring at the screen. A headline caught her eye: Infant Abandoned Beside Road.

Jesse's heart jerked at the sight of the familiar headline. He scanned the story he now knew by heart, then moved on to the next week. Amanda had moved closer and now stood at his side watching the screen. Behind him he heard a sound, a popping of gum and the scent of grape.

He didn't need to turn around. He knew Aimee Carruthers had probably seen the article on the screen. He also realized it would be impossible to keep anything a secret in a town this size—especially once he started asking questions. He would just have to find the answers fast.

In the next week's paper he found only a brief piece

on page one about the baby: Parents of Abandoned Infant Sought. It was followed by a plea by Sheriff Art Turner for the mother to come forward.

The article said the baby had been found in a cardboard box, wrapped in a pale blue blanket on Woodland Lake Road. Like the first story, the article didn't mention the gold chain or the strange heart-shaped pendant found on the baby or the name of the person who'd discovered the newborn beside the road.

Amanda pulled up a chair and sat down beside him as she read the article. Out of the corner of his eye, he saw her frown at the screen, then at him, but she said nothing as he scrolled the pages of the next week's paper.

The story of the infant had dropped to the third page. There was only a short piece titled, No Leads On Found Baby. The investigation had stalled. No one had come forward.

He moved to the next weekly paper but found no mention of the infant. Nor was there anything in the next paper. Or the next. He scanned the rest of June, July, August, all the way to December, 1971. The baby boy left beside the road had been forgotten.

So how had his parents come to adopt him?

Slowly, he turned back to the last story and reread it, finding nothing new of interest except that the baby had been found a quarter mile down the road from the old Duncan place.

He made copies of the stories with a growing uneasiness as he recalled his parents' reluctance to even talk about the night they'd found him beside that road. And their repeated concerns that he not dig in the past.

Aimee Carruthers was on the phone when they came out of the newspaper morgue. She stopped talking and gave them a nervous smile as she held her hand over the mouthpiece until they were out the door. When Jesse looked back she was hunched over the phone, talking hurriedly. He wondered how long it would take for everyone in town to know.

He cut across the street with Amanda keeping stride beside him. She didn't ask and he was grateful, but as he opened the door of city hall for her, he saw her look of concern and remembered her dislike for cops and her fear that he'd turn the ledger over to the police.

"Trust me," he whispered.

Her look was half plea, half warning.

He'd hate to ever cross this woman.

The police station was an anteroom off city hall, just large enough for two desks. A skinny redheaded young man stood behind the short counter, his freckles seeming to leap off his pallid face. A pair of red-rimmed pale-blue eyes peered at them with obvious interest as they entered. He wore a deputy's uniform and his name tag read: Deputy Lane Waller.

Lane Waller had just hung up the phone. Jesse suspected that Aimee Carruthers had called him. Now why would she do that, he wondered with a growing uneasiness.

"I'm looking for Sheriff Art Tucker?" Jesse said stepping up to the counter, hoping that the sheriff might still be around after all these years.

"Well, he shouldn't be hard to find." On closer inspection, the young man didn't look old enough to drive, let alone carry the loaded weapon at his hip. "You can find him where he always is this time of day."

"And where might that be?" Jesse asked when the deputy didn't go on.

"Oak Rest Cemetery on the edge of town," Lane said and chuckled heartily at his own joke.

Funny. Jesse tried to squash his disappointment in the sheriff's demise, but after all it *had* been thirty years. "How about the coroner?" Jesse recalled his name from the newspaper article. "Gene Wells?"

Again Lane shook his head. "Pushing up daisies as well."

"I suppose there isn't anyone around still who worked in this office thirty years ago?" Jesse asked, feeling like he'd hit a dead end already.

Lane Waller chuckled. "Not unless you count Hubert Owens."

"Who is he?" Jesse asked.

"Tucker's former deputy but he's—"

"If he's still alive, where can I find him?" Jesse asked, before he could be assaulted by another of Lane Waller's bad jokes.

He glanced at his watch. "He should be having his third beer by now over at the Corral Bar. He might even be half sober. Or awake."

The Corral was wedged between the local garage and the drugstore. Rough-hewn cedar covered the front in a western-looking log fence design. Beer signs glowed in the dusty window, illuminating a handful of spiky cactus plants covered with cobwebs and red Texas dust.

The bar was empty except for an elderly man on a stool, hunched over a glass of draft and a younger man washing glasses behind the bar. At the back, an old Patsy Cline tune played on the jukebox.

"Hubert Owens?" Jesse asked as he took the stool next to the man and Amanda pulled up one on the other side. Of course Amanda drew the man's attention.

Owens gave her a blurry, near toothless smile. "Most people just call me Huey," he said brightly and sat up a little straighter. He hadn't shaved in days and reeked of stale beer, sweat and tobacco.

"Mr. Owens, I understand you were a deputy in town thirty years ago," Jesse said.

Owens reluctantly turned to squint at Jesse, his look instantly suspicious. "What of it?"

"We're trying to find out about that little baby that was left near the old Duncan place thirty years ago," Amanda said turning on the charm, which was considerable. "Out on Woodland Lake Road?"

Hubert Owens swiveled his head back around to her. "Sure, sweetie, but what would a young thing like you care about that for?"

"I think that little baby might be someone I know," she said, her brown eyes turning to gaze at Jesse challengingly. "You probably don't remember much about the case…"

"The heck I don't, little lady. 'Member it like it was yesterday. Strangest damn—'scuse me—strangest darned thing to happen around here."

Jesse sat back on his stool and watched Amanda in the mirror with a mixture of irritation, amusement and gratitude. She was smart enough to have put two and two together and figure out what he was looking for. His admiration of her grew.

"What was so strange about it?" she asked conspiratorially.

Owens leaned toward her. Jesse could smell his beer-soaked breath from where he sat and knew Amanda was getting the full force of it. Well, she'd asked for it.

"Who'd leave a little baby like that in a box beside

the road?" the old man asked. "Didn't make no sense at all." He leaned closer to her. "And the note—" He shook his head.

"What note?" Jesse mouthed to Amanda in the mirror.

"There was a note?" she asked in a hushed, sexy voice.

The old man nodded smugly. "That part never got into the paper. Ya know ya always got to keep one piece of evidence back. That way when someone comes forward, wanting the baby, ya got something secret. If they can tell ya what's in the note, then—"

"What *was* in the note?" she asked trying to steer him back on track.

He glanced down the bar at the bartender. He didn't seem to be paying any attention but Jesse knew he was listening to every word.

"Guess after all these years it don't make no difference," Owens said. "And you seem like a nice enough girl." The old man seemed to zone out for a moment.

"Was the note handwritten?" Amanda prompted.

He blinked, then nodded. "Handwritten and kinda scrawled like the person writing it had been in a hurry. Said—and I'll never forget this—'Take care of my precious baby. I will go to my grave loving him.'"

The words squeezed at Jesse's heart.

"You probably had your suspicions about whose baby it was," Amanda said. "I mean, it would be hard in a town this size to hide being pregnant."

Jesse watched her work in the mirror, admiring how easily deception came to her. Must be something in the genes. The thought brought him up short as he wondered about his own genes.

Owens stared down into his beer. "Weren't no local

gal, I can tell you that." Owens glanced over at Amanda. "You know, you're the second person who's asked about that baby. Couple weeks ago—" He seemed to catch himself. He reached for his beer and drained it.

"Who else was asking about the baby?" Jesse asked.

Owens didn't answer. He looked around the empty bar. The bartender was busy washing glasses and didn't look up.

Amanda laid a hand on the old man's arm. "Who else was asking?" she whispered.

"That's just it," Owens said, dropping his voice. "What's a guy like that coming around here asking a lot of questions after all these years about some baby? Makes people nervous, you know. Ain't like we all ain't seen him in the paper."

"A guy like what?" Amanda asked.

Owens fidgeted on his stool for a moment, then looked over at her. Jesse watched in the mirror behind the bar as the old man whispered one word, "Mobster."

Jesse's eyes met Amanda's in the mirror. He'd seen her tense at the word, some of the color draining from her face.

"Which mobster?" she asked in a small strained voice.

"That Crowe fella, but you didn't hear that from me," Owens said and pounded on the bar with his empty glass. "If that couple was willing to take the baby, I don't see no reason to tell anyone about 'em. 'Specially someone like him."

"You're sure it was J. B. Crowe?" Amanda persisted.

"The one that's in the paper today," Owens said, sounding scared. "You think I don't know who I talked to? You think I don't know about that underworld stuff?"

"What did you tell him?" Amanda asked, a tremor in her voice.

"Don't know nothin'," the old man muttered, swaying a little on the stool. "Nothin' 'bout that couple that found the baby. Nothin' 'bout no baby. Nothin' at all." He winked at her, then his head dropped to the bar and he began to snore loudly.

The bartender came down to take Owens's glass. He didn't say a word but Jesse noticed how he also didn't meet his eyes as if he didn't want to get involved.

Behind them the door banged open. A man in a sheriff's uniform filled the door frame. He was large, his expression displeased. "I heard there might be a problem over here?" he said eyeing them.

The bartender shook his head. "No problem here, Sheriff Wilson."

Sheriff Wilson let his gaze run over Jesse, then slowed as it took in Amanda. The only sound in the room was Hubert "Huey" Owens's loud snoring.

Jesse got to his feet, figuring now was as good as any time to talk to the sheriff. But the man's wide face closed over. He tipped his hat to Amanda, then turned around and left as if in a hurry.

"What was that about?" she asked after the door had banged shut behind the sheriff.

"Beats me." Nor did Jesse plan to take it up with the sheriff. At least not now. He followed Amanda out of the bar. "Thanks for your help in there. You were good," he admitted grudgingly.

"No problem," she said and walked over to the curb. "Wanna tell me about it?"

"Not really," he said. "Not yet."

She nodded.

"Also I wouldn't take too much of what the guy said to heart," he told her, knowing all that mobster talk had upset her. "The baby was only a few hours old. Of course it was a local girl's. And that stuff about him recognizing the mobster from the paper—"

"Jesse."

Something in her tone stopped him. He joined her at the curb and saw that she was staring down at one of the newspaper racks. The *Dallas Morning News*.

Looking out from the front page was J. B. Crowe. He'd just been given some humanitarian award in Dallas.

11

An icy chill ran up his spine. Could J. B. Crowe have been in Red River? Asking about the baby? Asking about Jesse? But why?

He grabbed Amanda's arm and ushered her quickly across the street to the van. It wasn't until they were both inside that he said, "Right after I went to work for your father, he made a business trip." He heard the fear in his voice. "Do you know where he went?"

She shook her head. "I just know he was upset when he got back. What's going on?"

Jesse started the van. "I wish I knew."

At the town's only gas station, he called Dylan from the pay phone outside. He'd forgotten that Dylan said he would be on another case and out for a while. Dylan's sister Lily gave him the news, though. The fingerprints had come back on the photocopy of the newspaper article Jesse had given Dylan. There was a second set of prints on the paper. J. B. Crowe's.

Jesse stood for a moment in the phone booth, his heart pounding. J. B. Crowe had been up here two weeks ago asking about a baby left by the road thirty years before. Then he put the photocopy of the newspaper article under Jesse's door. Why?

Inside the classic old filling station, Jesse asked directions to Woodland Lake Road and the old Duncan place. The attendant eyed them warily as he pointed east, seemingly glad when the van pulled away from his pumps.

They quickly left the small town behind, the road running red to the horizon. Not far out, they picked up a creek. It twisted and turned its way through the brush beside the road, the day already growing hot and no shade except for a small puddle beneath the occasional tree they passed. Behind the van, dust boiled up into the faded blue of the Texas sky, the landscape as bleak as his reason for driving out here.

He tried to steel himself at the thought of seeing the spot where he'd been abandoned. A building appeared ahead. The old farmhouse sat on the hill, weathered and gray, a faint sign on the fence, Duncan. The old Duncan place.

He drove past it, wanting to see the curve in the road beside the creek a quarter mile farther where, according to the newspaper article, the baby had been found.

A golden Texas sun beat down on the red earth and van as he coasted down the hill. Crickets chirped from the bushes beside the creek and in the distance a hawk cried as it circled overhead.

He could see the bend in the road ahead, the wide spot next to it and the creek.

He slowed the van, trying to imagine what had happened in the hours, the days, the years before he was left in this lonely, desolate spot.

Braking, he brought the van to a stop, killed the engine and slowly opened his door. He could feel Amanda's gaze on him. She had said little since they'd left the bar. As he walked toward where he imagined he'd been left that night, he heard her open her door and get out.

There was a low spot beside the creek and road the width of a car. He stepped into the shade of the largest of the trees, his heart hammering in his ears. This had to be the place. He could see it, the darkness, the car coming up the road, stopping and the door opening as someone lowered the cardboard box to the earth. The door of the car closing quickly. The sound of the engine dying away in the distance.

It sickened him, frightened him and made him angry and grief-stricken all at the same time. Why? Why would his mother have done such a thing? If she hadn't wanted him, why not leave him on someone's doorstep?

Because she hadn't wanted anyone to know she'd given birth to him. She hadn't expected him to survive. She hadn't expected someone to find him. Then why the note? And the gold chain with the odd-shaped heart?

He closed his eyes, breathing in the unfamiliar scents, listening to the sounds of water and rustling leaves and birds high in the branches. Anger and pain and a horrible sense of betrayal filled his heart to bursting. And fear. There was more to the story. He could feel it. A woman who didn't want her child didn't write a hurried note, didn't put a gold heart in the baby's blanket.

And now J. B. Crowe had been asking about the baby. Knew Jesse was the baby. Why else had J.B. given him the copy of the newspaper article?

"This baby we're looking for," Amanda said, dragging him from his thoughts. "It's you, isn't it?"

He opened his eyes. She was standing in front of him. He blinked, fighting emotions that threatened to drop him to his knees. And he'd had the nerve to berate her for *her* genes. "Yeah." He told her about the McCalls, and how they had found him and raised him, about the copy of the newspaper clipping and the news that he was adopted.

"I'm sorry. You didn't know until yesterday?"

He shook his head.

"Oh, that must have been a terrible shock."

"You could say that." He was still reeling from it. And now to find out that J. B. Crowe put the copy of the newspaper article under his door. Worse, that J.B. had been in Red River asking questions about the baby.

"I don't know what to say." She reached over to squeeze his hand.

He didn't want her pity, but almost at once he realized that wasn't what she was offering.

"You and I have more in common than I would have ever thought," she said, looking at him as though seeing him differently now. "Only, I'd love to find out I was adopted."

She seemed to hesitate. "What does it have to do with my father?"

"I don't know." He met her gaze. "But I intend to find out."

He turned back to the van. That's when he saw the old Duncan place perched on the hill, caught the flash of the sun off one of the windows. He stopped and stared up at the house. "They could have seen it," he said. "Whoever lived there."

She followed his gaze and hugged herself as if suddenly cold. "It was at night, right? They could have seen the lights from the car. Maybe even seen the interior light come on."

He looked over at her, glad she was there with him. "I think I know who might have been living up there thirty years ago."

The house had seen better days and the yard was filled with falling-down outbuildings and broken-down equipment and vehicles.

Jesse slowed the van, his heart a hammer in his chest. His parents had warned him not to dig in the past. Obviously something had frightened them.

He pulled off onto the dirt track, the bumper of the van slapping down the tall weeds, and drove up to the house. Turning off the engine, he sat for a moment, listening. Crickets chirped in the tall grass, a hawk screeched overhead and, closer, he could hear a bee droning just outside the window.

The house was empty and looked as if it had been for some time. He opened his door. He didn't know why, but he needed to go inside the old rambling farmhouse. He needed to know how Marie and Pete McCall had found him. He had a pretty good idea that he was right about one thing at least.

"You might want to wait here." He'd half expected Amanda to argue.

"All right," she agreed, her gaze on the creepy old place.

Like him, she seemed to feel wary of the place. Just something in the air. A disquiet. A feeling of foreboding. As if some presence remained, a memory of something awful that had happened.

Jesse tried to shake off the feeling as he stared at the blank darkness where windows should have been on the second floor. Most of the glass was gone, leaving yawning openings and the dusty woven webs of spiders in the window frames.

He pushed open the already ajar door and was hit with the cold putrid breath of the house. He hesitated, telling himself there was nothing to be learned here. Dust and debris coated the worn wooden floor. A scurrying sound came from a distant room.

He peered into what had once been the dining room, the floor creaking under his weight. There were old clothes and books and newspapers and magazines piled in a corner. He dug a newspaper out of one pile and looked at the date. Newer than 1971.

He thought he heard a car engine. But knew it wasn't the van. He'd taken the key. And even if Amanda had another set, she wouldn't leave without the ledger in his pocket.

He moved deeper into the house where the shadows hunkered, dark and cold in corners. Something moved off to his right, making him jump. A rat scampered from a pile of clothing, disappearing around the corner into the next room.

As he climbed the rickety stairs to the second floor, he asked himself what he was looking for. Hadn't he seen enough of this place? He stopped in one of the old bedrooms. A rusted metal box spring mattress leaned against one wall, a pair of once blue curtains fluttered at the broken window, on the floor was a book with a watermarked brown cover.

He bent down to pick it up. An old Hardy Boys mystery, one he'd read as a boy, *The Secret of the Old Mill*. The pages smelled of mildew and dust as he flipped it open, trying to remember the story, trying to think of anything but the reason he was here.

Inside the cover of the book was stamped Red River Community Library. He flipped to the back and pulled out the library card. The book was long overdue. Thirty years worth. But he could still read the name of the person who'd checked it out. Marie McCall. His adoptive mother.

The wooden steps of the stairs creaked. He froze, listening. Another step creaked and another. Goose bumps skittering over his skin like a spider's legs. Someone was coming up the stairs.

"Amanda?"

No answer.

"Amanda?" he called a little louder as he moved back toward the stairs. Suddenly he wished he hadn't left her alone in the van. Not after everything they'd learned here.

He dropped the book and drew the weapon he'd taken from Amanda yesterday. Slowly, he crept down the hall toward the stairs. As he came to the corner, he heard the stairs at the top creak and saw a shadow spill across the landing floor. Not Amanda. Too tall and broad for her.

"Hello?" came a male voice, one he recognized just in time.

Hurriedly, he shoved the gun back into the waistband of his jeans and covered it with his shirt just as Sheriff Wilson topped the stairs.

"Ya know ya'll are trespassing?" the sheriff asked with obvious irritation.

"Just having a look around," Jesse said.

The sheriff nodded. "I heard you've been just looking around and asking a lot of questions, upsetting a lot of people."

Jesse wanted to take this conversation outside into

the sunlight, away from this house and everything in it, especially that presence that he'd felt, a presence like an albatross around his neck.

He did wonder, though, just who he'd been upsetting and why.

"Who are you and what business brings you to Red River?" Wilson demanded.

Jesse thought about telling the sheriff that he was a cop out of Dallas up here investigating the mob. But how would he explain Amanda? The last thing he wanted was the sheriff to know who she was. If the cop didn't already.

"Sheriff, I just learned that I might have been that mystery baby that was found around here thirty years ago." Jesse suspected he wasn't telling the sheriff anything he didn't already know. "I just want to find out who I am."

"No one around here knows. Or cares," the sheriff said with a coldness that surprised Jesse.

"My mother had to be one of the local girls—"

The sheriff was shaking his head. "Whoever left that baby wasn't from around here."

"How do you know that?" Jesse asked.

"You'll just have to take my word for it." The sheriff moved toward him, his hand on the butt of his weapon, a steely hardness in his eyes that made Jesse want to retreat a step.

"Jesse?" Amanda called from the floor below.

"Honey, I'm up here. I'll be right down," Jesse called out quickly. "My fiancée and I are on our way to get married in Oklahoma," he improvised and hoped Amanda went for it. "Her mama lives up there," he said loud enough he thought Amanda would hear.

He moved to get past the sheriff, but Wilson was a big man, thick through the chest with a head like a block of wood. The cop didn't budge and for a moment Jesse feared he wasn't going to.

"Jesse?" Amanda called again, definite concern in her voice.

"Up here, honey," he called again. "Stay there, I'm coming down. Those stairs are dangerous." He looked at the sheriff. "I thought it was important that I find out about myself before I got married," he said.

"Let me give you a little advice," the sheriff said quietly. "Some things are best left alone."

Jesse nodded. "I'm beginning to think you might be right about that."

"You can take it to the bank," the sheriff said and seemed relieved Jesse was seeing it his way. He stepped aside and let Jesse descend the steps to where Amanda waited, looking scared. She'd changed into other clothing from the back of the van. She now wore a silk shirt, slacks, sandals.

Jesse reached for her, realizing the sheriff was right behind him and could hear anything he said.

"Sorry, honey, I just got to looking around and lost track of time." He pulled Amanda into his arms. She came easily as if he'd held her like this a hundred times. "I guess we'd better get going if we hope to make your mama's before dark." He let go of her and stepped back, meeting her gaze.

"Where'd you say you were going in Oklahoma?" Sheriff Wilson asked Amanda.

"Lawton," she answered without hesitation, before shifting her gaze back to Jesse. "And we're going to be late, thanks to you. You know Mama's making dinner for us."

He put his arm around her shoulders and pulled her close, grateful she was such a quick study. "The last thing I want is to make your mama mad at me," he said with a laugh. Then he sobered as he glanced around the farmhouse. "Nothing here, anyway." Nothing but ghosts.

The sheriff settled his ham-size fists on his hips. "Glad to hear you're not planning to stay around," he said pointedly. "I assume you won't be coming back to Red River?"

Jesse shook his head. "We thought we'd honeymoon up north somewhere. Maybe Montana."

Sheriff Wilson nodded, his look colder than the inside of the old house as he walked past Jesse, headed for the door. "A good place for your kind."

Jesse felt a chill soul deep. His kind. "And what kind would that be, Sheriff?" he asked the cop's broad back.

But Sheriff Wilson either didn't hear, or didn't care to answer.

"Bastard," Amanda swore under her breath at the sheriff's retreating back.

Jesse walked her to the van without a word, opened the door for her, then climbed into the driver's seat. Sheriff Wilson stood by his car, watching them, waiting for them to leave.

"What the hell was that about?" Jesse demanded, looking over at Amanda. She had angry tears in her eyes.

"He thinks you're the son of a mobster," she said. She looked over at him. "Don't you see? My father was here asking about the baby. The sheriff thinks you're J. B. Crowe's son."

12

Jesse swore as he turned the van around and headed down the rutted path to the two-lane county road.

"I can see it in your face," Amanda said, her emotions raw and too close to the surface. Her chest ached from trying to hold back the well of feeling inside her. She wanted to strike out. Not at the sheriff. She'd met enough people like him in her life that she didn't care what he thought of her and her "kind." But Jesse—

"You're scared to death you might be the spawn of a mobster," she said, daring him to disagree.

He glanced over at her as he turned toward Red River and accelerated. The Texas sun-baked red dust kicked up behind the van, dark as a thunderhead.

Jesse's knuckles were white on the steering wheel, his jaw set in granite. She saw him glance in his rearview mirror, but she didn't need to turn to feel the sheriff's scornful gaze. She'd seen enough of them in her life.

"Frightening, isn't it," she said, her voice breaking. "After all the contempt you've had for me since the day you went to work for my father, just to think that you might have the same tainted blood as me."

He hit the brakes. The van went into a skid, coming to a stop in a cloud of red dust.

Before she could take a breath, he grabbed her and jerked her around to face him, his eyes dark with emotion. "You think I don't want to be related to you because of your genes?" he demanded loudly.

"Isn't that your greatest fear?" she cried, grabbing a handful of his shirt.

He let out a low growl, anger making his eyes as black as obsidian and just as bright. "Oh, yeah, that's a fear all right. I sure as hell don't want to be related to you. But not for the reasons you think."

She could see the pain in his eyes, his desire for her, his fear that she might always be forbidden to him. What surprised her was her own fear. She clung to his shirt, desperately wanting to tell him that he wasn't the only one hurting by this news.

He pushed her away from him before she could release her hold on his shirt. She heard the fabric tear and him let out a curse. Something fell out of his shirt pocket, making a slight tinkling sound as it dropped to the floor.

She watched him pick up the gold chain. It glistened for a moment in the sunlight. Long enough for her to see what dangled from the chain. She gasped at the sight of the unique-shaped heart, one she'd seen before.

He looked over at her. "What?" he demanded, sounding scared. "You recognize it?"

"My father has the other piece of the heart."

He stared at her, all his fears exploding like a bomb inside his head. "Your father has the *other* piece?"

She nodded. "He had the hearts made. There are only two like them in the world. They were made to fit together to form one heart. One perfect heart."

He barely heard her words, only the meaning behind them. His mother had put the gold heart in his blanket the night he was born and written a hurried note, hoping someone would find him. His father must have been the one who had left him in the box beside the road. The same man who had the matching gold heart.

"Then your father—"

She shook her head. "The heart belonged to my father's best friend." She seemed to pause as if for effect. "My father had the heart made for Billy Kincaid and the woman he was in love with."

"Billy Kincaid," he echoed.

"The Governor's little brother."

"The one who died," Jesse said.

She nodded. "When I was a little girl, I found a box with some old things in it. I was taken with the funny-shaped heart and my father told me the story."

They both turned at the sound of the vehicle coming up the road behind them. In the distance, the sun shimmered off the sheriff's car.

"Drive," she ordered. "We don't want another run-in with him."

Jesse couldn't have agreed more but he also desperately needed to know about the heart. He pulled back onto the road, his hands shaking. He wasn't J.B.'s son. He wasn't related to Amanda. Was she as relieved as he was? He glanced over at her.

She smiled and nodded. "I assume we are both relieved for the same reason."

"Both?"

She grinned. "Both."

"I also assume you want to hear about the heart first?" she asked.

"First?"

She laughed. "First." She glanced behind them. He followed her gaze. The sheriff's car had disappeared in their dust. "My father knew a jeweler and had the hearts made as a present for Billy and his girlfriend. He didn't want any others ever made like them so my father talked the jeweler into promising he never would. It was a promise I am sure the jeweler kept," she said knowingly.

Jesse had to agree.

"Billy and his girlfriend each wore one. The idea was that they would put the hearts together when they got married and he would put the one heart on her during the ceremony."

"But then Billy got killed."

She nodded. "Obviously before they could get married."

He drove through Red River almost without noticing and took the two-lane south, not sure where he was going, just far from the small Texas town.

"Who was the girlfriend?" he asked, holding his breath.

"My father never told me. I got the feeling that Billy had kept the romance quiet for some reason. I'm not even sure my father knew her well."

Was it possible J.B. hadn't known the girl was pregnant with Billy's son? He felt the skin on his neck prickle. The day J.B. had hired him—Jesse hadn't thought anything about it at the time. But J.B. had seemed in shock. Of course he would have been shocked; he'd believed his daughter had almost been killed by a hit-and-run driver.

But Jesse remembered now the way J.B. had stared at him. Almost as if the man had seen a ghost.

Ahead Jesse could see the outline of the town on the horizon. He'd be glad when it was in his rearview mirror.

"I know this sounds nuts, but I think your father recognized me that first day I went to work for him," Jesse said. "I think that's why he hired me, no questions asked. Why he left on a business trip the next day. He came to Red River. Started asking questions about me."

"That would explain the warm reception we've gotten here. I'm sure having a well-known mobster show up in town ruffled a few feathers, especially all the times my father's picture has been in the paper for one criminal investigation or another," she said.

He nodded. It would also explain J.B.'s fingerprints on the photocopy of the newspaper clipping. "Maybe he *didn't* know I existed until a couple of weeks ago. Or maybe he's the one who dumped the box beside the road for Billy, just assuming I would die."

"No," Amanda said with more force than he'd expected. "My father loved Billy like a brother. If he'd known about you, there isn't any way he would have allowed anything to happen to you, believe me. I know my father. He would have raised you himself."

He did believe her. "We have to find my mother," he said and looked over at her.

She nodded. "Jesse, I did lie about one thing."

The expression on her face almost made him drive off the road.

"I lied when I said I felt nothing but contempt for you." Leaning toward him, she put her hand on his thigh.

This time he did drive off the road. "Amanda?" He got the van under control again. "I'm a cop," he reminded her.

"And probably a Kincaid," she said. "And I'm a mobster's daughter. Nothing's really changed, has it?"

He shook his head. She was still dangerous and he still wanted her, wanted her more than he could have believed possible. "Nothing at all," he said and took the next side road down into the lush thick trees beside the river.

Her fingers trembled as she began to unbutton his shirt the moment he stopped the van beside the river.

"Amanda?"

"I need you, Jesse. I need you to hold me. To make love to me."

She touched a finger to his lips and shook her head. She knew all the reasons they shouldn't make love and one very good reason they should. As she slipped each button free, she exposed more of his muscular chest, his broad shoulders. Dark hair formed a V like an arrow to the waistband of his jeans. Desire stole through her, leaving a trail of heat to her center.

She wanted this man. Wanted his arms around her. Wanted to feel his bare skin pressed to hers. Wanted him in a primitive, carnal way, to possess and be possessed. And had for a long time.

That in itself scared her. She had never let any man close to her. Certainly not Gage, even though he'd fathered her baby.

With Jesse, it would be total surrender.

He looked at her as if afraid to touch her for fear of what they would do together, both wanting the same thing, both fearing it.

She leaned over and kissed him, her lips barely brushing his. "I think there's a blanket in the back," she whispered.

The river lapped at the shore under a canopy of green leaves. He spread the blanket on the grass. Water pooled next to the bank. He looked at her, the desire in his gaze almost as pleasurable as the anticipation of his touch.

He reached out to undo the top button on her shirt, his fingers grazing her skin. His eyes never left hers as he undid the next button, then the next.

Her heart pounded as he slipped the shirt from her shoulders and let it drop to the blanket, then slipped off one strap of her bra, then the other. Her nipples pressed hard and insistent against the thin cloth. She reached behind to unhook the bra. It fell to the blanket.

Jesse moaned at the sight of her round, full breasts dappled in sunlight. She stepped to him and pulled his shirt off. He hesitated only a moment before he drew her to him, skin to skin, wrapping his arms around her, holding her. He told himself this wasn't happening. He'd wanted it too badly. He could feel her heart, its emphatic beat keeping time with his own. He looked down at her. And wondered why she was giving herself to him.

Not for the reason he would have hoped, that much he knew. But did it matter?

She leaned up to kiss him, her kiss heated. She pulled away to shuck off the rest of her clothing, seemingly as anxious to make love to him as he was to her.

He watched her, enthralled, completely captivated as she stripped, then dove into the pool of water, droplets momentarily suspended in the air around her, her skin silky as the water that rippled over it.

"Are you joining me?" she called.

He took off his clothes, the ledger falling from his pocket onto the blanket. Then he followed her into the water.

The pool was waist deep, the water wonderfully cool,

the bottom a fine sand. He moved to her, pulling her into his arms, feeling her nakedness against his own. He dropped his mouth to hers. Her lips parted, welcoming him, as her body pressed to his and he enveloped her, the way the water enveloped them both.

His kiss left her breathless, the taste of him on her lips, the scent of him branded in her memory. She watched as he cupped the cool water in his hands and poured it over her breasts, letting it run down her belly to her navel, to the golden V between her legs. His mouth followed the path of the water.

Then he swept her up in his arms and carried her to the blanket beside the river. He made love to her, slowly, deliberately, passionately. She opened to him, surrendering to his touch, giving herself to him in a way she knew she would never give to another man.

He took her to dizzying heights, and finally crying out, she reached the zenith with him. She clung to him, tears blurring her vision at the realization that she would never see Jesse again after tonight.

He left her sated, sensuously serene, his body lying next to hers, the air around them cooling as he drifted off, holding her in his arms.

She waited, listening to his soft, steady breathing, the sound of the sighing boughs overhead and the murmur of the river. Then she looked over on the blanket to where the ledger had fallen out of his pocket.

She felt the serenity evaporate the way the water had on her skin, the way the sweat from their lovemaking had. She checked her watch. Earlier, while Jesse had been in the old Duncan place, she'd called Gage. The trade was set for tonight at an old bridge outside of Dallas. She could take off now, hide out and make the trade. Without Jesse. Just as she'd planned.

Carefully, she slipped from his arms and crawled over to the ledger. In the shade of the tree, she opened the small bound pages, her father's handwriting filling her with conflicting emotions. Through her tears, she saw that handwriting on all the cards he'd given her over the years, all the presents with loving notes attached, all the checks signed to her, gifts he'd given from the heart. And in this book, she saw his other life, the illegal, dishonest, deceitful, horrible one. She'd known some of his business dealings were illegal. She just hadn't known the extent of it.

She closed the book and sat looking down at it, remembering her plan to take the ledger and leave without Jesse, her plan to do this alone. Then she looked over at him. He was still sleeping, his dark eyes closed, his chest rising and falling. She felt a catch in her throat— in her heart. She thought of the little baby left beside the road. Of the man who'd saved her life last night. Of their lovemaking.

She couldn't fall for a cop. Let alone a Kincaid. Could she?

With a silent curse, she put the ledger back where she'd found it and, fighting the urge to curl up again in his arms, headed for the river to bathe before they had to leave.

Jesse opened one eye and watched her. He smiled to himself as he saw her change her mind and put the ledger back and walk into the cool water of the river. He had never seen a more beautiful woman. His heart convulsed at the sight of her, at her trust in him. They would make the trade together. But then she would take Susannah and leave the country. He'd lied to himself, believing making love to her once would be enough. Not one time, one day or one lifetime would be enough of this woman.

He watched her glide through the water, her naked body glistening in the sunlight, then he rose and followed her into the river. They still had a little time before they had to leave.

13

The sun left the sky infused with color as it sank into the horizon. Amanda changed the plates on the van from Texas plates to the Louisiana ones she had in the back. She stuck a couple of bumper stickers on the back: Proud to Be a Grandma and This Van Stops at Garage Sales, then she slapped up some gaudy stick-on blinds at the windows.

"Looks like a different van, doesn't it?" she said as she considered her handiwork. "I figured Sheriff Wilson called in the plates. Anyone looking for us will be searching for a tan van with Texas plates."

Jesse had to agree the van looked entirely different.

"Who do you think is looking for us?" he asked.

She shrugged. "Maybe no one. But there's no reason to take a chance. Not when I'm this close to making the trade for my daughter."

Jesse didn't buy it. He wondered who had her worried. Probably her father. Maybe Gage. Or whoever owned that dark car with the knocking engine.

"At least I know the van is clean," she said. "I checked it myself for tracking devices before we left Dallas." She produced a small box from the glove compartment.

"This detects any kind of bug or foreign electronic device, including a G.P.S."

He nodded and smiled. "Electrical engineering, huh?"

She shrugged. "I always liked gadgets. I rewired the intercom in the house when I was a teenager so my father couldn't spy on me. Getting around Daddy's expensive security system is child's play."

He doubted that.

On the edge of Dallas, he glanced in his rearview mirror, something he'd done so many times without incident that he almost dismissed the car coming up fast behind them.

"Get down!" he ordered, reaching for Amanda before going for the gun at his waist.

He pushed her to the floorboard as a dark-colored, expensive car closed the distance between them.

"Who is it?" she asked, her voice cracking.

He could see the fear in her eyes and knew she was worried that J.B.'s goons would find her and keep her from making the trade. "I don't know yet."

Jesse flipped up the rearview mirror and leaned back so his reflection couldn't be seen in the side mirror, either. "Just stay down." The car looked familiar. He laid the gun on his thigh, being careful to keep his speed the same.

The car following him swung out into the passing lane, then sped by as if Jesse were standing still. Jesse sat back as it zoomed past. There were at least three guys in the car.

"They're gone," he said and looked over. Amanda had moved to the back of the van and must have been looking out the tinted side window.

"I recognized one of them," she said as she climbed back into the front seat.

"One of Mickie Ferraro's men, right?" He'd heard the engine's distinctive knock as the car sped past. "It was the same vehicle that tried to run you down just last night in Dallas."

She stared at him. "Why?"

"For the ledger, I would imagine."

"But how—I know what you're thinking. Gage wouldn't—"

"The hell he wouldn't," Jesse snapped. "Who else knew about the trade?"

"The kidnapper."

"You really don't believe Mickie Ferraro is working with the Governor now?" he asked.

She fell silent. "It can't be Gage. He's determined to make the trade."

"But he doesn't need you. In fact, if you were dead, he would get Susannah, right?"

"He'd have to fight my father," she said. "There would be bloodshed but—" She seemed to hesitate. "It *would* put Mickie right where he wants to be with the Organization."

Jesse's head snapped around as he looked over at her, his eyes widening. "If something happened to you, your father would go to war with whoever he thought was behind your murder, right?"

She nodded.

"But wouldn't he suspect Kincaid rather than Mickie Ferraro?"

She seemed to pale. "You're worried about the trade tonight, aren't you?"

"Damned right, I am. I've been worried since the cops

showed up at the last one. Dirty cops, I'd wager. Except I don't believe they were your father's."

"What can we do?" she asked quietly.

We. Making love to Amanda had done nothing to exorcize the desire he'd felt for her. Instead, the desire had become a force to be reckoned with as if it had taken on a life of its own. He wanted more than ever to be her gallant knight and slay all her dragons. Especially that big, ugly one, Gage Ferraro and his hoodlum father.

He watched the road ahead, still worried that the car with the men might be waiting for them.

"I think Gage is too smart to try to pull something like that again," she said. "He wants the ledger too badly."

And why was that, Jesse wondered. To save his daughter? That didn't sound like the Gage Ferraro he knew. Nor did Jesse believe Gage was trying to get into J. B. Crowe's good graces. What *was* going on?

Whatever it was, Amanda and her baby's life hung in the balance.

He found a side road, one that would skirt around Dallas, and took it.

"Where are we going?" Amanda asked.

"I have to talk to Kincaid," he said, knowing she wasn't going to like it.

"Kincaid? You have to be kidding. Do you really think he'll even let you in the door?"

"I think he will, once he sees me," Jesse said. "I have a feeling I resemble my father."

"What makes you think that?" she asked.

"Your father's initial reaction to me," he said. "I misunderstood it that day I first met him."

"I assume my near accident was a setup?" she asked.

He didn't like the edge to her voice. "I'm a cop."

"So all is fair in the fight of good to overcome evil?" she asked.

He shot her a look, realizing that the lines had blurred considerably for him over the last few days. "I won't apologize for trying to bring down your father, but I was wrong to paint you with the same dirty brush." He reached for her hand and squeezed it. "If you don't want to see Kincaid—"

"No," she said. "I do." Her voice broke. "I want to make a plea for my baby."

"What if he didn't take her?" Jesse had to ask.

She said nothing, just stared out the windshield, as he drove south to Austin and the capitol.

It took several phone calls to find the governor once they reached Austin, then the person who answered the call refused to put Jesse through.

"Tell the governor it's about a close relative of his," Jesse said. A few moments later, Governor Thomas Kincaid came on the line. Jesse was sure the call was being traced.

"Yes?" Kincaid said, sounding old and tired and scared.

"I need to talk to you in person," Jesse said.

"What is this about?" Kincaid asked.

"You'll know when you see me," Jesse said.

Kincaid didn't hesitate long. "You know where I live?"

Everyone knew where the governor's mansion was. "I'm just around the corner. I can be there in two minutes. I think it's best if we come in through the back."

"We?" Kincaid asked.

Jesse felt an arrow of guilt pierce his heart. Kincaid thought this was about his daughter Diana. "Two minutes." He hung up and looked at Amanda. She looked scared. She still believed that Kincaid was behind the kidnapping of her daughter. She must feel as if they were going into the lion's den.

He took her hand. "We're in."

She gave him a tentative smile. "I hope you're right about this."

"Me, too," he said. "But I'll get us back out of there if I'm not. One way or another."

Kincaid met them at the back door, just as Jesse figured he would. Several "suits" stood in the shadows, obviously armed.

The governor looked as if he hadn't slept for days. Jesse knew he probably hadn't. The older man's gaze went first to Amanda, his eyes widening in surprise. Then he looked at Jesse. For a moment Jesse thought he might faint.

"Can we come in?" Jesse said. "We need to talk to you."

Kincaid stumbled back, motioning to the men that everything was fine, when Jesse knew it wasn't. All the color had gone out of the governor's face and his hand trembled as he opened a door and ushered them into what appeared to be a TV room, furnished with comfortable chairs and a large-screen television.

"Who are you?" Kincaid asked dropping into a chair, his gaze never leaving Jesse's face.

Jesse sat down next to Amanda on the love seat. He took her hand. Now that he was here, he didn't know where to begin. But Kincaid's reaction resolved any questions he might have had about his resemblance to his father.

"I believe I'm your nephew," he said. "Billy's son."

Kincaid leaned back in his chair and glanced at Amanda, distrust in his expression.

"Let me explain," Jesse said, realizing he had to lay all of his cards on the table. "My name is Jesse McCall. I'm a cop. An undercover cop. I've been working as J. B. Crowe's chauffeur the last couple of weeks." He filled Kincaid in on everything, including what he'd learned in Red River.

Kincaid shook his head as if in shock. "I'll admit the resemblance is uncanny but—"

Jesse pulled the gold heart from his jeans pocket and held it out to the governor. The older man's reaction erased any doubt.

"Oh, my God," Kincaid said, tears filling his eyes.

"My adoptive parents found this heart in my baby blanket," Jesse said. "I need to know who my mother is. I need to know what happened and how I ended up beside that dirt road."

"I didn't know she was pregnant. Billy never told me. But I did know how he felt about her. I never met her. Billy and I...well we were at odds over his involvement with—" He glanced toward Amanda.

"Billy and my father were best friends," she said haughtily. "Billy's death changed my father's life."

Kincaid nodded, no doubt thinking how his little brother's death had changed his, as well. He looked to Jesse. "If I had known about you, I wouldn't have let anything happen to you."

Jesse believed him. "What was my mother's name?"

"Roxie. Roxie Pickett."

"Is she still alive?" Jesse asked.

Kincaid shook his head. "She died two days after my brother. She killed herself."

Jesse felt as if the floor had fallen out from under him. For a moment he couldn't speak. "Her parents?"

"I think they still live in the old neighborhood," Kincaid said, his tone implying it was the same one where he and Billy and J.B. were raised. "I think the father's name was Frank. Frank Pickett. It's been so long. I can't remember the wife's name."

Kincaid stared at him, obviously in shock. "You look so much like Billy." He looked ill, not powerful, not frightening.

Jesse could see that Amanda had lost some of the anger in her expression. She just looked scared for her baby.

"I need to ask you about another child," Jesse said. "Susannah Crowe, Amanda's six-month-old baby."

Kincaid's gaze flicked to Amanda. "Your daughter is missing?"

"I wouldn't think that comes as a surprise."

Kincaid looked back to Jesse. "It does make things clearer though."

Jesse nodded. "Like her father, Amanda believes you're behind the kidnapping because the kidnapper is demanding evidence against J. B. Crowe."

Kincaid closed his eyes for a moment. When he opened them, they swam in tears. "I understand your frustration, Ms. Crowe. My daughter and her unborn baby are also missing. But I did not have your baby kidnapped. I wish there was some way I could make you believe that. Make your father believe that, if it is not too late for my daughter. I pray it is not too late for your daughter, as well."

Amanda stared at him, looking numb.

Jesse couldn't tell if she believed the governor or not. It didn't matter really what any of them believed. "I plan to find out who kidnapped Susannah Crowe," Jesse warned Kincaid. "If you're involved I will bring you down no matter who you are."

Kincaid nodded solemnly.

Jesse and Amanda rose. Kincaid pushed himself to his feet. He seemed awkward as if he didn't know what to say but didn't want Jesse to leave either. He held out his hand. Jesse shook it, feeling a strength that assured him his uncle would be fine. His uncle. That would take some getting used to.

"Will I see you again?" Kincaid said.

"Yes." Jesse followed Amanda to the door. "When this is all over, we'll both come back."

Frank and Molly Pickett lived in a neighborhood of Dallas that had seen better days. Rusted-out cars balanced wheelless on blocks, garbage cluttered the gutters and graffiti defiled the faces of the weathered buildings.

Amanda tried to imagine her father growing up here, let alone Kincaid. She shivered at the thought of the children who still grew up here and thought of Kincaid's programs to replace these neighborhoods with homes for the poor. She'd always thought his plan was political. Now she wasn't so sure.

"The van probably won't be here when we get back," Amanda noted as Jesse parked in front of the address he'd found in the phone book.

"Do you have some money?" he asked her. "A twenty and a fifty?"

She gave him a questioning look, but dug out the bills and handed them to him, then climbed out of the van after him.

Jesse approached one of the young men sitting on a stoop in the shade. "See this twenty?" he said to the man. "I have a fifty for you as well if I come back and that van hasn't been touched. It's better than what you're going to get from the guys who steal or strip these cars."

The man smiled at that and took the twenty. "Don't be long."

Amanda knew Jesse had no intention of being any longer than necessary. She could feel his tension when he put his hand on her back and led her up the stairs. She felt uneasy and knew it wasn't just the neighborhood that was making her feel that way.

Jesse rang the buzzer on the apartment marked Pickett. The sun beat down in waves of heat while a putrid stench rose from the rainwater and garbage lying stagnant in the gutter.

"Yes?" came an older female voice.

"Mrs. Pickett?" Jesse asked.

"Yes?" came the hesitant answer.

He looked at Amanda as if he didn't know what to say.

"We're friends of the family and just wanted to stop by," Amanda said into the speaker.

Silence. Then the crackle of the speaker. "Come on up, then," the woman said and buzzed them in.

Jesse shot her a look of gratitude and Amanda smiled, wanting to touch his face, hold him in her arms. She'd never felt like this about a man before. Safe. Protected. Cared for. And yet part of her held back, afraid. Afraid of the future. Some things were just too good to be true. And Jesse McCall was one of them.

At 2A, Jesse knocked. Inside the apartment came the sound of a radio. Jesse knocked again.

The door swung open. A small, white-haired woman appeared wiping her hands on the apron she wore. The apron was a bright, multicolored fruit pattern and each time she wiped her hands, she left a white flour handprint on the cloth.

"Sorry, I didn't hear your knock," she said and smiled cheerfully as she pushed open the door. "Come on in. I was just baking a pie." She turned on her heel and led them inside.

Amanda shot Jesse a look, taken aback by the woman's friendliness as they followed her into the kitchen.

"It's going to be a scorcher," the woman commented as they trailed her into the large homey kitchen where she picked up the rolling pin she had discarded and began to work at the golden dough on the floured board. The room felt warm and smelled of apples. "And it's only spring."

The apartment was surprisingly nice inside with a feeling that the people who lived here had no intention of ever moving again.

Amanda had never lived in a home like this. It tugged at something deep inside her. She spotted a photograph on the top of a buffet and glanced over at Jesse.

Jesse had seen the photo the moment he walked into the room. It was a young girl. He wondered if it was Roxie Pickett or some other little girl, maybe a sister.

"We're sorry to bother you—" Jesse began.

"Oh, it's no bother at all." The elderly woman looked

up then, meeting his gaze. "You say you're a friend of the family?"

He'd hoped, he realized, that she would recognize him. She didn't seem to. "Possibly even a distant relative. That's why we're here. To find out."

Molly seemed fine with that. "Everyone just calls me Molly," she said. "Nice to have a little company. Hardly ever see anyone. I'm sorry I don't have the pie done or I would offer you a piece."

"That isn't necessary," Jesse managed to say. "But it is a nice offer."

For a moment, he watched her work the crust, rolling it with practiced expertise until it was thin and smooth, the edges round. He had so many questions, he didn't know where to begin.

"I need to ask you about your side of the family," he said.

She smiled. "I'll tell you what I can."

He took a breath. "You're married to Frank Pickett, right?"

She nodded. "Have been for more than forty years," she said proudly.

"And your children?" he asked and immediately regretted it.

Her face clouded over for a moment, then cleared. "Had one daughter, but she died. Just had the one."

"And her name was Roxie?"

Molly looked up and appeared surprised. "That's right. Roxanna Lynn but everyone called her Roxie."

Jesse felt his heart pounding. "I suppose you have some pictures of her?"

Molly studied him as she wiped her hands again on her apron. "You want to see her?"

"Very much so," he said.

She seemed to hesitate, but only for a moment. "I have a photo of her on the buffet, but some more recent ones are in here." Jesse and Amanda followed the woman into a bedroom. "This was taken not long before—" she looked up "—when she was sixteen."

Jesse took the photograph in the tarnished frame and felt his heart hammer against his ribs. His mother. She took his breath way. Beautiful dark eyes, long dark hair. The face of an angel. Tears filled his eyes.

Noticing his reaction, Molly took the framed photo from him. "Will you tell me what this is about?" she asked, her voice sounding weak, scared.

His throat seemed to close. All he could do was stare at the other photographs on the wall. Many of Roxie. One when she was about eleven, standing holding up a fish for the camera, her eyes bright, a smile on her face.

Amanda saved him. "Mrs. Pickett—"

"Molly."

"Molly, your daughter had a baby just before she died," Amanda said.

Molly's gaze swung to Amanda's, but she said nothing.

"We need to know about the baby," Amanda said.

"There is nothing to tell," Molly said. "The baby died."

Fishing. Jesse realized most all of the photographs on the wall were of fish. Roxie at varying ages. Alone and with a man, a man who looked like her. Roxie's father. Frank Pickett. Jesse stepped closer to study the man in the snapshot, asking himself what he'd come here for. He knew now who his birth parents had been. Even his grandfather, he thought studying the picture.

Jesse only half listened to Amanda trying to talk to Molly about the baby as he dragged his gaze from the man's face to the cabin behind him and the weathered sign over the cabin door. He was trying to read the words, when something else drew his attention. Off to his right was a photograph of Roxie in her teens. Around her neck she wore a gold chain. The unusual heart dangled from the end.

"We know the baby didn't die," he heard Amanda say and turned his attention back to the room and the elderly woman wringing her hands in her apron.

Molly dropped into a chair. "You're wrong. The baby was born dead." She began to cry. "Frank was there. He said it was God's will, a baby conceived in sin, by a man like that."

"A man like that? You knew the father then? The man she was dating?"

Molly shook her head looking confused. "Roxie was only sixteen. She wasn't allowed to date. She met him secretly. Frank saw the heart around her neck—" She began to cry again. "He found out who'd had the heart made, then he knew who the father was, the father of this child born before its time."

"The baby came early?" Amanda asked in surprise. "Then the baby was born here in the house?"

Molly shook her head. "At Roxie's friend's next door." She got to her feet. "I have to finish dinner. My husband will be home from fishing soon. None of this matters anymore."

"I'm that baby," Jesse said, finally finding the words.

Molly swung around to face him, her eyes wide. Slowly she lowered herself into a chair again. "That isn't possible."

"I'm afraid it is," he said. Couldn't she see her daughter in him? Something around the eyes? He reached into his pocket and withdrew the heart. He held it out to her.

Molly gasped and put her hands over her mouth, her eyes huge above her fingers.

"The night he was born, someone wrapped him in a blanket and put him in a cardboard box," Amanda said, kneeling before the woman. "Roxie had just enough time to write a note and put it and the heart into the baby blanket. Then someone took the child away and left him in the box beside a dirt road north of here near Red River. Only, he was found before he could die."

Molly seemed to be gasping for breath. "Please go," she whimpered. "I don't want you upsetting my husband with all this."

"Let's go," Jesse said and took Amanda's arm to help her to her feet. "She doesn't want to hear this. And it doesn't matter who left me there. I found out what I needed to know."

"But Jesse—"

"Please," he said meeting Amanda's gaze. "Let's just get out of here."

She nodded, tears in her eyes. For a woman who didn't care about justice, she'd certainly tried hard to at least get at the truth for him.

He wanted to take her in his arms and hold her and thank her and make love to her again. And again. She was in his system now and he wondered how he could ever get her out. If he could bear to even try.

As he and Amanda came out of the apartment, Jesse felt numb. He'd gotten what he'd come for. Almost. He still didn't know who had left him beside the road. But what did it matter really? Maybe whoever had delivered him really did believe he was dead. Or maybe not.

He put his arm around Amanda as they descended the steps into the hot, horrible-smelling street. They'd found one baby. Now they had to find hers. Jesse promised himself that he could at least give Amanda the justice she deserved. He would get her daughter back and bring the kidnapper in. No matter who he was.

The van was still there. The young man was sitting guard on the steps halfway down. He didn't say a word, just held out his hand. Jesse put the fifty into his open palm as he and Amanda passed.

The feeling came out of the blue. That distinct prickle at the back of his neck. His feet had just touched the sidewalk, when he heard the screech of tires and a familiar engine knock.

"Get down!" he yelled as he dragged Amanda to the concrete behind the van. The sound of gunfire echoed off the buildings as the car sped past.

Jesse got off two shots. One took out the back window of the dark-green car. The other made a hollow sound as it pierced the trunk lid. Behind him, he heard the young man on the steps take off at a dead run.

14

Amanda rose slowly from the ground. "That was Mickie's men again, wasn't it?"

"Yes," Jesse agreed, opening the van door. The side of the van was riddled with holes. "Get in and stay down."

She slid in with him close behind.

He started the van and flipped around to go in the opposite direction. "They have some way of tracking us. It's the only thing that makes sense. Sheriff Wilson might have called in the plates on the van, alerting those cops who tried to arrest us the other night. Somehow they got to this van."

He drove a few miles, then pulled over. "You have a way of checking for a bug, right?"

She nodded, opened the glove box and pulled out her gear. She found the bug within a few minutes. "Someone would have had to put it on while we were in the Corral Bar talking to Huey. I should have checked the van again."

She tore the bug from the undercarriage of the van and smashed it, then climbed back in. Suddenly a thought hit her. "What if Mickie Ferraro has a very good reason for not wanting me to make the trade?" she asked when Jesse got back in.

He glanced over at her. "The ledger. You think there is something in there that incriminates him as well as your father?"

Her heart began to beat a little faster. "There has to be. But how does Mickie know about the ledger and the trade?"

"Those cops who tried to bust us last night," Jesse said. "They might work for Gage. Or they might also be on Mickie's payroll if the money is right. One of them could have spilled the beans about a ledger they were supposed to get from you—and where."

That would explain how Mickie's men had found her and almost run her down. "You don't think Gage—"

"Is hoping to get rid of both J.B. and his father and take over their territory?" Jesse asked sarcastically.

She leaned back in her seat, trying to figure all of the angles as Jesse drove toward the old Ballantine Bridge and the trade with the kidnapper.

"The only way it makes sense is if Kincaid is behind the kidnapping," she pointed out. "Kincaid could bust my father and Mickie and clear the way for Gage."

"Unless Gage is behind the kidnapping," Jesse said quietly.

She looked over at him, her heart pounding. Better than anyone, she knew what Gage was capable of. But not the kidnapping of his own child.

"He might want the ledger as insurance," Jesse said. "With it, he would control both J.B. and his father."

That was one possibility she didn't want to even consider. She would rather have believed Kincaid was behind the kidnapping. But she had to admit he'd confused her earlier when they'd talked to him. He didn't seem the kind of man who could kidnap an infant, but then her father didn't seem like the kind of man who could steal babies and sell them in the black market, either.

She tried not to think of Susannah. Or babies left in cardboard boxes beside dirt roads or sold on the black market. She'd convinced herself that Susannah's kidnapper would take good care of her daughter. That any kidnapper who took J. B. Crowe's granddaughter knew better than to harm the child.

But at the same time, she couldn't imagine anyone arrogant enough to mess with her mobster father and his family. That was another reason she was convinced the kidnapper had to be Kincaid. As governor, Kincaid might feel bulletproof.

But Gage had been furious at being exiled to Chicago. And equally furious with her.

Gage could be behind Susannah's kidnapping as much as she didn't want to believe it.

"You might be right," she said. "We might be dealing with Gage."

"Better than Mickie and friends. We're almost to the bridge."

"I'm frightened, Jesse," she admitted.

He smiled over at her, reaching out to cup her cheek in his hand. "Don't worry, I have a plan."

Now more than ever, he was convinced Gage had to be behind the kidnapping. It was the only thing that made any sense.

He drove toward the old bridge, anything but calm about the trade. Amanda had repeated the instructions Gage had given her earlier. Jesse had little option but to follow them.

It was her daughter's life at risk. He would do everything he could to protect her and Susannah, but without police backup. Alone. He had no other choice. He'd be afraid to involve the police even if she'd have let him. He no longer knew who he could trust.

And he desperately wanted the kidnapper. Wanted to nail the bastard. No matter what Amanda said about not caring if the man was brought to justice. Would she change her mind if the man was Gage Ferraro?

He looked over at her, wishing there was something more to say. It didn't help the ache in his chest at just the sight of her.

The Trinity River was running full from spring runoff. Water rushed between its banks, dark waves hurling tree limbs and debris downstream.

Ballantine Bridge was an old county bridge about twenty miles out of Dallas, a long span of steel covered with rotting boards over the Trinity River. The bridge had been closed to the public for years. A metal crossbar over each end allowed only pedestrian traffic—mostly fishermen.

Jesse stopped a good mile from the bridge, pulling the van off the road into a stand of dense trees. He could see the river through the branches, the water brown with silt and moving fast. He took one of the weapons, checked the clip on the other and handed it to her.

She stared down at the gun. "I'm not going to need this."

"Better safe than sorry. Put it in the waistband of your jeans in the back. Your jacket will cover it."

"I told you, Jesse, I don't care about the kidnapper," she repeated. "I just want my daughter."

"That's what I want too, sweetheart," he assured her. "But sometimes things go wrong."

"Nothing better go wrong."

He nodded at her warning and handed her the ledger from his jacket pocket.

She took it, her hands trembling.

"If it came down to catching the kidnapper or saving Susannah, you know I would let the kidnapper get away, don't you?" he asked.

She looked into his eyes and nodded, then leaned over to kiss his lips. He pulled her to him, holding her tightly as he deepened the kiss, overpowered by the taste and feel of her. A live wire of desire shot through him. Lord, how he wanted her. Reluctantly, he let her go.

"We'll get your baby back," he said to her, his palm cupping her cheek.

She nodded, tears in her eyes. "I know."

He wanted to tell her what he was feeling, but he couldn't even put it into coherent thoughts for himself, let alone words for her.

"Jesse—" She seemed to stop herself. "Be careful."

He nodded. "You, too. I'll be there when you need me." But even as he said the words, he knew that wouldn't always be true. He was a cop. She was a mobster's daughter. Once Amanda got her daughter back, she planned to skip the country. Jesse had no intention of spending the rest of his life on the run. After tonight, it would be over between them.

His heart ached at the mere thought, but he only had himself to blame. He'd done the worst thing he could have: he'd made love to her. And now the memory of their lovemaking would haunt him forever. He couldn't imagine the day he wouldn't want her, wouldn't remember her scent or the feel of her skin.

He climbed out of the van, stuffed the weapon into his

waistband and waited for her to slide behind the wheel before he closed the door. "Give me twenty minutes."

She nodded, and he turned and hurried off into the woods, telling himself that the next time he saw her, she would have her baby back.

Amanda waited, counting off the minutes with the steady thump of her heart. Finally she would get to see her daughter. To hold her baby in her arms again. To put all of this behind them.

But she didn't kid herself. She knew she would also be putting Jesse behind her. He wouldn't be going with her and Susannah. It shocked her how much that realization hurt. She had fallen so hard, so fast for a man who was all wrong for her. A cop. It was almost laughable. She couldn't have done worse. Even Gage would have been preferable in the world she'd grown up in.

But Jesse McCall was exactly the kind of man she wanted as a father for Susannah. Exactly the kind of man she'd dreamed of for herself, although she'd never imagined that such passion could exist between two people. Nor did she kid herself that she could ever find a man like Jesse or that kind of passion again.

The waiting was torture. When twenty minutes had gone by, she started the van and drove down the narrow gravel road. The river ran entwined in the trees off to her left. She followed it, approaching the bridge slowly, her heart in her throat. A half-dozen fears clouded her thoughts, fears for Susannah. Fears for Jesse. She couldn't bear the thought of losing either of them. But then she reminded herself, Jesse wasn't hers to lose.

The bridge glittered dully in the dying light. Dust settled deep and dark along the river's edge. Tree limbs drooped into the rushing water, pockets of darkness pooled beneath them as the daylight slipped away.

She brought the van to a stop just before the bridge, just as she'd been instructed, turned off the engine and climbed out. Across the expanse of steel and rotting timbers, she could see another vehicle parked on the other side. The car door opened. A man stepped out. He held a bundle in his arms.

She felt her heart leap. It took everything in her not to run across the bridge to him and rip her child from his arms. She listened intently for the sound of her baby, cooing, even crying. Any indication that Susannah was finally within reach.

But she heard nothing over the sound of the water surging under the bridge as she ducked under the barricade and started across. On the other side, the man did the same. They were to meet in the middle and make the exchange. She gripped the ledger in her hand and walked toward him.

As she grew closer, she could make out his features. She wasn't surprised that she didn't recognize him. Kincaid would use someone she didn't know. So would Gage. Not that it mattered now who'd kidnapped Susannah. Just as long as Amanda got her baby back, safe and sound.

But as she walked across the old bridge, the boards making a hollow sound beneath her soles, something cold and hard settled in her stomach, a fear she couldn't shake off. What if she was wrong? What if the person who had her baby wasn't going to give Susannah up easily?

She didn't dare look around for Jesse. She didn't dare stop walking. She could feel the gun digging into her back but she knew she wouldn't draw it, wouldn't fire it. Even though she'd learned to shoot, she'd never used a weapon against anything more than a paper outline of a man.

She was almost to the man when he stopped.

"Where is the ledger?" he called out to her.

She held it up for him to see.

"Lay it down and back up," he ordered. "I'll take it and leave the baby."

"No," she said, surprising him and herself. "We make the trade, eye to eye."

He shook his head. "No. You want the baby? Then you do it my way."

She took a breath. Susannah was so close, so close. She swallowed. What choice did she have but to trust him? She'd come this far. "All right." Hands shaking, she put the ledger down on the wooden boards that spanned across the bridge supports. Through a crack, she could see the river raging far below her. She felt dizzy and sick to her stomach with fear.

Slowly she backed up, one step at a time. The man waited until she had retreated a good distance before he advanced. She felt her heart thundering in her chest, her pulse so loud she couldn't hear the river anymore.

He approached the ledger lying on the boards, appearing wary. Carefully, he put the baby down, scooped up the ledger, took a quick look inside, then turned his back and began to walk quickly back to his car.

She could wait no longer. She took off at a run, tears blinding her, a cry in her throat as she rushed to her baby daughter.

Jesse slowly approached the vehicle on the far side of the river. He could see a man hunched down in the seat, hiding, waiting. For what? He had watched the first man cross the bridge to meet Amanda, carrying the baby in his arms, and waited, not about to do anything until Amanda had Susannah and the two were safe.

Once the man put down the baby and moved away, Jesse knew he had only a few seconds to get to the second man in the vehicle before the first man started back. If he could disable the man in the car, it would even the odds and keep the men from possibly reneging on the trade.

It bothered Jesse that the first man had taken no precaution to keep from being recognized in a police lineup. Were they so sure that Amanda would never press charges? Or were they planning never to give her the chance?

The moment the man surrendered the baby, Jesse moved quickly up the right side of the car. His hand had just closed over the door handle when he heard Amanda scream, a blood-chilling scream that set his heart pumping.

The man in the car sat up with a jerk and threw open his door. Jesse barely got out of the way before the man leapt from the car. Jesse recognized him instantly. Gage Ferraro.

Gage didn't even see Jesse behind him. All of his attention was on the bridge. Before Jesse could react, Gage took off running toward the first man—and Amanda.

With a curse, Jesse went after him, his heart in his throat. Was something wrong with the baby? Oh, dear God, don't let Susannah be dead.

Gage didn't seem to hear Jesse behind him over the rush of the water. Amanda had dropped to her knees in the middle of the bridge. The baby seemed to roll out of her arms. Her scream still echoed off the steel girders.

The first man was running hard back toward Gage and the car, the ledger in his hand. Jesse watched in horror as Amanda straightened and reached behind her.

The shot reverberated across the river. The man with the ledger jerked, stumbled and fell face first onto the bridge.

For a moment, Jesse thought she'd shoot Gage as well, but she lowered the gun as he ran toward her as if she thought he was running to her. If she did, she was dead wrong.

Gage rushed to the downed man, grabbed the ledger from the dead man's hand and turned around, already moving back toward Jesse before he saw him.

The look on Gage's face gave him away as much as his actions. Jesse saw Gage go for his gun. Jesse hadn't even realized it, but he already had his weapon in his hand. Amanda was still on her knees, out of his line of fire. He raised his gun, almost in slow motion and squeezed off a shot, then another. He could hear Amanda scream, "No!" A shot whizzed by Jesse's left ear and pinged off the steel girders.

Gage lost his grip on his gun as he fell. The weapon hit the worn boards of the bridge before Gage did and skittered off, dropping over the side into the river.

Gage was trying to get up as Jesse ran to him.

"Don't kill him!" Amanda was screaming. She'd gotten to her feet and had run toward them. She still had the gun in her hand and what at first looked like a baby dangling from the other. But as she drew closer, Jesse saw that it was a doll. Not Susannah, but a doll.

Jesse jerked Gage up to a sitting position. Gage had

taken a bullet in his side; he'd survive. The second shot had grazed his arm. "Where is Susannah?" Jesse demanded.

Gage shook his head. "I know my rights," he said recognizing Jesse for the cop who'd sent him up on the drug charge a few years ago. "I don't have to tell you anything."

"*I'm* not a cop," Amanda said behind Jesse. The quiet calm in her voice made him turn. She stood over Gage, the gun in her hand, the barrel pointed at Gage's chest. "Where is my daughter?"

"Our daughter," he growled.

The shot was deafening and too close for comfort. Jesse jumped back.

"The next one will be in you," Amanda said quietly.

Gage swore. "You can't let her do this," he cried to Jesse. "You're a cop. Tell her, I have my rights."

Amanda got off a second shot before Jesse could get to her. Gage let out a howl and grabbed for his knee. Blood spurted through the neat round hole in his pants.

"Where is my daughter?" she asked again, a deadly calm in her voice. Her eyes were glazed over. She appeared to be in shock.

"All right," Gage groaned.

Jesse reached for Amanda's gun but stopped as Gage began to talk.

"I don't know anything about Susannah," Gage said. "I just had to have the ledger." He was crying now, holding his knee. "It was the cops. They got me on drug trafficking. We're talking the Big House. I had to do what they told me to."

"You made a deal, your neck for Crowe's *and* your father's?" Jesse asked in disbelief. "For… what?"

"A lighter sentence," Gage said. "Maybe even minimum security."

"You never had Susannah?" Amanda whispered.

"When I heard through my sources in the Organization that Susannah had been kidnapped, I didn't know of any other way to get you to deliver something big on your father," Gage said between sobs. "I knew you'd do it for Susannah. So I pretended I'd been contacted by the kidnapper and that the ledger was the ransom."

"After everything *else* you did to me?" Amanda asked.

Jesse had forgotten about the gun in Amanda's hand until she raised it and aimed point-blank at Gage's chest.

"No, Amanda!" Jesse shouted as he grabbed for her. As much as he despised Gage Ferraro for what he'd done, Jesse was still a cop. He still believed in playing by the rules. No matter how hard they were to abide by at times like this.

But as he grabbed for Amanda's gun, he made a fatal error. He diverted his attention from Gage for just a split second. Gage kicked his feet out from under him, knocking the gun from his hands and sending Amanda's weapon into the river.

Jesse came down hard, then Gage was on him, wrestling for Jesse's dropped weapon, and at the same time trying desperately to hang on to the ledger.

Jesse got a grip on the gun as they rolled dangerously close to the edge of the bridge where no railing would prevent them from dropping to the raging river below. Jesse's head and shoulders hung over the edge of the rotted timbers. Gage banged Jesse's hand with the weapon in it on one of the bridge's steel guy wires and tried to force him over the edge.

With everything going against him, Jesse felt the gun slip from his grasp and knew he'd be dropping to the river next. He could see Amanda out of the corner of his eye. She'd run down the bridge a few yards and picked up what appeared to be a piece of pipe. She was running back toward them, but Jesse knew she wasn't going to make it in time. He felt the rotten edge of the timber give a little more under him.

He could grab for a guy wire as he fell—or the ledger. He grabbed for the ledger, knocking it loose from Gage's grasp. The ledger skidded across the wood along the edge of the bridge, headed for the river.

Gage let out a howl and dove for it, coming down hard on the rotted timbers. As Jesse grabbed the guy wires and pulled himself back onto the bridge, he heard the timber give way next to him and saw Gage fall.

Jesse scrambled to his feet and rushed over to where Gage had dropped over the edge. Gage had managed to grab hold of one of the girders with his free hand as he went over. He now dangled by one arm, his prize, the ledger, in the other hand.

"Let go of the ledger," Jesse called to him as he laid on his belly and reached down to take Gage's hand. He could see that Gage's fingers were slipping on the rusted metal. "Drop the ledger and give me your hand!"

Gage's pupils were huge. He glanced down at the roaring river far below him, then up at Jesse. With great reluctance, he released the ledger. It fluttered down like a dried leaf to the water below.

Gage started to lift his free hand toward Jesse's but it was too late. His hold on the metal gave. He fell, his scream finally drowned out as he disappeared like the ledger into the turbulent water.

Jesse let out a curse. As he got to his feet, he turned to look at Amanda. She stood staring over the edge after Gage, the piece of pipe in her hand, a look of shock still on her face.

"He never had Susannah," she said, her voice a whisper. "He never even knew where she was."

Jesse pulled her into his arms and hugged her tightly. "It's all right. We'll find her." But suddenly he felt numb with fear: why hadn't the real kidnapper demanded a ransom?

15

Jesse didn't know how long he stood on the bridge holding her. For a long time, she felt like a granite statue in his arms. Then she began to soften and tremble, then shake. The sobs rose as if coming from someplace deep inside her. He wrapped her in his arms and waited for the storm to pass, not knowing what else to do.

When she stopped crying, she quickly wiped her eyes and stepped from his arms. He saw the determination and strength come back into her.

"Amanda, something is wrong with all this," he said, when he was sure she was ready to hear it. "Why hasn't there been a request for a ransom?"

She stared at him in confusion, then shook her head. "I thought there had been. But if Gage was telling the truth…"

Jesse nodded. "Then there never was a ransom demand." Did that mean that whoever had taken Susannah didn't want anything from the Crowes? Suddenly he felt the hair on the back of his neck stand straight up. A chill skittered across his skin. He shivered as if he'd stepped on a grave. Maybe he had.

"Amanda, remember what Molly said about Roxie's

baby? About it being God's will, conceived in sin, the son of evil."

She nodded.

"Jesse, what are you saying?"

"Molly said Frank found out who the father was by tracking down the jeweler who made the hearts. *J.B.* had the hearts made. Wasn't that what you told me?"

"You think Frank thought J.B. was the father of Roxie's baby?"

He nodded. "Amanda, the man who grabbed your baby in the department store, could he have been Frank Pickett?"

She could only stare at him.

"It's a long shot," he told her as he quickly ushered her from the bridge toward the van. "If there was no ransom, no demand for money or favors or evidence, then why kidnap your daughter? Unless it was revenge. I know I'm probably crazy, but I think we'd better go talk to Molly Pickett again. Maybe we'll get lucky and her husband Frank will be home from fishing." It was dark by the time they reached Molly Pickett's apartment. This time a half dozen men loitered on the front steps, but Jesse didn't offer them money as he shoved his way past, drawing Amanda in his wake.

Jesse laid on the buzzer, but no one answered. He tried the door. To his surprise and uneasiness, it wasn't locked. "Molly?" he called as he pushed the door open and stepped inside.

Only one light glowed in the living room, a small desk lamp next to the phone. Otherwise, the room was pitch-black. He snapped on the overhead living room light. "Molly?"

No sound. Moving slowly, he searched the small two-bedroom apartment. It was empty. Worse, it appeared Molly had left in a hurry. The crust for the pie she'd been making was still curled around the rolling pin where it had been earlier. The apples, all neatly sliced in the bowl, had turned dark gray.

He glanced at Amanda. She motioned to the desk lamp. In the circle of gold light, the phone book lay open, the phone next to it.

Amanda moved to the desk. Jesse followed her. The yellow pages were open to the *F*'s. Firewood. Fireworks. First Aid Supplies. Fish and Seafood. Fishing Consultants. Fishing—Resorts. Fishing—Tackle and Supplies.

"Wait a minute," Jesse said, remembering the photo of Roxie and her father in front of a fishing lodge. He moved to the wall of photographs. Behind him, he heard Amanda pick up the phone, then the sound of the line being redialed. "I'm going to try the redial button," Amanda said. "Maybe Molly tried to call him after we left."

He found what he was looking for. The wooden sign over the cabin door with the words carved in it, Woodland Lake Resort. Behind him he heard the distant voice on the speaker phone say, "Good evening, Woodland Lake Resort."

"Woodland Lake," Jesse said with a curse as Amanda hung up the phone. "Red River is between here and the lake."

"Oh, my God, Jesse."

He nodded, that cold chill turning to ice as it moved like a glacier up his spine. "Frank Pickett. Molly said he was there at the birth. He must have been the one who left me beside the road."

"No wonder Molly was upset," Amanda gasped. "She really believed you were dead."

"Until I showed her the heart pendant."

"Oh, God. Jesse, she must have gone up to the lake when he didn't come home tonight. She thinks he has Susannah!"

"So do I."

They scrambled out of the building and down the steps to the van. Fortunately, all four tires were still attached as they leapt in. Jesse started the engine and popped the clutch, praying they could reach Woodland Lake in time, praying this wasn't just some wild-goose chase.

Woodland Lake Resort sat at the edge of the lake, a large old log lodge with boat docks, rooms and a restaurant. Amanda stayed in the van while Jesse ran in to ask how to get to Frank Pickett's cabin. She could only assume either Frank didn't have a phone at the cabin or he hadn't been answering it when Molly had called, so she'd called the resort looking for him.

Amanda sat perfectly still, trying to remain calm. She'd had such high hopes earlier on the bridge, now it was hard to hope at all. She was still shaken by finding the plastic doll wrapped in the baby blanket. How could Gage have done that to her?

She pushed him out of her mind and thought of Frank Pickett. She could understand greed. She'd grown up around it. But Frank hadn't asked for money.

She also had a good understanding of revenge. If Frank Pickett believed that J. B. Crowe had fathered his daughter's baby, he might blame J.B. for Roxie taking her life. An eye for an eye. A child for a child. After all, he'd left Jesse beside a dirt road to die.

But why not take *her,* J.B.'s child, if he wanted an eye for an eye? She felt a chill, remembering what Consuela had said about history repeating itself. Someone had tried to kidnap her when she was a child but had failed. Oh, my God, could it have been Frank Pickett?

If that were true then why had he waited so long? Or had something happened to remind him? She thought of recent articles in the paper about her father. The announcement that he'd been chosen for that stupid humanitarian award had come out in the paper the day before Susannah's kidnapping.

Oh, dear God. Jesse could be right. Frank Pickett could have Susannah.

The thought poleaxed her. What in God's name had he done with Susannah, a baby born of mobsters' children?

Jesse startled her from her dark thoughts as he leapt back into the van. He turned down a small dirt lane bordered by thick-leafed trees, the headlights cutting a swath through the darkness.

"It's just up the road a half mile," he said. "I want you to stay in the van. If Susannah's there, I'll get her and bring her to you. Amanda, are you listening to me?"

He glanced over at her and must have recognized the look on her face. He swore.

"Don't try to stop me, Jesse," she said softly.

He swore again. "Then stay behind me and do as I say."

She nodded. He had to know by now that she would move heaven and earth to just hold her baby in her arms again.

* * *

Jesse stopped the van in the middle of the narrow lane, blocking the road should anyone try to leave the cabin. Through the trees, he could see a light in the distance. Quietly he opened the van door and slipped out, closing it silently behind him. Amanda did the same.

They made their way through the darkness of the woods, following the flickering light spilling from the cabin. As they drew closer, Jesse could hear voices. The only weapon he had was the piece of pipe he'd taken from Amanda on the bridge. It was stuck up the sleeve of his jacket.

He inched closer, Amanda right behind him. He could hear Molly's voice, a thin whine, and a deeper voice, raised in anger.

"Go around to the back, but don't go in until I tell you," he ordered.

She nodded, that look in her eyes that told him she would do whatever she had to do.

He swore under his breath as he watched her retreat along the side of the small cabin wall until she disappeared into the darkness.

Then carefully, he rose and peeked in the window. Through a crack in the blinds he could see Frank. The man was pacing back and forth. Behind him, Jesse saw something that made his heart leap. A baby. Susannah lay on the couch wedged between two pillows. Her tiny legs and arms flailed the air. Thank God, she was all right.

Molly sat in a chair opposite the couch, wringing her hands, talking softly to Frank.

Keeping low, Jesse moved to the front door, reached up and cautiously tried the knob. It turned in his hand.

The door wasn't locked. He hoped to surprise Frank. Catch him off guard. And hoped that Frank didn't have a weapon in his hand at the time.

Rising, he quietly opened the door a crack. He could hear them now.

"Frank, please listen to me," Molly was saying.

"Everything's going to be all right now Molly," said the large man with graying dark hair. He stood over Susannah. "Someday little Roxie and I will go fishing together." Frank moved over by the baby and reached down to touch one perfect little hand. "My little Roxie."

Jesse would have gone in then but as Frank turned, Jesse saw the gun in the man's other hand.

"That's not Roxie," Molly said crying. "That's not your little girl."

Frank's face seemed to cloud. He jerked his hand back. "You're right. That's the spawn of that mobster. I thought I got rid of that baby." He sounded confused, near tears. "I thought I got rid of him."

"Oh, Frank," Molly wailed. "Please, let's take this baby back where you got it. Don't do this."

"It's too late, Molly," Frank said. "My Roxie killed herself because of that mobster. You know it's true. He did that to her. Made her pregnant. She couldn't bear it."

"You're wrong, Frank," Molly said.

Susannah began to cry, a few little yelps, then a steady wail. Jesse swore, knowing Amanda too well. He put his shoulder against the door, praying he could time it right.

Amanda heard her baby cry, a primal call that reverberated through her body. She'd already tried the back door. It was locked. She'd moved to one of the windows and found she couldn't get it unstuck. Now, she hurried to another window. It was partially open. She shoved it up enough that she could squeeze through.

She dropped into a large clawfoot bathtub and stood for a moment, listening. Susannah's cries clutched at her heart. She could hear voices. A man's. And Molly's.

"I saw the heart, Frank," Molly was saying. "He had that heart Roxie always wore."

"Got it from that damned mobster," Frank said, sounding angry. "That J. B. Crowe. Humanitarian, like hell."

"No, Frank," Molly said. "It wasn't him. I never told you because you didn't like any of the boys that came 'round, but it wasn't that one. It was the other boy. Billy. Billy Kincaid. I saw her with him once."

"Don't do this to me, woman," Frank warned.

"Oh, Frank, how could you have left Roxie's baby beside some road in a box? How could you have lied to me all these years? How could you have done something like this? Why now, Frank? Why now?"

"This isn't the first time, Molly," Frank said. "You think I would wait this long to get back at that monster? I almost got the other baby twenty-five years ago."

Amanda couldn't stand it any longer. She jerked open the bathroom door, praying that she could distract Frank Pickett enough that Jesse could get to Frank.

She saw the large, graying man standing over her baby. She didn't notice the gun or the woman sitting in the corner of the room crying. She rushed to her baby and scooped Susannah up into her arms before the man could react.

* * *

Jesse put his shoulder against the front door and burst into the room just seconds after Amanda. But it was already too late.

Frank was bringing the gun up, the barrel pointed at Amanda and the baby.

"No!" Jesse cried as he tried to get to Frank before he could pull the trigger.

It all happened so quickly. Molly trying to stop Frank, throwing herself out of the chair and at him. The sound of the gunshot, Molly being thrown to the floor, the sound of her head hitting the edge of the log coffee table, then silence.

At first Jesse thought Amanda had been shot. There was blood everywhere and Amanda was on her knees beside Molly, Susannah cradled in one arm, her hand on Molly's cheek.

Jesse caught Frank with a left hook and dropped the man, twisting the gun from the kidnapper's hand before he hit the floor beside his wife. Molly was on the floor lying in a pool of blood, her eyes open, her life gone.

Jesse rushed to Amanda and Susannah, seeing at once that both were fine. He shook his head at Amanda's hopeful look. Molly was dead.

He helped Amanda to her feet. She clutched Susannah in her arms. The baby had quit crying. She cooed up at her mother, kicking her tiny legs and flailing her arms. The look on Amanda's face as she gazed down at her baby almost dropped Jesse to his knees. He looked at mother and daughter, his heart bursting. Finally, Susannah was safe in her mother's arms. At least for the moment.

"Molly?" Frank said as he laid his head on her body.

"It's going to be all right, now, Molly. Everything is going to be just fine. Tomorrow I'll take you and Roxie fishing. You'd like that, wouldn't you?"

16

In the wee hours of the morning, the ambulance finally pulled away, the siren a low, mournful moan dying away in the distance.

"Frank has confessed everything," Sheriff Wilson told Jesse. "You're both free to go."

Jesse glanced to the van where Amanda lay curled in the back, her baby beside her, both having fallen into an exhausted sleep. Frank was under arrest. Molly was dead.

"Frank was never the same after Roxie killed herself," a neighboring cabin owner kept saying. "He was just never the same."

When the sheriff finally said he could go, Jesse got into the van and drove south. He called his boss on Amanda's cell phone and filled him in on everything that had happened, knowing he was going to catch hell over the decisions he had made. At one point, Jesse had held in his hands evidence against J. B. Crowe, something his boss wasn't likely to forget. Nor was Jesse likely to forget that his boss was the only one who had known he and Amanda had gone to Red River. Amanda didn't wake until he'd almost reached Dallas. With Susannah secured in the car seat she had packed in the back, she planted a kiss on the sleeping baby's cheek before slipping into the passenger seat next to him.

He could tell how hard it was to let Susannah out of her arms. What had ever made him think she didn't love her baby? Could have abandoned Susannah? Or pretended the infant had been kidnapped, using Susannah as Gage had?

"Where are we?" Amanda asked, glancing around.

"Almost to Dallas."

Her eyebrow shot up.

"I can't let you leave the country," he said hurriedly. He could feel her gaze on him.

"Can't? Or won't?" she asked.

"Can't," he said as he pulled over in the shade of a large tree alongside a city park. The sun was coming up, big and bright. It was going to be another hot one in this part of Texas.

He cut the engine and turned in his seat. "I've been thinking about this a lot."

"Yes?" she asked and waited.

His heart pounded with just the thought of what he wanted to say. Words he'd never uttered to another woman. But they seemed right. And yet, only a fool wouldn't realize the danger in what he was about to propose.

"Amanda," he said, taking her hand in his. "I *can't* let you go off alone with Susannah. You won't be safe. No matter where you run, either your father or Mickie Ferraro and his henchmen or someone else with a grudge against your father will be looking for you. There is only one place I can think of that you and Susannah would be safe. And that's with me."

* * *

Amanda held her breath, her gaze locked to his. He wanted to come with them. Was it possible he would give up being a cop to protect her and Susannah? She could feel her heart banging in her chest. For the first time in her life, she knew exactly what she wanted. This man. A family for Susannah. A normal life. She wasn't sure what that would entail—let alone how to get one—but she had the feeling that with Jesse, anything was possible. As long as he'd go with her and Susannah.

"With you?" she managed to ask.

And the next thing she knew, she was in his arms. His mouth found hers, his kiss soft and sweet and full of promise. He kissed her deeply, passionately, as if this morning was all they had. Then he drew back and gazed into her eyes, making her melt inside.

"I love you, Amanda. I want to marry you."

His words filled her, as satisfying as any she'd ever heard. "Oh, Jesse, my love." She hugged him tightly. "Oh, yes, I knew you'd come with us. We can go to Europe. Or maybe—"

He pulled back abruptly, his eyes dark, a frown furrowing his brows. "No, Amanda."

She stared at him, uncomprehending. Hadn't he just told her he loved her? Hadn't he just asked her to marry him?

"We can't run all our lives," he said. "What kind of life would that be for Susannah? For us?"

"What are you saying?" she managed to ask.

"We stay here."

She gaped at him. "Are you mad?" Finally, she'd met the man of her dreams and he was stark raving crazy.

"It's the only way," he said grabbing her upper arms,

forcing her to face him. "Listen to me. I've thought about this. I've thought about nothing else since we made love. I've been crazy for you since the first time I laid eyes on you. But these past few days, I've fallen in love with you. I can't imagine life without you."

"But Jesse—"

He put a finger to her lips. "Sweetheart, running away won't help. Your father would find us. Or Mickie. Amanda, we need your father's protection."

"Now I know you've lost your mind," she cried. "You aren't suggesting—"

"Your father loves you, Amanda. He loves his grand-daughter. I think you realize now that he wouldn't harm you or Susannah. I'm not saying you can change him. Or change his past. I'm not saying eventually he won't go to prison for some of the things he's done. But I believe he will try to be a better man for the two of you and for right now, that's enough."

"He would never allow me to marry a cop," she said emphatically.

Jesse grinned. "There's only one way to find out."

"He'll kill you!" she cried.

"His future son-in-law? I don't think so. You forget, I'm Billy Kincaid's son and J.B. knows it."

She cupped his wonderfully handsome face in her hands. "Do you really believe it's possible that we could have a normal life?" Yet even as she asked the question, she knew it just might be. For that, she would do any-thing. Even go back to her father's.

"Well?" Jesse asked. "I promise it's only temporary."

She pulled his face to her and kissed him lightly on the mouth. "You make me believe anything is possible."

* * *

Possible or not, it was the only option Jesse could come up with. They couldn't run. J.B.'s resources were too far-reaching. And as far as Jesse knew, Mickie Ferraro still hadn't given up trying to kill Amanda. J.B. could make sure that Mickie was stopped. The Crowe compound could be a temporary sanctuary. Or the lion's den, Jesse thought as he neared the gate.

Jesse didn't believe for a minute that J. B. Crowe could change. Or would want to. Not for all the love in the world. Not even for his daughter's. Or granddaughter's.

But Jesse knew if he could get J.B.'s blessing, he would be able to protect Amanda from not only the mob—but from J.B. himself. As for Mickie Ferraro, if Jesse knew J.B., the mobster would take care of Mickie once and for all.

All Jesse knew was that he and Amanda and Susannah couldn't run the rest of their lives. Nor could they ever hide from the mob. Their only hope was going inside.

He knew he was taking a hell of a chance, but he had Amanda and Susannah. And he was Billy Kincaid's son. Jesse just hoped that was enough.

J.B. had placed a new guard at the gate now, a man Jesse had seen before, a man who'd seen him as well. The guard recognized Amanda immediately. His gaze went from her to Jesse, then to the back of the van where boxes and suitcases were piled high, to the seat where Susannah, now awake, smiled and laughed as if she'd already forgotten those few days in April 2001 that she'd been lost to her mother.

Excitedly, the guard called up to the main house on

a cell phone, announced who was at the gate, then held the phone away from his ear. Jesse could hear J.B. yelling from where he sat.

"Yes, Mr. Crowe," the guard said when he got the chance. The gate opened and the guard motioned them through hurriedly.

J.B. was standing outside when they drove up. Neither Death nor Destruction seemed to be around, but Jesse would bet they weren't far off.

"Remember," Jesse whispered. "He loves you." But did J.B. love her enough to accept Jesse's terms? That would be the question.

Amanda nodded and opened her door. She'd never seen her father scared. Nor had she ever seen him cry before. He pulled her into his arms and hugged her tightly and she hugged him back. Jesse was right. J. B. Crowe was her father. Good or bad.

Amanda felt Jesse behind her. He'd gotten Susannah out of her car seat and now held her in his arms. He was looking down at Susannah's little face and smiling in a way that made her heart purr.

Without a word, Jesse handed Crowe his granddaughter. J.B. took her, holding her awkwardly, and Amanda realized this was the first time he'd actually held Susannah. She stared at the pair, wondering just what the power of love could accomplish. Because in her father's eyes she saw his love for her. For his granddaughter.

After a moment, she took her daughter from him. "There is a lot I need to tell you," she said.

"Yes," her father agreed. He looked to Jesse.

"You know who he is, don't you?" she asked.

"So it is true," J.B. said. "You're Billy's son."

Jesse nodded. "I'm in love with your daughter. And I'm a cop."

J.B. nodded slowly. "I see. Perhaps we should step inside."

Epilogue

It was to be the biggest wedding of the year, maybe of the century. J. B. Crowe had spared no expense. The guest list was huge and as varied as any wedding in history, from mobsters to cops to the governor himself. Even Olivia flew home from New York for the affair and to help with the hurried arrangements. Few people had ever been inside the Crowe compound. Most would never see it again.

But for one day, J. B. Crowe would open the doors and let the world in to see his only daughter marry the man she loved. The story had broken on page one of the Dallas papers and quickly spread across the country. *Governor Kincaid's Cop Nephew to Marry Mobster's Daughter.*

The story about Mickie Ferraro's accidental drowning in White Lake got buried on a back page of the same day's paper, but Jesse saw it and knew Ferraro's death had been no accident. J.B., good to his word, had taken care of it. Just like he had the wedding.

Jesse had watched J.B. with his daughter and granddaughter, pleased with the mobster's acting job. J.B. had seemingly convinced Amanda that he wanted to change.

That he could change. She seemed deeply touched by her father's acceptance of a cop into the family.

Jesse could tell that she also wanted to believe that J.B. really hadn't had anything to do with Diana Kincaid's disappearance. Or the black market baby ring. J.B. swore his men had been operating it independently of him and he would see that it was stopped at once.

"I want to change," J.B. had told Amanda. "You have to admit, letting a cop marry into the family is a start."

Amanda had leaned up to give her father a kiss on his cheek, her eyes full of tears.

"I just want you and Susannah to be happy," J.B. had said.

That, Jesse thought, Amanda *could* believe. But for those few days before the wedding, Amanda seemed to enjoy the closeness she and her father shared. Like a lull before a storm, Jesse thought.

One night over a glass of brandy in his study, J.B. told them about the night he went to see Roxie, the night Jesse was born. He saw Frank leaving in his car. Even thought he heard a baby cry. But he'd been too upset over Billy's death to understand what he'd seen, what it meant.

Like everyone else, J.B. had believed the baby died at birth. That Roxie had gone into premature labor after hearing about Billy's death and because of complications, lost not only her baby, but later her will to live.

J.B. often held his granddaughter and seemed to take great pleasure in having the house full of life. Sometimes Jesse would catch him watching his daughter and granddaughter, a sadness in his gaze.

Even Eunice and Malcolm treated Jesse as if he was family. Consuela cried a lot, her happiness running over, as she made wonderful meals and raced about waiting on them as if they were royalty.

"Amanda and I will be leaving right after the wedding," Jesse reminded J.B. Amanda didn't want her baby raised behind fences and bars. She desperately wanted that normal life that Jesse had promised her. And Jesse planned on it beginning right after they were married.

J.B. had only nodded. It was obvious he didn't want to lose his daughter, but maybe part of him realized he already had.

Jesse took Amanda up to meet his parents the day after their return to the Crowe estate. Amanda took to them instantly and they her, just as he'd expected.

"You made a huge hit with my folks," Jesse told her on the way home.

"They are wonderful."

"They sure loved you and Susannah. As soon as we get married, they'll be expecting us to have more children. What do you think?"

She'd smiled. "I think we should start working on it soon. I've always liked the idea of a lot of kids, close in age. I can't believe I've finally gotten the large family I've always dreamed of. Your brothers and sisters are great."

He'd laughed. "We'll see how great you think they are when you see them every holiday and every birthday and every—"

She interrupted him with a kiss. "I can't wait."

"Soon," he'd promised and he'd seen something in her gaze… She knew, he thought. She knew he'd made a deal with her father.

And he knew that when J.B. went back to business as usual, Amanda would wash her hands of her father once and for all. And maybe, like him, she knew it was just a matter of time.

But she never said anything. Nor he.

He'd had a long talk with his parents about what he'd found out in Red River. They had never known who his real parents were but had always feared they might be people who would come after Jesse some day.

He loved Marie and Pete McCall even more now, knowing that they had adopted him, knowing what they had gone through all those years, worrying about the biological parents possibly showing up one day.

He and Amanda had also visited the governor and his wife a few times in Austin. Jesse told him about Brice and the other cops who'd come after them that night, unsure just who the cops worked for, and Jesse's suspicions about his boss. Kincaid had promised to look into it. He'd also offered Jesse a job on a special government task force, making it clear that he still planned to shut down organized crime in Texas.

While he'd heard from his daughter Diana and she was safe and swore she hadn't been kidnapped by J. B. Crowe, Kincaid wasn't sure if he could make the wedding or not. Jesse understood.

On the big day, when all the wedding preparations had been made and the Crowe compound had changed more dramatically than even J. B. Crowe himself had appeared to, J.B. called Jesse down to his study.

"I want you to have this," J.B. said, handing Jesse the heart and chain that Billy Kincaid had worn until his death.

Jesse put the two odd shaped hearts together for the first time. They formed a perfect small heart of solid gold. "Thank you, J.B. I can't tell you how much this means to me."

The older man had nodded awkwardly. "Promise me you'll look after my girls."

"I promise," Jesse said.

Outside music played on the large lawn and a crowd began to gather. Dressed in his tuxedo, Jesse went down to stand at the altar with his two brothers as attendants, and wait for his bride. He held the heart in his pocket, balled in his palm, a reminder of the past—and his hopes for the future.

Then he saw Amanda coming behind the long line of bridesmaids, three of them his sisters. She took his breath away.

His beautiful bride appeared at the end of the long runway with J.B. by her side. Jesse wanted to remember J.B. this way, he thought. A father escorting his only daughter down the aisle.

When they reached Jesse, J.B. handed Amanda to him, a warning look in his eye.

"Make my daughter happy," J.B. whispered.

"I'm sure going to try."

When the preacher finally pronounced them man and wife, Jesse lifted Amanda's veil and kissed his bride, then he pulled the heart and gold chain from his pocket and held it out to her. Tears welled in her eyes as she slipped it over her head, the two hearts finally united.

"Forever," he said, against all odds. And as he and Amanda walked down the aisle, he had the strangest feeling that Billy and Roxie were watching. And that they heartily approved.

* * * * *

We hope you enjoyed reading
LAW AND DISORDER
by *New York Times* bestselling author
HEATHER GRAHAM
and
SECRET BODYGUARD
by *New York Times* bestselling author
B.J. DANIELS

Both were originally Harlequin® series stories!

From passionate, suspenseful and dramatic
love stories to inspirational or historical,
Harlequin offers different lines to
satisfy every romance reader.

New books in each line
are available every month.

Harlequin.com

I N T R I G U E

*One night, when Mary Cardwell Savage is lonely, she
sends a letter to Chase Steele, her first love. Little does
she know that this action will bring both Chase and his
psychotic ex-girlfriend into her life...*

Read on for a sneak preview of
Steel Resolve *by* New York Times *and* USA TODAY
bestselling author B.J. Daniels.

The moment Fiona found the letter in the bottom of Chase's
sock drawer, she knew it was bad news. Fear squeezed the
breath from her as her heart beat so hard against her rib
cage that she thought she would pass out. Grabbing the
bureau for support, she told herself it might not be what she
thought it was.

But the envelope was a pale lavender, and the handwriting
was distinctly female. Worse, Chase had kept the letter a
secret. Why else would it be hidden under his socks? He
hadn't wanted her to see it because it was from that other
woman.

Now she wished she hadn't been snooping around. She'd
let herself into his house with the extra key she'd had made.
She'd felt him pulling away from her the past few weeks.
Having been here so many times before, she was determined
that this one wasn't going to break her heart. Nor was she
going to let another woman take him from her. That's why
she had to find out why he hadn't called, why he wasn't
returning her messages, why he was avoiding her.

They'd had fun the night they were together. She'd felt as if they had something special, although she knew the next morning that he was feeling guilty. He'd said he didn't want to lead her on. He'd told her that there was some woman back home he was still in love with. He'd said their night together was a mistake. But he was wrong, and she was determined to convince him of it.

What made it so hard was that Chase was a genuinely nice guy. You didn't let a man like that get away. The other woman had. Fiona wasn't going to make that mistake, even though he'd been trying to push her away since that night. But he had no idea how determined she could be, determined enough for both of them that this wasn't over by a long shot.

It wasn't the first time she'd let herself into his apartment when he was at work. The other time, he'd caught her and she'd had to make up some story about the building manager letting her in so she could look for her lost earring.

She'd snooped around his house the first night they'd met—the same night she'd found his extra apartment key and had taken it to have her own key made in case she ever needed to come back when Chase wasn't home.

The letter hadn't been in his sock drawer that time.

That meant he'd received it since then. Hadn't she known he was hiding something from her? Why else would he put this letter in a drawer instead of leaving it out along with the bills he'd casually dropped on the table by the front door?

Because the letter was important to him, which meant that she had no choice but to read it.

Don't miss
Steel Resolve *by B.J. Daniels,*
available July 2019 wherever
Harlequin® Intrigue books and ebooks are sold.

www.Harlequin.com

HIEXP0619

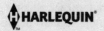

"I've been assigned to go back to Florida. To stay at the Frampton Ranch and Resort—and investigate what we believe to be three kidnappings and a murder. And the kidnappings may have nothing to do with the resort, nor may the murder?" Brock McGovern asked, a small note of incredulity slipping into his voice, which was surprising to him—he was always careful to keep an even tone.

FBI assistant director Richard Egan had brought him into his office, and Brock had known he was going on assignment—he just hadn't expected this.

"Yes, not what you'd want, but, hey, maybe it'll be good for you—and perhaps necessary now, when time is of the essence and there is no one out there who could know the place or the circumstances with the same scope and experience you have," Egan told him. "Three young women have disappeared from the area. Two of them were guests of the Frampton Ranch and Resort shortly before their disappearances—the third had left St. Augustine and was on her way there. The Florida Department of Law Enforcement has naturally been there already. They asked for federal help on this. Shades of the past haunt them—they don't want any more unsolved murders— and everyone is hoping against hope that Lily Sylvester, Amy Bonham and Lydia Merkel might be found."

"These are Florida missing-person cases," Brock said. "And it's sad but true that young people go to Florida and get caught up in the beach life and the club scene. And regrettable but true once again—there's a drug and alcohol culture that does exist and people get caught up in it. Not just in Florida, of course, but everywhere." He smiled grimly. "I go where I'm told, but I'm curious— how is this an FBI affair? And forgive me, but—FBI out of New York?"

"Not out of New York. FDLE asked for you. Specifically."

Don't miss
Tangled Threat *by Heather Graham,*
available September 2019 wherever
Harlequin® books and ebooks are sold.

www.Harlequin.com

Love Harlequin romance?

DISCOVER.

Be the first to find out about promotions, news and exclusive content!

Facebook.com/HarlequinBooks

Twitter.com/HarlequinBooks

Instagram.com/HarlequinBooks

Pinterest.com/HarlequinBooks

ReaderService.com

EXPLORE.

Sign up for the Harlequin e-newsletter and download a free book from any series at **TryHarlequin.com.**

CONNECT.

Join our Harlequin community to share your thoughts and connect with other romance readers! **Facebook.com/groups/HarlequinConnection**

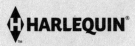

HARLEQUIN®

ROMANCE WHEN YOU NEED IT

HSOCIAL2018

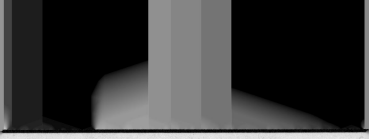

Earn points on your purchase of new Harlequin books from participating retailers.

Turn your points into **FREE BOOKS** of your choice!

Join for FREE today at
www.HarlequinMyRewards.com.

Harlequin My Rewards is a free program (no fees) without any commitments or obligations.

MYR18